PENGUIN BOOKS

# Tom Clancy's Firing Point

Thirty-five years ago, Tom Clancy was a Maryland insurance broker with a passion for naval history. Years before, he had been an English major at Baltimore's Loyola College and had always dreamed of writing a novel. His first effort, *The Hunt for Red October*, sold briskly as a result of rave reviews, and was then catapulted on to the *New York Times* bestseller list after President Reagan pronounced it 'the perfect yarn'. From that day forward, Clancy established himself as an undisputed master at blending exceptional realism and authenticity, intricate plotting and razor sharp suspense. He passed away in October 2013.

Mike Maden grew up working in the canneries, feed mills and slaughterhouses of California's San Joaquin Valley. A lifelong fascination with history and warfare ultimately led to a PhD in political science focused on conflict and technology in international relations. Like millions of others, he first became a Tom Clancy fan after reading *The Hunt for Red October*, and began his published fiction career in the same techno-thriller genre, starting with *Drone* and the sequels, *Blue Warrior*, *Drone Command* and *Drone Threat*. He's honored to be joining The Campus as a writer in Tom Clancy's Jack Ryan, Jr, series.

www.tomclancy.com
facebook.com/tomclancyauthor

Tom Clancy's

# Firing Point

MIKE MADEN

PENGUIN BOOKS

PENGUIN BOOKS

UK | USA | Canada | Ireland | Australia
India | New Zealand | South Africa

Penguin Books is part of the Penguin Random House group of companies
whose addresses can be found at global.penguinrandomhouse.com

First published in the United States by G. P. Putnam's Sons 2020
First published in Great Britain by Michael Joseph 2020
Published in Penguin Books 2021

001

Set in 11.68/14 pt Garamond MT Std
Typeset by Integra Software Services Pvt. Ltd, Pondicherry
Printed and bound in Italy by Grafica Veneta S.p.A.

The authorized representative in the EEA is Penguin Random House Ireland,
Morrison Chambers, 32 Nassau Street, Dublin Do2 YH68

A CIP catalogue record for this book is available from the British Library

PAPERBACK ISBN: 978–1–405–94731–2
OM PAPERBACK ISBN: 978–1–405–94732–9

www.greenpenguin.co.uk

MIX
Paper from
responsible sources
FSC® C018179

Penguin Random House is committed to a
sustainable future for our business, our readers
and our planet. This book is made from Forest
Stewardship Council® certified paper.

In valor, there is hope.

— TACITUS

# Principal Characters

## United States Government

**Jack Ryan:** President of the United States
**Mary Pat Foley:** Director of national intelligence
**Arnold 'Arnie' van Damm:** President Ryan's chief of staff
**Scott Adler:** Secretary of state
**Admiral John Talbot:** Chief of naval operations
**Dick Dellinger:** U.S. Consulate (Barcelona, Spain), Public Diplomacy Section

## The Campus

**Jack Ryan, Jr:** Operations officer/senior analyst
**Gavin Biery:** Director of information technology
**Gerry Hendley:** Director of The Campus and Hendley Associates
**John Clark:** Director of operations
**Domingo 'Ding' Chavez:** Assistant director of operations
**Dominic 'Dom' Caruso:** Operations officer
**Adara Sherman:** Operations officer
**Bartosz 'Midas' Jankowski:** Operations officer

## Other Characters

### United States

**Buck Logan:** President, White Mountain Logistics + Security
**Kate Parsons:** Oak Ridge National Laboratory scientist

### Spain

**Laia Brossa:** Centro Nacional de Inteligencia (CNI) agent
**Gaspar Peña:** CNI supervisor

# Prologue

'Alive, not dead.'

That was the order. Jack got it. Rijk van Delden – if that was his real name – was the only link between the Iron Syndicate and the nameless merc outfit the syndicate hired for their dirtiest hits. The merc outfit was their real target. Find van Delden, find the outfit.

Simple as that.

But van Delden had been hard as hell to find. Impossible, actually. Until a lead, finally, that led them here tonight. Their one and maybe only chance to grab him.

'Alive, not dead' meant keeping the big Dutchman alive so they could find and eliminate his murderous organization.

The only problem with that was van Delden was one of his outfit's heavy hitters. The six-foot-six killer possessed serious combative and tactical skills. The giant Dutchman had put more men in the ground than a gravedigger's shovel.

'Don't even think about taking this monkey on by yourself. Get eyes on him, call for backup, sit tight till the rest of us show up. Savvy?' Clark said in their brief before The Campus team split up. All hands were on deck for this op: John Clark, Ding Chavez, Dom Caruso, Adara Sherman, Midas Jankowski, and Jack Junior.

They all headed in different directions across the steel mill's huge complex of buildings. Too much ground to cover for them to buddy up. They had to go it alone to find the guy. And fast.

Van Delden was in one of a dozen possible places on two hundred acres of property, and scheduled to leave within the hour, according to their source. They couldn't risk missing him here tonight. If he shook loose, he'd be back in the wind the minute he left and they'd lose the only shot they'd ever had at rolling up his crew.

Alive, not dead, was tonight's mission but it seemed like a pretty good idea for him and the rest of the team, too, Jack thought, as he made his way through the cavernous shell of the integrated steel mill. The cold night fog looming over the port outside stopped at the doorway, the air inside tinged with the acrid smells of rust, ozone, and burnt coal.

Jack Ryan, Jr, was a big, blue-eyed white guy striding confidently through the dark, hangar-size structure. He didn't look that out of place beneath his stolen white safety helmet, clipboard, and paper mask. He moved fast like he had something to do, which he did. The steelworkers were too busy flying several hundred tons of molten slag in giant ladles lumbering overhead to pay attention to him.

Jack sweated beneath his shirt. It was an industrial volcano inside the sweltering building. At least the team had Sonitus Molar Mics. Without bone conduction for reception, he wouldn't be able to hear the others calling out their sitreps on his comms. The infernal din of pounding hydraulic hammers, roaring diesel motors, grinding steel, and blaring alarms was a near sensory overload.

'I'm thirty seconds from target,' Dom whispered on his way to the plant manager's office.

'Copy that,' Clark said.

Jack took two steps at a time up the yellow steel staircase to the 'pulpit' – the automated control room for the hot-steel processing facility, high off the floor. The grated treads led to the landing just outside the control-room door. With his back against the corrugated steel wall, he did a quick check around him. Helmeted workers below were focused on the job, not him.

From the landing, a steel-grating walkway ran parallel along the windowless steel wall of the pulpit where Jack stood. On either end of the east–west walkway was a catwalk. Both catwalks ran north, parallel with the tracks of the huge ladles moving slowly along beneath them. Each ladle brimmed with nearly two hundred tons of molten steel heading toward the vacuum degassers on the far side of the building.

In the middle of the steel control-room door stood a small, face-size observation window.

'I'm in position,' Jack whispered.

'Copy,' Clark said as a siren wailed overhead.

Jack stepped over to the door's observation window.

He scanned the room. In front of the big picture windows overlooking the mill floor, five young South Korean technicians sat at their monitors chatting excitedly, pointing at virtual gauges on their screens.

Scanning right, Jack saw Park, the oldest Korean in the room, standing in the corner, round and silver-haired beneath his safety helmet. Jack recognized Park from his file photo. He was the steel firm's CEO and biggest shareholder, and a man in serious trouble with Japan's largest yakuza syndicate, the Yamaguchi-gumi. Their source inside the syndicate said Park was reaching out to van Delden for protection tonight.

Jack leaned over to see who Park was talking with.

And there he was.

The giant Dutchman towered over the diminutive Korean, his long, granite face focused on Park in earnest discussion.

3

The Dutchman's gaze shifted briefly toward the window. His eyes locked with Jack's.

*Shit.*

In the blink of an eye, van Delden's big Glock 17 was in his hand. Jack ducked as the barrel sparked. The door glass shattered just above his head.

'Found him,' Jack barked in his comms as he crouched low and pressed hard against the heavy steel door. He felt more rounds thud against the metal, like someone was pounding the door with their fists.

'Sit tight,' Clark said. 'We're on our way. Five mikes, max.'

'Copy that.' More bullets crashed into the door near Jack's ear.

'Don't hurt him, Jack.'

'Copy that –'

*WHUMP!*

The big man slammed into the door. The steel cracked against Jack's skull and knocked him back a little. But Jack was wedged hard against it. The door only budged open an inch. He slammed it back shut with his shoulder.

Jack heard the last shards of the shattered window glass breaking above him. He glanced up just in time to see the black steel slide of the big Glock wedge through it, then angle down, thick fingers wrapped around the hilt. The Glock fired three earsplitting shots that *chinged* the grated steel floor near Jack's feet before Jack could react. Jack turned and grabbed the hot slide with his left hand and twisted it upward just as van Delden fired another shot into the steel rafters overhead.

The hot barrel burned Jack's hand as he squeezed but he caused the last shot to fail because the slide couldn't fully eject the brass.

With his left hand still gripped around the Glock, Jack pulled his SIG P229 Legion Compact SAO with his right hand and smashed the steel butt against the Dutchman's thick wrist, breaking it with a sickening crack.

The massive paw dropped the Glock and yanked back through the shattered glass. Jack kicked the Dutchman's gun over the edge.

'Status?' Clark asked. 'Still got eyes on?'

'He ain't going nowhere –'

*WHUMP!*

Van Delden crashed against the door again before Jack could brace himself. The steel door blew open, tossing Jack backward, dropping him to the grated landing.

Jack raised his weapon to put a bullet in the Dutchman's knee but the man's giant steel-toed boot kicked the gun out of Jack's hand, and sent the SIG sailing over the edge, clattering onto the cement floor far below.

Jack's hand exploded in pain, as if it had been smashed with a sledgehammer. His momentary focus on his aching hand cost him dearly as the same big boot raised high and smashed down into Jack's gut, knocking the wind out of him. Jack gasped for air and clutched at his belly as the boot raised up a third time, aimed squarely at his skull. Jack rolled away at the last second, the sole of the massive boot clanging against the steel near his ear.

Jack rolled again just as the Dutchman launched a kick at his skull and missed. Van Delden lunged forward for a final, fatal steel-toed shot to Jack's temple, not seeing Jack's three-inch Kershaw spring-assisted blade until it plunged into his inner thigh.

Van Delden screamed and grabbed his leg to stanch the blood. He stumbled away past Jack before The Campus operative could strike him again, limping west along the walkway as Jack struggled to stand.

'Jack, we're close. Stay put,' Clark ordered. Jack shook the pain out of his hand as he grabbed a couple of deep breaths, his stomach aching like he'd been gut shot.

'Jack? You copy?'

Jack glanced up just in time to see van Delden turn the corner north, heading away from the pulpit.

'Copy,' was all Jack said.

He sure as hell wasn't staying put.

He had his orders. 'Alive, not dead.'

But Jack knew there was a long, nasty road of hurt between the two, and he was happy to take the big man along for the ride.

Jack thundered along the steel grate, racing after the giant operator. Even wounded, the big man was fast as a feral cat.

Jack turned the corner, running past the giant ladle of molten steel crawling along on its track ten feet below him. Even from here, the searing heat made his skin tingle, like standing too close to a campfire on a cold night.

'Van Delden! Halt!' Jack shouted over the noise of the giant ladle motors grinding overhead.

Van Delden limped farther along, leaning heavily on the rail, one bloody, massive hand gripping his thigh. He finally stopped as Jack charged up behind him.

'Turn around, asshole,' Jack said, finally able to pull his backup gun, a striker-fired SIG P365 SAS micro-compact nine-millimeter.

The thick shoulders turned. On the dimly lit platform, the Dutchman's rugged features glowed in the seething light of the lava-like steel approaching them. The backs of Jack's legs itched with the heat through his trousers.

Jack pointed his pistol at the big man's chest.

The Dutchman grinned.

'Afraid to pull the trigger, little man?'

'Oh, hell no. But I've got my orders.'

'Tough guy, huh?' The grin disappeared as he winced in

6

pain, his trouser leg soaked in blood. He raised himself up to his full height – five inches taller than Jack. His broad chest was like an oak barrel, and his tree-trunk arms bulged beneath his shirtsleeves.

Jack's finger tightened on the trigger. 'I won't kill you, but if you make a move, you're gonna be pissing through a straw for the rest of your life.'

The Dutchman's eyes searched Jack up and down, calculating speed and distance to target.

'Clark, you copy?'

'I copy. You have the tango in sight?'

'I'm sitting on him. Hurry the hell up.'

'Almost there. You good?'

The air roared with the noise of the automated crane hauling the giant ladle just below them. Jack caught the glow of the white-hot steel in the corner of his eye.

'I'm good. But van Asshat is in a world of hurt.'

'Who sent you?' van Delden asked.

'Nobody you'd know.'

'What do you want with me?'

'You're the link to an outfit we're interested in.'

'Interested how? You are police?'

'Not exactly.'

'Do you know who I work for?'

'Your outfit contracted for the Iron Syndicate.'

'The syndicate is dead.'

'I know. We're the ones that rolled them up. It's your organization we're going to take apart next, thanks to you.'

'Ha! You *really* don't know anything about us, do you?'

'No. But I promise you, within the hour you'll tell me.'

Van Delden gritted his teeth, grimacing with a strange *fuck-you* smile at Jack.

'Something strike you as funny?' Jack asked.

7

The big Dutchman suddenly frowned, confused. He punched himself in the jaw. One, two, three times. Jack heard his teeth crack even above the noise.

'What the hell is wrong with you?'

Van Delden's desperate eyes darted around – searching for some kind of a weapon or another way out. The Dutchman's bloodied fingers tightened around the steel railing.

Jack suddenly realized that the much larger man could use the railing as leverage to throw his bulk at him, even on that bad leg. If one of those meaty fists clocked his jaw, he'd be lights out.

Jack stepped back. 'Don't move.'

Van Delden inched closer.

'Afraid, little man?'

Jack shook his head. 'No one's pointing a gun at *my* nutsack.'

The Dutchman smiled again, a sliver of sunlight in a storm cloud. But then it faded.

'What are you willing to die for, little man?'

'What kind of a stupid –'

In a single, vaulting leap, van Delden threw himself over the railing.

Jack lunged at the man to grab him, but he was too late.

The big Dutchman plunged feet first into the glowing ladle ten feet below. His massive frame barely rippled the blistering surface, the white-hot liquid swallowing his last, sharp cry.

Jack stood at the railing staring at the bucket of molten steel inching relentlessly forward as Clark, Dom, and Adara came racing up behind him.

'Where the hell's van Delden?' Clark asked, leaning over the railing. 'I told you we needed him alive.'

'I know,' Jack said, holstering his pistol. 'But he had different plans.'

# October 18

# I

## *Aboard the container ship Jade Star*

Second Officer Luis Loyola stood outside on the starboard bridge wing, vaping a sweet menthol Juulpod. He admired the blanket of stars shimmering across the black velvet sky.

His seaman's eye suddenly caught the breaking wake of what was probably a dolphin's fin racing toward the hull far down below, then watched it dip beneath the blue-black water, night feeding. He smiled. Amazing animals. And always a good luck charm.

The ship's bow surged toward a waxing moon blazing like a searchlight, illuminating the dark Pacific waters in every direction, all the way to the horizon, or so it seemed. Out here in the South Pacific, he couldn't see the lights of any nearby ships of any size; his radar had indicated the nearest fishing vessel was some 140 kilometers away. He might as well have been on the surface of Mars for the solitude he craved tonight.

The ship was sailing on a smooth sea at fifteen knots – a little more than half its rated speed – to save expensive bunker fuel. The 102,000-ton (deadweight) vessel was powered by a 93,000-horsepower, two-stroke diesel engine thrumming far belowdecks. It was burning 90 tons of fuel a day at current speed as it drove the ship's thirty-foot-diameter copper alloy, six-bladed propeller.

He cast a quick glance at the deck, stacked with red, blue, and green shipping containers. In fact, the *Jade Star* was fully loaded with 8,465 twenty- and forty-foot shipping containers, including South Korean industrial pipe and fittings, washing machines, refrigerators, car parts, rubber tires, X-ray machines, and, strangely, seven hundred liters of human blood.

The ship was also illegally carrying three hundred tons of ethylene and other combustible chemicals, used in a variety of manufacturing applications. The legal restrictions for recommended storage and transportation precautions were ridiculous and prohibitively expensive relative to the cost of the chemicals themselves. He wasn't worried about their safety. As the ship's administrative officer, he was duty bound to be aware of such things. But if stopped and searched, he alone would be the person charged with the crime.

But all of that was of little concern at the moment. He was off the clock now, and couldn't give a damn about what they were hauling. His only concern was that his son's birthday was yesterday, and as far as he knew, his *puta* ex-wife hadn't bothered to give the boy the quadcopter drone he had sent him last week.

Loyola loved his life at sea, but he loved his six-year-old son even more. He was torn. It was the sea that had cost him his marriage, or so his wife said, blaming her whoring with every swinging dick in Lima on him not being around to satisfy her womanly desires.

*¡Hija de puta!*

He took a long drag on his Juul, then watched the breeze sweep the vapor cloud away into the darkness. If he didn't quit the sea, he might lose his son altogether. Besides, he hadn't had a pay raise in three years, let alone a promotion, and neither was on the horizon. He had thought about quitting many times, but as shitty as the non-union wages were, they were still better than anything else he could manage from a desk job back home in Peru. At least this way he could save up money for his son's future, even if he missed his son growing up.

He felt a dark despair falling back over him again and thought about the bottle of Golden Blue Korean whiskey he had stowed away in his cabin. His drinking had gotten worse this trip, and it was probably time to back off. His last fitness report by that *maricón* captain had warned him about his drinking but that asshole didn't understand the pain he was feeling.

Loyola took another deep breath of salt air, and forced his mind to forget his troubles. For all of the pain of being a sailor, there was nothing like standing out on the bridge on a night like this. He'd sailed around the world a dozen times, and seen things on land and at sea that no civilian would ever see. Not bad for a street kid who used to hustle cigarettes and lottery tickets in the filthy Lima slums.

Loyola took another long, thoughtful pull. Yes, perhaps he would try to find some kind of job at the port, nearer the boy. Maybe even teach him how to play *fútbol,* as his father had taught him. And with the money he'd already saved up, perhaps a house out in the country where the boy –

A thundering blast deep beneath the vessel threw Loyola to the deck, slamming his skull against the steel bulkhead. Stunned, Loyola crawled to his knees as the breaking hull tore apart with a scream of shattering metal. He was tossed against the rails of the bridge wing, cracking his ribs, but his desperate hands wrapped around the nearest post to keep from falling several stories into the ocean. The air filled with the wail of alarms and klaxons.

He tried to blink away the blood pouring into his eyes from the wound in his broken scalp. He watched in horror as the bow and six hundred feet of ship behind it broke away and plunged headlong into the sea. The rear section where he lay surged ahead, still under power, and crashed into the upended hull in front. Steel containers spilled out of their holds and into the water, and a dozen screaming crewmen along with them.

Secondary explosions ignited the incendiary chemicals, enveloping the shuddering wreckage in unquenchable fire. Within minutes the entire ship and its cargo were lost, sent plunging into the depths of the warm Pacific.

There were no survivors.

# October 24

# 2

## *Barcelona, Spain*

Jack stood at the bar of L'avi, his favorite restaurant in Barcelona. It was located in the El Born district of the old city, called the Ciutat Vella in Català, the language of Catalonia, the semi-autonomous region of Spain. It was also a locals' favorite, which was saying something, because *catalanes* really knew how to eat and drink, and did so quite often, late into the night.

Jack took another sip of sweet, red Spanish *vermut*. Van Delden's suicide was a distant memory, thanks to his time in Spain. It had been a week since Jack woke up in a cold sweat in the middle of the night reliving it. Now numbed to the horror of the Dutchman's excruciating death, Jack still couldn't help but wonder what kind of organization inspired that kind of fearsome loyalty.

Jack had loved his time in Madrid but he was utterly captivated by Barcelona. He could see himself living in this city, despite recent events. Spontaneous mass protests of hundreds of thousands of people had shut Barcelona down several times in the days before he arrived but lately all was quiet. Jack sensed there was still something in the air.

Most protesters favored Catalonian independence from Madrid, but not all. Independence wasn't the only issue. The rage that had driven freedom-loving people into the streets was the recent sentencing of Catalonian independence politicians to long prison terms by Madrid. Spain still lived under the long shadow of Franco's Fascist dictatorship. Though Spain was now a democratic republic, heavily armed riot police battling barricades of unarmed Catalonian civilians elicited hard memories from the earlier times. It was an emotional response, not a rational one, Jack thought, but modern politics was only about emotions in the Western world these days, including here.

The protests changed nothing. Madrid still held all the cards because it held the monopoly of force. Barcelona was a city on the edge of another eruption, which made it all the more interesting as a place to be.

At six-one, Jack's broad-shouldered frame towered over most of the locals who crowded the place at lunchtime, which throughout Spain lasted until at least three o'clock. The energy level in here was somewhere between a late-night disco and a rock concert.

Jack could hardly hear himself think above the din of excited diners jabbering away in a half-dozen languages, particularly Català – its own unique mix of Spanish, Italian, and French. Català was one of the many things that made Catalonia separate and distinct, which was why Franco had outlawed the language during his regime.

Jack had little more of the language than *si us plau* or *gràcies* in his vocabulary, but even using those few words was enough to elicit a smile from appreciative locals, particularly those favoring independence from Madrid. If all else failed, Jack knew the words for the tapas he loved best – especially *bombas* and *pa amb tomàquet*. In a worst-case scenario, a finger jabbed onto a menu item along with a smile would always do the trick.

Today was Jack's last day in Spain. Despite the highly social atmosphere, he was by himself. The life he lived as a covert operative wasn't amenable to long-term relationships, at least, not for him.

He'd seen the pretty blonde at the other end of the bar when he first came in, and saw her check him out. She wore no wedding ring and appeared to be by herself. She had a Bluetooth stuck in her ear and engaged in a very occasional conversation with someone on the other end of the call. Between shots of bubbly cava and bites of crispy *croquetas de jamón*, she tossed subtle, sidelong glances at him in the mirror that stood behind the counter.

Even if she was interested in him, he was already packed for his American Airlines flight back home tomorrow. He only traveled with a laptop and a buffalo leather satchel crammed with a few days' worth of clothes. He preferred washing his things to throwing them out and buying new ones, unlike a famous fictional character he admired.

The only thing he needed to remember to grab in the morning was his dog-eared copy of George Orwell's *Homage to Catalonia,* which was the reason for his stop in Barcelona. He'd first read the book in college and its last, prophetic pages had haunted him for years. When Gerry Hendley told him to take a few weeks off after his last mission with The Campus in South Korea, he decided to revisit the idea of Spain, and in particular, the Spanish Civil War. He loved being an off-the-books operator for The Campus – the 'black side' operations of the financial firm Hendley Associates, carrying out missions for the American government that otherwise couldn't be handled through normal channels.

But lately, Jack had been considering the words of an old Jesuit professor he'd bumped into in London a few years back. His subconscious was nibbling on the edges of an idea to go back to school and get his doctorate in history, just like his dad.

Maybe.

Nothing on this trip persuaded him to quit The Campus.

The work was too important and too damned exciting. But he also had to admit he had been utterly captivated by his time in Spain and experiencing it through a historian's eyes, rather than through the green glow of night-vision optics while chasing tangos. It was one thing to read about a great historical city like Barcelona but something else altogether to stand inside a nine-hundred-year-old church with the bones of Crusader knights entombed beneath the stones at your feet.

He plopped the last of the glistening *pimientos de Padrón* into his mouth. The small green peppers fried in olive oil and dusted with sea salt practically melted on his tongue. He seriously considered ordering another *vermut* but decided to just finish the one he had and pay the bill. The clock was ticking and he had a timed entrance ticket to the Picasso Museum, which was just up the narrow, medieval street of Carrer de Montcada. It was the last item on his list before leaving tomorrow.

He raised a finger to the passing server who set his check on the bar in front of him. Jack counted out the bills he needed to cover the tab along with a generous tip. He noticed he still had a few euros left in his wallet and decided to toss those into the tray as well. He didn't need euros in Virginia and the young server was working her ass off. God bless her.

*Adéu, Barcelona.*

# 3

His bill paid, Jack polished off the last swallow of his drink when he happened to catch a glimpse of a striking young African American woman as she edged her way into the restaurant, clearly looking for someone.

*Renée Moore?*

Jack couldn't believe it was her, after all these years.

They'd had a few senior finance classes together at Georgetown and, as often happened when two smart, attractive people spent a lot of time together, fell into an intense but brief relationship. Renée Moore was the most career-minded woman he'd ever met, and that was saying something coming from a household of highly accomplished Ryan women. But her mind was set on conquering Wall Street. She was perfectly gentle but crystal clear when she broke up with him: She wasn't looking to get married. Ever.

Jack hadn't seen Renée since they'd both graduated seven years ago. He had often wondered if she could have been the one who got away because she had so many of the qualities he most admired in women. But then again, her top priority was earning a Wall Street fortune. His wasn't. Jack believed in living for things worth dying for, and money wasn't one of them.

He'd actually thought of reaching out to her a couple of years ago for a Costa Rican banking project he was tackling as a 'white side' analyst at Hendley Associates. Moore had a first-rate mind and an incredible work ethic. She would have been perfect for the gig. He'd even thought he might be able to convince her that things like duty, honor, and country were just as significant as making a billion dollars by the time she was thirty. But every time he thought about picking up the phone, he didn't. Most people's loyalties were only to their own ambitions. That didn't necessarily make them bad people. But if his dad taught Jack anything, it was that the only life worth living was a life of service to others.

And like the Man said, you can't serve two masters.

Above the din of happy diners, Jack shouted her name. She began searching the crowd until she spotted him, which wasn't hard, given his height. A luminous smile lit her up for a moment, then it turned to confusion as she made her way over to him, squeezing her five-foot-six frame next to him at the crowded bar. She reached up and gave him a hug.

'Reneé, I can't believe it. What brings you to Barcelona? To this place?' Smile lines creased around Jack's blue eyes.

'For a second there, I thought maybe it was you, but –'

He could barely hear her above the noise. He raised his voice. 'Can I get you something to drink? The tapas here are unbelievable.'

'No, thanks.' She glanced around the room, clearly searching for someone, occasionally standing up on her tiptoes.

'Can't find who you're looking for?'

She turned back to Jack. 'Sorry, I'm being rude. How have you been? You look great – put on a few pounds of muscle since I last saw you.'

'Yeah, hitting the weight room every now and then,' Jack said.

She touched his face, a familiar gesture. 'The beard's new. I like it.'

'Tell that to my mom.'

He wanted to tell her how gorgeous she looked, too – better

than he remembered. But he knew that wasn't going to go anywhere, and he wasn't looking to seduce her. He was just genuinely glad to see her.

The pretty girl with the Bluetooth at the end of the bar seemed happy to see her, too. She kept glancing back and forth between her second cava and Moore.

'What are you up to these days?' Moore kept scanning the room and checking the door.

'Hendley Associates. A small, private-equity firm in Alexandria. You?'

'I'm a VP with a tech startup in California called CrowdScope.'

'Tech? I thought you'd be in finance.'

'I am, just the other side of it. It's a fintech firm.'

'Sounds exciting. What happened to Wall Street?'

'Been there, done that.'

Jack's Apple Watch beeped. 'Oh, man. I gotta run.'

'Hot date?'

'No. Just the museum. I've got a timed entry. Any chance we could grab a drink later? Or maybe dinner?'

She turned back around and smiled at him. 'Yeah, Jack. I'd really like that.' She reached into her purse and pulled out her business card. 'Call me around seven. We'll find a place to meet. Okay?'

'Perfect.' He glanced at the address and phone number, then pocketed it.

'How long are you in town for?'

Jack shrugged. 'Leaving tomorrow.'

'Too bad.' Her smile faded. 'I've missed you, Jack. I'm so glad we bumped into each other. What a crazy coincidence.'

Jack ignored the screeching voice of the catechism nun in his head telling him that there was no such thing as coincidences.

'Try the *vermut* here. And the *tortilla*. It's fantastic – hell, everything is. Well, gotta run. I'll call you later.'

'Make sure you do.' She threw another hug around his neck and kissed his bearded cheek. *'Adéu.'*

*'Adéu.'*

Jack gently pushed his way through the crowd of people, heading for the exit. He cast another glance at Moore at the bar, still searching for someone, and the Bluetooth blonde, still watching her. As he stepped through the doorway, a short, heavyset man about his age with shoulder-length hair and thick, Warby Parker tortoiseshell glasses bumped into him.

'Sorry, man,' he said to Jack as he passed.

*'No hay problema,* slick,' Jack muttered, thinking nothing of it.

Finally breaking through to the narrow street, Jack checked his watch. His online ticket would get him into the museum in five minutes, which was perfect timing.

A glance in the window of a small jewelry store across the narrow street gave Jack the nearest shot for quick surveillance detection. The only person who caught Jack's eye in the glass was a guy about his size and age, with short-cropped blond hair, a long, crooked nose, square face, and deep-set hazel eyes. He also had a Bluetooth in his ear.

It was a lot of data to acquire in a short glance, but that was how Jack had been trained by John Clark, The Campus's director of operations.

Like Jack, the man was catching a glimpse of him as well in the same glass, or so it seemed. They held each other's gaze for less than the blink of an eye before the man turned casually away and headed south in the opposite direction. He was just another tourist on the phone, Jack supposed, but his mind registered the man's strong, athletic gait as he turned a corner onto Passeig del Born.

Jack turned north and headed for the museum.

Three steps later, he was dead.


Or so he thought.

The concussive force from the blast inside L'avi had nowhere to go but out the front door and into the narrow street between the heavy stone walls in a rushing tidal wave of pressure. Shop windows shattered for a dozen yards in each direction.

The sound of the explosion was like a shotgun blast in Jack's unprotected ears. The pressure from the detonation behind Jack was heavy enough to knock him forward, slamming his head into a wall, but he managed to stay on his feet.

He turned, dazed, and staggered back toward the direction of the explosion. Broken bodies lay in the narrow street in front. He didn't stop to help them. They were dead.

Blood and shredded flesh spattered the wrecked doorway as he picked his way through the debris and into the restaurant. The ringing in his ears muted the anguished cries and moans of the few survivors. Jack's limited emergency medical training under the watchful eye of Adara Sherman kicked in, but without a medical kit there wouldn't be much he could do. He stepped around the wounded and the dead, pushing past overturned chairs and tables, desperately searching for Moore. His eyes finally fell on her crumpled form, one arm twisted unnaturally against the hinge of her elbow, her blouse torn away by the blast.

Jack fell down at her side, broken plates and glasses crunching beneath his weight. Her swollen face oozed blood from her nose, mouth, and ears. He laid a hand on her neck to check for a pulse, certain she was dead, but her bloodshot eyes suddenly startled awake. Jack nearly shouted for joy that she was still alive. Her swollen lips began to whisper.

'Babe, it's me, Jack. Lie still. An ambulance will be here soon.'

Moore's dimming eyes pleaded with Jack. She tugged on his shirtsleeve with the bloody fingers of her one unbroken hand. He leaned in close, his ear next to her mouth. He saw her eyes fluttering, and the whites suddenly showing. But with her last, ragged breath she managed to whisper a single word:

'Sammler.'

# 4

*South Pacific*
*On board the Russian Federation Navy submarine* Glazov

Captain First Rank Nikolay Grinko read the notice a third time and swore.

It wasn't a complicated instruction. Far from it. The extremely low frequency transmission (ELF) from the ZEVS transmitter near Murmansk was only capable of sending out minimal communications.

The ELF data rate was so low that submarine comms were limited to receiving messages only from Murmansk, and those were little more than 'bell ringer' notices. The microscopic data rate had always seemed ironic to Grinko. The ZEVS transmitter was the most powerful in Europe. It required up to 14 megawatts of electricity fired through two sixty-kilometer-long antennas in order to generate an 82 Hz signal with a massive wavelength of 3,686 kilometers. Only China's ELF transmitter – five times the size of New York City – was larger and more powerful.

The low data-transmission rate was the trade-off for the ZEVS's capacity to send a signal through several hundred feet of polar ice or ocean water almost anywhere on the planet. The *Glazov* was currently submerged at 137 meters below the surface of the Pacific, deep enough to avoid any surface sonar detection from air or ships. A submarine like his only survived by remaining undetected. ELF was designed to help him remain so.

Unless, of course, the bell ringer message was telling him to surface and receive new instructions from a high-density satellite communication, which it was.

Grinko swore again.

'No mistake?'

'No, sir.'

Grinko searched the man's eyes for any sign of doubt. There was none. He wasn't surprised.

The senior enlisted man standing in front of him was utterly reliable, as were the rest of his crew. The information systems technician – Grinko still called them radiomen – didn't write the new orders; he only delivered them.

'Thank you. Dismissed.'

The man quietly closed Grinko's cabin door. Grinko couldn't believe it. What was the point of changing position? The first test of the latest version VA-111 Shkval 3 ('Squall') supercavitating torpedo had gone perfectly and, equally important, undetected by the opposition. It had taken all of his crew's best efforts to avoid them to arrive on station.

Propelled by a solid-fuel rocket motor and a terminal guidance system, the new Shkval 3 had achieved underwater speeds approaching three hundred miles per hour and struck its target with a range in excess of twelve miles.

Keeping the weapon secret meant the Americans couldn't develop defenses against it. Why risk being found now by moving? For what purpose?

Grinko rubbed his clean-shaven face, resigned to his fate. Submarine captains in the Pacific Fleet carried out orders from Vladivostok HQ, not the other way around. So be it. He picked up his phone and called his XO, issuing the order to redeploy to the new coordinates.

Grinko's resignation turned to confidence. He was

captain of one of his nation's most advanced submarines, carrying some of its most potent weapons. Vladivostok was handing him another opportunity to demonstrate to the arrogant Americans that their dominance at sea was at an end.

# 5

## Barcelona, Spain

*Who the hell was Sammler?*

'Sammler' was the last thing she ever said, and last words mattered the most, Jack told himself as he gently closed Moore's eyes. His hand hovered over her breathless mouth. He touched her lips.

A last good-bye.

Still wet with her blood and his skull pounding with a near-migraine headache, Jack glanced over at a middle-aged woman lying against the bar, whimpering in Spanish. Her eyes were shut against the blood oozing onto her face from a scalp wound and the stabbing pain of her injured left hand. Sirens screamed in the distance.

Jack dashed over to her side. He snatched up a handful of paper napkins from the floor and pressed them hard against her scalp wound. He took her one good hand and switched it for his.

'*Su mano, empujar aquí,*' he said. 'No, not *empujar.* Sorry. I don't know the word. Just . . . press hard.'

But the woman understood Jack's middle-school Spanish well enough. She pressed her good hand hard against the makeshift bandage as Jack took her other hand and inspected it briefly before pulling out a large shard of glass from her palm. It bled, too, but not as badly as the scalp. Jack pulled another stack of napkins from a dispenser lying next to him, compressed it into her palm, and folded her hand into a fist.

'Hold this, tight, okay?' Jack said, as he turned around to see who else he could help, his clothes even bloodier now than they were a moment ago.

On the floor just a few feet away he saw Moore's purse. A few cautious pedestrians crept into the wreckage of the restaurant, faces white with terror but eager to help. Ambulance sirens screamed just beyond the door.

As tires screeched to a halt outside, Jack reached down and picked up Moore's purse, its contents scattered on the floor. He dug through the nearly empty purse looking for her smartphone, thinking that whoever this Sammler was, maybe he'd called her earlier or she had his contact information stored on her phone.

Spanish EMTs charged through the doors with medical gear in hand, followed by four local police, their uniforms marked GUÀRDIA URBANA.

One of the cops, bearded and burly, saw Jack standing in the middle of the carnage, rifling through Moore's purse like a looter, and began shouting at him in Català.

Still dazed by the blast and numbed with grief, and with his ears ringing and a headache crushing his skull, Jack couldn't make out a single word of what the cop was saying, but it wasn't hard for him to figure out the guy was pissed.

More sirens blared outside and more tires screeched to a halt as even more police and EMTs arrived, charging through the broken doors.

Jack pointed at Moore's corpse. 'She's my friend. I'm just looking for –'

But the big cop pulled his baton and charged at Jack, his eyes raging.

Jack dropped the purse but something in him snapped. His friend was dead and he'd nearly been killed. *And now this asshole is calling me a thief.* Jack squared up to take the guy down as the cop raised his baton.

'*Parì!*' – Stop! a woman's voice called from behind.

The big bearded cop froze in mid-swing. He and Jack turned around to see a woman about his age in jeans and a leather jacket flashing a badge. Her shoulder-length hair was neat but not fashionable, and her small frame was trim like an athlete's. Despite his headache, Jack saw the pistol in a shoulder rig beneath her coat. She barked another order at the cop towering over her. He argued with her, pointing his baton at Jack.

She turned toward Jack. 'He says you're a looter. Is that true?'

'No. I was looking for the phone of my friend . . .' Jack's voice trailed off, his legs wobbly. He pointed at Moore's corpse. Unexpectedly, tears welled in his eyes.

The woman with the badge softened, but only slightly. She took Jack by the elbow.

'Let's go outside and get you checked out.'

Jack sat on the stone stairs of the back entrance to the big Gothic church, Santa Maria del Mar. He was just a hundred yards from the restaurant, facing a *placeta* – a small plaza. A uniformed EMT examined Jack's eyes with a penlight under the watchful gaze of the woman with the badge. A police helicopter's rotors hammered low overhead.

Hundreds of spectators had gathered in the area but had been pushed back behind yellow police tape and barricades. A local TV journalist stood among them, interviewing people claiming to be witnesses to the tragedy.

The plaza was filled with several ambulances and police vehicles, forming a staging area for medical treatment and a preliminary investigation of the blast. Jack saw police cars and vans marked from several departments – Mossos d'Esquadra, Guardia Civil, Policía Nacional – blue lights still flashing on most of them.

The EMT gave Jack one last cautious glance as he pocketed his penlight. 'No headache?'

'No. I'm fine,' Jack said, lying.

The EMT's eyes narrowed with disbelief. '*Estàs segur?* You are sure?' He scratched his thin beard tinged with gray.

'Yeah, really. Thanks.'

'I think it is best you go to hospital. Get X-rays, at least.'

'No, I'm good.'

'You know, it cost you no money for medicine here.'

'It's not that. I just don't want to go. I'm fine.'

'Then it is necessary for you to see a doctor when you get back to the States, *vale*?'

'I will. I promise.'

The EMT looked over at the woman and shrugged his reluctant approval, then dashed off with his medical kit to another victim.

'My name is Laia Brossa. I work for the Centro Nacional de Inteligencia – CNI, for short. That's our version of the FBI and CIA, how you say, rolled into one. Who are you?'

Still seated on the steps, Jack stuck out his hand. She took it. 'My name is Jack Ryan. *Mucho gusto*' – Nice to meet you.

'*Igualmente.*' Brossa pulled out her smartphone. 'Do you mind if I record our conversation? It's easier than taking notes.'

'Not at all.'

'And you said your friend Renée Moore was killed inside?'

Jack lowered his head and nodded.

'Yes.'

She patted his shoulder. 'I'm very sorry for your loss.'

Jack raised his head. 'Yeah. Me, too.'

'She was an American as well?'

'Yes.'

'And how is it you survived the blast, Mr Ryan?'

'I was outside. I had just left to go to the Picasso Museum. If I'd waited another thirty seconds, I'd probably be dead, too.'

'You are very lucky. And what brings you to Spain?'

'I'm sorry, I don't know why you're asking me all of these questions.'

'Because it is my job.'

'Your job is to find out who killed my friend, and all of those other people.'

'We already know. It was a terror group called Brigada Catalan. They claimed responsibility just a few minutes ago on the Internet, while you were getting checked out.'

'I read about them in the news. They haven't done anything like this before. Just a lot of talk, right?'

Brossa shrugged. 'Every terrorist who kills talks a lot before they start killing, yes?'

'Yeah, I guess so.' Jack glanced up at the flags hanging from several of the private terraces around the square. Most had patriotic gold flags with four red stripes – the official flag of Catalonia – but a few had the addition of a Cuban white star on a blue triangle – the flag of the independence movement. In the last few days, Jack had hardly seen any Spanish national flags here in Barcelona. In Madrid, just the opposite.

'But these Brigada Catalan people, they haven't been violent, not like this. It's a political movement, not a terrorist one, if I'm not mistaken,' Jack said.

'Until today,' Brossa said, surveying the flags. She muttered something in Català to herself. She turned back to Jack. 'You are well read on Catalonian politics for an American. Quite unusual.'

34

'We're not all idiots,' Jack said, instantly regretting the comment. Most Americans weren't idiots. They just didn't pay attention to other countries because their own country was so huge and had plenty of its own problems. And not every American double-majored in history and finance at an elite university like Georgetown.

'I apologize if I offended you,' Brossa said.

'Not at all. I'm sorry for my bad manners. Almost getting killed has put me in a lousy mood. The only reason I'm up to speed on Brigada Catalan is because I happened to read an article about them in *El País* yesterday. In English. So, yeah, maybe I'm just another American idiot, too.'

'Somehow, I doubt that. So tell me, what brought you to Spain? Ms Moore? She was your woman?'

'No, nothing like that. Just friends. We hadn't seen each other in years. It was a pure coincidence that she walked into the restaurant.'

'My father says there is no such thing as coincidence,' Brossa said.

Jack smiled, despite the headache.

'Something funny, Mr Ryan?'

'Not really.'

'And the reason you are in Spain?'

The real reason he was in Spain was for R & R from missions he'd run for The Campus in Poland and Indonesia in the past several months, and to clear his mind from the death of his friend Liliana, and van Delden's suicide. But Brossa wasn't cleared to be read in on any of that.

'I studied a little history in college, and read Orwell's *Homage to Catalonia* – do you know it?'

'Of course.'

'We didn't cover the Spanish Civil War in depth in class. I wanted to fill in the gaps by seeing it for myself.'

Brossa eyed Jack up and down, trying to decide if he was bullshitting her or not.

'And did you find what you were looking for, Mr Ryan?'

'I came to find out more about the war, but I wound up falling in love with Spain. It's a fantastic country.'

'Where have you been in Spain?'

*Chasing a couple of arms-smuggling shitbirds in Seville with The Campus last time I was here,* Jack reminded himself.

'It's been a short trip, unfortunately. Just Madrid, and then here.'

'You must come back, then, and see the rest. Galicia, Andalusia, the Basque region – Spain is not just one country, but a collection of many smaller ones.'

'Already on my bucket list, believe me.'

'So, Mr Ryan –'

'Please, call me Jack.'

'*Vale,* Jack. Can you tell me what you last saw or heard before the explosion? Any protesters outside? Anyone suspicious?'

'The place was packed for lunch. Everyone seemed to be having a good time. I'd say half locals, half tourists, maybe? I heard German, French, Norwegian, but mostly Català.'

'You are very observant.'

'Just a curious tourist.'

'L'avi is very popular. One of the best in the city. I eat there often myself. No shouts of *Visca Cataluña!* before the blast? Or anything else that would indicate a motive for the attack?'

'No, nothing like that. People were just eating and drinking and having a good time when I left, then suddenly – well, you know the rest.'

'And your friend? What does she do? Why was she in Barcelona?' She pronounced the word *Barcelona* like an American – the *c* sounding like an *s,* unlike the Castilian

36

Spanish of Madrid, which turned the *c* into a lispy *th* sound – Bar-*thuh*-lona.

'I really don't know. Business, maybe. I'm pretty sure she was there to meet somebody.' Jack reached into his shirt pocket and handed her Moore's business card.

'Who was she meeting there?'

'I don't know.'

*Renée didn't, either, judging by the way she reacted when she first saw me,* Jack thought. Like maybe she thought *he* was the contact, but then she knew it wasn't him. That meant she didn't know what he looked like – and it was probably a guy.

'The last thing she said to me before she died was a name. "Sammler." Maybe that's the guy she was meeting.'

*Or, the man who killed her.*

'First name?'

'She didn't say.'

Brossa read Moore's business card. 'CrowdScope? What is that?'

'A Silicon Valley fintech startup.'

'Excuse me? "Fintech"?'

'Companies that apply new technologies to financial transactions, like using data analytics to acquire new customers, or robo-investing. That kind of thing. Renée was a financial wizard.'

'May I keep this?'

'Of course.'

'Do you happen to have your passport with you?'

'Yes.' Jack pulled it out of a front zippered pocket of his cargo pants, stowed away against pickpockets, which were rife in the city.

Brossa examined it, flipping pages for visa stamps. She snapped a picture of the page with Jack's information and passport number before handing it back to him.

'And you, Jack? What do you do?'

'I'm in finance, too. But not fintech.' He pulled out his wallet, fished out a business card, and handed it to her. 'I'm a financial analyst with Hendley Associates, out of Alexandria, Virginia.'

'Interesting work, I imagine.'

'Numbers always tell a story, if you know how to read them.' *Something Paul Brown taught me years ago.*

Brossa's cell phone rang. 'Excuse me, Jack.' She turned away and spoke into her phone. A short exchange. Jack watched her in his peripheral vision. She ended the call and sighed.

'Jack, I'm sorry, I have to go. Is it possible you are staying in Barcelona for the next few days? I have more questions for you, and you are one of the few surviving eyewitnesses.'

Jack didn't know if he could extend his stay at his Airbnb, or if Gerry would give him the extra time off, but there was no way in hell he was going back home until he found out who killed Moore, and until he was certain her killer would be brought to justice. Helping this CNI agent would be the easiest way to ensure both.

'Of course. But I need you to do me a favor.'

'If I can.'

'I need you to look into this Sammler guy for me. I think that name is going to be important for solving this case.'

Brossa gave him another searching look. Finally, her first, small smile.

'I'll be in touch.'

# 6

It was a twenty-minute walk from the *placeta* where he'd been treated for his injuries back to his Airbnb apartment in Barceloneta, the old workers' neighborhood down by the beach that had recently been revitalized.

The explosion at the restaurant had put authorities on edge. Blue lights from police cars and motorcycles flashed at every intersection and helicopters hovered protectively around the Ciutat Vella.

Despite predictions to the contrary, no massive rallies for Catalonian independence spontaneously materialized. Jack didn't know if the peaceful protesters were afraid of suffering violence or being blamed for more of it if another bombing attack occurred tonight.

In this part of town, tourists seemed completely unaware of what had occurred just a kilometer away, only an hour before as they flocked past the restaurants, hotels, and *gelaterias* on Passeig de Joan de Borbó approaching the sea. Despite his attempts to clean up back at the church, some of the more observant did notice his bloodstained clothing.

His head still pounding, Jack ducked into a tiny Carrefour Express for some aspirin and bottled water. He popped a couple and washed them down with a long gulp as he crossed back into the alley toward his place, willing himself up the fifty-seven narrow, winding marble stairs to his door on the third floor.

Still feeling like he'd been dragged behind a car on a rocky dirt road, he stripped off his clothes and hit the small but generous shower, letting the steam and hot water work their magic. He couldn't stop thinking about Moore and the light fading from her dimming eyes. Such a waste. A brilliant and beautiful woman who happened to be in the wrong place at the wrong time.

He toweled off, trying to solve a couple of mysteries about her. A fintech kinda made sense – finance was her thing. But a Silicon Valley startup? He remembered distinctly her dream of running, if not outright owning, a white-shoe Wall Street investment firm. Both of her parents were corporate executives and had groomed her for the same life. She never struck him as the entrepreneurial type. On the risk-reward continuum, she was heavily slanted toward the latter.

Maybe something went sideways in her career? Had to start over? And what would a Silicon Valley tech executive be doing in Barcelona? Possibly on vacation, like him, but not likely. She didn't have the wide-eyed look of a tourist. She was all business in her demeanor, and clearly on a mission to find whoever it was she was supposed to meet – someone she had obviously never met before, which is a strange way to do business.

His headache finally ebbing from the aspirin and shower, Jack reached into the fridge and grabbed a can of Mahou Radler, a *clara* – a Spanish beer mixed with lemon soda – which he'd come to crave these last few days. He plopped down at the little kitchen dinette that served as his office space and opened up his laptop, encrypted for security by Hendley Associates' IT director, Gavin Biery.

It was just five o'clock in the afternoon, local. He pulled up the contact information for the U.S. Consulate in Barcelona in order to call them and tell them about Renée, in case the Spanish authorities hadn't yet done so. He discovered that the consulate had closed to the public at one p.m. He could call a 24-hour hotline but he wanted to do it in person. He decided to pay them a visit first thing in the morning.

He then Googled Moore's company, CrowdScope, and found the corporate website. It was about what he expected: 'Optimizing capital investments and business solutions through big data analytics,' blah, blah, blah. Standard corporate speak, stock photos, and bullet points. Nothing interactive. He clicked on the 'Who We Are' tab and found Moore's contact information. She was listed as 'Vice President of Marketing,' just as she was on her business card.

*Marketing?*

Her phone number and a CrowdScope e-mail address were also given. It was a lot of information but didn't really say much, but that was pretty common these days. Style over substance. Corporate clickbait.

It was eleven a.m. EST and Jack saw that Gavin was online back in Alexandria. He dialed Gavin's direct number on his smartphone.

'Jack! I was just getting ready to shoot you a text. I read about the explosion in Barcelona. You weren't anywhere near it, were you? The photos online looked pretty bad.'

'Yeah, that's why I'm calling.'

'You okay?'

'I'm fine. But a friend of mine was there and got killed.'

'Oh, jeez. I'm so sorry.'

'I'm sure you've got better things to do, but I wanted to ask you a favor.'

'Name it.'

'I'd like you to do a little digging into my friend for me. I'll send over the contact information and some links. I'd like to know more about the company she was working for, and more important, see if you can find a connection between her and a guy named Sammler – last name, I'm sure, no first. Phone records, OSINT, whatever you can find out about this guy, and what he had to do with Renée.'

'What kind of connection should I be looking for? You think this Sammler guy is tied to the bombing somehow?'

'Not sure. But his name was the last thing she said before she died, so I figure he must be important to her, and maybe he might have an idea about what happened.'

'Sounds like you were nearly killed yourself.'

'Not really,' Jack lied.

'I'll jump right on this. Things are pretty quiet around here right now. The whole team is still out on vacation, just like you. Even Gerry, so I've got time to kill.'

'Thanks, Gav. I really appreciate it.'

'Question for you. Did you see any CCTV cameras in the restaurant? What was its name?'

Jack chided himself. Why didn't he think of that? Maybe the explosion rattled his skull harder than he realized.

'The name is L'avi.' He spelled it out. 'And yes, I did see cameras. Three of them. It would be awesome if you could get your hands on those tapes. Might tell us everything we need to know.'

'Won't be easy.'

'Any chance you can hack the restaurant's computer and grab them?'

'Not if the computer has been blown to smithereens. And most likely, the videos are on digital cards or even actual digital tape if the system's old enough. I'm guessing the local police have already recovered whatever survived the blast.'

'I'm betting the cops don't have it. My guess is the CNI might – those are the people who interviewed me after the blast. I'll be seeing my contact again tomorrow, I'm sure. I'll see what I can do on my end.'

'I'll call you if I find anything. Just watch yourself, okay?'

'You know it.'

Jack drained his *clara* as he put an e-mail together for Gavin with links to CrowdScope and everything else he could think of and sent it off. He sent another e-mail to Gerry, informing him he was extending his stay in Spain for a few more days but Gerry's auto reply bounced back, informing Jack that Gerry wouldn't be back in the office for another week. He took that as permission to hang around. He'd ask for forgiveness later, if needed.

Jack then remembered about extending his stay at his place – packing up and moving would be a pain in the butt. He shot a quick message through the Airbnb site and his landlord responded minutes later, telling Jack he was thrilled to extend his stay for another week. Jack paid for the extension online in advance then remembered to put his return airline ticket on hold.

He also thought about his mom, who was not only a world-class eye surgeon and ophthalmologist but also a heck of a psychic, as all good mothers were. She always seemed to know when he or one of his siblings was dancing on the edge of something that could hurt them. He dropped her a text telling her that he was far from the explosion she'd probably heard about on the news and that he was coming home soon. It was the kind of lie he could only pull off in a text because she would have seen right through him if he was standing in her presence.

Thank God for texting.

Satisfied he'd gotten a jump on things, he grabbed another *clara* from the fridge and dropped back in front of his computer. He'd only really glanced at the Brigada Catalan article and its brief references to other recent events connected to them. Since he had some time to kill, he decided to dig deeper. If Brigada Catalan was responsible for Renée's death, he'd do everything he could to help Brossa track them down.

What the CNI agent didn't realize was that if she wasn't able or willing to deliver the justice that Renée deserved, he'd find a way to do it himself, one bullet at a time.


Two hours later, Jack shut his computer, his eyes watering from the river of facts about Catalonian independence he'd just been wading through. Gavin hadn't called him back and he was hungry, so he decided on a hole-in-the-wall stand-up pizza joint around the corner for carryout.

He snagged up his apartment keys and headed out, still processing what he'd just read. The Catalonian independence movement was anything but monolithic. But it was pretty clear the source of the current troubles was Catalonia's 2017 independence referendum, which passed by an overwhelming ninety percent of the vote – despite Madrid's attempts to disrupt it. Madrid declared the whole thing illegal and jailed the offending members of the Generalitat – the local legislature – and the rest of the Catalonian independence politicians fled, including the president, seeking asylum abroad.

The officials in the European Union sided with Madrid against the Catalonian independence politicians. Brussels still had Brexit on its mind, not to mention the French Yellow Vests, the Italian Lega, Ireland's Sinn Féin, and others, and wholly supported Madrid's actions. This only fueled Catalonian frustrations. The EU constitution promised self-determination and, certainly, voting rights, and both appeared to be violated in equal measure by both Madrid's heavy-handed actions and Brussels's failure to recognize Catalonia's claims.

According to what Jack read in the press, that's when Brigada Catalan was born.

Of course, history was the context for all of this.

Catalonia had a distinct and separate national identity going back as far as the Roman era and the fifth-century Visigoth kings who succeeded them. They lost their independence and were absorbed into the Spanish empire by the Bourbon king Philip V, who conquered them in the beginning of the eighteenth century.

In the 1930s, under the Spanish Republic, Catalonia was granted increasing autonomy, but the Spanish Civil War ended that dream. Catalonia had been the heart of the resistance to Franco's final overthrow of the Republican government in 1939. In revenge, the Fascist Franco regime suppressed their language and culture for decades.

Complicating everything else, Catalonia had always been the industrial heart of modern Spain and its most prosperous region. Consequently, Madrid had always taken a disproportionate share of its tax base from the region, another source of local resentment.

Since Franco's death, Catalonian rights had been largely restored, and Català was now the primary language taught in its schools. Despite these reforms, Catalonian nationalists pressed for complete independence from Spain and the creation of an independent Catalonian state. Other regions in Spain, particularly the Basque, had expressed similar desires decades before and resorted to a bombing campaign that was ultimately subdued by Madrid.

Spanish nationalist parties in Madrid wanted both order and central government, and saw Catalonian nationalism as a threat to the Spanish state. If Catalonia seceded, other regions in Spain might follow.

Europe and the rest of the world were struggling with the centralism-nationalism debate. The benefits of national and regional integration were obvious — especially for the political elites and transnational corporations – but always at the cost of local identity and autonomy.

The subtext to all of this, Jack noted, was the tendency of politicians on both sides of the Catalonian argument to exploit the passions of their people in exchange for their own political power. Separatist politicians weren't willing to accept Madrid's previous offers of even broader rights of Catalonian autonomy, even as Spanish nationalists stoked the fears of their followers in Madrid and elsewhere.

Politicians' tendency to serve themselves at the expense of their communities wasn't unique to Spain. The United States suffered too many such fools, playing to identity politics at the expense of the national interest. Jack knew his father was the rarest breed of politician – the reluctant servant.

In truth, most people just wanted to live their lives in peace and prosperity. This was particularly true in Barcelona, where life was very good for locals and visitors alike.

Brigada Catalan rose up out of this confusion and frustration. They proclaimed that if democratic elections were no longer respected by Madrid and the will of the majority of Catalonians ignored, then violence was the 'only viable alternative to Madrid's totalitarian, Francoist, and Fascist rule.' Their online manifesto claimed solidarity with other independence movements throughout history, including the American Revolution, but leaned heavily on Latin American revolutionary sloganeering – in part, Jack believed, because so many Latin American immigrants lived and worked in Barcelona and throughout Spain.

Jack entered the small but pristine Kitchen Barcelona on Carrer de la Maquinista, and queued up behind a couple of locals. The air smelled of fresh-baked crusts, gooey cheeses, and ripe, spicy olives. He felt like he was cheating by eating Italian food, but it was owned and operated by local *catalanes,* which technically made it Spanish food. Besides, it was freaking good.

The place was barely shoulder wide between the glass case and the stand-up bar on the wall. The handsome, flour-dusted pizza chef stood just beyond another doorway, shoveling pies one at a time into the only oven in a kitchen not much bigger than a broom closet. Jack had been here once before — it was fresh, fantastic food, and the cute girl behind the counter had both an awesome sleeve tattoo and an excellent English vocabulary.

Jack didn't worry about Brigada Catalan attacking this place — it was too small and too out of the way. But the killers who murdered Renée were out there in the city somewhere and he knew they would strike again until Catalonia won its independence or until they died fighting for it.

If Jack had anything to say about it, it would be the latter.

# 7

## *Mountain View, California*

They were both lean and narrow-shouldered, with medium brown hair, brown eyes, and fair complexions, which was why people who first met them assumed they were siblings. But Chris and Cari Fast were married, first meeting, then dating, and eventually falling in love all at the Google AI quantum labs in Mountain View. They even recited their wedding vows standing beneath Stan, the iconic full-size *T. rex* skeleton on the Googleplex campus, surrounded by friends, family, and pink flamingos.

The childless, forty-two-year-olds loved not owning a car. It wasn't that the two senior Google scientists couldn't afford any luxury vehicle they wanted, or the insane insurance rates, or even a full-time driver to avoid the hassles of Bay Area driving.

Riding bikes, ridesharing, and not owning a car was really about keeping a low carbon footprint, and equally important, demonstrating their public commitment to combating climate change. For trips to the city, they always used Uber, including tonight's benefit gala for their favorite local no-kill animal shelter.

Uber's convenient phone app was on the front page of both their iPhones (only Nooglers – new Google employees – thought that Android phones were required at the Plex). Despite the fact that they didn't own a luxury vehicle, they certainly enjoyed the experience of riding in one, which was why they always opted for Uber Lux. Tonight was no different, and in truth, they needed the extra space, since they were bringing their companion dogs, a miniature Maltese named Cookie and a papillon – often mistaken for a long-haired Chihuahua – named Louis (with a silent *s* in the French manner) after the Dustin Hoffman character in the movie of the same name.

All four stood expectantly on the wide, tree-lined suburban street outside their one-story mid-century rancher as the roomy Cadillac Escalade glided to a halt at the curb. Cari double-checked her Uber app, confirming the make, model, and license plate of the vehicle. The smiling, well-built young Nigerian who opened their doors was the driver listed on the app as well.

*Good to go,* she thought, as the four of them climbed into the backseat. They were greeted with bottled Fiji waters and organic treats for the dogs. There were bright smiles and wagging tails all around as the big SUV pulled away from the curb.

They had no idea it was going to be the night of their lives.

# October 25

# 8

Walter Reed National Military Medical Center
Bethesda, Maryland

*Where do we find such men?* he asked himself.

President Ryan stood over the bed of Lieutenant Corporal Brad Shaffer, 3rd Battalion, Marine Raider Regiment.

*Men? Kid doesn't look old enough to shave.*

It never ceased to amaze him. The fate of the Republic had always been held in the strong, skilled hands of young war-fighters like Shaffer.

They all seemed to be young these days. Or maybe he was just getting to be that old.

'You shouldn't have gone to all the trouble, sir,' Shaffer said.

'It's my honor, son. You did a helluva good thing out there.' Ryan nodded at the Navy Cross he'd just pinned to the boy's hospital gown. 'Your folks will get word about that today.'

The chief of naval operations (CNO), Admiral Talbot, stood next to POTUS. 'Unfortunately, the citation won't include any details of your mission, nor will it be released to the press because the mission is still classified.'

'Understood, sir.'

Ryan added, 'But I hope you know how grateful the nation is for your sacrifice.'

'My boys woulda done the same for me, sir.'

President Ryan had read Shaffer's service jacket. *'For conspicuous gallantry and unyielding courage in the face of overwhelming enemy forces in defense of his team,'* the secretary of the navy had written in Shaffer's citation.

It had cost the boy dearly.

The after-action report read like a Don Bentley novel. It was an operation in Niger. Two of Shaffer's team were wounded, and one killed in an ambush by Boko Haram forces, tipped off by a local police captain on their payroll. Shaffer had single-handedly saved his brothers-in-arms by *advancing* into enemy fire, taking out a KPV 14.5 heavy machine gun and an RPG, then laying down covering fire until the Black Hawks arrived.

As far as Ryan was concerned, the boy deserved the Congressional Medal of Honor, but that wasn't his call. And in his experience, men like Shaffer didn't do what they did for medals. They did it because that was the job they were trained to do, and they were determined to do it, no matter the cost.

It frustrated Ryan that one in five meritorious citations were privately awarded these days. Valor should be celebrated, not hidden. But he understood the rationale. There were so many classified missions around the globe that even some members of the congressional oversight committees were surprised to find out where and when they occurred, let alone how frequently. Such was the price of eternal vigilance. The enemy never slept and never stopped moving until young war-fighters like Shaffer dropped them in the dirt. Ryan worried that there were too many bad guys out there, and not enough Shaffers willing to hunt them down.

'I understand you threw ball in high school,' Ryan said, trying to change the subject. 'You follow the Nats this year?'

Shaffer smiled beneath his facial bandages. 'Nah, sir. I'm a Georgia boy. Braves all the way.' He held up the amputated stump of his right arm. 'Doc says they're going to wire me up with some new bionic LUKE arm. Guess they're gonna make me a cyborg. After I muster out, I'm gonna try out for Atlanta, 'cuz I'll be throwing two-hundred-mile-per-hour pitches with that bad boy.'

'The Braves would be lucky to have you. But trust me, the Nats are the way to go,' Ryan joked.

Shaffer grinned. He was missing a few teeth. 'I'll talk to my agent.'

'Anything else I can do for you?' Ryan asked.

'You done more than enough, sir. I'll make out fine. With all the pretty lady doctors and nurses around here, I got no complaints.'

Ryan laid a hand on the boy's good shoulder. 'You need anything, I've left a card on the nightstand with my secretary's private number. Okay?'

'Yes, sir.'

Ryan leaned closer. 'I'm serious.'

The boy nodded. 'Thanks.'

Ryan stiffened, fighting back the tears welling in his eyes. He snapped his hand to the corner of his eye, the crisp salute he'd learned as a young Marine lieutenant decades ago. The CNO was caught off guard – senior ranks didn't salute junior ranks – and Ryan was the C-in-C. But he sure as hell appreciated him doing it and he joined in.

Shaffer was stunned. But he returned the salute smartly with the remains of his left hand.

'See you at the ballpark, kid,' Ryan said with a wink before turning and leaving.

Ryan was lost in thought as he and Admiral Talbot made their way across the ward toward the elevators, two Secret Service agents in step behind them.

Ryan knew that every time a soldier went into the field on his orders – or under the authority of his office, even if he wasn't aware of the specific mission – he bore the responsibility for the outcome, and he took that responsibility seriously. Sending fragile young bodies into hostile, high-kinetic environments entailed enormous risk and these magnificent kids willingly accepted that risk, even if they didn't fully understand the real cost until they actually had to pay it.

It was his job to make sure they didn't have to pay that cost or to be damned sure it was worth it when men like Shaffer paid it in full. The longer he was on the job, the more certain Ryan was that it should be the old men that went to war. The young had too much to lose.

Ryan didn't notice the admiring stares of the doctors and nurses as he passed by. It was hardly the first time he'd been to the critical-care unit but his obvious compassion for the wounded warriors always made an impact on the staff, who were even more dedicated to their recovery than he was.

'A private word with you, if I may, Mr President?' the CNO asked as they stepped into the elevator.

'Of course.' Ryan looked toward the senior agent in charge of today's presidential detail, Ruby Knox, herself a former Marine. 'Meet you in the basement.'

'Yes, sir.' Knox spoke into her cuff mic, informing the rest of the detail of the change of plans. She was warned the first day she was assigned to SWORDSMAN by Gary Montgomery, the special agent in charge of the Presidential Protective Division (PPD), otherwise known as 'The Shift,' that she needed to be flexible. This President wasn't about ceremonies and calendars but instead focused on the task at hand, including today's unscheduled visit to Walter Reed. Normally, Gary would have been the point man on an off-campus visit like this one but he was on a fly-fishing trip with his daughter in Montana and the honor fell to her.

God, she loved this job.

Knox keyed the panel on the security elevator so that it would proceed directly to the basement garage, bypassing the intervening floors.

As the stainless-steel doors shut behind them, Ryan turned to the admiral. 'So, John. What's up?'

'Our people over at MDA' – the Maritime Domain Awareness element of the Office of Naval Intelligence – 'bumped up a report to my office this morning that needs your attention.'

'You got it.'

'To make a long story short, the Royal Australian Navy received a report of a possible ship sinking in the South Pacific. The *Jade Star* was a Panamanian-flagged commercial vessel, sunk with all hands on board. The vessel's AIS signal disappeared immediately, which was how they got the call.'

Talbot didn't have to tell the President, a former CIA analyst and national security adviser, that international maritime law required every vessel over three hundred tons to broadcast Class A automatic identification system signals. AIS provided a host of self-reported data, including GPS coordinates, speed, port of destination, and the like, all supported by dozens of AIS-enabled orbiting satellites.

'I'm sorry to hear it,' Ryan said. 'The cause? Did Sibbers pick up anything?' Ryan was referring to SBIRS, the Space Based Infrared System.

'No, sir.' He explained why SBIRS failed. Ryan understood but wasn't pleased. But that was a conversation for later.

'Shit.' Ryan rubbed his hand through his hair, thinking through the implications. 'What do your people suspect happened?'

'The only data we have to go on at the moment is the flotsam the Australians were able to recover from the wreck. A few floating containers, even fewer corpses. Three, to be exact.'

'Cause of death?'

'Drowning, trauma. Two victims had burns. Could be from the cause of the sinking or from the vessel itself if it caught fire and exploded.'

'No eyewitnesses?'

'No, and no survivors.'

Talbot continued. 'The cause remains unknown. Ship sinkings aren't all that unusual. Over the last decade, an average of a hundred ships over one hundred gross tons are lost every year, mostly through weather, onboard accidents, or human error. The last two options were MDA's first assumption as to cause. Then they started digging around.'

'And?'

'By their count, six ships in total have gone down in the last eight weeks in the area, averaging over seventy thousand deadweight tons each; that isn't easily explained. It's obviously a big concern.'

Ryan frowned. It sure as hell was. Ninety percent of the world's international commerce was transported by nearly sixty thousand merchant ships crewed by over a million sailors. A threat to global shipping was a threat to the global economy.

'Any pattern to the sinkings?'

'Right now, it looks like it's limited to the South Pacific and only commercial cargo vessels. Six different flags, all different cargoes, none hazardous or environmentally sensitive, at least that we know of. I'll circle back to you with more details when I get them.'

Ryan's eyes narrowed. 'Why are we just hearing about this now?'

The elevator dinged and the doors slid open to the basement garage.

The armored Cadillac limo, affectionately known as

'Stagecoach,' stood idling in the distance, flanked by two PPD agents still out of earshot. Weighing in at nearly ten tons, the vehicle featured five-inch-thick windows, eight-inch doors with electrified handles, and a supply of blood matching Ryan's type, among many other survival features.

'The owners of the vessel reportedly called in to the destination port and said the *Jade Star* wouldn't be docking there. No explanation given. The weird thing was, they made that call *after* the explosion. Of course, the port didn't know that at the time.'

'A cover-up.'

'Apparently. One of the MDA techs got curious. She decided to find out what other AIS signals had vanished over the last several weeks, and had also canceled their port arrivals after the fact. More cross-checking showed that five other vessels had disappeared in that manner.'

'What do the other shipping owners say happened?'

'That's the weird part. When we contacted them, they refused to respond. A couple of them even denied losing their vessels altogether.'

'That doesn't make any sense.'

'No, sir. It doesn't.'

'So what do you need from me?'

'Turns out, one of the ships that went down was leased by White Mountain Logistics and Security.'

'That's Buck Logan's outfit. He's one of the good guys. Took over from his father several years ago.' Ryan chuckled. 'You ever meet Buck's dad, Scooter?'

'No, sir. But I've heard stories.'

'Trust me, they're all true. He was a six-five, two-hundred-forty-pound lineman for the UT Longhorns, back when they wore leather helmets. Ran an infantry platoon with the Fifth Marines in Korea. He came home and built a trucking company that Buck expanded into a worldwide operation. They don't make 'em like that anymore. So, what's the story with Buck?'

'He hasn't been any more cooperative than the other ship owners. In fact, he hasn't responded to any of our inquiries. Given his special status, I was hoping you might have a word with him.'

'If you're asking me to get involved, you must think Buck is hiding something.'

'That's the suspicion. More to the point, we need to know why he's hiding it.'

'And you think he'll tell me.'

'That's a pretty good bet from where I'm standing, sir.'

Logan had a big GOP fundraiser scheduled next month in Houston, where his company was based. More important, White Mountain Logistics + Security was one of the country's largest civilian defense contractors, providing nearly a billion dollars' worth of transportation and operational support to the DoD every year. In effect, Ryan wrote his paycheck.

But if Ryan called Logan and Logan lied, that would put Ryan on the horns of a dilemma. Unless Buck had broken the law, he wasn't compelled to discuss the situation with anybody, including the President of the United States.

On the other hand, why wouldn't he want to talk about it? Buck would have to tell the truth to Ryan if he didn't want to lose his contracts with the federal government – no way he'd spend tax dollars with a known liar. But shutting down White Mountain right now would put a lot of men and women in uniform at risk, and that was something Ryan couldn't abide, either.

'I'll call him and see what I can find out,' Ryan said as he climbed into the armored Cadillac.

'I appreciate that, sir. And also, what you did for young Shaffer today.'

'Compared to what he's sacrificed for us? I haven't done a damn thing. Keep me posted on this situation.'

'Will do, sir.'

Ryan had been scheduled for a lunch meeting with the secretary of agriculture but he'd bumped it for Shaffer. He'd asked Arnie van Damm, his chief of staff, to apologize to her and to reschedule for tomorrow. He pulled a protein bar out of his briefcase. It would have to do for his midday meal today.

'Where to, sir?' the driver asked.

Ryan cracked open one of the bottles of water that were always sitting in the cupholder in front of him. Time enough to grab a quick workout in the White House gym before his three o'clock with Senator Burns.

'Back to the barn, please. There's a stack of iron calling my name.'

'Yes, sir.'

Stagecoach pulled out of the shadows and into the dull light of a gray autumn day. Ryan's heart was heavy with both pride and grief over Shaffer's sacrifice, knowing the battles the boy was now going to have to endure. Over the next several months he faced a number of corrective surgeries for his face and prosthetic limb fittings, followed by months of painful PT and training.

But the bombshell the CNO just dropped in the President's lap was what occupied his mind, spinning with the terrible possibilities. Maybe Buck Logan would have the answers he needed.

He pulled out his phone and called Betty Martin, his long-time personal secretary, to place the call to the big Texan.

# 9

Jack arrived without an appointment when the doors opened at nine o'clock, which was probably a mistake. A number of people were already queued up for business, mostly Spaniards, according to the passports they displayed at the security check-in.

The three-story beige Mediterranean-style building looked more like a producer's home in Beverly Hills than a federal facility. It felt oddly comforting to know he was standing on a patch of U.S. soil even though it was smaller than the average Walmart parking lot. He suddenly felt a pang of homesickness, which surprised him.

In the lobby, Jack put his name and the purpose of his visit on the waiting list: 'To report the death of an American citizen.' He was promptly moved to the front of the line.

After showing his passport to the very pleasant young Spaniard behind the counter, he was given a visitor's tag to wear. She then escorted him to a waiting room on the second floor.

Moments later, a middle-aged brunette with green eyes, a kind smile, and sensible shoes approached him.

'Mr Ryan? I'm Debbie Mitchell, the consular officer.'

Jack shook her hand. 'Nice to meet you.'

She escorted Jack into her small but tidy office and took a

seat behind her desktop computer. 'Can I get you a coffee or something to drink?'

'I'm fine, thanks.'

'I understand you have some bad news to report.'

'Yes, a friend of mine, an American citizen, was killed yesterday in the bombing over in the El Born district.'

'I saw the bombing on the news last night. I didn't realize an American had been killed. No names have been released. Were you there?'

'I had just left.'

'Thank God you're okay. I'm so sorry for your loss.'

'Thank you.'

Mitchell turned to her computer. 'Would you mind giving me his or her name?'

'Sure. Renée Moore. Renée Michelle Moore, I believe.'

Mitchell typed in the information. 'You wouldn't happen to know her passport or Social Security number, would you?'

'Sorry.'

'Age?'

He wasn't exactly sure. Close to his. 'Thirty, plus or minus a few, I'd guess.'

'Race?'

'African American.'

Mitchell typed a few more keys, then stopped. She frowned at her screen for a moment, then glanced up at Jack, offering an awkward smile.

'Uh, Mr Ryan. Would you mind waiting here for just a moment?'

'Sure.'

'If you'll excuse me.' Mitchell rose from behind her desk and headed out the door, clearly on a mission.

Jack sighed. This was the part he worried about.

He wouldn't trade his name for anything in the world but being the President's son carried a few disadvantages in life, including unwanted attention, especially from U.S. government officials. His folks had done a fantastic job of shielding his identity from the public when he was younger, and both the Feds and Hendley Associates had worked miracles, constantly scrubbing the Web and almost every public and private database of any kind of reference to him and his siblings, particularly photographs, or any other information that might link him to his famous parents.

But sometimes a stray file lingering on a hard drive in some vast server farm had been missed. Nearly a hundred million photos and videos were posted just to Instagram every single day.

That lingering file could be anything. Someone's uploaded yearbook that he had signed years ago or a cell-phone shot taken when he passed by unawares. It wasn't the intentional posting that worried people. It was the accidental stuff, obscure and unimportant, that interested sleuths might find and exploit to their advantage.

Whatever it was, something in Mitchell's computer had sent her scurrying to the consul general or some other high-ranking official.

Moments later, a gentleman appeared in the doorway. 'Mr Ryan,' Mitchell said, 'this is Mr Dick Dellinger. He'll be taking over the rest of the interview. If you'll excuse me. It was nice to meet you.'

'*Igualmente*,' Jack offered. His middle-school Spanish was improving.

Dellinger looked to be in his forties. He was shorter than Jack by four inches and at least forty pounds lighter. But Dellinger's fierce brown eyes behind the rimless glasses and the knotty biceps beneath his tailored shirt told Jack this was a guy who knew how to handle himself.

He shook Jack's hand before perching on the edge of Mitchell's desk, giving him a height advantage over the larger, younger man.

'Mr Ryan, I'm so sorry to hear about the loss of your friend Renée Moore. What happened?'

'I was already at the restaurant when Renée walked in. We exchanged business cards and planned to get together later for a drink. I left, and moments later the bomb went off. I rushed back in, and she died.'

'My God, that's awful. Any idea who might have done it?'

'A woman I spoke to last night said that Brigada Catalan had claimed responsibility.'

'What woman was that?'

'She was with the Spanish CNI.'

Dellinger's eyes narrowed. 'So you spoke with Spanish authorities about Ms Moore?'

'Yeah, why?'

Dellinger shrugged. 'I'm just surprised they haven't contacted us about her, that's all. It's a professional courtesy. You talk to anybody else?'

'About Renée? No. Just her. She was on the scene pretty quickly, along with a dozen other uniformed officers from different departments.'

'Barcelona is a relatively small town, especially in the old city, and the cops here are pretty good. I'm not surprised they showed up like that, especially with everything going on these days.'

'Yeah, I've been reading about the protests, and the independence movement.'

'A lot of Americans have canceled their vacations because

of the protests.' Dellinger smiled, a thin line across his clean-shaven face. 'I take it you weren't concerned?'

'No, not at all.'

'Did Ms Moore happen to tell you why she was in Barcelona?'

'Not really. My impression was she was in the restaurant to meet somebody.'

'For what purpose?'

'She didn't say.'

'She didn't tell you who she was meeting?'

Jack felt the heat rising on the back of his neck. At least this wasn't about his dad. But why the hell was he being interrogated?

'No, she didn't.' Jack didn't add, *And she didn't know who it was, either.*

'Did she tell you what her line of work was?'

'She said she was with a fintech company called Crowd-Scope, out of California.'

'So she was here on business?'

'I really don't know. She didn't say.'

'And you're here on vacation, I take it?'

'Yeah. I've always wanted to visit this part of the world.'

'And what's your line of work, if you don't mind my asking?'

'I was going to ask you the same thing, Mr Dellinger.'

'Fair enough. And please, call me Dick.'

Dellinger pulled up a chair and sat down across from Jack. 'I'm with the consulate's Public Diplomacy Section. I work with the student exchange programs, university lecture series, you know, the cultural stuff.'

Now it was Jack's turn to smile. 'Field trips with high school students, wine tasting with the faculty wives — that sort of thing?'

'Pretty much. It's not exciting work, but it's important, or at least I like to think so.'

*Bullshit.*

And they both knew it.

'Now it's your turn, Jack.'

'I'm a financial analyst with Hendley Associates. We're based out of Alexandria, Virginia.' He pulled a card out of his wallet and handed it to him.

'So, you were both working in finance.'

'Yes, I guess so. I actually met Renée at Georgetown. We had a couple of business classes together. She was phenomenal with numbers.'

'You've known her for several years.'

'Yeah. But I hadn't seen her since we graduated.'

'Pretty close with her while in school?'

'What is it you really want to know, Dick?'

Dellinger sat back in his chair, tenting his fingers in front of his narrow face.

'We take the death of American citizens very seriously. I'm just trying to get all the information I can so that we can be sure that all Americans in Spain can live and travel safely here.'

Jack's phone vibrated. 'Excuse me.' He pulled it out of his pocket. It was a text from Brossa: MY OFFICE 10 AM?

Jack checked the time at the top of the screen. He could just make it. He texted back. ON MY WAY.

'Problem?' Dellinger asked.

Jack stood, ending the meeting. 'Not at all. Gotta run, chief.' Jack stuck out his hand as Dellinger stood. He gripped it.

Yeah, the guy could probably handle himself.

'Thank you for bringing this information to our attention, Mr Ryan. I hope the rest of your stay in Barcelona is uneventful. And please don't hesitate to call me if you need any kind of assistance.'

'I appreciate it.'

Jack turned to leave.

'Oh, just one other thing, Jack. Who did you say you met with from CNI?'

Jack grinned. 'I didn't.'

# IO

## Washington, D.C.

'Mr President, Buck Logan is on the line for you,' his secretary said.

'Thanks, Betty. I'll take it from here.'

'Yes, sir.' She clicked off the line. One advantage of a heavily armored limo was the near utter silence inside the cabin. Perfect for calls.

'Buck? Jack Ryan here.'

'Mr President, it's quite an honor. How's the weather in your neck of the woods?'

'Swampy, with yellow rain in the forecast and another shitstorm on the horizon.'

Logan laughed. 'Gawd, how I hate D.C.!'

'It's not always my favorite place, either, but we serve where we're stationed, right?'

'Yes, sir. Speaking of which, how can I serve you?'

'Listen, Buck. I've just had a very disturbing brief from Admiral Talbot.'

'Talbot's a good sailor. You can trust his judgment.'

'I do. But let's cut to the chase. I understand his friends have had a hard time reaching you. They want to have a talk.'

There was a pause on the other end of the line. It didn't take an FBI profiler to figure out what that meant.

'Really? About what?'

'I think we both know the answer to that, Buck.'

'I'm sorry, Mr President. I'm not sure I do.'

'Admiral Talbot believes you recently lost a ship, or at least a ship licensed to carry your cargo.'

Another pause.

'I'm sorry, Mr President, that's news to me.'

Ryan frowned. Why in the hell would Logan lie about something like this? Could Talbot be mistaken? Not likely.

'You sure, Buck?'

'Believe me, if something happened to one of my shipments, I'd be madder 'n a scalded cat.'

*Interesting.*

'Well, I suppose Talbot's people might have got their wires crossed. Sorry to bother you, Buck.'

'Never a bother, Mr President. By the way, I'm really looking forward to the Andrews fundraiser on the eleventh, if you can still make it.'

Ryan didn't remember any fundraiser on the eleventh, let alone one at Joint Base Andrews.

'I'm sure it's on the calendar. I'll have Betty confirm later.'

'Thank you, Mr President.'

'Take care of yourself, Buck.'

'You, too, sir.'

Logan rang off.

Ryan double-checked the calendar on his phone. He was right. There was no fundraiser at Andrews or on the eleventh.

That meant Buck Logan was in trouble.

# II

*Barcelona, Spain*

Jack grabbed a cab to the Guardia Civil annex just west of the old city, a ten-minute walk from the famous Las Ramblas boulevard, frequented by tourists and pickpockets from around the world.

He passed by a small café with a single entrance, its steel door rolled up to let diners and sunshine into the half-dozen tables inside, all occupied, and crowded with people devouring churros and hot chocolate for breakfast. The restaurant was part of the same building that housed the Guardia Civil.

Jack entered through a double-wide vehicle entrance gate and showed the security guard his passport before heading up to the second-story suite of offices subleased to CNI. They had established a temporary presence in the city when the protests first began.

'Jack, thanks so much for coming by,' Brossa said, ushering him into her office. Her smile was pleasant enough but she also looked exhausted, even fragile. Her shoulder holster and pistol hung on a coatrack behind her secondhand steel desk.

'Coffee?' She pointed at the American-style coffee maker, quite unusual for Spain.

'Sure.'

She poured him a cup from a freshly brewed pot she had on a stand near her desk. Though spartan like almost every other government office he'd ever been in, the room – one of dozens inside the renovated nineteenth-century neoclassical building – had an old-world charm, with its high ceilings, bronze-and-glass light fixtures, and tall, heavy oaken doors.

Jack was glad for the meeting and the hospitality but he wanted to get down to business. The interrogation by Dellinger had already put him in a foul mood. If Dellinger was running the student exchange program, Jack would eat his Georgetown Hoyas sweatshirt. Dellinger was CIA, no doubt, and maybe even chief of station, judging by his age and demeanor.

Now his bad mood was getting worse. It felt like the investigation was already behind schedule and the longer it took to get things rolling, the less likely it was that Brossa or anybody would ever find the dirtbags that killed Renée.

Brossa took a sip of her coffee. 'So, tell me, Jack, what exactly does a financial analyst do?'

'Nothing as interesting as what you do. A lot of reading, mostly corporate balance sheets, quarterly earnings reports. And crunching numbers. Pretty dull stuff.'

'You must be good at your job.'

'There's always room to improve.'

'Your boss is a very important man, yes?'

'Gerry Hendley is a brilliant investor and a former United States senator. He's been a great mentor to me.' Gerry's name was better than an Amex black card when it came to impressing the right people.

'Ah, that explains why I was told to cooperate with you as much as possible in this investigation.' Her voice dripped with resentment.

'Let me guess. Gerry is friends with your boss – or more likely, your boss's boss.' Jack hadn't spoken to Gerry but his boss's existing relationships and reputation were enough to open doors even here in Spain.

'I was informed that Mr Hendley has known the director of my agency for many years.'

'I just want to lend a hand, Ms Brossa. Anything I can do to help solve Renée's case.'

'You do realize I can't divulge anything to you that would harm the Spanish national interest.'

'I wouldn't ask you to.'

'Good.' She pulled out a photograph from a file folder and handed it to Jack.

It was the Bluetooth blonde.

'Do you recognize this woman?'

Jack nodded. 'Yeah, I do. She was standing on the far side of the bar yesterday.'

'Her name is Noèlia Aleixandri. She's a member of Brigada Catalan. Or was. She was killed in the blast. But this confirms who was behind the bombing.'

'Too bad she's dead. She could have given you more information. Strange that she got caught in the blast.'

'New terror groups always go through a learning phase when they become violent. Perhaps she accidentally detonated it.'

'She was on a Bluetooth the whole time she was there. Maybe you can find out who she was talking to.'

'There was no phone on her person.'

'What about the Bluetooth?'

Brossa checked the notes on her phone. 'No Bluetooth, either.'

'I know I saw the Bluetooth, and I know she was talking to someone.'

Jack's jaw tightened, trying to keep his temper in check. He knew what he saw. Was she jerking his chain? Or were these Spanish police just careless idiots who couldn't run an evidence locker?

73

Or . . . did someone take them?

'Too bad.' Brossa flashed an indulgent smile. 'Without that phone, we can't know who was on the other end, can we?'

'No, I guess not.' Jack took another sip of coffee, his mind searching for answers. He suddenly remembered the guy with the crooked nose outside in the street, also on a Bluetooth.

A coincidence, probably.

Jack held up the photo. 'Is this my copy to keep?'

'Of course. I am cooperating with you, yes?'

*Not really.* Jack pocketed the photo. 'Thanks.'

'Have you thought about tracking her movements over the last few days?' Jack asked. 'It might lead you to where she bought the phone, and then you can access her account and find out who she was talking to.'

'Track her how?'

'Surely you guys have access to the city's traffic cameras.'

'Yes, of course. But I would have to convince my superior that a phone really did exist. Then he would have to convince somebody in the Barcelona traffic department to release the tapes. But then we'd have to get a court warrant to do so since Ms Aleixandri hasn't been charged with a crime and such surveillance is considered a violation of personal privacy.'

Jack took a sip of coffee to swallow his frustration. 'How long would all of that take?'

Brossa snorted, a kind of laugh. 'This is España – and, worse, Barcelona. My department represents the national government. We're already in a turf war with the local authorities. Imagine if a federal agent from Washington, D.C., asked for cooperation from a deputy sheriff in Alabama on the brink of your civil war.'

*Interesting reference,* Jack thought. 'So, never, I take it?'

Brossa shrugged as she put her cup back down. 'No, not *never*. But at least a week, most likely two.'

'Can't you convince them that this is urgent?'

She shook her head. 'In my country, two weeks *is* urgent.'

Jack glanced up at the painted tin-paneled ceiling, trying to come up with a different tack. In a couple of weeks, a case like this would turn ice cold. The only chance of catching whoever did this was to grab them by the short hairs now, and preferably yesterday.

'Have you had a chance to go over the CCTV footage from inside the restaurant?'

Brossa's face narrowed. 'How do you know about the CCTV tapes?'

'I have eyes, don't I? There were three cameras, each in one of the ceiling corners of the dining area. I wouldn't mind taking a look at them myself. Maybe I'll recognize somebody.'

'I didn't know financial analysts were so . . . observant.'

'Don't blame me. My mother is an eye surgeon.'

Brossa smiled. 'Tell me about your family.'

He couldn't risk being too specific even if it was just a friendly question, which he doubted. 'I have one older sister who's a doctor like my mom, and two younger siblings both still in high school. They're all brainiacs. I'm pretty sure I was adopted.'

'You have a big family. And your father? Is he still alive?'

By leaving his dad out, he only made him more obvious, Jack realized. Dumb mistake. 'Oh, yeah. He and Mom are happily married. He was a history professor.'

'Which is why you love history, yes?'

'Probably.'

'He is retired?'

'No, he went to work for the government. He's kind of a bureaucrat. How about your family?'

'I am an only child. My mother died in a car wreck ten years ago.' Her eyes reflexively turned toward the smartphone on her desk.

'I'm so sorry. I can't imagine getting a phone call like that.'

Her eyes searched his face. 'You don't miss much, do you?'

'I'm a people watcher.'

Brossa's mouth pursed. She clearly didn't like that answer. She took a sip of coffee.

'Yes, it was a terrible phone call. The worst. I was very close to my mother. But such is life, yes? We are born to die. The goal is to live well while we can, don't you agree?'

'I do. And your father?'

'He was a teacher, too, like your father. He taught English for twenty years.'

'That's why your English is so good. Perfect, actually.'

'Thank you. I try.'

'He is still with you, I hope.'

'Yes, thank God. He was a great teacher and a great father. I am very lucky.'

'If you don't mind my asking, why do you keep referring to him in the past tense?'

Brossa's eyes suddenly clouded. She turned in her chair, partly hiding her face as she wiped the corner of her eye with her fingers.

Jack stared at his hands, giving her a moment. She took a deep breath and faced him again, snatching a napkin from the coffee tray.

'My father taught English for twenty years, though it was his third language, and worked as a translator for the government for ten years prior to that. But about a year ago, he just stopped speaking it. Whether he understands and

76

pretends not to, I'm not sure. I don't think so. One time, I had a friend at the office call him in English and tell him that his daughter had been rushed to the hospital and that he needed to come see her. You know, a little test? But my father kept repeating in Català that he didn't understand what my friend was saying. He said over and over, "I don't speak English." My friend believed him. The neurologist told me this is possible for a man in my father's condition. *Demència.*'

'That must be hard on a linguist to lose a language like that.'

Brossa sat up, willing herself to stop the theatrics, wiping her proud, upturned nose with the napkin.

'I don't think so. He doesn't seem frustrated when he hears it and doesn't understand it. And he doesn't try to speak it at all. It's almost as if he decided to BleachBit that part of his brain. He is a proud Catalonian man, and Català is his first language, his heart language. It's who he most authentically is. Perhaps the death of English in his brain is just a function of his changing biochemistry, or perhaps he is merely retreating into what is most familiar and comfortable to him. Or perhaps it is a little of both.'

'Is his situation getting worse?'

She nodded, her eyes clouding again.

'I'm so sorry.' *And that's why you dread your phone calls now.*

'Finding someone to care for him during the day while I'm at work is difficult. He's becoming increasingly stubborn. I'm always afraid the next call will tell me something terrible has happened to him.'

'No family to help out?'

'He has a sister but she lives in Australia with her family, and has no wish to take him in. His brother is deceased.'

'It must be hard.'

She shrugged but shook her head. 'It's not hard to love

77

him or to care for him. It's just our new normal. But I have a job to do. I am a daughter, but I am also a patriot. Two loyalties, yes?'

'Both equally important.'

'So you understand?' She seemed surprised.

Jack did understand. He couldn't imagine how hard it would be to have to choose between serving his father or serving his country. He was lucky that the two were so perfectly aligned in his life.

'My dad says that loyalty is destiny. Who and what we love determines the shape of our lives. But like the Man said, you can't serve two masters.' He was thinking about that a lot these days.

'You can, but just not well, I'm afraid.'

They sat in silence for a moment. Jack was eager to push on, but she was still clearly decompressing. When she gathered herself together, she stood and refilled their coffee cups, signaling that she was back on track.

'Anything else we need to talk about, Jack?'

Jack flashed his best smile. 'Well, since you ask, I was wondering when you were going to let me see the CCTV tapes.'

Brossa nearly spat coffee out of her nose as she giggled.

'I don't think that is going to be possible.'

'Why not? Maybe I can be of some use. Like you said, I'm observant.'

'I am afraid you cannot see them. It's official business.'

'But I was there, and I was nearly killed. Don't I have a right to see them?'

'It is my job to find the bombers, not yours. Unless you think you can do my job for me?'

'Me? No, not at all. I'm sorry if that's what you think I meant. I just genuinely want to help. Anything I can do to help find Renée's killers.'

78

'We found one already, Aleixandri. We will find the rest, I assure you.'

He heard the edge in her voice. He decided to back off and try to find another way in.

Brossa beat him to the punch.

'Ms Moore was a beautiful girl.'

'Very. And even smarter.'

'And you knew her in college?'

'Yes. We were friends.'

'A girl that smart and beautiful. You were intimate with her?'

He didn't see that one coming.

'We were . . . close, for a while.'

'And you still have affection for her. Is that why you are so determined to find her killers?'

'Yes. Anything wrong with that?'

'*Vale.* I can understand that. But you must let me do my job.'

'Understood. Speaking of which, did you find out any information on this Sammler guy?'

'Interesting you should ask. Yes, I can share that with you.'

Brossa pulled out her phone. She opened her e-mail and read from it.

'In the last five days, there have been three Sammlers in España. One is an American woman named Martha Sammler. She arrived in Madrid two days ago on a Rick Steves' tour and was in Toledo yesterday. She was never in the vicinity.

'Next, John Sammler, a Canadian citizen, was in Barcelona yesterday morning. Today he is in Tunis.' She looked up from her phone. 'And he is an eleven-year-old traveling with his maternal grandmother, Maria Busquets.'

'And the third?'

'*Vale,* that one is interesting. Karl Sammler, a German businessman from Düsseldorf. He was traveling in Spain but we don't have any records of his travel destinations. We cannot be sure if he was in Barcelona until we speak with him. He is back in Germany now, and my office in Madrid is sending an agent to speak with him this afternoon.'

'You'll keep me informed?'

'If it is related to the case.'

'Thank you.'

'I'm curious, Jack. You said you came to Spain to study the Spanish Civil War. What did you learn?'

'Do you want the long answer or the short one?'

'How about both?'

# 12

Jack leaned back in his chair, folding his hands in his lap like a college professor, a gesture he'd accidentally picked up from his dad.

'Okay, the shortest version is this: Most politicians suck.'

Brossa snort-laughed again. 'Hard to argue with that.'

'The less-short version reminds me of a line in Antony Beevor's book *The Battle for Spain.*'

'Yes, I know it. It was a huge bestseller here.'

'He said the Spanish Civil War was the only war in which the losers got to write the history, and he's right. In the West, we saw that war as purely good versus evil – freedom-loving Republicans fighting a hopeless war against Franco's unbeatable Fascists. A real David versus Goliath story. If Americans know anything about that war it's based on the book or the movie *For Whom the Bell Tolls.* Do you know it?'

'Hemingway. *Sens dubte'* – Without a doubt. 'I love it. It is both terribly romantic and tragic, which is very Spanish.'

'It wasn't an accident Gary Cooper got cast for that film. He's an actor who played a lot of American cowboys. The whole movie plays like a western. We Americans love underdogs. The Republicans play the role of the helpless peasants fighting shoulder to shoulder with the International Brigades for democracy. They're up against Franco's Fascist war machine backed by Hitler's Condor Legion and Mussolini's Blackshirts.'

'Which was true.'

'Which *was* true, but not the whole truth. The Republicans

fought the Fascists, yes, but they were also murdering each other. The Spanish Stalinists were the worst. Their goal was to advance the interests of the Soviet Union, not Spain, and they imprisoned and killed the Spanish communists and anarchists who actually wanted a real socialist revolution here.'

'Crimes were committed by both sides, though far worse by the Fascists.'

'Agreed. But that's only the tip of the iceberg. It's the contradictions of that war that tell me the most about it.'

'Which contradictions?'

'Franco claimed to be fighting for Catholicism but his crack troops were Riffian Muslims. He also claimed to be fighting for Spanish nationalism but his military campaign relied heavily on German and Italian troops and arms to win.

'At the same time, the Republican loyalists claimed to be fighting for freedom and democracy against Fascism while they were murdering priests and nuns, burning churches, and slaughtering their political opponents. Worse, all of their material support came from Stalin, the most murderous tyrant in modern European history.'

'I'm impressed. You know a lot about our history. It was a very difficult and confusing time for us. In my own family, one side fought for the Republic, and the other side fought for Franco. I even had a grandfather who fought with the División Azul in Leningrad for Hitler – but he was no Nazi and no Fascist. He was just a poor man who couldn't find any other way to feed his empty stomach. He used to joke how expensive the terrible German rations were.'

'The Germans made him pay for his rations?'

'No, the Russians did. He lost his left eye to shrapnel, and three fingers of his right hand to frostbite.' She laughed.

82

'That never stopped him from sleeping with many beautiful women.'

'The bottom line for me is that it seems like a lot of what's going on in Barcelona right now is still connected to the civil war.'

Brossa nodded. 'Yes, it is. The independence issue was important for us before *la guerra* and it was never fully resolved, and really, neither was the war itself. Do you know that there are still two hundred thousand Spaniards lying in unmarked graves from the civil war? Can you imagine such a thing in civilized Europe?'

'Yeah, I can.'

Jack's mind drifted back again to the slaughter of the Yugoslavian civil wars – and every other holocaust that had swept the continent since the Thirty Years' War. 'Civilized Europe has been a slaughterhouse since before they invented the word *Europe*. The reason Europeans have dominated the globe for the last five centuries is because they have a particular genius for organized violence.'

'You sound like a history professor. I imagine just like your father.'

Jack wasn't sure what to do with that comment, so he ignored it.

'The Spanish Civil War reminded me that history repeats itself.'

'In what way?'

'When the people believe the justice system is no longer just, that the politicians are above the laws they make, that the government serves the interests of the ruling class instead of the middle and working classes; and when the history and culture and language of the people are denigrated and denied – these are the conditions that make a society ripe for civil war.'

'You have just described the feelings of millions of Catalonians,' Brossa said as she took her last sip of coffee.

'Not just here. It's a movement sweeping all over the world. And I suspect it might even change the world, sooner rather than later.'

'For better or for worse?'

'The jury's still out on that one.'

Brossa's phone vibrated. A voicemail. She checked it, frowning.

*Worried,* Jack was certain. Something personal.

'Please, take it,' he said.

'Excuse me.'

She listened to the message. Whatever she was hearing – a woman's anxious voice was all Jack could make out – darkened Brossa's face. She deleted the message.

'Everything okay?'

'I hate cell phones.' She tossed it on the table like it was a dirty diaper. She began rubbing her forehead, stressed, gathering her thoughts.

'Maybe I should go.' Jack stood.

'Yes, thank you.' Brossa stood, too. 'I will call you when I learn of anything. When are you leaving for home?'

'Not until I'm satisfied Renée got her justice.'

Brossa reached for her shoulder holster and slipped it on. She gave him a pitying look.

'This is España, Jack. You might be here for a long while.'

# 13

Jack left through the Guardia Civil's double-wide gate and turned toward the little café next door. The place was still jumping. But something about the college-age kid sitting near the door bothered him. Slacks, shirt, tie.

Not a tourist.

Jack turned into the café, grabbed an empty chair from the next table, and sat down next to the kid, startling him. An empty chocolate-smeared demitasse cup and a plate littered with churro crumbles were on the table in front of him.

'What's your story?' Jack asked.

'*Perdón, señor?*'

Jack shook his head. Pointed at his left hand. 'Not a lot of Spaniards wear Texas Aggie class rings.'

The kid reflexively raised his ring hand and stared at it. 'Wow, good catch.'

'So, who are you, who sent you, and why are you following me?'

'Name's Sam Davis. I was in the break room at the consulate when Mr Dellinger grabbed me and told me to follow you.'

'Why?'

'He said to just keep an eye on you and report back what I found.'

'And what did you find?'

'That you came to the Guardia Civil building, stayed about twenty minutes, and left.'

Jack leaned closer, lowered his voice. 'Look, Sam, no offense. But you kinda suck at being a spy.'

'I'm not a spy. I'm here on a semester internship with the Office of Agricultural Affairs. I'm an international business major. But when Mr Dellinger says go, you go.'

'He's your boss?'

'Not exactly. He runs the student exchange programs, but he's a pretty big deal around the consulate. He and the CG spend a lot of time together.'

'Well, head back to your office and tell Mr Dellinger you followed me here and you saw me leave. Got it?'

'Got it.'

Jack stood and snatched up the bill for Davis's breakfast. 'Next time, try the pancakes. And if I ever see you again?'

Davis stood. 'You won't.'

'Good.'

Jack watched the kid slink away. Davis was almost the same age he was when he joined The Campus. He couldn't help but grin.

*Was I ever really that green?*

Jack pulled out his wallet but it was empty. He put the kid's bill on his credit card instead.

He decided to head back to his place and see what he could dig up on the dead bomber on his own, hoping like hell Noèlia Aleixandri was her real name, while he waited for Gavin's call.

Lost in his thoughts, he didn't see Crooked Nose following far behind him, shielded by a Chinese tour group.

Jack sat on the rooftop terrace of his apartment. It was a warm day with a slight breeze from the sea. The building itself contained several other apartments, but Jack's had exclusive access to the terrace through a separate stairwell. It had become his favorite thing about the place, with views of both the Mediterranean to the south and the old city to the north. It even had a great Internet connection. At night, he could see the lights from the basilica on the high mountain north of Barcelona. The terrace had a stout table and chairs that sat beneath a sturdy aluminum awning frame, though the awning itself was nowhere to be seen. It didn't matter. The sun was warm and welcoming this time of year, not a beatdown like it could be in the summer, according to the travel books he'd read.

The dead bomber's name and face appeared in the Spanish language newspapers and, as far as Jack could tell with his poor Spanish, all of them reported essentially the same terse information, probably from the same press release that authorities sent out on a case like this.

Noèlia Aleixandri was twenty-three years old at the time of her death. She had been a journalism major at the Universitat de Vic, a small city up north near the Pyrenees where she was born, before dropping out two years ago. She had been a student activist involved with the independence movement while in school, 'but never violent, and never arrested for anything criminal,' according to her grieving mother.

Too bad, Jack thought. A bright young woman with a promising future, blown to hell by her own negligence, or someone else's.

It was the someone else that really interested him. Getting hold of her cell phone would open that door, and Gavin was just the guy to do it.

Time for a phone call. He headed back downstairs to the relative security of his apartment. No telling who might overhear his conversation with Gavin about the bombing and draw the wrong conclusions.

# 14

'Jack! That's so weird. I was just about to call you. You won't believe the stuff I've found.'

Gavin's high-pitched voice squealed with the enthusiasm of a teenage gamer winning a Fortnite competition. But the portly, fiftysomething bachelor – who actually *was* a Fortnite player – was a world-class programmer, hacker, and researcher, and the brains behind Hendley Associates' considerable IT department.

'Surprise me.'

'Well, where should I start? I'll do the good stuff first. Your friend's company, CrowdScope? It's a CIA op, and Renée Moore was CIA.'

'What? You're sure?'

'Hell*oo*? It's me. Of course I'm sure.'

Jack couldn't believe it. Moore had never mentioned government service. The one time he'd raised it with her, she'd laughed in his face, incredulous. 'Where's the money in that, Jack?'

He wondered what had changed her mind.

On the other hand, Silicon Valley made perfect sense as a CIA station. Google, Twitter, Facebook, Instagram, and the other giant social media networks constituted the most successful intelligence-gathering operation the world had ever seen. They collected and dissected terabytes of personal data from their billons of users around the world – almost always provided by the users themselves, and with their own consent.

Why try to compete with that kind of data harvesting and analysis when you could simply infiltrate those preexisting networks?

Thanks to Snowden, everybody knew that the Intelligence Community had secured the cooperation of many of the technology firms early on. Companies like Google, Amazon, and Microsoft had billions of dollars' worth of contracts with the federal government, including the agencies of the Intelligence Community and the Department of Defense.

But a combination of bad press, customer concerns, and activist outrage had resulted in a pushback against covert and even overt cooperation by these firms with the American government. These companies' loyalties were to their bottom lines, not national security. It wasn't surprising that the CIA had decided to try to find another way in. God knows how many foreign powers used platforms like Facebook and Twitter to covertly influence domestic and world opinion. If he ran the CIA, Jack would focus his efforts on infiltrating and influencing Silicon Valley as well.

'What can you tell me about Renée? What was she doing at CrowdScope – or in Barcelona?'

'That's the crazy thing, Jack. I have access to a lot of databases – including ones I'm not supposed to have access to. But whatever your friend was up to, and whatever operations CrowdScope is conducting, I can't get close to it. I think even their firewalls have firewalls. I tried tiptoeing around some of their defenses and set off a few alarms. If I'm not careful, I'm going to get hauled away by a CIA snatch team and dumped in an offshore prison somewhere.'

*So Renée wasn't just in federal service,* Jack thought.

*She was all the way in, up to her neck.*

'If CrowdScope is that important, and if Renée was part

of it, whatever she was up to in Barcelona must be kryptonite.'

'Are you thinking what I'm thinking?' Gavin asked.

Jack heard paper crinkling. 'Snickers or Almond Joy?'

'Snickers, baby.' Gavin took a bite and spoke with a full mouth. 'It's the PowerBar of gamers everywhere.'

'So, I'm thinking the bombing in Barcelona wasn't a terror act at all. Maybe the real target was Renée. What about you?'

'A definite maybe. But, Jack, there is one other possibility.'

'What's that?'

'Maybe the real target was you.'

'Why me?'

'Why not you? Besides the fact you work for Gerry Hendley and you're the son of the President of the United States – a fact we've managed to hide, but it's still a fact that someone could have discovered. You've killed, captured, or jailed enough bad guys on your own in the last few years to put you on a dozen hit lists. Remember van Delden? The Iron Syndicate?'

Jack surely did. The Iron Syndicate was an international crime organization with tentacles reaching into almost every security organization on the planet. They'd put a bounty on Jack's head – or technically, for the collection of his severed head – two years ago. Thanks to his time in Poland with Liliana, the Iron Syndicate was largely dismantled and its members dead, in jail, or on the run.

*God rest your soul, Liliana.*

'I appreciate the thought, Gav, but I'd be really surprised if they were after me. I've been wide open the whole time I've been in Spain. There were dozens of better opportunities to take me out without any collateral damage.'

'Collateral damage is a great way to hide a crime, you know.'

'I think you're reaching.'

'Just keeping an eye out for you.'

'I appreciate that. More than you know. But it seems to me that Renée is the obvious target. As near as I can tell, she'd only just arrived in Barcelona. Maybe you can find out when and where she flew in from. That might give us a clue as to her assignment.'

'Sure thing.'

'Thanks. You said you had other stuff you've discovered besides Moore's CIA connection?'

'Oh, yeah, I almost forgot. I was thinking about the CCTV tape. Any luck with your CNI contact?'

'I tried. No go.'

'Well, no worries on that account. I hacked their server —'

'You did what? How?'

'Oh, Jack. I'm hurt. You doubted me?'

Jack shouldn't have been surprised. Gavin was a one-man wrecking machine when it came to hacking. Even NSA-level encryption didn't stop him. He usually found his way around technological firewalls by exploiting the failings of the human operators. Gavin idolized the Israeli agents who destroyed the centrifuges at the Natanz nuclear facility. They did it by dropping a Stuxnet-infested flash drive on the ground, knowing that an OCD Iranian scientist would pick it up and insert it into one of the air-gapped computers.

'I never doubt you, Gavin. You only manage to astound me.'

'Oh, you know. All in a day's work.'

Jack rolled his eyes. Gavin's gloating practically oozed through the phone. 'So what did you find on the CCTV tapes?'

'I only had time to download an hour's worth before their IT people discovered I was snooping around. I know you know this, but there's video-editing software on the secure Hendley cloud server you can use to check out what I downloaded, along with some facial-recognition software that might help.'

Gavin had built an entire suite of proprietary investigative tools that members of The Campus could access remotely for occasions just like this. Gavin was more than happy to do the work himself but usually there was far more of it to do than even an extraordinary technician like Gavin could handle. He not only built the suite of tools, he trained the team on them as well. They couldn't come close to Gavin's talent on the really technical stuff, but for grunt work like reviewing hours of video or audio transmissions, it was better to put less skilled hands on the oars.

'Gavin, I can't believe it. That's perfect. Post it up on the Hendley cloud as soon as you can and I'll start going through it.'

Gavin's mouth was full of Snickers bar again. 'Already done.'

'Okay, okay. You're obviously one step ahead of me.'

'That goes without saying.'

'Then let me throw you a curveball. I'm sending you something now.'

Jack texted the photo of the Bluetooth Blonde Brossa gave him and links to the stories he'd found about her. He gave Gavin a minute to look it over.

'Sounds like you already know who she is. What do you need from me?'

'I saw her at the restaurant just before it blew. She was on a phone. My bet is that it's a burner phone. The CNI says they don't have it.'

'They might be lying.'

'Could be. But for now, I'll give them the benefit of the

92

doubt. Any chance you can break into the citywide camera system and track her movements? If she bought that phone herself, you might be able to find the store where she got it. From there, we might be able to run her down.'

'Yeah, that'll be fun. I've got a new automated tracking software I wrote that I want to try out – it lets the computer do all of the monotonous stuff.'

'Thanks, Gav. I couldn't do this without you.'

'No question about that.'

'So, you said that you had some bad news?'

'Oh, yeah. I nearly forgot. I chased down this Sammler guy you asked me to look into. I couldn't come up with any-body who had any obvious ties to Moore. Sorry about that.'

'Don't sweat it. My Spanish source came up short, too. Though apparently there was a German national by that name in Spain a few days ago and she's chasing him down.'

'I saw him, too. Already checked him out. He's not the guy. Are you sure you heard the name right? Could she have said "Samuels" maybe? Or "Stattler"? Something like that?'

'I heard it right. Renée made sure of that.'

'I don't mean to offend you, but maybe she was hallucinat-ing toward the end, or losing oxygen to her brain. She might have said "Sammler" but that might not mean anything at all.'

'It's a possibility.' Jack's hopes began to fade. 'Unless the Spaniards pull up something on Sammler, I'm afraid he's a dead end for now.'

# 15

*Washington, D.C.*
*Diplomatic Reception Room, The White House*

'Show him in, please.' Arnie van Damm, the President's chief of staff, cradled the phone, then stifled a yawn. His suit was rumpled from a long day that always began before Ryan's, and Ryan always started early.

'Can I get you a cup of coffee?' Ryan smiled. 'Or maybe a can of Ensure?'

Arnie wiped a smudge off his rimless glasses with his tie. 'Did I ever tell you that my old man used to work the graveyard shift at the steel mill to make extra money so he could put me through college so I wouldn't have to work late nights?'

'You call this work?' Ryan pointed at the elegant Federal period room around them. The two old friends sat on gold silk wingback chairs in front of a roaring fireplace with the iconic Gilbert Stuart portrait of George Washington hanging over the mantel. The panoramic wallpaper surrounding the room had been installed by Jacqueline Kennedy, and every important president, prime minister, and potentate from the last fifty years had either stood or sat in this room at some point.

Ryan was in a pair of jeans, Sperry Top-Siders, and a Fly Navy sweatshirt, having come straight down from the family residence. He was already in bed and propped up on his pillows next to Cathy and only a few pages into Lieutenant

Colonel Rip Rawlings's latest when Arnie called forty minutes ago. He wasn't all that surprised by the call but grew concerned when Arnie told him Buck Logan was actually on his way over. Ryan assumed he'd be getting a call from the big Texan. He wasn't expecting a personal visit.

'Must be damned important,' Arnie said.

Ryan agreed.

The phone call with Logan that morning was odd, to say the least. When Ryan had asked Logan about his sunken ship, he denied it happened. According to Admiral Talbot, that was a lie. And then Logan insisted on mentioning the nonexistent Andrews fundraiser – not a lie so much as a statement that was demonstrably false.

It took about a heartbeat and a half for Ryan to figure out Logan's coded message. *I just told you an obvious lie about the fundraiser so that we both know I'm lying, and that way, you know I just lied to you about the sunken ship.*

And that's how Ryan knew Logan was in trouble.

Given the dramatic meeting about to happen, he assumed that meant *big* trouble.

Ryan had given Arnie a heads-up about Logan while he was still in transit from Walter Reed. Arnie was almost always the first call Jack made when the excrement hit the oscillator because his chief of staff was about the sharpest pencil in the drawer as far as politics was concerned. Arnie had been chief of staff to three presidents, including him from the beginning. The crow's feet around Arnie's pale blue eyes were deeper, and his bald scalp a little paler and flakier, than when he'd first met the man. But Arnie's mind hadn't aged. Arnie might have looked a little like Merkin Muffley, the hapless American President in *Dr Strangelove,* but he was General Chesty Puller when it counted on the political battlefield, and Ryan couldn't ask for more than that.

It was Arnie's suggestion to meet in the Diplomatic Reception Room rather than the Oval. It was nearer the family residence so Jack wouldn't have to walk so far at the late hour and it was still on the first floor for Logan's convenience.

As always, Arnie thought of everything.

One of the double doors opened and an electric wheelchair rolled into the room.

Jack and Arnie stood as Buck Logan wheeled in their direction. Ryan watched Logan's bodyguard, a six-foot-five slab of meat in a tailored suit, take a position outside next to the PPD agents stationed there before the door closed again.

'Mr President, I'm so terribly sorry to inconvenience you,' Logan said as he pulled to a stop. He removed his gray felt Stetson. His bright blue eyes contrasted with his thick but short-cropped silver hair. He was five years younger than Ryan but the deep lines in his rugged face aged him considerably.

'I knew you had the smarts to figure out what I was trying to tell you. And I can't thank you enough for allowing me to inconvenience you at this ridiculous hour.'

Ryan smiled. 'It's a little past Arnie's bedtime, but I think it all worked out.'

Ryan shook Logan's hand. The Texan's grip was crushing. The former Naval Academy tight end had been nearly as big as his bodyguard when he played football. Tragically, a catastrophic spinal cord injury from a late hit by Notre Dame in his senior year put him in a wheelchair forever, ending both his collegiate football career and his dream of following in his father's footsteps into military service.

As physically impressive as he still was, Buck Logan's greatest strength was his first-rate mind. His father had built a great regional trucking firm after the Korean War, but it was Buck who transformed it into a global logistics operation, with land, sea, and air assets. To satisfy his longing for military service, Logan had also built a top-tier private military contracting outfit. Altogether, Buck had forged White Mountain Logistics + Security into one of the largest and most reliable private-sector contractors servicing the DoD and several other federal departments.

But despite his outsized achievements in business and academics – he finished his USNA degree in civil engineering with a 4.0 – Buck still lived in the long shadow of his famous father.

Logan nodded at Arnie. 'Then my apologies to you as well, Mr van Damm.'

'Please, it's just Arnie.'

'Can I get you something to eat? Drink?' Ryan asked.

'No, sir, I've already put you out. I'll be brief.' Logan motioned to the two empty wingback chairs. 'Please, don't stand on my account.'

Jack and Arnie took their seats.

'So, Buck, what's this all about?' Ryan asked.

Logan sat up straighter in his motorized chair. 'First of all, let me get it off my chest. As you've already figured out, I lied to you this afternoon, Mr President, and I can hardly forgive myself for that. But the truth of the matter is, I didn't have much of a choice. I'm in one hell of a pickle, and I'm afraid my personal security situation has been compromised. I just didn't feel comfortable speaking with you on an unsecured line. Lucky for me, I own a fleet of private planes, so arranging an unscheduled flight up here wasn't a problem, and I wanted to look you in the eye when we spoke.'

'I can appreciate that, Buck. So, let's get to it. What's going on?'

'The bottom line is that one of my ships – technically, a

ship I was leasing for a single transport – was sunk seven days ago in the South Pacific.'

'Why lie about it?' Arnie asked.

Logan reached around behind his chair, pulled a file folder out of his seat pocket, and handed a couple of e-mail print-outs to Arnie.

'As you can read there, that sinking was no accident. I was sent that note seventy-two hours before it happened. I was told to transfer ten million dollars in Bitcoin to a Dark Web address or else they'd sink one of my shipments. What concerns me is that they must have known it wasn't my ship – only my cargo. Not many people have that information.'

'And that's why you believe there's someone on the inside of your organization – and why you couldn't speak on the phone.'

Logan grinned. 'That's why I'm your biggest supporter in Texas, Mr President. Sharp as a tack, and blunt as a hammer.'

'Why didn't you contact us when you received this threat?' Arnie asked.

Logan laughed. 'Are you kidding me? What was I going to do? Come crying to you guys because somebody said something mean to me? A non-specific, non-credible threat? What could you have done to prevent it? I've got operations all over the globe. It's not like you were going to put Marine detachments on all of my ships or provide me with destroyer escorts.

'Besides, for all I know, this was sent by some "Nigerian princess" riding a laptop somewhere in Romania.'

Logan blew air through his bleached white teeth, his face reddening. 'Nobody's gonna push Buck Logan around – sure 'n hell ain't gonna squeeze ten million U.S. government dollars outta his wallet with a goddamn e-mail!'

Jack and Arnie exchanged a look. Logan was losing it right in front of them.

Logan saw their reaction.

'Sorry about that, gentlemen. I'm a little off my game, as you can well imagine. I lost seventeen million dollars' worth of civilian cargo – mostly drilling pipe, steel fittings, generators. Nothing for Uncle Sam, mind you. Not to mention the poor bastards who went down with the ship, whoever they were.'

'You have insurance, don't you?'

'Flip over to the second page. After the sinking, I was contacted again. Told in no uncertain terms: Do not contact your insurance and do not contact the authorities or more sinkings will follow. Given the circumstances, I was inclined to believe them.'

Logan pointed at the pages again. 'You can see there, they listed out every one of my scheduled shipments for the next thirty days, and each one of my flagged vessels. I lose a few more of those, and I'm ruined, no matter what I do.

'If I don't file insurance claims on the *Jade Star* cargo, I'm out of pocket on the losses. And if I do file a claim, my insurance rates will skyrocket and then these bastards said they'd sink another one. If they sank a second boat, I'd have to file a second claim, and then my insurance would get canceled. And if that happens, then I can't carry goods and I'm out of business. Either way, my pooch is royally screwed.'

'What are you going to do now?'

'Cross my fingers and pray. Three days ago, they sent me another letter demanding *twenty* million dollars – ten for the first letter, and ten for not believing them.'

'What did you do?' Arnie asked.

'I paid the bastards. What else could I do?'

'Have they threatened any more of your ships?'

'No, they said this was a one-time payment.'

Arnie pressed further. 'And you actually believe them?'

'Whoever these shitheads are, they're smart. I doubt I'm the first one they've done this to and probably not the last. It's one thing to swipe a few apples from the neighbor's tree but there's no point in cuttin' it down 'cuz then the apples run out.'

'You don't know how right you are, Buck. There have been several other unexplained sinkings, along with yours,' Ryan said.

'I'll be damned.'

'They must have been threatened the same way you were,' Arnie said. 'Same conditions.'

Logan's eyes narrowed. 'Who else have they hit?'

'Big companies with deep pockets, like yours. All in the Pacific, just like yours.'

'And they haven't said anything, either?'

'No. You've told us the most – and that wasn't a hell of a lot,' Ryan said. He leaned forward. 'No idea at all who's behind this?'

Logan shifted around in his chair.

'I've thought long and hard on this. Could be a political group. Could be a religious outfit. Or it might just be your run-of-the-mill, greedy-ass pirate. They all have the same motive: money. The question is, what do they want to do with that money?'

'Something tells me you've ruled all of those out,' Ryan said.

'Motive ain't enough. You gotta have the means, which tells me we're talking about a blue water navy. As I've noo-dled on it, I think we're talking about the Russians.'

'Why the Russians?' Arnie asked. 'That seems like a real stretch.'

'Is it? The South Pacific is a far piece out in the middle of nowhere. Who else has the reach? North Korea has a navy, but mostly coastal vessels, and their deepwater stuff is mostly secondhand Cold War crap from the Russians. China has the reach but it's all tangled up in Hong Kong right now and their navy is playing footsie with us in the South China Sea. And last I heard, there sure as hell ain't no flip-flop-wearing Somali pirates running around in the Cook Islands.'

Logan leaned forward. 'But the Russkies have eight deep-water surface vessels and eighteen-plus submarines just in their Pacific Fleet – hell, they got more subs in their navy than we do.'

'I'll grant you they have the means,' Ryan said. 'But what's their motive?'

'That's what I can't quite figure out. Maybe they've had some kind of breakthrough in their underwater operations or their hypersonic anti-ship missiles and they're running real-world tests. Any Russian-flagged ships sunk?'

'No.' Ryan wondered if Logan was onto something. 'Not U.S.-flagged or Chinese-flagged, either.'

'But you're missing the obvious, Buck. They hit you up for cash,' Arnie said. 'That's not a military operation.'

'Are you kidding me? Russia is run by the world's richest gangsters. They love money, the dirtier the better. What better way to hide their testing program than to pretend it's a piracy operation – and make some serious bank on the side doing it?'

Ryan and Arnie exchanged another look. Maybe Logan wasn't crazy after all.

'You said you think you have an insider on your hands. What are you doing about it?' Arnie asked.

Logan shifted around in his chair again, unable to get comfortable. It was obviously a losing battle.

'I've got my most trusted security people sniffing around to find out who the backstabbing sumbitch is, but no luck so far.'

Arnie held up the blackmail threat. 'Your IT people must have searched for the source of this e-mail? Chased down the Dark Web bank account address?'

'Jumped right on it. But you know that computer stuff – VPNs and firewalls and such. They couldn't find anything we could grab ahold of. And we all know how good the Russians are at that kind of thing.'

'You never struck me as a man who left his fate in the hands of others,' Ryan said.

Logan grimaced, obviously in some discomfort. 'Believe me, I'm not. I'm going on the offensive and putting my security team on this. I'll find the bastards who did this, come hell or high water, and God help them when I find them.' Buck pointed a meaty finger in their direction. 'You two gents have to color inside the lines, I don't.'

'If it really is the Russians, you're taking on a helluva risk,' Arnie noted.

'No worries on that account. I have a few arrows in my quiver I'm not afraid to loose.'

'We can't sanction any illegal activities,' Arnie said.

'No, we can't,' Ryan said. He stood, ending the meeting. 'But if you do find out anything, Buck, you be sure to let us know.'

Buck smiled and winked. 'Will do, Mr President. Will do.'

# 16

*Philippine Sea*

The *Don Pedro* was lashed by heavy rains in a rolling sea, making a steady five knots beneath a hard gray sky. The wiper blades slapped away the salt water sheeting the bridge windows where the captain stood, joking with the first officer. It was a powerful storm by any measure but according to the weather radar would pass within the hour. The large, purse-shaped tuna nets were stowed away and the booms secured while the deck crew huddled dry below playing cards, grabbing shut-eye, or cleaning weapons, waiting for it to pass.

Héctor Guzmán was no sailor but the rise and fall of the boat in the running swells had no ill effect on him as he sat in his small, private cabin, staring at a laptop screen.

Dark, beardless, and with a long sharp nose that flared at the base, Guzmán's looks favored his mother's purely Indian ancestry. But he was a head taller than anyone in his village, and stronger than any man by the age of fifteen, the genetic gift of his father's mixed Spanish and German heritage. His badly pockmarked face was puckered with divots and irregular scars, like a rotted orange skin punctured by shoe spikes. With such a face, he paid double for whores who would have him willingly. The whores who wouldn't he took by force and made them pay dearly in other ways.

The men under his command both on and off the water assumed his facial defects were the product of battle – a shotgun blast to the face, or perhaps even burns. It added to his reputation as a fearsome and indestructible fighter, both of which were true. But in fact, the scarring was merely the aftermath of a virulent skin condition from his childhood.

Guzmán examined the photo on the laptop intensely, a pair of wireless AirPods stuck in his ears. It was the blue eyes and dark beard in the photo that caught his attention.

'Who am I looking at?' Guzmán demanded. 'He looks like an operator.'

'According to our contact at the CNI, he is an American by the name of John Patrick Ryan, Jr,' the operator said through the AirPods, his throaty vowels betraying his Russian accent. 'He goes by the name of Jack. Works as an analyst for a privately held financial services firm, Hendley Associates, owned and managed by an ex–American senator by the name of Gerald Hendley. Apparently, Ryan was an acquaintance of Moore and that is his interest in the case.'

Guzmán scowled at Ryan's picture. He had only just learned about van Delden's death secondhand, and that a man matching Ryan's description was involved. He doubted it was possible this Ryan guy in Spain was the same guy who killed van Delden in South Korea, but his instincts told him to pay close attention.

The Russian operator's name was Bykov, one of Guzmán's smartest. He had a real genius for killing. Munitions and remote-controlled detonations were his specialty. The Slav's deep-set hazel eyes and flat face were offset by his crooked nose. Bykov was concerned enough about the situation in Barcelona to reach out and that was worrisome. Ryan had been in touch with the American consulate, twice met with an agent of the CNI, and made contact with Moore just before the explosion.

'He's not an operator? Not with any agency?'

Guzmán's own English was superb, and nearly without accent, taught to him by a spinster Baptist missionary lady who served in a nearby village when he was a child.

'We did not find anything else on him in our database, which is extensive.'

It was extensive, Guzmán agreed. And expensive. One of his best investments. If this Ryan character wasn't on it, it was possible he had been scrubbed. That made Ryan even more problematic.

The boat yawed violently beneath Guzmán. 'That's all you have on him?'

'I have his home address in Alexandria, Virginia. His driver's license says he's one hundred and eighty-seven centimeters tall, and weighs eighty-nine kilograms, and by the looks of him, I'd say that was all muscle.'

His old friend van Delden was a physical monster, second to none in close-quarters combat, but this Ryan guy was no wimp, either, according to Bykov's description. Was it possible a financial analyst was able to take out his number two? No. Impossible.

'There is one other thing. The CIA bitch told Ryan the name "Sammler."'

'What does Ryan know?'

'Nothing, according to our CNI friend. Moore just mentioned the name to Ryan as she died.' Bykov chuckled. 'Last thing she thought about before going tits up.'

'Something isn't right about this guy.'

'I did a little of my own checking on Hendley Associates. They handle big international accounts, mostly corporate, sometimes individuals. In my experience, these high-end finance guys hide their identities as best they can because they work with a lot of shady characters. It gives them an advantage in negotiations and protects them from the more dangerous elements. I've seen it before.'

Guzmán scratched his beardless chin. 'I don't buy it. This Ryan *cabrón* "accidentally" shows up to a meeting with a CIA agent that he already knows just as she's about to meet the target? The next day he goes to the U.S. consulate and meets with the CIA chief of station while he is also working with the CNI. You really think this is just a finance guy?'

'If you feel he is a threat, I can make him a borscht easily enough.'

Guzmán grinned at Bykov's little joke. Making Ryan a borscht was the Russian's way of saying he would make the man into a blood-red soup, dissolving his corpse in a barrel of acid, the same way the Mexican cartels disposed of their opponents – sometimes before they were dead. It was a gruesome but effective way of destroying DNA evidence.

Something told Guzmán that Bykov was right. And the Russian operator was, after all, the man on the ground.

But if Ryan worked for a big financial firm run by an American ex-senator, that meant he had powerful and influential friends. If Ryan really was just a financial analyst and had no real connection to the operation in Barcelona, it would be an unnecessary mistake to eliminate him – an 'unforced error' as they said in American baseball, which he loved with a passion.

Yet, Bykov was onto something. If Ryan was a threat, he needed to be eliminated. Things were too far along now. They couldn't afford to have Ryan throw sand into the gearbox. Whether Ryan was merely a businessman or a security operative, if he posed a threat, he needed to be eliminated. But Guzmán needed evidence that Ryan was, in fact, a threat. More important, he needed to know if Ryan was responsible for van Delden's death.

'What do you propose, Bykov? You're the man on the ground.'

'When Ryan left the restaurant, our eyes met, though only briefly. Perhaps it was an accident. Perhaps not. But he has the look of a predator and that makes me nervous.'

'Was he carrying a weapon?'

'Not that I saw, though I admit, I didn't have much time to observe him.'

'Your recommendation?'

'Kill him.'

Bykov was a good operator, not prone to panic. Like all of the others under Guzmán's authority, he had previously served with a national military organization before selling his combat experience to the private sector.

Guzmán was different. He'd been forcibly retired from the Guatemalan Army.

He joined as early as he could to escape the grinding poverty of subsistence farming in the highlands. At first, Guzmán was mistaken for another dull campesino, but his incredible physical and intellectual skills stood out from his first days in uniform.

A born hunter, he moved swiftly and silently through the bush, his bloodied machete an extension of his wiry arm. More important, his cunning mind seemed perfectly tuned for small-unit tactics.

But it was his capacity for violence that made him truly stand out, and he was immediately accepted into the Guatemalan elite Special Forces unit, the Kaibiles. He not only raised and killed his companion puppy – a notorious initiation ritual in Kaibiles training – he gladly skinned and roasted it over an open flame, and devoured it in front of his approving officers. He daily proved himself a dedicated warrior in service of the unit, eager and able to carry out the most difficult orders in the government's war with the cartels.

Guzmán rose through the ranks, one of the Kaibiles' most competent and trusted commanders, whose instincts on the battlefield were matched only by his steadfast devotion to the men under his command. These were the reasons why his unit was selected to fight in the Democratic Republic of the Congo. His troops dominated the field, and in true Kaibiles fashion, showed no mercy to their enemies, military or civilian. When charges were raised by international rights groups, the Palacio Verde – Guatemala's White House – demanded Guzmán punish the enlisted men involved. He refused.

For his devotion to his men, he was forcibly cashiered from the Army. But it was that devotion that compelled two dozen of his best fighters to follow him into private employment, even out here, to the very depths of the merciless sea. And it was that devotion that bound another seventy-odd operators to him today, including Bykov.

Guzmán blew out a long breath, thinking. He had a reputation for completing his missions and fulfilling his contracts to the letter, a record he was proud of. A point of honor, in fact. This particular contract they were working on was the most difficult and dangerous of his career.

It was also the most lucrative.

He also had the reputation of protecting the lives of his men at whatever the cost in blood or treasure. It was Guzmán's point of honor to always ensure that both mission and men were protected.

When the two came into conflict? Normally, he sided with his men. But fulfilling this contract was especially important.

'Bykov, I want you to step up your surveillance of this

Ryan asshole. Take it as far as you need to without touching him and report back to me tomorrow. If necessary, we'll snatch him and find out what he's really up to before we let you toss him into the pot. *¿Me entiendes?*'

'Perfectly.'

'Good.' Guzmán ended the call. He zoomed in on Ryan's photo, studying the young face.

If Ryan was responsible for van Delden's death, he needed to suffer badly.

# 17

*Barcelona, Spain*

Renée Moore had been killed only yesterday. Her murderers might have already fled the country. Time was their ally, his enemy. So Jack kept pushing. It was his only hope of getting justice for his friend.

Jack rubbed his tired eyes. After hours of reviewing the CCTV images Gavin had secured, he still wasn't sure what he had, if anything. No audio didn't help, either.

Part of the problem was that he didn't even know what he was looking for. The story Brossa and the CNI had settled on was pretty straightforward. A bomb was clearly detonated inside L'avi and a member of the terrorist group known as Brigada Catalan, Noèlia Aleixandri – the Bluetooth Blonde – was inside at the time.

All of that was verified on the digital file. The explosion itself destroyed the only working camera. Before the explosion, the blonde was standing at the bar not too far from him.

Brigada Catalan's motives were well known, thanks to its radical online manifesto. It had claimed credit for the attack in social media just minutes after the explosion. Jack could tell by Brossa's demeanor that she felt the case was closed. In a way, he couldn't blame her. Cops and case officers liked closing cases, and the easiest ones to close were the simplest ones. Occam's razor and all of that.

But his review of the digital files had raised a few questions he couldn't quite answer.

The Bluetooth Blonde arrived at L'avi approximately twenty-five minutes before Jack showed up. She first appeared in the camera as she entered through the only door and proceeded to the back, out of camera range. She returned about eight minutes later. Jack assumed that was a bathroom stop.

What stood out was the small backpack she wore when she entered the restaurant. He hadn't noticed it when he saw her yesterday and now he knew why. She came out of the restroom still wearing the backpack but set it at her feet when she stood at the bar.

He enlarged the video image and replayed it several times. Owing to the poor image quality, he couldn't tell if the backpack's dimensions changed between the bathroom and the bar. He made himself a note to ask Brossa if they had determined the location of the bomb explosion. If the blast originated in the rear of the restaurant, especially the restroom, then Aleixandri would most likely be the bomber.

But there was something about the woman. She didn't strike Jack as a suicide bomber. Most suicide bombers were visibly nervous just before an attack, fearing either detection or death or both. That was one of the reasons groups like ISIS often used unsuspecting children or mentally impaired people for such missions, their suicide vests detonated remotely by their handlers.

Aleixandri carried herself with confidence. If she had been nervous, she sure hid it well. In the moments before she died, she wasn't shouting revolutionary slogans or behaving erratically in any way.

No, the more he thought about it, he was certain Aleixandri wasn't the bomber because of her behavior.

All she was doing was watching Jack exit out of the door. And talking.

That Bluetooth headset never left her ear. It looked like she was watching him exit the restaurant and telling someone about it.

Why? And how was the explosion connected to him leaving?

And if she wasn't the bomber, who was?

He could think of a couple of possibilities. It could have been someone else in L'avi. Since Brigada Catalan had taken responsibility, then it would have been another Brigada Catalan member. According to the newspapers, it wasn't a large group. Wouldn't all of the Brigada Catalan members know one another?

Yeah, most likely, unless they were organized into smaller cells. But that was a long shot.

If the bomber was in the restaurant *and* Aleixandri knew him, she either never saw him – or her, Jack corrected himself – or didn't know he had a bomb. Otherwise, she would still be nervous about being detected or her impending death. Or both.

Jack scoured the digital file several more times, searching for someone who looked like a bomber but nobody in range of the camera seemed to fit that profile.

Damn.

Even if the bomber wasn't in the restaurant, the bomb was. And the bomb had to be detonated.

How?

A timer made sense if all you wanted to do was strike during the hours-long lunchtime to produce the maximum casualties.

The only reason to use a remote detonator was for a targeted assassination.

So the question really boiled down to this: Was a timer

used for a general terror strike? Or a remote detonator to kill a specific target?

The latter seemed the least likely. A single bullet in the back of the head in a dark alley was far more efficient than an explosion in a crowded space.

All Jack knew for certain was that his friend Renée had been killed in the blast and that she was a CIA agent who came to the restaurant to meet with somebody she didn't know. She arrived at the restaurant, and within minutes of her arrival, the bomb exploded.

If she was the target, then the attack succeeded. But why would Brigada Catalan want to kill her?

The CIA hunted down global terrorist organizations like Brigada Catalan. But why would a CIA agent based in California come to Barcelona to investigate a new, small, and regional independence organization that had no history of actual violence until the explosion itself? That just didn't add up.

If the CIA wasn't investigating Brigada Catalan, what other reason would Brigada Catalan have to kill Moore? He'd have to think about that one some more.

The other thing that bothered him was the timing of the explosion. If Renée was the target, why not explode the bomb the moment she came in? Why wait several minutes?

Jack replayed the entire tape all over again.

Aleixandri was clearly talking to someone on the Bluetooth, though infrequently. She could have been talking to her mother about her health or the utility department disputing an electric bill or selling phone-sex services right there at the bar.

But Jack's gut told him she was talking to the person who detonated the bomb.

Jack really needed to figure out who that was.

He wished he could read lips – that would be a heck of a skill to acquire at some point. Of course, if she was speaking in Català it wouldn't do him any good.

Gavin had talked about a program called LipNet. The software was more accurate than human lip-readers who only read and translated one word at a time. LipNet analyzed an entire sentence of spatial-temporal lip movements. It then decoded those spatial-temporal lip movements with a deep learning algorithm. In short, LipNet taught itself the 'lip language' of the person it was observing as the person was speaking.

But the shitty video quality prevented that and the camera shots were all overhead from a static rear angle and didn't capture enough of her mouth.

Another dead end.

Now what?

# 18

Jack yawned. It wasn't time to throw in the towel just yet.

His memory was sharper than the crappy CCTV video files. Aleixandri had checked him out on several occasions in the mirror behind the bar. She was interested in him. But interested *how*? His vanity last night assumed it was sexual. Now he wasn't so sure.

He also remembered that Aleixandri checked out Renée when she came in. Was that because Renée was so attractive? Or because he and Renée knew each other? Or because she was obviously searching for someone else? Or was it all of the above?

Or maybe she knew Renée was CIA.

It was impossible to know the reason. All that mattered was that she was tracking Renée, and if his gut was right, doing it for the guy or gal on the other end of her Bluetooth.

Jack shook his head, frustrated. If she knew Renée was the target, why wasn't the bomb exploded right then and there?

Because maybe Renée wasn't the target.

Or maybe Renée wasn't the *only* target.

Jack bolted to his feet.

*Idiot! Why didn't you see that before?*

All Jack could find in the cupboards of his Airbnb apartment was Nescafé instant coffee but that would have to do. He boiled up a pot of bottled water and knocked back a couple of cups to clear his mind before dropping down in front of his laptop.

He ran the video again from the moment Renée came into view. There was no doubt in his mind that Aleixandri had a reaction to seeing Renée. That confirmed the idea that Renée was a target, but now the challenge was to figure out who the other target could be.

Jack played the video again. Aleixandri watched him the whole time. A few steps after he exited, the room erupted and the camera died.

Was Gavin right? Was he the other target of the bombing?

He played it again. No doubt about it. She was watching Jack exit the doorway, and moments later, the bomb went off.

But that made no sense. If he and Renée were both targets, why wasn't the bomb set off when they were *both* inside the restaurant? Why set it off as he was leaving?

Was Aleixandri supposed to leave before the bomb went off? But Aleixandri made no move to leave at any point, not even when Jack was exiting through the door.

No, it was clear. The Bluetooth Blonde had no idea that bomb was going to explode.

Jack backed the tape up to the moments just before the explosion.

His eyes fell on Renée. She was talking to the bartender, probably ordering a drink just as the bomb exploded. He backed it up. Froze the image one frame before the explosion. The last moment of her short life. He enlarged the image. His heart broke all over again.

He started to touch her face on the screen but stopped short. Now was not the time to grieve.

He shook it off.

*What am I missing?*

Aleixandri watched Jack leave. Why? Was she waiting for him to leave? Why would she do that?

*Damn it!*

No reason. No reason at all – if the bombing wasn't about him.

Then why was she watching him leave?

Jack ran the tape again. *Funny how the thriller movies never tell you how boring this work really is.*

He watched himself head out the door. She's watching him leave . . . and . . . she's still watching him leave – even after he's gone.

Wait. One more time.

Yeah. He leaves. She seems to still be watching the door. Why? To make sure he's really gone?

*Holy shit.*

That guy.

The one that bumped into him. Short, tortoiseshell glasses, long hair. An American. Or at least an English speaker. 'Sorry, man,' he said when they bumped into each other.

Aleixandri was watching *him*. Sorry Man.

Jack toggled the arrow keys, advancing the video by individual frames, back and forth, back and forth.

Instead of watching himself leave, he focused on Sorry Man.

Sorry Man takes a couple of steps into the restaurant.

Renée orders a drink at the bar.

Aleixandri is speaking.

The room erupts in an explosion.

The camera dies.

Jack grabbed the best image of Sorry Man's face he could and uploaded it onto The Campus cloud drive.

From the same drive, Jack opened up The Campus facial-recognition program.

Besides having access to the U.S. government's vast

database of over seven hundred and fifty million faces, Gavin's program hacked several other foreign government facial-recog databases. This expanded Gavin's program's reach by orders of magnitude. China alone had recorded each of its 1.4 billion people and probably every tourist, business executive, exchange student, or any other *wàiguó rén* that had entered the country, legally or otherwise.

Jack initiated The Campus facial-recog program and sat back. It could take several hours to do its thing using the 2-D image he uploaded. In the near future, more and better cameras producing true 3-D and thermal images, along with gait, skin, and even hair analysis, could make facial recognition both ubiquitous and nearly infallible.

The program suddenly alerted.

The alert snapped Jack back to reality. A reality that, at times, sucked. Especially now.

According to the nearly infallible software, Sorry Man didn't exist.

# 19

*Barcelona, Spain*

Jack killed the software alert telling him that Sorry Man didn't exist in any database that The Campus had access to.

He could choose to believe the software or his own lying eyes. Of course Sorry Man existed. But he existed in the same kind of space that Jack did. A man who wasn't supposed to be found.

That fact alone told him Sorry Man was an important part of the puzzle. Maybe the most important part. Certainly the missing part.

A FaceTime window from Gavin opened up on his screen.

'Dude, you look thrashed.'

Jack grinned. 'Let me guess. They were running *Fast Times at Ridgemont High* at the Bijou Theater again.'

'Better still, laser disc. It's a classic.'

'What do you have?'

Gavin grinned ear to ear. 'I found your perp's cell-phone store. Even have the date and time stamp.'

An encrypted zip file popped up on Jack's screen. He opened it. He watched a high-angle view of Aleixandri walking into an Orange telecom store on Ronda de Sant Pere, a tree-lined street located just steps from the Urquinaona metro stop. Convenient.

'Can you get a shot of her inside making the purchase?'

'You're killin' me, Smalls. I can't work miracles.' Gavin

took a long swig from a Big Gulp cup just slightly smaller than a kitchen trash can.

'You're selling yourself short, Gav.'

'I was lucky to find this traffic camera shot. By the way, here's another one.'

Another file popped up on Jack's screen. The time stamp showed it was taken thirteen minutes later. Aleixandri exited the store with an Orange branded plastic bag, presumably with a prepaid phone inside since it only took her a few minutes to get it.

'Okay, that's good enough for me. Great job. Seriously.'

'No big deal.' Gavin shrugged, slurping on his straw. 'Anything else? I've got time to kill before the next Battle Royale tournament.'

'Well, since you're offering. There's this.' Jack sent over a file of Sorry Man. 'Can't find this guy on our face-recog software.'

'You sure?'

'Ran it twice.'

'Huh. That's interesting. He looks like a couch-surfing goober.'

*He looks just like you, Gav, only twenty years younger,* Jack thought, biting his tongue.

'What do you think?'

'I think I've got two hours before I suit up for war. I'll see what I can do.'

'Thanks, buddy.'

'You staying out of trouble, Jack? I mean, I don't mind looking into this stuff, but you're on your own over there and you're not authorized to do anything. I don't want you to get into the middle of something you can't get out of, especially without any backup around.'

'Just trying to scratch an itch, that's all. The locals seem to be a little shorthanded, so I figure we should help them out so they can do their jobs and I can get home.'

Gavin frowned. Jack wasn't sure if it was out of concern for his safety, or because his mouth was wrapped around the straw, sucking out the last, rattling gurgle of the empty Big Gulp.

'"Head on a swivel," Clark always says,' Gavin said just before he logged off.

'You, too.'

Jack was grateful Gavin was on his team. He'd hate to have the middle-aged computer genius coming after him, and worse, he'd hate to not have Gavin as a resource. He tried to imagine Clark back in the day, racing around the ancient capitals of Eastern Europe crumbling behind the Iron Curtain without benefit of cell phones or high-speed Internet. How did those old guys do it with just a pocketful of change and one of those old paper phone books for comms?

Crazy.

Jack stared at the photo of Aleixandri leaving the Orange telecom store. He had the address. Should he pay a visit? What could he do? The clerk wouldn't divulge any personal information about the woman, assuming she gave him an authentic name and ID, which Jack doubted. And breaking in after hours made no sense. He needed access to the electronic records that would identify the phone – an electronic serial number, system identification code, or mobile identification number, and, ideally, all three – and those wouldn't be located inside the store.

But he couldn't just sit on this, either.

The only person who could help him was Brossa. It would make an excellent bargaining chip, too.

He picked up his phone and called her, hoping to catch a late-night meeting. But she didn't pick up, so he left a voicemail.

'I know how to find the bomber.'

# 20

*Bavarian Alps, Germany*

She leaned the motorcycle hard right into the steeply wind-ing mountain curve, her heart racing faster than the brushless DC three-phase electric motor accelerating between her thighs.

For her, speed was sex.

The only sound she heard inside her helmet was the rush of cold night wind. The carbon fiber, all-electric Saroléa Manx7 sped along in utter silence. An extravagant gift from her doting father, the Belgian bike wasn't even in production yet. It was everything she dreamed of – and the perfect escape from her lab in München. At work, the project con-trolled her.

Out here, she was free.

The bike was flawless, and stunningly fast. Unlike a gasoline engine, an electric engine accelerated near instantaneously – the same way an electric light turned on as soon as the switch was flipped. The Saroléa could go from zero to one hundred kilometers in three seconds. As soon as the mechanical limi-tations were addressed, the time between full throttle and full speed would approach zero.

Fast as light.

She leaned left into the next curve, her leathered knee nearly touching the ice-slicked asphalt. The grippy tires held firm.

She laughed.

Thank God no other vehicles were on the two-lane road this late at night.

Otherwise, she'd be dead.

She straightened up out of the turn and saw the long straightaway pointing toward the next turn and the starlit sky beyond.

She twisted the throttle full open.

The bike bolted forward. The speedometer jumped. The engine was software-limited to just 240 km/h. It was capable of far more than a human could handle.

Well, most humans.

But she wasn't stupid; 240 km/h was a handful, even for her.

The Saroléa was nearing 150 km/h. She dared not take it further. In the next two seconds she needed to ease off the throttle and gently brake, then lean hard right into the next curve.

She eased the throttle.

The bike accelerated.

From 150 km/h to 270 km/h in the blink of an eye.

*What happened?*

The turn was on her. Faster than she could react.

Joy turned to terror.

She jammed the brakes.

Too late.

The man in the BMW coupe on the next ridge watched it all through his night-vision binoculars. He had timed the signal transmission perfectly.

The woman and the bike separated just moments after they launched into the air. He lost track of both as they tumbled into the rocks three hundred meters below.

Too far away to hear her scream.

Too bad.

# October 26

# 21

*Washington, D.C.*
*The White House*

President Ryan convened the emergency meeting of a very small and select national security team in the Situation Room.

Only Secretary of Defense Robert Burgess, Secretary of State Scott Adler, Director of National Intelligence Mary Pat Foley, Admiral John Talbot, and Arnie van Damm were present. They all sat in the high-backed leather chairs clustered on one end of the long mahogany table, Ryan at the head. Thick ceramic mugs with the presidential seal stood at each place, brimming with hot coffee or tea.

'Thank you all for coming on such short notice,' Ryan said, a pair of reading glasses perched on the end of his nose. 'I want to keep today's meeting brief. Given the gravity of the potential threat, the fewer people that are in the loop, the better. You've all been briefed about my conversation with Buck Logan.

'I don't need to tell any of you what's at stake. Like the historian said, Whoever commands the seas commands everything. And while I don't yet consider this to be a direct national security threat, I do see it as a challenge to our capacity to protect the sea lanes and our global economic interests.'

SecDef Burgess added, 'If the Chinese or our allies in the Pacific aren't already aware of the situation, they soon will be. They'll be watching how we handle this. Our failure to solve this problem will erode confidence among our friends and embolden the PLAN' – the Chinese Navy.

'If this thing escalates, it could panic global markets and destabilize the entire global economy,' SecState Adler said.

'Our job is simple, but not easy,' Ryan said, folding his hands on the table. 'We need to figure out who's behind this, how they're doing it, and how we're going to stop it.'

Ryan turned toward Admiral Talbot. 'John, you're up.'

Talbot clicked his laser presenter. The monitor showed four graphical images of satellites in geostationary orbit around the Earth.

'Let's start by trying to answer the "how" first and maybe that will get us to the "who." Before we begin, let's discuss the national-technical means at our disposal.

'What you're looking at here are the four SBIRS, Space Based Infrared System satellites, deployed by the Air Force Space Command. This is the backbone of the OPIR missile defense early-warning system. SBIRS provides us with an unblinking infrared eye – a global persistent stare. These satellites deploy the most sensitive infrared sensors in our inventory and are designed to detect primarily missile launches.

'SBIRS enabled us to determine that it was an SA-11 Gadfly missile launched from Russian-backed rebel territory in Ukraine that shot down Malaysia Airlines Flight 17. SBIRS tracked the missile from launch origin through trajectory to the final explosion that killed all 298 passengers.'

'Amazing,' Arnie said.

The admiral continued. 'As it turns out, SBIRS is also able to pick up other man-made and natural heat events, such as conventional explosions, volcanic eruptions, artillery fire, and even midair aircraft collisions.'

'Was SBIRS able to detect any explosions related to the sinking of these ships?' Arnie asked.

Talbot shook his head. 'The four SBIRS satellites are in geostationary orbit.' He drew a circle around one of the SBIRS satellites with his laser pointer. 'Unfortunately, the satellite positioned over the Asia-Pacific quadrant failed three months ago. Its replacement is being readied and is expected to arrive on station early next year.'

'In other words, the almighty, all-seeing eye in the sky got a cataract,' Foley said.

Talbot nodded. 'Yes, ma'am. One of them did. Some sort of a software glitch. But in truth, as I said before, SBIRS is primarily designed for detecting significant heat signatures – high-energy events like burning LOX rocket fuel. Even if SBIRS had been fully functional, it's not clear that it would have alerted us to the sinking events.'

'I don't understand,' Arnie said, frowning deeply. 'Wouldn't an explosion large enough to sink a ship generate enough heat to be detected?'

'That's a very good question, Mr van Damm. Let me be more specific. I'm referring to two possibilities. First, even if SBIRS had detected an explosion, it may not have conformed to the heat signature of a missile launch. So the event would have been stored as data and not brought to our attention.

'These infrared satellites are enormously sensitive and are picking up hundreds if not thousands of heat events every day. We couldn't possibly respond to each of them or even sort through them with the human eye – which is why we use high-speed computers and complicated algorithms to do that automatically.

'The second reason why SBIRS may not have alarmed is because of the type of ordnance. For example, if it occurred underwater, like a mine, the thermal effects would have been significantly reduced. Like lighting a flare at the bottom of a swimming pool.'

Ryan leaned on the table, folding his hands. 'If SBIRS had been in operation, it also could have detected an anti-ship missile launch, which would have answered even more questions for us.'

Talbot nodded. 'Yes, sir. Air, land, sea, or sub-based launches could have all been detected.'

'A damn lucky coincidence for the bastards behind all of this,' Arnie observed.

'Coincidence, or good planning,' Ryan said. 'I'm not sure which yet.'

'SBIRS is just one part of MASINT,' Foley said. 'What has MASINT told us?'

Measurement and signature intelligence assets, including SBIRS, were the ground, sea, air, and satellite systems that provided real-time tactical and strategic intelligence gathering. MASINT assets deployed a wide range of seismic, acoustic, thermal, optical, and other sensors capable of detecting any and all forms of kinetic events. Some assets covered entire continents; others were tasked with missions as small as a few meters. Most were targeted at known threat vectors like North Korea or the Middle East.

'MASINT hasn't shown us anything, ma'am. Gamma waves, X-rays, radio waves, infrared, sonar, radar – nothing along the entirety of the electromagnetic spectrum locates any kind of air or sea combat vehicle in the vicinity of these sinkings.'

'No indication of nuclear, chemical, or biological attack?' Ryan asked.

'None that we detected remotely. Putting assets on-site

would give us a more definitive reading. These locations are way the hell out in the middle of nowhere.'

Ryan turned to Admiral Talbot. 'You've just told us what we don't know. Let's change tack and talk about the facts we do know.'

'Yes, sir.' He clicked his laser pointer and a live digital map popped onto one of the other wide-screen monitors. It displayed the Pacific Ocean with arrowhead-shaped graphical images of current vessel shipping traffic. A key in the bottom right-hand corner showed vessel type by color. Cargo ships were green, fishing vessels were pink, oil tankers were red, and so forth.

'What you're looking at is a live display of vessels broadcasting automatic identification system, AIS, signals all over the Pacific.

'The vessels are equipped with transceivers that transmit a variety of ships' data including name, speed, location, et cetera. AIS is both land and satellite based, and supplements other ship-based navigational aids such as radar, gyrocompass, and Global Navigation Satellite System receivers.'

'How many ships broadcasting AIS are we talking about?' Ryan asked. 'Globally?'

Admiral Talbot widened the screen to show the entire globe. Tens of thousands of multicolored 'arrowheads' appeared on every ocean, most congested around the coastlines of every continent, save Antarctica. The North Atlantic and western Pacific were particularly congested.

'Approximately one hundred thousand vessels broadcast an AIS signal yearly, though of course, not every such equipped vessel is currently at sea.'

Arnie whistled. 'That's a lot of damn boats to keep track of.'

'It is.' Talbot clicked his laser pointer and all of the 'live' arrowheads disappeared. All that remained on-screen were six green cargo ship arrowheads overlaid with red $X$'s. He pointed to each of them as he spoke.

'These are the locations of the six vessels sunk in this remote region of the South Pacific. It's an area of approximately one thousand square miles located about three thousand miles due south of San Diego and the same distance due west of Peru. The sunken ships all sailed under five different flags of convenience. No witnesses or survivors. No known means of destruction, though it appears the destruction was total. Based on our analysis, each ship was sunk by a single, catastrophic strike.'

'Don't ships of that size have "black boxes" like passenger aircraft?' Arnie asked.

'Yes, otherwise known as voyage data recorders. Some are designed to float free of a vessel but most are fixed. It's entirely possible somebody boarded each vessel and disabled or removed the VDRs. The other possibility is that a massive event could destroy a ship and send it to the bottom without allowing enough time for the VDR to broadcast a distress signal.'

'If we find the wreckage, can we send down divers and recover the VDR?'

Talbot highlighted the first wreck. 'This one is located in the most shallow area at just five thousand and sixty-five feet. Almost a mile.' His laser pointer ran to another. 'The deepest location is nearly seven thousand feet below the surface. A human diver simply isn't possible.

'Our only chance is to get a deepwater submersible into the area. A visual inspection of the wreckage would be possible – but only if the submersible is able to navigate the tangle of steel, cables, containers, and other debris that might block its ingress.'

'But if we do recover the VDRs? That'll tell us what we need to know, right?' Arnie asked.

'Unfortunately, most of the information a VDR would provide would only duplicate the AIS data we already have. Some VDRs record sound and radio transmissions, which could prove useful if the ship communicated with whoever attacked it. On the other hand, a sophisticated intruder on board the vessel would know to erase the data with a simple magnet.'

Arnie frowned with frustration. 'But in general, are you confident that these six markers are the likely locations of the sunken ships?'

'Assuming the vessels weren't simply boarded, their AIS turned off, and then sailed to a distant location, then, yes, "likely locations" is a good bet.'

# 22

'To summarize,' Ryan began. 'We're fairly confident we know where these ships were sunk but we still don't know how. John, what's your best guess as to the weapons platform? Maybe that will get us closer to "who."'

'If you put a gun to my head? A submarine makes the most sense.'

'Why?'

'My gut. Nothing more. I know what boats can do and this fits the profile.'

'Does IUSS tell us it's a sub?' Ryan asked. He was referring to the Navy's submarine detection program, the Integrated Undersea Surveillance System. IUSS included SOSUS, garage-size hydrophone arrays planted on the seabed, and SURTASS, plane-based sonar buoys and towed array ships.

'The short answer is, IUSS sensors weren't available in the area of the sinkings.'

Ryan shook his head, smirking, and leaned back in his chair. 'Of course not.'

'Another coincidence, boss?' Arnie asked.

'For what it's worth, we did pick up a Russian ELF transmission a few days ago. They don't use it very often so we pay attention when they do.'

'ELF?' Arnie asked.

'Extremely low frequency radio transmission. It's used to communicate with submerged submarines over huge distances – almost anywhere on the planet. I'm not saying

134

the ELF transmit is connected to this but it's one more hash mark in favor of my gut.'

'Buck Logan thinks the Russians are behind this,' the President said. 'I'm not convinced, but if you think it's a sub, it's worth discussing. Let's start with why it could be the Russians.'

SecDef Burgess said, 'They certainly have the national-technical means to do so, especially if it's a sub. And they've just launched the K-329 *Belgorod,* assigned to their Pacific Fleet.'

'Is it in the area?' Foley asked.

'No, but it doesn't have to be,' Talbot said. 'The *Belgorod* is an Oscar-II class submarine, the longest in the world – bigger even than the *Red October,* which was a *Typhoon*-class. But the *Belgorod* isn't a missile boat. It's a "special mission" boat, designed specifically to carry two deepwater submersible research vessels along with six Poseidon torpedoes.'

'Poseidons?' Adler asked.

'Nuclear-powered drone torpedoes with an estimated range of over six thousand miles, and an operational depth of up to ten thousand feet,' the admiral said. 'The Russians claim that Poseidon can reach underwater speeds of a hundred knots whether it's carrying a hundred-megaton nuclear or a conventional warhead.'

'Poseidon sounds like a doomsday machine,' Arnie said.

'It's meant to sound like one,' Talbot said. 'In reality, their speed and payloads are probably less than advertised. But even so, they can evade our defenses, which makes them a formidable weapon.'

'Do you think the Poseidon is the most likely weapon?' Foley asked.

'No, ma'am. It's too new and too expensive for them to waste on something like sinking cargo ships.'

'What other subs do they have in the area?' Ryan asked.

'The *Glazov* was launched six weeks ago and assigned to the Pacific Fleet. It's an improved Kilo-class diesel-electric boat. Probably the quietest boat they've ever put in the water, SSK or otherwise.'

'How quiet?' Foley asked.

'Remember the *Krasnodar* incident a few years back?' Talbot said. 'That boat was also an improved Kilo class, only this new one is even better.'

Ryan shook his head, frustrated at the memory.

President Yermilov had announced to the world, and to NATO in particular, the launch of the *Krasnodar* and its mission to fire its Kalibr cruise missiles into Syria. NATO tracked the boat – which conveniently ran on the surface – all the way from its home port in the Baltic to the Mediterranean Sea. Somewhere off the coast of Libya, it submerged and disappeared. It was only found again after it launched its cruise missiles at targets in Syria. It then resurfaced and headed for its new home base in the Crimea. NATO had taken to calling the *Krasnodar* 'the Black Hole.'

'Where is the *Glazov* now?'

'We're not sure, sir. NRO satellites tracked it leaving port six weeks ago, and passed it off to the Japanese. They assigned the *Toryu* to keep an eye on it. The *Toryu* is one of Japan's new lithium-ion AIP diesel-electric boats – the most advanced in the world. But three days later, the *Glazov* submerged and slipped the leash. We're not exactly sure where it is now but it was last seen heading in the general direction of the area in question.'

Ryan pointed at the map. 'Given its operational capabilities and the locations of the sunken vessels, you think the *Glazov* is the most likely culprit?'

'Right now, it's the only candidate. The fact it carries

Kalibr-M cruise missiles and supercavitating Shkval torpedoes doesn't exactly fit with a whale-watching mission profile.'

SecDef Burgess held up his hands. 'I'm sorry, I'm just not buying this. Are we saying the Russian government has gone into the piracy business?'

'If by "piracy" you mean we're chasing a bunch of Ivans with parrots and peg legs, my guess would be no,' Ryan said. 'But given Buck Logan's experience, I'm comfortable calling these criminal actions "piracy."' Ryan scanned the table. 'But if anybody here says "arrr" I'm canceling lunch.'

That elicited a much-needed chuckle around the table.

'But it seems odd for the Russians to engage in this kind of behavior,' SecState Adler said.

'Could be a cover or a feint. Could be they want us to believe we're chasing pirates instead of Russian subs,' Arnie suggested.

'Why? What cover? What feint?'

Arnie shrugged. 'Testing new weapons systems – or testing ours? Or a feint to draw us into this area while they do something else on the other side of the globe? Or trying to throw confusion into our ranks?'

'I think the President already alluded to the real reason,' SecDef Burgess said. 'We've put economic sanctions on them for years. Loss of trade hurts them. Perhaps this is their way to dry up global trade on our end. Tit for tat.'

'I've got a better reason,' Ryan said. He pointed at Admiral Talbot. 'You're the one that brought up the *Krasnodar*. At the time, we all agreed Yermilov pulled that publicity stunt to embarrass NATO. But we figured out a little later it was actually a piece of theater meant to sell the improved Kilos to Third World customers like Egypt and India.'

'That's right. And it worked. We put sanctions on the

Russians, and they turn around and sell their Black Hole Kilos to every regional competitor who can cough up the rubles. Makes our job a whole helluva lot harder.'

'So, this *Glazov* sub is doing the same thing? Sinking commercial ships to prove its worth?' Arnie said.

'It's only a theory,' Ryan said. 'And right now, five bucks and my theory will only buy you a cup of burnt coffee. And there's one other little problem.'

'What's that?' Arnie asked.

'How in the hell do you find an unfindable boat?'

'So let's continue the "who" conversation,' Ryan said. 'Someone tell me why it's *not* the Russians.'

'What if the sinkings weren't caused by a sub?' Arnie asked. 'What if it was done with an explosive device smuggled on board? That could be the work of a terrorist organization.'

'But no terror demands have been made,' the SecDef countered.

'Cash has been demanded – lots of it – and those assholes need a shit-ton of loot to carry out their operations. We've done a good job of drying up their primary funding sources. Maybe this is their response to our efforts,' Arnie said.

'Terrorists aren't out of the question,' Foley said. 'But it's kind of a reach, if we're talking about the usual suspects.'

'Even Houthis are flying aerial drones these days,' Arnie said.

'Not in the South Pacific.'

'What about the Chi-Comms? They have deepwater boats, don't they?' Arnie asked.

'We have all of their submarines accounted for,' Talbot said.

'How?'

Talbot smiled and winked. 'Sorry, Arnie, but you're not cleared for that one.'

A few chuckles burbled around the table.

Slightly irritated, Arnie pushed back. 'What about the NORKs? Those assholes are always up to something, and as I recall, they have over six hundred combat vessels in their fleet, including subs.'

'All true, Mr van Damm, but most of their surface fleet is limited to coastal operations — gunboats, patrol boats, and amphibs. We estimate they have seventy operational diesel subs and some of those have deepwater capability. But most of those are Soviet and Chi-Comm surplus, which I wouldn't trust to sail the Potomac. I wouldn't rule them out entirely, given their tenacity, but I wouldn't put them anywhere near the top of the list.'

'What about regular, run-of-the-mill pirates?' Foley said. 'They've been quite active over the last decade.'

Talbot spoke as he flashed his pointer at the piracy hot-spots on the coasts of Africa, the Gulf of Oman near the Arabian Peninsula, the Strait of Malacca, and the South China Sea.

'Pirates are typically indigenous locals. Their SOP is to seize vessels or hostages for ransom, and their weapons inventory is limited to small arms. Given the location of the incidents in the South Pacific and the catastrophic destruction of the vessels and crew, I'd rule them out.'

'So where does that leave us?' the President asked.

'The fact that only cargo vessels have been targeted intrigues me,' Foley said. 'There's a lot of money in the oil industry. I'm surprised they aren't hitting tankers. Some of the big ones now carry in excess of five hundred thousand deadweight tons of petroleum.'

'According to Logan's ransom letter, these jokers want to

keep things out of the public eye.' Ryan leaned on the desk. 'Remember the *Exxon Valdez*? Imagine the global outrage if it was known that our pirates sank an oil tanker and destroyed an entire coral reef? There would be instant demand to find and prosecute them.'

'So it's just cargo ships,' Foley said. 'Under what flags?'

'Panama, Liberia, the Marshall Islands, Cyprus, and Moldova. Owners can avoid union wages and Western labor and environmental regulations.'

'Not Chinese-flagged? Or Russian?' the SecDef asked.

'Not to my knowledge, though several carried goods manufactured in China. One vessel was carrying a shipment of Chinese antibiotics.'

Ryan's eyes narrowed. That was a sore subject with him, and one he'd been raising with the American pharmaceutical industry over the last year. Nearly eighty percent of all pharmaceuticals globally were now made in China, including prescription drugs, antibiotics, and over-the-counter medicines, along with the chemical precursors needed for just about everything else. Not a single penicillin factory existed in the United States anymore.

'So why not Chinese- or Russian-flagged ships? Is it just because our pirates don't want to pick a fight with a real fighting navy?' Ryan asked. 'Or does the fact that Russia and China haven't been hit make them our leading suspects after all?'

'Wait a sec,' Ryan said. He turned toward the admiral. 'Didn't you say *Glazov* put to sea six weeks ago? And it's still out there?'

'Yes, sir.'

'And what kind of underwater endurance does it have?'

Talbot pulled up a file on *Glazov* and flashed its photos and specs on a monitor.

'Our estimate is that they can stay under for two weeks without surfacing, and have a patrol range of forty-five days before they need to restock and refuel.'

Ryan jumped to his feet. He marched over to the other monitor still displaying the locations of the sunken ships in the South Pacific.

'Okay, let's assume just for the sake of argument that the *Glazov* is our culprit. If it's operating in this area and it's at the end of its forty-five-day endurance, where the hell does it resupply out here in the middle of nowhere? There aren't any Russian naval bases in the area.'

'Good question,' Talbot said. He stared at the map for a moment. 'There's gotta be a sub tender in the area.'

'Is there?' Ryan asked.

'Not to my knowledge.'

'Can you change back to the live screen and zoom in here?' Ryan pointed at a spot in the remotest part of the South Pacific.

'Roger that.' Talbot pulled up all of the ships broadcasting AIS signals.

Ryan touched one of the arrowheads with his finger. 'What's this?'

Talbot put his pointer on the arrowhead. A text box appeared. 'That's the *Penza*. It's Russian-flagged and registered out of Vladivostok.' There weren't any other specs on the readout. The *Penza* AIS only put out what it wanted to communicate.

'Give me just one minute,' Talbot said as he snatched up his tablet and tapped a few virtual keys searching a database. When he slid his finger across the tablet it threw a still photo of the *Penza* onto another wall monitor. A black-and-red rusted cargo ship. The white multistory bridge stood on the aft end. The deck featured two powerful cranes.

'The *Penza*'s a multipurpose vessel. One hundred meters long, nearly eleven thousand tons' displacement. Transports wet and dry cargo. You can see the two twenty-five-ton derricks for lifting.'

Talbot's face broke into a wide grin.

'Son of a gun. That's the tender.'

Ryan nodded. 'And if that's a tender, then the *Glazov* is our boat.'

'What are our chances of finding a "Black Hole" boat like the *Glazov*?' Ryan asked the admiral.

'The *Glazov* is relatively small and optimized for silent operations. We'd have a better chance of pulling a winning lottery ticket once a day for seven days in a row than we do finding it. But you know what they say – you can't win if you don't play.'

Ryan smiled. 'Then let's play. Where are the *Theodore Roosevelt* and CSG-9 right now?'

'The *Roosevelt* carrier strike group is one hundred and fifty miles southwest of Hawaii.'

'That's Admiral Pike's command, isn't it?'

'Yes, sir. David's top drawer.' Talbot was pleased but not surprised that his commander in chief knew the names of his most important commanders in the field.

'How long to get them to the area in question?'

'At thirty knots, I'd estimate three days.'

'Unless you can think of a reason not to, let's send them that way. Putting seventy-five-hundred pairs of eyes on the situation can only be a good thing, not to mention the ASW capabilities they'll bring with them.'

'Roger that, sir. Admiral Pike will jump all over this. A French attack sub sank his boat and most of his CSG off the coast of Florida in an exercise in 2015. The French bragged about it on Twitter until we made them pull it down. He's never gotten over it. He'll be glad for the rematch – in real time. May I make one other suggestion?'

'Shoot.'

Talbot highlighted another arrowhead sailing halfway between Chile and New Zealand. 'That's the *Luzon,* a *Ticonderoga*-class cruiser, one of our newest. She has ASW capabilities, including two Seahawk helicopters. We can divert *Luzon* into the area to start a search almost immediately.'

'Do it.'

The President crossed over to his chair and laid his hands on the headrest. 'I think we've taken a pretty good first swing at this thing. Now we have to wait until the *Luzon* reports back. I wish this was the only thing on our plates today, but we all have other things to attend to, so I'm calling it for now. Thank you all again for your time and input.'

With the meeting declared over, Ryan's team shuffled out. Before the SecState exited the room, Ryan called after him.

'Scott, a word, if you don't mind? I have one other idea.'

# 23

'What can I do for you, Mr President?' SecState Adler said.

'Scott, I want you to set up an appointment with that new Russian ambassador ASAP.'

'You mean Christyakov? The one whose credentials you haven't accepted yet?'

'Yeah. That one.' Ryan rolled his eyes. The chief of protocol had vetted the man. Christyakov was apparently no more odious or problematic than the other ambassadors in Yermilov's diplomatic corps. Ryan wasn't eager to accommodate yet another crony of the Russian president, even if he was Yermilov's most important diplomatic officer.

'If you don't mind my asking, why the change of heart? And why now?'

'I want his rear end in a chair across from the Resolute desk so I can get the measure of him. If the Russians really are up to something in the South Pacific, he might know something about it, and with any luck, I can shake it out of him.'

'Not literally, I hope.'

'Don't be so sure.'

Yermilov had just appointed the nephew of Russia's largest petroleum conglomerate, GazNeft, to the American post, a man with no diplomatic experience whatsoever. That was fine with Ryan. He was more than happy to steal candy from a spoiled Russian baby.

'My people on the Russia desk say there's more to him than meets the eye. He might be harder to rattle than you suppose.'

'A diplomatic credential does not a diplomat make.'

'That's just the thing. He's not like most diplomats.'

'Then it should be an interesting conversation. If a Russian sub is behind all of this mess, I intend to find out, and convince him to tell Yermilov to back off. Frankly, Scott, I'm worried about the bigger picture here.'

'Are you referring to the Snow Dragon exercise next week?'

'Yeah. And that's just one piece of a larger puzzle.'

Snow Dragon would be the largest joint Chinese-Russian naval exercise ever held, and it was taking place in the Bering Sea. Snow Dragon was part of an alarming trend of cooperation across the spectrum by both governments hostile to American interests. Snow Dragon in particular was aimed at the Sino-Russian drive to exploit Arctic natural resources and newly opened Arctic shipping lanes.

In the relationship – Ryan likened it to a shotgun wedding between the Hatfields and McCoys – Russia brought to bear its technological and engineering expertise in Arctic oil and gas production. China brought its enormous banking and credit reserves to fund those operations, including a GazNeft facility now pumping over sixteen million tons of super-cooled liquefied natural gas from beneath the polar ice.

The Chinese Politburo had released an official white paper six months earlier outlining their plan to create the 'Polar Silk Road,' an extension of its global Belt and Road Initiative. The BRI was China's grand strategic plan to bring about a Eurasian economic zone. This would ultimately lead to political and military integration of the Eurasian landmass, an existential threat not only to the United States but also the rest of the world.

The Polar Silk Road through the Arctic would shorten the sea route from Shanghai to Hamburg by more than three thousand miles. A major military exercise in the Bering Sea within shooting distance of Alaska gave a whole new meaning to the idea of a new 'cold' war.

'Let's get this Christyakov his papers, and then we'll see what he's made of.'

'I'll get right on it, Mr President. Any chance I can watch? I've never seen two scorpions in a bottle fight it out before.'

'It's better if I handle this on my own. It won't take long for either of us to find out who has the bigger stinger.'

# 24

*Marin County, California*

The modest two-story ranch was set back three hundred feet off the two-lane asphalt road, surrounded by stands of cypress and pine.

Marin County Sheriff's Office vehicles stood either in the uncut grass or on the gravel road surrounding the home, including the coroner's meat wagon. Yellow crime-scene tape marked SHERIFF'S LINE DO NOT CROSS was strung across the broken-down porch, blocking the entrance.

Sergeant Ralph Browning watched the CSI team taking pictures, documenting the crime scene. The nude and desecrated corpses of Chris and Cari Fast were nailed to the wood floor, their outstretched limbs crucified to the pentagrams drawn in their own blood. White blowfly larvae were already hatched and squirming in the soft tissues of their mutilated eyes, open mouths, and abused genitals.

Thirteen black waxen candles had melted in dark pools in the circles around them. Their two small dogs were nail-gunned to the peeling walls and SATAN RULES! was written in blood beneath the furry corpses.

Sergeant Browning stood next to the young deputy who'd been called by a suspicious neighbor. He'd seen a lot in his years on the force, including a couple of head-on collisions. This was the first time he ever felt like throwing up.

'I thought they only did this shit in the movies. You ever seen anything like this before, Sergeant?'

'In twenty-two years on the job, I never seen nothing like it.'

'Makes me think I need to start going to church again.'

'First lesson on the job: People are evil.'

Sergeant Browning checked his watch. The FBI agent should be arriving at any moment. The Feebs had put out a bulletin on the two missing Google scientists after they failed to report to work. Browning was the point man from the investigations division heading up the case. He called it in to the FBI field office in San Francisco after the bodies were identified. Nothing was to be removed from the crime scene until one of their agents arrived. 'National security' was the only explanation given or needed.

'One of the techs said that the woman's Uber app had been hacked. Fake driver, fake car. Is that true?'

'Looks like it.'

'Kinda ironic, isn't it? A couple of computer geniuses getting hacked?'

'I'm going outside for a smoke,' Browning said, the bile in his throat rising from the stench. He was getting too old for this shit. He already had a hard time sleeping. After today, he might never sleep again.

His ex-wife told him he should've retired two years ago. As usual, she was right, he thought as he lit up a Marlboro, trying not to think about the horror inside.

## 25

*Barcelona, Spain*

Jack arrived at the consulate ten minutes early for his appointment with Dick Dellinger. He wanted a face-to-face meeting and a phone call wouldn't cut it. Nothing like being in the room to get a read on somebody. E-mails and texts could be ignored.

Jack needed Dellinger's attention badly. His back was against the wall. He'd hit a couple of major dead ends, first on this Sammler guy and then on Sorry Man.

At least now he had Dellinger's attention as he sat across from him, the man's dark brown eyes locked with his.

'What is it that I can help you with today, Mr Ryan?'

'Yesterday, you said I should contact you if I needed any assistance.'

'Of course, that's why I'm here – and why I cleared my schedule so that I could meet with you on short notice.'

'And I really appreciate that. You also said that you take the deaths of Americans very seriously.'

'I do.'

'Then if you don't mind my asking, what the hell is going on with the Spanish government? Why are they dragging their feet on this investigation?'

'Dragging their feet? It's only been two days since Ms Moore was killed, so if you'll pardon my French, you need to cool your jets, son. Besides, this is Spain. Spaniards only have two gears in the gearbox: slow and siesta. Don't get me wrong, they do a good job, but they do it on their own damn time.'

'If Renée were your friend, your daughter, your wife – you'd say the same thing?'

Jack wanted to gauge Dellinger's reaction. Was Renée important to Dellinger? That would confirm he was a CIA operative like her.

Dellinger didn't miss a beat. He was a slick customer. Too slick. He didn't take one second to process the question in order to try and imagine Renée as an intimate acquaintance. That meant he was either blowing smoke or he didn't have to imagine her as important to him because she already was.

'Yes, of course I'd say the same thing.'

'You're not telling me something.'

Dellinger sighed.

*Processing?* Jack wondered. *Or spinning up his bullshit generator?*

'Look, Jack, you're a smart guy. You know how the world works. You probably have heard about the independence protests going on, haven't you?'

'Yeah, sure.'

'Well, Spain's politics are very delicate and raw right now, especially when it comes to the separatism issue. Ms Moore's death sits right in the middle of the controversy, so we – the American government – must tread very carefully. Spain is an important member of NATO, and the alliance itself is feeling some tension. So we can't be seen as pressing too hard, one way or the other. There's a bigger picture here to consider.'

Dellinger leaned forward on his desk for emphasis. 'But trust me, Jack, the Spaniards are working the case. I'm keeping close tabs on things. I have friends in the Spanish government. In fact, I have a contact at the CNI and I was actually planning on putting a call in to him later this afternoon. If I find out anything that I'm allowed to tell you, I'll give you a call and fill you in. Is that acceptable?'

'Sure. And I appreciate it.'

'Good, Jack.'

Dellinger stood. So did Jack. They shook hands, but Dellinger held his grip with a strong hand. There was just a hint of violence behind the man's smiling eyes, confirming the idea in Jack's mind that Dellinger was old-school CIA.

'I want you to know that I'm as committed to finding Ms Moore's killers as you are, Jack, and I'm not going to stop until I do. Do you believe me?'

Jack squeezed a little harder, and let the violence in his own soul leach into his gaze.

'I believe you, Dick. And I hope you believe me when I tell you that I'm holding you personally accountable. So for both our sakes, light a fire under somebody's tail over there, will ya?'

'I'll do my best, Jack. Trust me on this.'

Jack turned and left the office, heading for the stairs. Something his dad once told him when he was a little boy came to mind.

*Never trust the man who tells you to trust him.*

# 26

*Houston, Texas*

The White Mountain Logistics + Security corporate head-quarters was located on the twenty-third floor of a downtown high-rise. Buck Logan chose it, in part, for the helipad on the roof. He hated wasting time and there was no bigger time suck on the planet than Houston traffic.

Logan also maintained operational facilities outside of Houston at a compound that included his own private airport, weapons-testing grounds, and even a game preserve. But Logan found over the years it was easier to do business with Houston's elite in their native habitats inside the concrete bunkers and asphalt jungles of the sweltering Texas metropolis.

Today, Buck sat with his brain trust in his own high-tech version of the White House Situation Room. The conference table was built from the oaken deck planking from the Imperial German Navy battle cruiser SMS *Lützow,* scuttled at the Battle of Jutland in 1916.

The walls of Buck's situation room were also adorned with priceless naval artifacts from history, and memorabilia from his midshipman days at the U.S. Naval Academy before his tragic football accident. His father's beloved Marine Corps had pride of place on its own separate wall, including one colorized picture of the old man in blood-smeared snow camouflage, a cigar stub clenched in his smiling teeth and his face blackened with a five o'clock shadow. He looked like an actor straight out of central casting for a Hollywood war movie. In fact, he'd just spent three sleepless days and nights in a running gun battle with Chinese 'volunteers' at the Chosin Reservoir, leading his men in a desperate action that earned him both the Purple Heart and a Navy Cross.

Buck Logan worshipped his father, his employees knew, and it was no secret that of the many priceless weapons in Buck Logan's personal arsenal, none was more precious to him than the battered, ivory-handled .45 Colt M1911A1 his father carried on his hip in the war. It was also no secret to those in the room that Buck felt as if he never lived up to the image of his larger-than-life father despite overcoming his enormous physical disability and building out a great, multi-national business that was unimaginably larger and more profitable than his father could have ever conceived.

Following the meeting with President Ryan the day before, Buck called an emergency meeting of his own 'kitchen cabinet,' the five most trusted people in his organization, each the head of White Mountain's most important divisions. They sat in low-backed leather chairs around the table, Buck at the head, of course. He was so tall in his torso that a visitor could be forgiven for thinking he'd elevated the floor on his end of the table to make him look taller. Each division head had a tablet in front of them.

'Here we are in the situation room, and we've got ourselves one hell of a situation, people,' Buck said. 'We ain't gonna sit on our hands and wait for the other shoe to drop but we sure as hell ain't gonna step on our dicks, neither –'

He glanced over at Diedre Nunn, the head of his IT division. 'Do I need to call HR before or after I issue you a formal apology, Dee?'

The retired Navy commander, who'd spent half her service time in the company of randy men at sea, smiled indulgently.

'Not necessary, sir. But I wouldn't object to a bottle of Baileys Irish Cream on my desk by EOB today.'

Logan grinned. 'Done. Hell, I might even join you for a tipple or two.' He turned to the rest of the table.

'You all have been briefed on what's happened. I also need you to know that I've made a promise to the President that we would do what we can to tie a knot in the tail of the sumbitches that have screwed us, and, now pose a threat to our great nation.'

Buck scanned the room. Every head nodded in agreement. These were good people, excellent administrators, and, most important of all, patriots to the core. Each of them had served in military uniform except for Phil Werley, his governmental liaison. But he'd done his turn in government service, first in the CIA and later as one of the deputy directors in the ODNI, reporting directly to Director Foley. Logan personally recruited Werley out from underneath her with a salary offer that nearly popped the man's eyes out of his head.

Logan continued. 'We are not the U.S. government, which means we don't have their resources, but it also means we don't wear their handcuffs. We're gonna push the limits of the law – maybe even wiggle our toes over the line every now and then – and find out who these people are, and take both offensive and defensive measures to protect our property and our people.' He pointed at Werley. 'And we're going to turn over every scrap of information we uncover to Ms Foley and let her run with it, even if it hurts us. Understood?'

Werley nodded. 'I'm sure we can find a way to pass along our intel without compromising our methods or sources. We don't want to hurt the reputation of the company, especially with her. Seventy-five percent of our revenues are government contracts.'

'I don't give a shit about contracts. This country faces a threat to our vital national interests on the high seas. What's good for America is good for us. If we have to take it in the shorts, so be it. Now, let's get down to brass tacks.'

Buck turned to Joe Gannon, a retired rear admiral and former deputy commander of the Military Sealift Command.

'Joe, I want an inventory of every ship we run, and every ship we lease in the future – let's be damn sure there aren't just voyage data recorders on board, but I want *topside* VDRs, you know, the ones mounted on floating buoys? Ship goes down, those things stay on top and belt out a distress signal.'

'We'll begin the inventory today. I'll see to it personally.'

'I also want live video on all of my vessels, forward, aft – hell, 360 degrees. Good cameras, too, not the cheap shit. Anybody or anything gets within a thousand yards of our boats, I want a picture. And I want these images displaying here' – Logan pointed up at one of the giant 4k screens – 'right up there on the big TV. How many boats do we have now?'

'Thirty-seven that we own and operate. Of those, twenty-two are either in or scheduled to enter the Pacific in the next forty-eight hours. None of those will travel within three hundred nautical miles of the other sinkings.'

Logan turned back to his IT director. 'Dee, do we have the means to broadcast images like that globally, twenty-four/seven? Put them up on that screen, that picture-in-picture thing? I'd love to keep an eye on things in real time, if possible.'

'It shouldn't be a problem. If anything, storage of that amount of data will pose the biggest challenge. But it's the kind of challenge that enough money can handle.'

Logan shrugged. 'Done. We can keep each ship's data for a week, then dump it. That should be long enough, shouldn't it? No, scratch that. Make it a month's worth, just in case. If a boat goes down again, I want that video evidence available to assist in the investigation and capture.'

Nunn typed notes into her tablet. 'My team will take point on the technical side and make the necessary purchases.' She turned to Admiral Gannon. 'And we'll coordinate with your people to set up the install schedule and the rest of the details, if that works for you.'

Gannon nodded. 'Done.'

Logan frowned. 'I don't want this to take six months or even six weeks. I want it done in the next thirty days, at most. Even sooner, if possible. I don't care if you gotta fly your tech people out to Timbuktu to get these things put on, I want it done pronto. Am I clear?'

Nunn and Gannon nodded.

Logan turned his withering gaze toward Kyle Reicher, former Army major, 75th Ranger Regiment, and head of his security division.

'Kyle, I want you to start thinking about how we're going to put at least three of your best people on each of our ships, each team member doing eight-hour shifts. We also need to talk about what security measures you can come up with.' Logan smiled. 'And so as not to play footsie with you, I mean *kinetic* measures: anti-air, anti-sea, anti-pirate, anti-sumbitch. Any goat-humpin' muttonhead gets over, on, under, or near one of my boats, I want a 5.56 round shot through his damn skull or a Stinger shoved up his exhaust pipe.'

'I have a few ideas, Buck, but we're a little shorthanded at the moment. Our operations in Africa –'

'To hell with our operations in Africa. Unless doing so puts our guys or any of the people in our care at risk, I want you to strip away everyone and everything that isn't nailed down over there and get it deployed to where it really matters. Understood?'

'HUA, sir.' *Heard, understood, acknowledged.*

The emergency meeting went on like that for another hour.

Werley was damned impressed by Logan's command of the facts, and his determination to get ahead of this thing. Logan was pushing hard. It would be a hell of a test for whoever was out there sinking his ships to stand up to the effort Buck was putting into this. He could imagine Buck as a young tight end at the academy trying to smash his way across the goal line on a fourth and goal play against overwhelming odds.

He'd always been impressed with Buck Logan, and that's why he left government service to join his organization – well, that, and a mid-six-figure salary plus stock options. But today Buck really showed his stuff. Werley thought he would have made a fine admiral or Marine general. He even seemed presidential in this moment of crisis. Who knows? If Buck had gone into military service, it would have been the perfect platform for a presidential bid, much like the twelve previous presidents who achieved general's rank before reaching the White House. Werley had even heard rumors among the old hands at White Mountain that that was the plan old Scooter had made for his son.

It was a crying shame. Buck Logan might have pulled it off. So much potential cut short, and so early. *How does he even live with that?* Werley wondered.

No matter. He needed to touch base with his old boss, DNI Foley, and fill her in on today's events. Buck didn't need to be informed he'd be making that call but Werley knew the man was smart enough to know it would probably happen. He'd let her know that Buck was doing his part to win this war – or whatever the hell it was.

## 27

*Barcelona, Spain*

Getting into Ryan's apartment cost Bykov a hundred euros, but it was worth it. The Guatemalan maid cleaned several Airbnbs in the Barceloneta neighborhood. He had bribed her before for just fifty, but she got smart and decided he could afford double. She also threw in a quick roll in the sheets of the place she was cleaning when he came to pick up the keys, and that alone was worth the hundred. Besides, it was Guzmán's money, not his. So really, it was a freebie for him.

Ryan's apartment building had its own front door lock, and then the third-floor apartment had yet another keyed lock. Bykov could have picked them both but it was daylight and the cops in the city were on edge with the rumor of another mass protest in the afternoon. More than three hundred thousand people were expected to rally at the old post office across from the marina where the big, multimillion-dollar yachts were crowded into their berths.

Besides the blue-and-white Mossos d'Esquadra cars cruising the neighborhood, a storefront police station was just around the corner with a couple of official Vespas parked out front.

Bykov slipped a white paper mask over his face and pulled on a black Nike ball cap as he charged up the narrow, twisting marble staircase, two steps at a time. This was a working-class neighborhood so nobody should be home. If there were other Airbnbs in the building he might bump into a curious tourist and he didn't want to reveal his face or he'd have to kill them and dispose of the body.

A real pain in the ass.

It was easier to wear a mask.

More important, if Ryan was some kind of an agent or operator, he might have a camera planted in his place for security. It would be a disaster if Ryan uncovered his identity – the opposite result of what Bykov was attempting today.

Standing in the postage-stamp-size hallway next to the shoulder-wide miniature elevator, Bykov got to work. The heavy door lock chunked open with a twist of the big brass skeleton key and Bykov slipped in, pushing open the thick wooden door with his big hands gloved in latex.

Inside, he glanced around the small kitchen and living area on the bottom floor of the two-story unit. His practiced eyes searched for any small portable video cameras that might have planted but he saw nothing.

Bykov checked his watch. His hired lookout had eyes on Ryan, who was with the CNI agent at a restaurant in the Jewish Quarter. He was instructed to call Bykov as soon as Ryan left. Even if Ryan grabbed a taxi it would take him at least twenty minutes to get back here, and closer to thirty if he walked. That was more than enough time to get the job done. He set the alarm on his watch for twenty minutes and got to work.

The kitchen counter was within arm's reach of the front door. Ryan kept a clean place. A few dishes, glasses, and cups were washed and neatly stacked on the counter. Too bad. Those would have been a good source for the DNA samples and fingerprints he was looking for.

However, it was doubtful Ryan did a thorough cleaning of the kitchen, and the stainless-steel faucet would still be covered in fingerprints. He removed a latent-fingerprint-lifting sheet from his coat pocket, peeled off the protective paper, and pressed it against the knobs, but the decorative plastic surfaces were too uneven to pick anything up. He crumpled up that film sheet and stuck it into his back pocket, then pulled out a fresh one and pressed it against the smooth stainless steel of the long spout. He pulled it off and examined it. There were fragments of prints, at best. Nothing usable. *Damn it.*

He saw a closed laptop on the small kitchen table. Unless Ryan was OCD, he wouldn't have cleaned the keyboard. That was the jackpot he was looking for.

If Ryan was an operator, there was every chance his laptop was designed to engage the onboard camera and record whoever was using it. The only problem with that kind of security system was that it depended on a total idiot to open the laptop all the way – and Bykov was no idiot.

The Russian mercenary lifted the laptop lid just enough to be able to access the keyboard, but not enough to take the laptop out of sleep mode and activate the camera. He was also careful not to move the device at all, or anything else in the apartment, for that matter, since Ryan might have used some kind of security app like Photo Trap, which overlaid 'before' photos with a live photo of any object to determine if it had been moved. Bykov used Photo Trap himself when he traveled.

He gently swabbed the keyboard with three different swabs, then placed them in a plastic ziplock bag for storage. He then removed a latent-fingerprint-lifting sheet from his coat pocket, peeled off the protective paper, and carefully placed the film on the laptop surface on either side of the touch pad, then removed it. He grinned beneath his mask when he saw several partial whorls, most likely from the palms.

He stored that one away and placed two more lifting

sheets across the bottom row of keys – the space bar, control, option, command, and arrow keys – then pressed the laptop lid down to put pressure on the lifting sheet. After carefully raising the lid a minimal distance again, he gently peeled away the lifting sheets and inspected them as well. He even captured a few partials on the lid itself.

Success.

Bykov headed upstairs toward the bathroom. There were plenty of places to check for more fingerprints, including the toilet's flush handle and the fixtures on the bathroom sink and in the shower. But it was Ryan's DNA he was looking for now.

Despite his personal distaste, he also gathered up the spent tissues in the wastebasket, pubic hairs in the shower, and bits of hair from Ryan's electric razor – also a fingerprint source – hoping for any DNA samples he could find. Most security agencies kept DNA files of POIs. Maybe this Ryan character's snot was on record somewhere his people could access. If nothing else, his people had access to several commercial ancestry DNA sites. It was hard for him to believe that people actually paid to give up their DNA and other important personal information to complete strangers, many of whom sold that information to interested parties.

The last thing Bykov did was plant a couple of voice-activated listening devices. Each was the size of a one-euro coin and had a twenty-hour battery life. He could record anything he heard with his receiver while listening live. Chances are they would yield nothing and it would require him to break into the apartment again to retrieve them. All that meant was spending another hundred euros of Guzmán's money and thirty minutes of pleasure with the Guatemalan woman.

He was willing to make that sacrifice.

Bykov's watch alarm signaled at exactly twenty minutes.

He did another quick survey of the place to make sure he hadn't disturbed anything and then checked the small hallway through the door peephole to make sure no one was outside. Satisfied, he exited the apartment, pocketing his gloves and mask before he hit the street in case a policeman happened to be driving past.

There wasn't one. It was a clean op.

Or so he thought.

# 28

Jack met Brossa at a small family restaurant on the Carrer dels Banys Nous, a narrow pedestrian street in the old Jewish Quarter. They sat in a corner in the far back, away from the others. Jack sat with his spine against the rough-hewn stone walls, and he kept an eye on the far front entrance beneath the ancient timbers that lined the low ceiling.

'This part of the building was a cattle barn three hundred years ago,' Brossa explained as she dipped a fried churro into the cup of hot chocolate. 'The restaurant itself is only one hundred and forty years old.'

Jack had the same thing in front of him – another Spanish delicacy he'd come to love. The chocolate was thick, almost like a liquid pudding, and made with only water – no milk. It wasn't as sweet as American hot chocolate, and the churros were only lightly dusted with sugar, but it was plenty sweet. He'd just devoured a Spanish *tortilla,* another surprise he'd discovered. Essentially a slice of potato, egg, and onion casserole cooked in olive oil. It was a staple of Spanish cuisine – breakfast, lunch, and dinner.

'I'm going to be running a lot of miles when I get home after this trip,' Jack said as he plopped the last piece of churro into his mouth. He'd already run the beach that morning in Barceloneta to burn off yesterday's calories. He thought he'd lost his appetite forever after jogging past the ancient nude sunbathers on the southern end of the beach near the Hotel W. They were all old men, mostly fat and leathery. A few of them were engaged in too-revealing Warrior poses or dick-flapping calisthenics. He was mad at Brossa, too, for not calling him back. He let go of his temper and recovered his appetite when she called an hour ago and invited him to breakfast.

'The voicemail you left on my phone last night said you knew how to find the bomber,' Brossa finally said, wiping her small mouth with a napkin.

Jack was surprised she'd taken this long to ask him. Back home, an agent in her position would have led with that question – and skipped the meal altogether. Another reason Spain was really growing on him.

'Yeah, I think I do. The clue we're looking for is the phone Aleixandri was speaking on.'

'The one you said you saw – or, more accurately, the Bluetooth you saw. The one we couldn't find.'

The edge in her voice was unmistakable. Did she doubt him? Or was it the obvious exhaustion that was wearing on her?

'I think you mean the phone that was taken from the crime scene,' Jack countered.

'Who would do that?'

'The guy on the other end of the call? Maybe he snuck back in during the chaos and grabbed it.' *Or maybe someone in your organization,* Jack wanted to say.

Brossa wiggled her head. It was cute. Her way of weighing something in her mind, he supposed.

'Unlikely. But I can ask some of the officers if anyone suspicious or unidentified came into L'avi that night.'

Jack handed her a piece of notebook paper.

'What's this?'

'The address of the phone store where Aleixandri bought her burner phone.'

'And you know this . . . how?' Brossa's dark-rimmed eyes narrowed.

Jack had thought about showing her the pictures and video Gavin had snagged from the traffic camera but then he'd have a lot of explaining to do, including Gavin's criminal act of hacking the city's computer network. He'd hoped the address and the approximate date and time of purchase would be enough to pique her curiosity.

Apparently, it had just pissed her off.

'My financial firm has certain technical resources . . .'

Brossa darkened. 'Stop bullshitting me, Jack. We both know you're CIA or some other alphabet agency.'

'No, I'm not. Scout's honor. Hendley Associates does a lot of international business with high-net-worth clients. Some of those clients are victimized by criminal elements and we want to protect them. But in some cases we become suspicious about the origins of their high net worth, and that's when we want to protect ourselves. For those reasons, we have developed a very competent security team – sort of like an in-house private-detective agency.'

Brossa crossed her arms, her face set in stone, obviously doubting every word.

'The location of the phone store with a time of purchase for Aleixandri is very difficult information to collect. I don't believe a private company like yours could manage this.'

'Why is that so hard to believe?'

'Because you still haven't told me the truth about yourself.'

'What haven't I told you?'

Her face scrunched up in a half-frown, half-grin. 'How am I supposed to know that? Don't they teach logic in American schools?'

*The Catholic ones I went to sure did,* Jack thought.

'I haven't lied to you, I promise.'

'I believe that. But I didn't accuse you of lying to me. I said you haven't told me the truth – the *whole* truth. That's what they say on American TV dramas, yes? "I swear to tell the truth, the whole truth, and nothing but the truth."'

'You're obviously driving at something. Spit it out.'

She looked him up and down. 'I'm around Special Ops guys all the time. You look just like them. The way you walk, the way you carry yourself. Your eyes constantly scanning for area threats – including the front door of this restaurant. You're a spy, Jack, or some kind of operator.'

'Look, Laia. I'm telling you the absolute truth, the *whole* truth, when I tell you that I do not work for the CIA or any American government agency. I'm a private citizen, that's all.'

Jack's eyes burrowed into hers, faking his sincerity as hard as he could.

In fact, he was telling her the whole truth, depending on what the definition of *whole* was. Or *truth*. He wasn't on the government payroll. The Campus was a private outfit working for a private firm. That was all completely true, wasn't it? The fact that they did it all on behalf of the American government was a mere technicality.

Despite his flawless internal logic, his fake sincerity wasn't quite hitting the mark. Jack doubled down.

'Sure, I work out a lot, and I do MMA stuff for fun, so, yeah, I probably can handle myself in a fight. And I took Tony Blauer's Be Your Own Bodyguard one-day training course because my job requires me to travel around in some pretty shady places.

'And, if I'm being completely honest, I'm pretty good with a gun because I grew up with guns. After all, I'm an American, aren't I?' He smiled to sell the joke.

No sale.

He pressed on. 'I enjoy shooting guns at my local gun

range and besides that, my grandfather was a Baltimore police detective, so guns are part of my family history.

'But that's about as exciting as my life gets. My day job is really boring. All day long I read 12b's and ferret out investment opportunities for my firm and my clients. I buy and sell a few stocks every now and then. I'm just a regular guy who's really pissed off that an innocent woman was massacred and nobody is being held responsible for it.'

Jack was good at reading people. It was a skill his dad had taught him to cultivate, and that Clark had honed to a razor's edge. Clandestine work was even more about people than it was about weapons and tactics. He hated the fact he'd become such a gifted and practiced liar. He justified his deceptions as simply a means to accomplish a mission or to save a friend or protect an innocent or, in this case, find Renée's killers and get her justice. He never lied for his personal benefit. Lying was just another valuable tool in his tool belt. But still, something always died a little inside of him, no matter how small or well intended the lie. Such was the gift – and curse – of a Jesuit education.

Brossa's hard face softened, her shoulders lowered. She sighed through her nose, and even smiled a little.

'I believe you, Jack.'

'Thank you.' *So why do I feel like a dirtbag?*

She glanced at the paper again.

'If you promise me you have done nothing illegal, perhaps I can use this information to get a warrant and obtain the store records of her purchase. That would allow us to identify the phone and her account, then acquire the metadata.'

'Which would allow you to begin to figure out who she was talking to, and where that person was. That's the asshole you're after.' He hoped she didn't notice he didn't make the promise.

Brossa shook her head. She picked up a churro and pointed it at him. 'No, Jack. That's the asshole *you're* after, and you're using me to do it.' She dipped her churro in the chocolate before taking a crunchy bite.

'I'm only trying to help. So is my company. We have a lot of resources.'

Brossa chewed, her eyes searching Jack's for an answer to a question she hadn't asked him.

She finally found it. She swallowed and reached into her purse, sliding a photograph across the table.

Jack picked it up. He hid his surprise, poker-facing as hard as he could. He didn't want her to know he'd seen this face before.

It was a grainy photo of Sorry Man. Same tortoiseshell glasses, same shoulder-length hair. A screen grab from the same angle as the one Jack had, only tighter – no doubt grabbed from the same camera footage Gavin had found.

'Who is this?' Jack asked. Gavin hadn't found the man yet, either. He was glad he didn't have to lie to her about that at least.

'That's what we want to know as well. Any ideas?'

Jack shook his head. 'No.'

'You never saw him?'

'I did. We bumped into each other as I was heading out. I think he said, "Sorry, man."'

'In English?'

'Sounded American, or maybe Canadian.'

Brossa pushed her half-empty cup of chocolate away and leaned back in her chair. 'That's more information than we've been able to come up with.'

'What about his personal identification?'

Brossa sighed. 'I probably shouldn't tell you this, but then again, I was instructed to keep you informed as the case advanced, wasn't I?'

'You seem annoyed by that fact.'

'I have enough to do without babysitting a rich American finance guy.'

'I'm a lot of things, but rich ain't one of them. I'm sorry that hanging out with me is such a pain. I get it, I really do. You have a job to do and I'm just one more complication. But please believe me, I'm only here to help.'

Brossa bit her lip. He watched her guard fall as she brushed her curly hair away from her face.

'I'm sorry, Jack. I'm being very rude. I have a lot of things going on in my life besides this crazy job of mine.'

'It's okay, I understand. Anything I can do to help – I mean, besides the case?'

'That is kind of you to offer, but no.' She shook her head, suddenly embarrassed by her moment of weakness.

She sat upright and folded her hands on the table in front of her. 'So, as I was saying about this man's personal identification . . . well, he had none. No wallet, no credit cards, no passport, no – how do you say it, "pocket litter"? – no cell phone, no Fitbit, nothing. Absolutely nothing to help us identify him.'

'You must have taken his fingerprints?'

'We did, and ran them through our databases, including Interpol. Nothing.'

'If he's from the EU, he has a chipped passport and probably uses facial recognition at the automated ePassport gates. Did you check there?'

'We did. No luck.'

'Airport cameras? Trains?'

'Nothing.'

No wonder Gavin hadn't called him yet.

'You must have some ideas,' Jack said.

'Perhaps he was connected to the bombing.'

'You think he's Brigada Catalan?'

'We think we have a complete list of their membership – names, addresses, and pictures. His face wasn't on that list. But we know BC is rumored to be connected to al-Qaeda, the Macedonian UÇK, and a few other terror gangs. Our suspicion is that he was with one of those other organizations.'

'There are a lot of agencies around the world with detailed records of AQ membership. Have you passed this photo around to them?'

'Yes, it's been sent out, but no luck yet. There is another possibility I've been playing around with.'

Brossa leaned in closer. 'Perhaps BC isn't behind this bombing at all.'

'What do you mean?'

'You've been reading about the civil war, and you seem well read on current Spanish politics. There are pro-nationalist and pro-Franco groups that hate the idea of Catalonian independence and would certainly hate a group like BC.'

'And you think one of these groups might have set BC up for the bombing – even though BC claimed credit for it?'

'Anybody can post anything on social media these days.'

Jack waved the photo of Sorry Man. 'Can I keep this?'

'Give it to your "private investigator" and let me know what he finds.' Brossa stood, ending the meeting.

Jack stood as well. 'And you'll keep me posted on the burner phone?'

She smiled with the corner of her mouth and shrugged. '*És clar* – of course. We are helping each other, right?'

# 29

Brossa knocked on the tall open door of her supervisor, Gaspar Peña, twenty-five years her senior and a native of Madrid. He was a little round in the middle but it was well hidden by an expensively tailored suit, a gift from his new wife, half his age. Despite his reputation as a ladies' man, he never treated Brossa with anything but paternal affection.

'Come in, Laia. And close the door behind you.'

He smiled and waved her in with his hand, pointing at the chair across from his desk. 'I have good news.'

Peña came around to the front of his desk and sat on the corner as Brossa took a chair. She forced a smile beneath her dark-rimmed eyes.

'What's the good news, sir?'

Peña held his grin for a moment longer. 'The Guardia Civil has a credible lead on Brigada Catalan. They are planning a big meeting tomorrow to discuss future plans, and better still, we know exactly *where* they are meeting.'

Brossa brightened. 'That's fantastic news.'

'And it gets even better. The Guardia Civil will lead the assault —'

'But, sir, this is my case. I should be leading the raid.'

Peña flicked his hand in a dismissive way. 'No, no, no. We're going to let the door-breakers do their thing.'

Brossa jumped to her feet. 'That's not fair.'

'Laia. You understand politics, don't you?' He gestured at the walls around them. 'It's no accident we were assigned temporary offices in this building. We were brought down to

Barcelona to partner with Guardia Civil to help them deal with this *independencia* insanity. They provide the muscle, we provide the brains.'

'Is this because you're trying to protect me?'

'No, not at all. You have the most important job. While those brutes are smashing the furniture, I need a calm, steady hand on the helm supervising the arrests and the crime scene investigation. If we are going to shut down these idiot separatists, we need solid convictions – not bodies on a coroner's slab. We can't afford to make any martyrs out of these killers. And we can't afford to lose any courtroom trials because somebody wasn't smart enough to collect evidence properly.' Peña's fatherly smile widened. 'Don't you agree?'

Brossa's jaw clenched. Spain was one of the last countries in Europe still struggling with women's equality. On the surface everything was equal, but in reality, many people in the culture still held a paternalistic view of women and their roles in society. It wasn't just the *catalanes* who were struggling for independence in Spain these days. But today wasn't the day to fight back. Solving the case and bringing the criminals to justice was more important.

'Yes, of course. You know best about these things,' Brossa said. 'But I'll be kitted out anyway.'

Peña grinned ear to ear. 'Excellent!'

He scrambled back behind his desk and pulled up a name on his computer. 'I'll put you in touch with Captain Asensio, the assault team leader. Call him and he'll read you in to the details.' He glanced up from the keyboard, a worried expression on his face. 'And not a word of this to anybody, yes? We don't want anything to get out and spoil the party.'

*I'm not an idiot.* Brossa knew this news would be music to Jack's ears but her loyalty was to her country, not pushy

Americans, no matter how sincere – or handsome – they were. He would just have to wait until after the raid.

'No, sir. Not a word.' She stood. 'And thank you for the opportunity to serve.'

'I have complete confidence in you, Laia. We all do. Someday, no doubt, you'll be sitting behind my desk – perhaps even running the entire agency. But we build the house one brick at a time, yes?'

'Yes. One brick at a time,' she agreed as she headed for the door. *And a brick against your thick macho skull, too.* She smiled to herself as she closed the door behind her.

Now all she had to do was make last-minute arrangements to take care of her father while she was on the raid.

# 30

*London, England*

Mari Moon's eyes watered.

She had marched through the open loft door and hit an invisible wall of pure stench. It was the rancid, unmistakable smell of rotting flesh, stale urine, and fecal material, the latter two in a molding, clumpy puddle on the floor just below the blackening feet. It stopped her in her tracks.

The naked corpse hung by the neck from one of the wooden beams supporting the low ceiling of the wide, open living area. The swollen face of the middle-aged body was pale green and marbled with its protruding eyes and tongue, both forced out by the gases arising from the feverishly working bacteria within. The rest of the corpse was increasingly green, tending toward brownish-black the farther down she looked, the blood pooling and darkest in the lower legs and feet.

Moon began taking short breaths through her mouth, shutting off her nose. She was an internal security investigator, not a cop, and certainly not a coroner.

'Agent Moon?' the man asked, approaching her, his steely blue eyes softening. He knew her only by the title and name she'd given on the phone, neither of which was true. He wore a stylish Brioni sport coat and Crockett & Jones loafers, she noted. Rather posh for a London detective. His poise and posture, along with the silver in his neatly trimmed hair and mustache, suggested confidence and experience. She would take advantage of both.

'Yes. I'm looking for DCI May.'

'That would be me.' He smiled. 'Travis May. Pleasure.' They shook hands. He saw the pale color of her face. 'My apologies for the unpleasant redolence.'

'We appreciate the sensitivity and speed with which you responded to the incident.'

'When we found his GCHQ credentials, I knew we had to contact you immediately.' His eyes narrowed. 'National security and all of that.'

*You have no idea,* Moon thought. Dr Stanley Hopkins was one of the most important researchers in one of the world's most important intelligence agencies, Britain's equivalent of the NSA. 'Can you read me in, briefly?'

DCI May turned toward the corpse, his manicured hands clasped behind his back. 'The residents across the hall reported a foul smell early this morning to the building superintendent, assuming it was a sewage line backing up somewhere.'

'I'll need their names and contact information.'

'Of course.'

'Please continue.'

'As I was saying, they traced the odor to this apartment, opened the door, and you know the rest.'

'How long has Dr Hopkins been dead, in your estimation?'

'Rigor has subsided, and judging by the lividity and the state of decomposition, we estimate four days, possibly more.'

Moon nodded, thinking. Hopkins had been missing for five days. Alarm bells began ringing seventy-two hours after he failed to appear at two critical departmental meetings. The future of Britain's cybersecurity rested on his shoulders. Or did.

May continued. 'The corpse in the bedroom matches that timeline as well. We'll have something more definitive for you once we get them back to the lab.'

'Another corpse? Who?'

'Joseph Okwi. A Ugandan national here illegally. Part of a male prostitution ring. He's been arrested twice in the last three years. The SOCO' – scenes of crime officer – 'believes it was a drug overdose.'

'And we can assume the two deaths are related?'

'I've seen it before. There's a wedding ring on Dr Hopkins's hand. Something went wrong here with Mr Okwi, Hopkins panics, doesn't know what to do, instantly imagines the scandal, his wife – children, I suppose – and he's over-whelmed at the prospects of trials, jail, shame. He isn't the first person to take the easy way out.'

Moon glanced at the corpse. 'I'm not sure I'd call that easy.'

'Yes, quite.'

'And the laptop?'

He nodded toward a large, imposing figure standing guard at a small desk where Hopkins's laptop rested, unopened. 'It's in the custody of Sergeant Lavin. It hasn't left his person since we spoke.'

Moon glanced back at the corpse. The iron-hard urgency set in her face faded for a moment. She knew Stanley Hopkins, his charming wife, Sally, and their three adorable young children. She had dined with them only just last month, cel-ebrating Sally's birthday. Stanley was indeed a brilliant mathematician on the far frontier of quantum cybersecurity. But he was obviously a devoted husband and father, too – something you can't fake. Drugs, sex, and suicide just didn't fit his profile.

'You just never know about people, do you?' DCI May said, reading her mind. 'It's a tragedy, certainly. You knew him?'

Moon stiffened, realizing her mask had slipped. 'Who else in your department knows about any of this?'

'Myself, Sergeant Lavin, two SOCOs, two constables. Why?'

'Has any evidence or any material been removed from the loft?'

'Not yet.'

'My department is taking over, as a matter of national security. Top priority.'

DCI May's genteel charm suddenly hardened into something else.

'This is *our* case, Ms Moon. It's simply not possible –'

'Commissioner Grimes will be in contact with you shortly to verify. I want you to gather up your people and vacate the premises immediately. I need you and your team to forget all of this, and to never discuss it with anybody or put any of it in writing under penalty of law. There was no Stanley Hopkins or Joseph Okwi. There was no forensic evidence and no laptop. There was no crime and no suicide. Am I clear?'

The muscle in May's jaw clenched. 'Perfectly.'

'Excellent. And one more thing.'

'Ma'am?'

'I was never here.'

# 31

### Barcelona, Spain

Jack called for a taxi – ride-hailing services like Uber were unavailable in the city. The driver was Colombian and spoke no English, but it wasn't a problem. Jack showed him his apartment address on his phone and off they went.

The driver was friendly enough and tried to make conversation with Jack. As they made their way toward the old city, he slowed his Spanish down enough that Jack could actually understand him somewhat. The man was from Bogotá and had been living in Spain for seven years, and also that he had a wife and two small *niñas* at home.

The Colombian cursed as the traffic suddenly halted near the Plaça de Catalunya. It wasn't hard to guess why. It was another protest, one of several that had erupted over the last month, drawing hundreds of thousands of citizens from all over the region.

The sidewalks were jammed with people, many of them wearing the white-starred red-and-yellow flags of Catalonian independence draped over their shoulders like capes. A lot of young people, Jack saw, but also parents pushing strollers or walking with their school-age kids. Scattered throughout were middle-aged folks and also senior citizens who ambled more slowly with their canes and patriotic hats.

The longer they sat there in the cab, the bigger the crowd became, all moving toward the historic plaza. Many carried handheld flags. A few waved banners proclaiming liberty and democracy or demanding free speech or the release of political prisoners. A few banners were anarchist, and fewer still flew the hammer and sickle.

Mostly people were laughing and talking excitedly. People were flowing through the streets past both sides of the taxi like a rock in the middle of a river. No one was angry or screaming. No fist pounding, no sloganeering, no lighting of Molotov cocktails. There was an incredibly positive energy in the air. Jack didn't see or sense any rage or revolutionary impulse. If he didn't know any better, he'd swear these people were headed to a sold-out FC Barcelona soccer match.

The taxi driver turned around. Jack didn't need a Spanish dictionary to figure out what he was going to say.

'Yeah, I get it. Time to get out and walk.' Jack checked the meter and pulled out his wallet, glad that he'd stopped by an ATM on the way to breakfast with Brossa. He counted out enough bills to pay it along with a twenty-percent tip, though he'd been told that tipping taxis wasn't necessary in Spain. He didn't care. He was raised to respect working-class people and to show it by being generous whenever possible.

Jack opened the door carefully so as not to bang into one of the protesters streaming by. He leaned back into the taxi and thanked the driver, wishing him *buena suerte, amigo* because he was going to be stuck here for hours and was gonna need it.

Jack joined the crowd as tens of thousands of people flowed toward the grand square. He could see the armored riot police and their vehicles positioned on one end of the plaza. He'd read about earlier protests and some of them had turned violent because of hooligans trying to cause trouble. But today was different. Or so he hoped.

But a thought suddenly crossed Jack's mind. With so many people crowding into the area, and traffic-jammed streets fronted by crowded restaurants, shops, and apartments, this would make one hell of a target for Brigada Catalan.

Jack wasn't afraid of an explosion so much as the panicked response of several thousand people if a bomb was detonated. As much as he'd like to hang around and actually observe the unfolding of a mass democratic protest – he'd never witnessed anything like this in person – he thought better of it. Anything could go wrong, and usually did at times like these. The last thing Jack wanted was to get clubbed or pepper-sprayed by an anxious cop fearing for his life and just trying to do his duty. He decided to get back to his place.

He checked his phone and found out where the underground metro station entrance was and tried to move in that direction. He might as well have tried swimming up the Niagara Falls. The closer he got to the entrance, the more people he was bumping into and the more densely packed they became, which made them less likely to move out of his way. He almost got into a fight with a couple of guys who thought he was trying to cause trouble. The underground metro station was still a hundred feet ahead but its street-level exit was spewing out people like a gushing fire hydrant. He abandoned the idea of the metro altogether.

It was time to find the least crowded side streets and hoof it. Jack made it two blocks when his phone vibrated. He popped in his AirPods.

'Gav, how are you, buddy?'

Gavin's hippo yawn roared in Jack's ears.

'Oh, man, sorry about that. I missed my nap today.'

'Yeah, I hate it when that happens. What's up?'

'I think I found your guy, Sorry Man. His name is Dylan Runtso. Actually, *Dr* Dylan Runtso. He got his Ph.D. from Princeton in quantum physics. He was traveling under a fake name and passport so it took me a while to ID him, and like you said, he's been scrubbed from the standard facial-recog databases. Sorry it took so long.'

'Are you kidding me? Nothing to apologize for. This is fantastic news. Once again, I bow to your genius.'

'Don't start bending over yet – wait, that didn't come out right. What I mean is, I don't have much more than that. He has Special Access Program clearance, along with SSBI, ANACI, and a half-dozen other clearances I didn't even know existed until today. He's supposed to self-report when he travels abroad, but from what I can tell, the only international destination he listed was Toronto for a science conference.'

'Nothing for Spain?'

'Nada.'

'I saw what you just did there, *hombre*.'

'Had to try.'

'So, what's he working on that he needs these uber-top-secret security clearances?'

'No idea. He was self-employed as a consultant – and you know how I feel about those guys. Mercenaries, as far as I'm concerned. Pick up some government expertise at a decent wage, then turn around and sell your contacts to the highest bidder.'

'Sounds like he used to work for our Rich Uncle.'

'Before becoming a consultant, he was with a project code-named RAPTURE.'

'What happened?'

'He resigned about a year ago. The Feds are keeping track of him, sort of.'

'He must be something special if he's still on their radar. What's RAPTURE all about?'

'No idea. I started tiptoeing around it and set off a few alarms. If I hadn't VPN'd all over the place, I would have been the one who got the two a.m. visit from an NSA Q Group team instead of the dumb bastards at a fuzzy-fetish porn hub in Bucharest.'

'I don't even want to know what that means. Just tell me you know another way to get in.'

'A project with this level of security is waiting for a guy like me to come snooping around. It's gonna take some time if I don't wanna get caught. They don't serve Slim Jim Bacon Jerky in the supermax in Colorado, and you know how I love me some Slim Jims.'

'Find out what you can about RAPTURE, but don't take any unnecessary risks. I wish I could tell you that this is all about a national security issue but I'd be lying. I'm just trying to do what's right for a friend, and the thread just happens to be pulling on this RAPTURE thing. There's no point in you getting into trouble over it.'

'Don't worry about me. I love a challenge even more than I hate solitary confinement. I'll get back to you when I find out more. Besides, if she was your friend, she was my friend, too.'

'I appreciate it. Hey, one more thing. Maybe we should pass along Runtso's name and his death to someone over at the State Department. It's only fair to his family.'

'I was thinking the same thing. But I'll do it anonymously so I don't have to face down a bunch of questions neither of us want to answer.'

'As always, you're ahead of the curve, Mr Biery.'

'That's exactly what my mom always says.'

'Smart lady.'

'But a terrible cook.'

Gavin rang off and Jack pocketed his phone, the good news picking up his gait.

# 32

Jack finally reached his apartment building after a long and circuitous walk through the winding, narrow streets of the old city. He turned the skeleton key in the lock and pushed through the heavy wooden door.

He closed it behind him, his eyes automatically scanning the room for any signs of entry, as he was trained to do. He'd kept his head on a swivel the whole way down from Plaça de Catalunya, and despite the crowds, was fairly certain that no one had been following him.

Nothing seemed out of order as he tossed his keys onto the small kitchen table. He reached into the fridge and grabbed a *clara,* popping the frosty can open as he sat down at the table.

He took a long pull of the lemon beer to slake his thirst after the walk home, trying to clear his mind. Maybe Brossa was right. What good was he actually doing here? He did believe she would do everything in her power to solve the case, and besides, he had a life to get back to, and duties with The Campus to fulfill.

He flipped open the laptop, waking up the screen, and tapped in his security code to access the machine. By force of habit, he double-clicked an innocuous file folder titled 'Travel Tips,' and inside that file folder tapped on another subfolder titled 'Vaccinations.'

The Vaccinations folder opened up a surveillance program linked to the four miniature, motion-activated, wide-angle video cameras he had hidden around the apartment.

Jack nearly spat *clara* through his nose when he saw the flashing green dot in the corner of the menu bar.

According to the display, someone had been in his apartment just thirty-five minutes ago.

The split-screen window displayed all four camera images, each with its own player controls. Activating the first camera automatically activated the other three, and all four were programmed to run for sixty minutes and then shut off unless activated again.

Jack watched his front door open and a man in a white paper mask and a black Nike hat enter his place. One of the cameras on the first level was placed in a fern on the top of the kitchen cabinets for down-angle view. The other was wedged between the cushions on the couch in the living room for the up angle.

Something about the man seemed familiar. The build, certainly. A white guy, big and fit, like an operator. His movements were economical and deliberate.

But his features were mostly hidden by the mask and the ball cap. He waited for his face to turn fully toward either camera. When he did, Jack froze the image and zoomed in.

The man clearly had short hair because none was spilling out beneath his hat, but the mid-ear sideburns were blond, for sure. There were a lot of blond people in the world, so that didn't exactly narrow things down, though not so many here in Barcelona.

Jack zoomed in farther on the eyes, just peeking over the mask.

Hazel eyes. Deep set in a square face.

Not so common.

He had a hard time remembering anyone that had them back home. The only pair of hazel eyes he'd seen in Spain that he could remember was from the other night, in the window reflection outside of L'avi, and they were also deep set in a square face.

Could this be Crooked Nose?

Had to be.' There was no way to know for sure with that paper mask covering his nose and mouth but it was a fair bet, given his body type.

He wouldn't be here if he wasn't a hostile. Why steal information when you can ask for it? And why come here unless he was connected to the bombing?

That made him BC or, if Brossa was right, some other terror organization.

*What does he want from me?*

Only one way to find out.

Jack let the video run to see what his old friend was up to. It only took a few moments to see that the man wasn't paying a social call. Within minutes he had gathered up enough genetic material and fingerprint fragments to satisfy a dozen crime labs. But all of the collected biological data was only as good as the database he had access to, and the records in it, specifically, Jack's.

Chances were, Crooked Nose would come up way short. With all of the effort exerted by others to scrub Jack's identity from public and private records, his anonymity was virtually guaranteed.

Reassuring himself of this, Jack was suddenly cold-slapped back into reality as Crooked Nose turned from DNA collection to planting listening devices in his apartment.

*Holy shit.*

DNA and wireless listening devices?

This dude was pretty serious about getting intel on him. Even small, wireless civilian LDs were easy enough to come by – Alibaba and Amazon had plenty to choose from. These were smaller. Probably mil-spec.

What was this guy hoping to hear? Conversations with Brossa, most likely, but also any information about his identity or any organization he might be working with.

The DNA snatch was an interesting twist. On the one hand, it meant Brigada Catalan either had their own serious hacking skills, a government agency plant, or a relationship with an organization that had either of those assets.

But then again, personal information was digital gold, especially of government personnel, and millions of hackers were mining for it every day.

Some hackers worked for other governments, like the one-hundred-thousand-plus digital thieves inside China's cyberespionage programs. They were believed responsible for the recent theft of nearly twenty-two million records from the U.S. government's personnel database, including digital images and fingerprints.

Worse, the medical records of at least one hundred and fifty million Americans had been stolen by still other entities. That was a lot of data that could be used to uncover people wanting to hide their identities.

People like Jack.

Private criminal organizations like the Russian Bratva or the Iron Syndicate needed that kind of information, as well. One of the ways they protected themselves was by identifying local and national police and security personnel in order to guard against them, bribe them, or kill them. And selling those identities to other interested parties was a highly profitable business.

In fact, it was becoming increasingly difficult to hide anyone's identity these days, a subject that Jack Ryan, Jr, had struggled with for several years. Because of his unique status, anonymity was required for him to be able to operate. But the proliferation of everybody's digital footprints, including people like Jack who consciously avoided making them, was growing exponentially.

Where things had gotten really crazy was the genetic stuff. Besides the general collection of DNA materials by governments, private DNA ancestry companies had been compromised, either through voluntary cooperation or by hacking.

In Gavin's latest security briefing, he pointed out it didn't matter if Jack had never submitted his spit tube to one of those companies. If close relatives had done so, their genetic connections could still lead to him, or at the very least, blow his cover by their actions or online activities.

The only good news was that it was also possible for the good guys to break into these DNA databases and either delete or alter the genetic records to protect their people or create whole new cover identities.

Things had become so complex on both offense and defense that Gavin created a separate digital identity unit within his division. While Jack's unique identity situation had top priority, every member of The Campus needed the service. Gavin's unit spent as much time wiping out the new digital footprints that crept up nearly every day as building credible digital 'legends' for their people for future use on operations as needed.

As Jack watched the last of his surveillance images play out, his DEFCON alert jumped a couple of pegs.

Brigada Catalan, or whoever this guy worked for, had a serious hard-on for him. Why? Was Gavin right?

Was he the bombing target all along?

Jack once read a story about the B-17 'Flying Fortress,' America's first four-engine bomber, and the U.S. Army Air

187

Corps' workhorse throughout World War Two. It was one of the most sophisticated airframes of its time, comprised of advanced, multi-featured engine, flight, and navigational systems. Early in its development it suffered a catastrophic crash and investigators determined that the pilots forgot to release a simple locking mechanism on the flight control system. This led to the conclusion that the B-17 was simply too difficult and complicated for humans to handle.

But the surviving test pilots felt the airplane was too important to abandon. They came up with a revolutionary solution to the B-17's complexity challenge: the preflight checklist. The checklist saved the B-17, which helped win the war against fascism in Europe and the Pacific.

And a checklist might have just saved Jack's life.

Checklists and routines – doing the same things the same way every time – were drilled into him during his formative training at The Campus by John Clark.

Though not a scholar by any means, Clark was highly intelligent – genius IQ, according to his service records – and well read. His checklist lecture included Aristotle's famous dictum *We are what we repeatedly do. Excellence, then, is not an act, but a habit.* Not that he needed Aristotle to prove his point. Clark credited his own iron disciplines of habit and hard work as the primary reasons he not only survived but prevailed in countless undercover missions against overwhelming odds behind enemy lines in Vietnam and the Iron Curtain.

So when Jack came through the door, the first thing he did was check his surveillance system.

*Thank you, Mr C,* Jack said to himself as he took mental note of the locations of the planted bugs.

Jack faked a yawn and ambled over to the sink for a glass of water, letting the faucet run while he came up with a plan.

He popped on the television set in the front room just ten feet away from the open kitchen and flipped channels until he found an English-language movie station and turned up the volume.

He then carefully removed the laptop from the kitchen table and sat down on the couch with it, and texted Gavin quietly. According to his surveillance cameras, the intruder hadn't planted any software or other surveillance devices on his computer so it was safe to communicate this way.

Thankfully, Gavin was almost always connected, even when he was asleep. He happened to be in a Fortnite competition but Gavin's high sense of duty and fierce loyalty to his friends overrode all other concerns, even when he was technically off the clock.

Jack filled Gavin in on what had happened and a plan he'd come up with to deal with the asshole who'd planted the listening devices. Gavin liked it because it let him get involved in field operations without actually having to be in the field. Gavin was a computer genius but also smart enough to recognize his considerable limitations. The inability to engage in lethal violence was one of those limitations. Surviving such lethal encounters was another. Going into the field with Jack Junior would challenge both because when he got his war on, someone was going to die.

# 33

Jack climbed the stairs to the upper level of his loft apartment and headed for the bathroom.

One of the planted audio devices was located behind the toilet. He took a leak – it wasn't an exercise in tradecraft, he just really needed to bleed the lizard after the beer.

He flushed the toilet, then turned on the shower. There also happened to be a radio attached to the wall above the toilet with small speakers located high in two corners of the closet-size bathroom. Jack found a Euro Pop station and turned up the sound, then headed back downstairs as quietly as he could. He also moved the laptop to the floor beneath the kitchen table, where another listening device was located. He then exited the apartment with every bit of stealth he could muster. Neither time nor noise was his friend right now. He had to move fast and silently for his plan to work.

Jack climbed the shoulder-wide staircase up to his private rooftop terrace.

His building was attached to two other apartment buildings – one a story higher, the other a story lower – on the north and south side of his building. Several more apartment buildings of varying heights ran together, forming the rest of the city block.

His building was bounded by narrow streets on both sides. His front door faced the eastbound street. There was no door to the westbound street.

At the ends of the city block, streets ran north and south.

Jack was careful to stay away from the walls that bordered his terrace. He was uncertain where the hazel-eyed intruder might be, or any other operatives he might have deployed to keep the block under surveillance.

Jack had a chance to look at one of the listening devices without disturbing it. Thankfully, it wasn't a recording device, but rather, a live feed. That meant Crooked Nose or one of his minions had ears on, and given the size of the miniature transmitter, that meant the listener was close – a hundred meters away, at most.

He crouched low and inched close to the east side of the building facing the Mediterranean Sea, just a few blocks away. He pulled out his pocket-size Nikon monocular, one of those small, innocuous checklist items Clark insisted they carry when traveling. The most likely location of whoever was listening would be in one of the many cars parked on the streets below.

Jack raised himself up just high enough to sight the Nikon down the north side of the street that ended just a block up. The buildings fronting the street were tall enough to cast shadows against the sun, so the car windows weren't blinded by glare.

Near as he could tell, there wasn't anybody sitting in any of the cars in that direction. Nor in the other.

Jack then scooted low across the terrace to the west side of the building and repeated the exercise. He spotted a woman walking a small terrier on one side of the street, and a South Asian man emptying the garbage from the back door of a restaurant. Neither appeared to be the tango in question.

Jack then turned his monocular to the southbound direction.

Bingo.

Across the intersection, approximately seventy-five yards away, an Audi sedan was parked in the lead position, and a man in a black Nike hat sat in the driver's seat, his window down and his elbow resting on the door. An audio headset was perched on his head. The face was square and the eyes were deep set, and most important, the long nose looked like it had once been broken.

Crooked Nose.

Had to be.

There was one way to test his assumption.

Jack put in his AirPods and pulled out his smartphone. 'Gav, I'm on the roof. You ready?'

'Yeah, I think I've got something that'll do the trick.'

'Fire away.'

Jack put his monocular on the man. A moment later, walrus and seal noises exploded in Jack's ears – a cacophony of roars, chuffs, screams, squeals, and bellows. It sounded like a pride of angry, flatulent lions fornicating inside a small public restroom. The noise was simultaneously hilarious, weird, and perfect to elicit the response Jack was hoping for.

Crooked Nose shook his head and tapped his headphones, his face twisted in a frown of utter confusion.

Bingo times two.

Gavin was running a crazy soundtrack through Jack's laptop speakers directly beneath one of the planted listening devices. It was so strange and unexpected it caught the guy off guard.

'Love the soundtrack, Gav. But you should see a doctor for that intestinal issue you obviously have.'

'Funny, Jack.'

'Good job. I'll take it from here.'

Since the dude in the car was on the same side of the street as the building's only exit, Jack had to find another way down to the street if he didn't want to be seen.

Jack pocketed his AirPods and phone as he ducked back over to the west side of his building and scanned up and down the row of adjacent buildings looking for a way down. There weren't any fire escapes. But there was an option.

The only problem was, how to get to it?

The sturdy aluminum awning frame on his terrace was bolted to his stairwell wall and, luckily for him, to the wall of the taller south-facing building. Jack stepped onto one of the wood-slatted chairs, up onto the outdoor table, then pulled himself up onto one of the aluminum awning struts where it was bolted into the taller wall.

Now he stood high enough to reach the roof of the next building. He hauled himself up onto it and made his way across three more rooftops, two lower, one higher, until he reached the roof of a building undergoing renovation.

Jack crossed over to the scaffolding attached to the west side of the building – the opposite side of the block where Crooked Nose was stationed – and climbed his way down to the street out of his sight line.

A gray haired woman carrying groceries saw him emerge from the netting covering the scaffolding and offered him a polite smile. Jack smiled back and waited for her to turn a corner before he sped away.

He ran all the way to the end of the street, careful not to show himself at the intersection. He waited until a large delivery van rumbled by and used its intervening bulk to block the line of sight between him and the intruder, now examining his headphones for malfunction. Jack sped across the street and all the way down the next block so he could come around behind Crooked Nose and surprise him.

He turned the corner once, and then once again, carefully crouching down low behind the line of parked cars in case Crooked Nose was checking his rearview mirror.

It took Jack another minute to make his way between parked cars, still ducking low behind vehicles or into doorways, trying all at once to not be seen but to not appear to any nosy neighbor like a thief or a terrorist on the street.

Inch by inch he made his way forward, still formulating his plan of attack. He needed to grab this guy and find out who he was and who he was working for.

Jack was twenty yards behind the man's vehicle on the opposite side of the street, hidden inside of a doorway, waiting for his chance. He got it when a green Mercedes diesel tour van rumbled up the street, its right turn signal flashing.

Perfect.

Jack jogged alongside it, waiting for it to make its rolling stop at the corner. Just as it made a sharp right, Jack dashed straight at the open car door window and threw a hard punch at the side of the man's close-cropped head.

Either Jack wasn't as stealthy as he'd thought or the man had preternatural peripheral vision, but either way the man's head ducked out of the way of Jack's punch. Jack's momentum practically tossed him through the open window just as Crooked Nose's iron-hard hands grabbed Jack's arm like a blacksmith's vise and pulled him farther into the car.

*Oh, shit!*

With his upper torso halfway into the Audi and his right arm trapped in the man's grip, Jack lost all of his leverage, robbing him of the power to launch any kind of a punch or even an elbow strike. His left arm was free but his own body and right arm blocked his left from doing any kind of damage.

The only good news Jack's brain could register in the nanosecond that followed was that the man's attempts to punch Jack's lights out also faltered because of Jack's awkward position. The adrenaline surging into Jack's bloodstream heightened his senses and fueled the years of CQB training driven into his muscle memory. Jack sensed more than saw the man loosen his grip and reach for a Kydex-holstered pistol, giving Jack's right elbow – the hardest bone in the human body – just enough distance and leverage to drive itself into the man's previously broken nose.

The man cried out as the cartilage cracked and blood spurted onto Jack's sleeve, giving Jack enough time to reach around with his left hand and grab the man's gun hand.

The two of them struggled to punch and grab, like two fighters boxing inside of a phone booth. It would have been comical if there hadn't been a loaded pistol in a holster just inches away from Jack's face. The man's powerful legs were wedged against the floorboard and he began using them for leverage to work himself free to get enough distance between him and Jack to reach the gun and pull it out and blow Jack's brains out all over the windshield.

As the man's body began pulling away, Jack's only defense was to grab the man's shirt and pull him back toward him. Crooked Nose only pushed back harder, inching away from Jack, his right hand making its way to the pistol.

Jack's big right hand opened up, and he clawed the man's face, gouging at his eyes. The man screamed again, his panic giving him a surge of strength. His gun hand turned into a fist and slammed into the side of Jack's skull but Jack turned his claw hand into a fist and threw a couple of short, sharp jabs into the man's forehead.

Jack didn't see the man's gun hand punch the starter button but he heard the engine roar to life. Jack twisted and turned, trying to land harder punches but his big frame wedged in the tiny car window blunted any force he might have generated. The gun hand slammed the car into gear and his foot stomped the gas.

The car lurched forward, tires squealing. Pain shot through Jack's torso as it twisted, whipped around by the car's momentum. Jack yanked himself away as hard as he could, and the combination of his remaining strength and the vehicle's trajectory freed him from the other man's grip. He crashed to the ground.

Jack scrambled for the next car and dove behind it, expecting Broken Nose to pull his weapon and begin shooting, but the squeal of tires and the stink of burning rubber told Jack to turn around just in time to see the Audi disappear around the corner.

Jack picked himself up off the pavement, the pulled muscles and bruising injuries providing yet another painful reminder that everyone has a plan until they get punched in the face, or in his case, tossed out of a moving car.

Jack made his way back to his apartment, informing Gavin on his AirPods that things hadn't quite worked out the way he'd planned. Gavin commiserated with him, and suggested Jack get the hell out of Dodge before the intruder came back with some friends.

Jack agreed. As he quickly gathered up his stuff, Gavin made arrangements for him at a luxury hotel in L'Eixample, the part of town just north of the old city that had some of Barcelona's trendiest shops and bars.

The first thing Jack did was snatch up the listening devices, smash them under his boot, then toss them into the trash underneath the sink.

He then grabbed everything he'd packed for Spain and crammed it into his leather satchel, then shoved his laptop into its carry case. He pulled out a hundred-euro note and left it on the kitchen counter as a tip for the cleaners.

He dashed out the front door and into a waiting cab that

Gavin had summoned. He'd text the owner later with an excuse for an emergency back home and thank him for the extended stay.

In the taxi ride over to the hotel, Jack formulated another plan – one that he hoped would survive another punch to the head.

A plan that might even keep him from getting punched in the first place.

He needed to identify Crooked Nose definitively, including an actual name. He saw the man's uncovered face inside the Audi but the only photo he could give Gavin was a masked face.

Was there anything Gavin could do with it?

He uploaded the photo and called him.

'Well . . . hate to brag,' Gavin said, 'but yeah, not really a problem.' He then began to explain the work being done at places like Google's DeepFace, and the FBI's Next Generation Identification project, and how 'machine-learning algorithms were being married to neural networks to measure and compare the fourteen major points of facial recognition, and how it was possible using –'

'Gav, can you just ballpark this for me?' Jack finally interrupted.

'Sorry. Sure. Even though the guy's nose and mouth are covered with that mask, there's still enough of his face to determine the depth of his eye sockets, the distance between his eyes, the overall shape and format of his face, and a few other points. That gives us a sixty-nine percent chance of re-creating the rest of his face.'

'Seriously?'

'If this mystery man of yours is in any database we have access to, we have a really good chance of finding him. But it's gonna take some time.'

'Speaking of which, any more progress on identifying the Dylan Runtso project? RAPTURE?'

'Still working on it.'

Jack heard the frustration in his voice.

It matched his own.

# 34

Brossa sat on a chaise lounge on the patio of a modest, two-story stucco rental on a hillside in the Sarrià–Sant Gervasi neighborhood. She overlooked the city below bathed in the soft, fading light of a cool evening. Her father, Ernesto, was already fast asleep in his bed. The caretaker she'd just hired over the phone, a *mexicana*, should be arriving within the hour to spend the night, and watch over him while she was away on the raid tomorrow.

She had just finished up a piece of *tortilla* her father had left in the refrigerator and was now sipping a glass of Espinaler *vermut,* her favorite. Her kit was ready and packed for the early morning flight up north. Time to unwind a little and forget her troubles.

Her phone vibrated on the glass tabletop. She swore under her breath when she saw Jack's number. She started to reach for the phone, then decided against it. Too many people – *too many men,* she corrected herself – were putting too many demands on her lately. Jack was nice enough but he was also too presumptuous. If he really was a civilian and not an American agent, he was the most aggressive tourist she'd ever met. Even if his passion was fueled by his sense of justice for his friend, it was still a thorn in her side that she didn't want to deal with at the moment. Tomorrow night or even the next day would be soon enough to speak with him, and she would have good news for him after the raid.

The phone stopped vibrating as she poured herself a little more *vermut,* irritated by Jack's interruption of her last quiet moment. The phone buzzed again, signaling a text. *Not Jack, please,* she thought as she picked up the phone.

She swore again. The text was from Jack. Against her better instincts, she opened it. It included a picture of a man's face taken at an odd angle by what appeared to be a security camera of some sort. He wore a black Nike ball cap and a mask covered his face. The only distinguishing feature she could discern was the glare of his hazel eyes.

Beneath the picture Jack had written THIS MAN IS YOUR BOMBER. I DON'T KNOW WHO HE IS BUT HE WAS AT L'AVI.

She started to call him for more details. How did he know it was the bomber? Where did he get the photo? But she decided against it. The picture was hardly enough to go on. If Jack was right, she'd see the man tomorrow when she arrested him. If he wasn't there, she'd deal with him and Jack some other day.

She set her phone back down on the glass table and sat back, savoring the last of her drink. She watched a flock of seagulls winging toward her, away from the sea.

A storm was coming.

# October 27

# 35

The heat from the turbine felt warm on her neck in the cool of the predawn morning as Brossa climbed into the Eurocopter EC135. Within moments she was at altitude and winging her way north.

Twenty minutes later the chopper set down on the grassy airstrip in Gurb. The airstrip was fit only for ultralight and small civilian aircraft, and in this case, a helicopter. She grimaced at the sight of the six URO VAMTACs – Spanish versions of Humvees – with their Browning M2 12.7x99mm NATO machine guns. She had spoken with Captain Asensio by phone yesterday and thought they had agreed to a quiet insertion, rather than a provocative show of force. Clearly he had changed his mind. The CNI was an intelligence-gathering unit, not a law enforcement agency per se.

She wasn't entirely surprised by the change of plan, either. Asensio began his career as a Spanish Army paratrooper in Afghanistan before transferring to the Guardia Civil. Quiet insertions weren't exactly his style.

Fortunately, the captain wisely decided not to assemble his assault team in Vic, a hotbed of Catalonian separatism. He'd even had the good sense to move his combat vehicles at night to avoid detection.

Vic – pronounced *Bic* locally – was a small, ancient city of some thirty thousand people and the capital of the district. It was also the gateway to the Pyrenees Mountains, toward which they were soon headed. Brossa had been in the main square market just last week. It was a festive affair, crowded with farmers and merchants selling their infinite varieties of delicious cheeses, olives, and *jamón* to locals and tourists alike. But the surrounding windows and balconies above the square were festooned with banners demanding the release of the Catalonian prisoners, independence flags, and even revolutionary slogans.

A police killing here, even an accidental one, could turn Vic into Spain's own version of Sarajevo and ignite another bloody war.

Brossa thanked the pilot, a woman, and her copilot before stepping onto the grass, lowering her head instinctively as the composite fiber blades spun overhead. As soon as she cleared the rotor radius, the chopper lifted back into the air with the roar of its twin turbo engines and headed back to Barcelona. The blast of warm air from the turbines felt even better in the crisp mountain air.

Brossa approached Captain Asensio, waiting by his command vehicle and kitted out like his men in green combat BDUs, a tactical vest with armor plate, and a Kevlar ATE bump helmet. She noted the H&K USP pistol on his hip but his subordinates all carried the H&K MP5 nine-millimeter submachine guns strapped across their chests. They looked less like a police operation than a full-on military strike force.

Standing next to Asensio was a man in his forties with fierce brown eyes behind his rimless glasses. He was shorter than Asensio but obviously physically fit and wore a tactical armored vest over his civilian clothes.

'This is Mr Dellinger. He's with the American consulate and will be observing today's events.'

'*Mucho gusto*, Agent Brossa,' Dellinger said, shaking her hand.

'*Igualmente*, Señor Dellinger.' Brossa nodded at the tactical vehicles. 'Change of plans, Captain? I thought this was a simple arrest.'

'New intelligence reports suggest they are heavily armed. I had to make adjustments.'

'We need to take them alive.'

He nodded toward one of his troopers behind a heavy machine gun. 'A show of force will make them think twice about resisting. The cowards will piss their pants and drop their weapons when they see us pull up in these.'

Brossa wanted to argue, but what was the point? Asensio was in charge of the tactical operation. She was only in charge of the arrests and crime scene investigation.

'Anything else, Agent Brossa?'

'We should get moving. No telling how long they'll be hanging around.'

'Agreed.' He barked orders into his comms and the six diesel engines coughed into life. The captain pulled open the door of his command vehicle and Brossa climbed in for the ride up into the high granite mountains above, Dellinger right behind her.


The abandoned eighteenth-century two-story farmhouse was built with rough-hewn granite stones from the surrounding mountains, as were two of the smaller outbuildings nearby, both in severe disrepair. A fourth building, a crumbling cow barn, was mostly wood. The ancient dairy farm stood at the end of a dirt track that ran off the small, winding asphalt road leading up from Queralbs, less than five miles from the French border.

Captain Asensio reviewed his plans with Brossa over their headsets inside the roaring VAMTAC. He pointed out the approaches his men would take on the infrared photographs his drone operator had made the day before. The narrow road would be blocked on both ends a half kilometer out, and his troopers would approach on foot to maintain the element of surprise.

A sniper team was already in position on the hill behind the farmhouse and reported that thirteen tangos – nine males, four females – had arrived the evening before and were still in place. At least one AK-47 and two Beretta 92FS pistols had been spotted through the windows. The sniper had permission to take out any RPG or other heavy-weapons operator on sight but to otherwise maintain fire discipline until ordered into action.

'There won't be any problems,' Asensio assured her with a confident grin. 'It will be sweet and easy, like a sip of your grandmother's sangria.'

*Flirting? Now? Seriously?* she said to herself.

'Oh, Captain. If you only knew my grandmother.'

Over the captain's objections, Brossa jogged along with the rest of the assault team, approaching the farmhouse under cover of the surrounding trees and low rock wall. Dellinger remained behind in the company of a young private as ordered.

According to the sniper team, no lookouts had been posted outside of the building, though men frequented the windows, smoking cigarettes and drinking coffee. It was just after seven a.m. now, and everyone inside the farmhouse appeared to be awake.

The captain raised a bullhorn to his mouth. 'Attention! You inside! You are surrounded by the Guardia Civil. Come out with your hands empty and over your heads!'

His second-in-command, Vázquez, another combat veteran, ordered the remaining four VAMTACs forward at top speed.

Panicked, angry voices shouted inside the building, as the ground-floor window shutters slammed shut.

Asensio swore under his breath.

'Easy, eh?' Brossa said.

The captain jabbed a finger into her tactical vest.

'No matter what happens, you don't move from this spot until I give the command for you to advance or I'll shoot you myself. Understood?'

Brossa forced a single nod of her head in reluctant compliance, swearing silently to herself at the man's arrogance.

The four VAMTACs roared up closer, skidding to a halt in a cloud of dust. They formed a ragged line some hundred meters from the house, machine guns pointed at the ancient stone walls.

'I won't make the offer again,' Asensio shouted in the bull horn. 'Leave your weapons inside and come out with your hands over your head or we're coming inside to get you.'

'Go away, *porcs feixistes!*' – fascist pigs! – a man's voice shouted from inside, hiding behind a second-story wall. 'We are assembling peacefully, as is our right under the Spanish constitution!'

'You are all suspects in a mass murder,' Asensio replied. 'I have a warrant for your arrests. You have two minutes to comply.'

'That is a lie! We are innocent!' the man shouted.

Asensio whispered a command in his comms, and the four heavy machine guns racked in unison.

He cast a sidelong glance at Brossa. 'You'll see. They'll come right out, the cowards.'

Brossa checked her Casio G-Shock. The second hand swept the dial twice.

Nothing.

'It's been two minutes –'

Asensio cut her off with a chop of his hand in the air. He put the bullhorn to his mouth.

'Time's up! We're coming in! If you resist, we will shoot.'

A young man with long hair and a full beard appeared at one of the second-story windows, waving a white pillowcase in his hand. From here, he didn't look to be more than twenty years old, Brossa thought.

'Hey, *feixisto*! We called our lawyer. She is on her way from Vic. She will be here in thirty minutes. Let her see the warrant. If it is legal, we will comply.'

Brossa let out a sigh of relief. 'Excellent.'

The captain ignored her. He whispered a command. 'Vázquez, we will advance on my order in thirty seconds. Get ready to –'

Brossa yanked his arm. 'Stop! What are you doing?'

'Hold!' Asensio ordered before whipping around. 'What the hell are *you* doing? This is my operation!'

'Our orders are to take them all alive, for questioning.'

'And that is my intention.'

'But they just said they would comply. All we have to do is wait for their lawyer.'

The captain shook his head, his eyes raking over her smaller form in a derisive inventory. He could barely hide his disdain.

'You damn desk jockeys don't have the first idea about field operations. "Wait for their lawyer"? How do you know they called a lawyer? Do you know if they even *have* a lawyer?'

'I don't. But thirty minutes won't cost us anything.'

'Really? What if instead of calling a lawyer they called in for armed reinforcements? Have you thought of that, Agent Brossa?'

'I say we wait and see what happens.'

He shoved a thick finger in her face. 'And I say, if you

interrupt this operation again, I'll zip-cuff your pretty little ass and put you facedown in the dirt, and then I'll report you to Peña for endangering this mission and my men. *¿Me entiendes?*'

Brossa jabbed her thin finger into his tac vest. 'You and I are going to have a little talk when this operation is over, *cabrón*. Go ahead and do your thing. But once we're inside, I'm the boss, and if you dick around with me in there, you'll be the one up for court-martial.' Her eyes narrowed, and she added in her native tongue, '*M'entens?*'

Asensio grinned, admiring her sand. 'Agreed.' His face hardened. He pointed at the ground 'Stay here until I call you in. That's an order.'

He turned around to face the farmhouse. 'Vázquez. Ready?'

'Ready.'

'Smoke. Now.'

A half-dozen smoke grenades arced through the sky, thudding in the dirt in front of the house. They each popped, belching out billowing clouds of reactive granular aluminum and perchloroethane, completely blocking the view between the house and the assault team.

'Wait for it,' Asensio growled in his comms. 'On my count. Five, four, three . . .'

The farmhouse and its outbuildings sat in the middle of a small open field, its grasses fed by a burbling creek that ran the length of the property behind the house. Three hundred meters behind the house was a steep, tree-studded hill where the sniper team lay in hiding.

The front of the house faced the winding asphalt road with no obstructions from the front door up the dirt track all the way to the road.

The asphalt road had been cut out of the side of the

mountain, which was why its far side was bounded by a steep wall of granite, the top of which was heavily treed. The straight-line distance from the top of the granite wall to the ragged row of VAMTACs down below was less than forty meters.

Well hidden and in camouflage, Bykov – a combat veteran on four continents – followed the captain's attack with a veteran's eye and listened in on Asensio's tapped comms through an earpiece. He hardly needed the latter. Popping smoke was textbook, and completely predictable.

So was the sound of the helicopter rotors beating the air, approaching right on time. Peña was as good as his word.

Forty meters from that height was an easy throw.

Bykov pulled the pin and let fly.


'Wait for it,' Asensio growled in his comms. 'On my count. Five, four, three . . .'

He glanced up as he counted, shocked by the sudden appearance of the bright yellow news helicopter overhead.

'. . . two, one . . .'

The small, round green M67 grenade thudded in the dirt twenty meters from Asensio. He recognized the sound immediately – he'd thrown plenty of them himself in the Sand Box. Six and a half ounces of Comp B explosive would shred its steel casing into deadly white-hot shards in a matter of seconds.

'GRENADE!'

The M67 exploded, throwing shrapnel in a lethality radius of five meters. A private standing thirteen meters from it went down, his left calf cut to ribbons. Other shards spanged against the nearby VAMTAC.

'Go!'

*

The four machine guns mounted on the VAMTACs opened up, hitting the windows, keeping tight fire lanes so that the troopers could advance without getting hit by them. Blue-on-blue 'friendly fire' casualties were a soldier's worst nightmare.

'Go, go, go!' Asensio commanded, charging forward, taking the lead, eight of his men advancing behind him toward the front of the house. Six more charged in from the other three directions. Another eight of his troopers took up covering positions, weapons pointed at the house, still shrouded in white smoke.

Brossa fought the urge to follow – until she couldn't. She pulled her pistol and charged forward toward the house through the haze.

She heard Asensio bark another order in her comms but her ears picked up the distinctive sound of spoons popping on flash-bangs. Tossed through windows, each of the devices blew in half a second, blasting an ear-busting 175 decibels of noise and a blinding two million candlepower of light.

Brossa broke through the last of the dissipating smoke toward the open space on the wall next to Asensio. He saw her approaching, and barked an angry order at her, waving her away.

'Get back!'

The house erupted.

White light blinded her, and the world went dark.

It happened so fast, Brossa didn't really know what hit her. All she knew was her ears rang and her head hurt like she'd been on a three-day drunk. She was propped up against a tire of one of the VAMTACs, and one of the troopers, the assigned medic, was blotting a minor cut on her face with an antibacterial swab.

There were other troopers around her, more badly

wounded than she, but none critically, and already bandaged. They smoked and laughed.

She blinked her eyes to clear them, only to see Asensio towering over her, his dark eyes glaring at her.

'You disobeyed my orders and nearly got yourself killed.'

Brossa pushed the medic away and climbed to her feet.

'How many dead?' she asked.

'None of my men, thank God.' He crossed himself.

'Inside?' she asked hopefully.

He shrugged. 'All of them. The cowards.'

'Show me.'

His eyes narrowed. 'I don't recommend it.'

'I'm not your little sister, Captain. Show me.'

Captain Asensio led the way, his boots crunching on the shattered glass and wood splinters in the dirt. They reached what was left of the porch. The door had been blasted off its ancient iron hinges, fragments of it still clinging to the thumb-width nails.

The stone walls still stood, mostly. The heavy granite had done its work. The thick walls had contained the explosion, much like a firecracker tossed into a coffee can – or more accurately, a coffee can full of grasshoppers. Even from here Brossa could see the blood and hair and brain matter embedded into the ancient gray stones.

It was the wooden structures inside that had given way. The ceilings, support beams, and staircases collapsed in on themselves or, in the case of the roof and window casings, blew outward in large, jagged shards, scattered around the meadow like trash after a rock concert.

Body parts, too. A foot still inside of a shoe lay near the creek. A bloody bone fragment was wedged in the front grille of one of the VAMTACs.

The smell of burnt wood couldn't hide the stench of the shattered torsos inside. She knew that beneath the rubble lay buried thirteen broken bodies, entrails spilling out onto the rough-cut boards, blood and waste seeping into the cracks.

Once the rubble was cleared away, the mangled remains could be removed. It would be dirty work putting them all back together again. But it had to be done in order to identify them.

The yellow helicopter circled high overhead, no doubt shooting more camera footage, perhaps even live, Brossa worried. Its blades beat out a dark tattoo that rang off the mountaintops.

'Can't you get rid of it?' Brossa asked.

'I called it in to my commanding officer. He's working on it.'

'How did they find out?'

He shrugged. 'They're vultures. They can smell death a kilometer away in parts per billion.' He motioned toward the smoldering wreckage inside. 'There's nothing you can do here. I've already called in my crime scene people. Let them handle this.'

'I have a job to do, Captain. So do you. Get out of my way.'

# 36

*Oak Ridge, Tennessee*

Ted had the good sense to leave without a word, shutting the door quietly behind him.

Forty-two years old, with short red hair and dark green eyes, Kate Parsons was as hard and efficient as the Peloton bike she rode every morning. She was in the middle of her live forty-five-minute HIIT ride when he approached her, his eyes warm and welcoming. But a single icy glance from her sent him slinking back to the bedroom to grab his stuff and leave without a shower or even a cup of coffee.

Parsons didn't care. She'd met Ted – or was it Tad? – on a run yesterday afternoon on the dirt service road in the rolling hills just beyond the Spallation Neutron Source facility. He was testing titanium jet engine parts at the SNS, the head of his own company, the name of which escaped her. Their eyes locked as she ran by. That was enough for the shirtless man to turn around. He finally caught up to her, his six-pack abs glistening with sweat and his eyes full of longing. Thirty minutes later they were in her bed, where she taught him her favorite form of high-intensity interval training.

Finally spent, he passed out.

This morning, she left him sleeping and got up to ride. The RAPTURE project was on her mind as it had been constantly for the last three years. It was her baby, and the only one she would ever have. Perhaps it was even her only true love. She didn't need a husband or an infant to care for;

her ambitions were loftier than dirty diapers and forgotten anniversaries.

When loneliness struck, men like Ted always appeared. Her momentary despair seemingly exuded musky phero-mones in her wake, drawing the nearest stallion to her loins when she most needed him.

She began toweling off in the cooldown part of the ride, still turning the crank on her Peloton. She was deeply satis-fied that she had ranked number one on the leaderboard of 2,948 other riders who had finished the same harrowing workout. Not unusual. She almost always finished on top. She flipped through her history screen. She ranked number one in a dozen other recent rides, and never lower than num-ber three in five more. Not bad for a woman who worked an average of eighty hours per week.

Number one was important in Parsons's world. Always had been, in everything, including physics as she clawed her way up in what was largely a man's world. She took after her late father, also a physicist, and was less like her mother, also dead and gone. The dowdy homemaker, mother of seven, and church organist had given up a full ride to Berklee Col-lege of Music to marry her dad.

Parsons's kitchen was white marble and stainless steel, spotless and organized like the rest of her house and her life. No art hung on the walls because the only beauty she cared about was the invisible quantum particles she manip-ulated, or the chiseled obliques she'd carved out of her own torso. She had no pets and no friends ever came to call, nor had she any need to visit or be visited by her siblings or their children.

Still only a quarter to six, Parsons fired up her Vitamix with her premeasured containers of organic coconut milk, protein powder, and micronutrient supplements. The machine roared and whirred like a particle accelerator. She didn't hear her phone vibrate on the snow-white Carrara marble countertop but the light from the text window caught her eye. The contact info read 'RHODES,' her boss at ORNL. EMERGENCY MEETING MY OFFICE AT 8AM TOMORROW. PLEASE CONFIRM.

She did. It wasn't like it was a request. But that didn't matter to her at all. There was an emergency and she was needed. There was no one else who could fix it because that's what she did. There were a lot of emergencies and a lot of emergency meetings, especially of late. This was nothing new. That was the nature of government projects with evolving mandates, shortened deadlines, and oversight committees chaired by people who thought quarks were the sounds that ducks made while they were fucking.

Just another emergency that really wasn't an emergency, unless you were Dr David Rhodes, the RAPTURE project manager, a position she'd once held in function if not title before he arrived on the scene.

She'd fix this emergency, too.

The Vitamix stopped roaring and whirring and she poured her protein shake. Food was only fuel to her. She was a machine, a well-conditioned, efficient, and, she daresay, an attractive one.

She picked up her phone again to text Tad, asking if he was free tonight.

Or was it Ted?

# 37

*Washington, D.C.*
*The White House*

President Ryan stood in front of the Oval Office fireplace with a portrait of an austere George Washington hanging over the mantel.

Ryan had a smile plastered on his face, a look his wife, Cathy, characterized as 'sincerely phony.' It was the smile he flashed with practiced perfection at every important state function including this one, the receiving of Ambassador Christyakov's credentials.

The two men both stood facing the flashing cameras, right hands held in a firm handshake, left hands holding the exchanged documents, putting the official and historical act on digital record. The official White House press photographer had already taken several good shots, then quit the room. It was the Russian state photographers that were still grinding away.

The event was a bit of a coup for the new ambassador. Maksim Christyakov was only thirty-nine years old and stood half a head taller than Ryan, with thick blond hair and dark blue eyes. He looked more like a Viking than the squat Soviet diplomats Ryan had known as a young analyst. But of course, Christyakov was Nordic. The Rus people were formally known as the Viking Rus, Scandinavians who raided the Black and Baltic Seas during the Middle Ages, settling along the Volga. Russians and Belarussians derived their very name from them.

It was quite a physical contrast. Such optics mattered these days, unfortunately. Perhaps they always did. But Ryan knew the Russian state Internet bots would push this image out into the ether with relentless enthusiasm. Score one for the Russians in the beauty department, Ryan supposed.

In truth, Christyakov's appointment to the position was a remarkable achievement for a man without prior diplomatic experience. The well-connected Russian was part of the New Wave reforms that President Nikita Yermilov had recently instituted in his pro-democracy and anti-corruption drive. A joke, if there ever was one, Ryan thought, as the LED flashes fired.

'I think that should do it,' Scott Adler said gently, as he stepped between the two camera operators and the President.

Ryan scanned the room. It was crowded with Christyakov's fawning retinue, along with a few of the SecState's senior executives and staff. The President flashed a look at Adler he knew all too well.

'Ladies and gentlemen, thank you for attending our brief ceremony.' Adler pointed at the door. 'There are refreshments waiting for you in the Diplomatic Reception Room, if you'll follow me.'

Ryan watched the parade of people file out behind Adler and waited for the Secret Service agent to close the door behind them before he spoke with the ambassador.

Today's meeting was a real challenge.

Buck Logan thought the Russians were behind the piracy crisis, and right now, that was the best hypothesis. Admiral Pike's carrier strike group would arrive on scene in a few days and put eyes on the situation. Ryan wanted answers sooner, if possible.

There was nothing Ryan wouldn't do to protect the nation and to serve its best interests, including war, if it came to that. Too often it had come to war for other men who sat behind his desk and even for him in the recent past.

Whoever was sinking these ships in the South Pacific had to be stopped. Action was necessary. War was an option.

Today's meeting could lead to the latter.

'Congratulations, Mr Ambassador. How does it feel?'

The handsome Russian smiled. 'The ceremony itself was rather anticlimactic, to be honest. We exchanged pieces of paper and took pictures.'

'Welcome to the club.'

'The honor for me today was to finally meet you in person, Mr President. Your reputation in my country is stellar.'

'I find that hard to believe.'

'Yes, your file is quite thick. "Brilliant, ruthless, cunning. Perhaps our country's greatest nemesis," it reads in part. But these are values my superiors respect greatly, as do I.'

'"Nemesis"? You make me sound like a comic book villain.'

Christyakov grinned infectiously.

'In Russia, Captain America *is* a villain.'

Christyakov's English was faultless, as were the porcelain veneers on his million-watt smile. The diamond-studded watch on his thick wrist was probably worth more than the one-bedroom fixer-upper shack he and Cathy had purchased just after they got married.

'Coffee? Tea?' Ryan asked the younger man as he stood at the small service table. He pointed him to the chair across from the famous presidential desk. The Russian fell into it like it was an old friend.

'Coffee, if it's not too much trouble. Cream, no sugar.'

Ryan poured two cups, dumping too much creamer into the Russian's. He liked his black, the way that God and the Department of the Navy intended it.

Ryan handed Christyakov his cup and took his seat behind the desk.

'How do you like Washington, Maksim?'

'I find it to be a city of "Southern charm and Northern efficiency."'

Ryan smiled to himself. If he was quoting JFK, he got the quote completely backward. *Or perhaps he was just being polite?*

'If I'm being perfectly honest, I find it to be neither on most days,' Ryan said.

Christyakov leaned forward in his chair. 'The architecture is stunning, and the women are gorgeous.'

Well, he got that right, at least.

'I appreciate your time today. I think it's important we get to know each other. Scott Adler speaks highly of you.'

'That is kind of the secretary to say. He is a very skilled diplomat and is held in the highest respect among my colleagues and superiors.'

'Scott is a good diplomat, and an outstanding negotiator. But his most important quality to me is that I can trust him completely.'

'A rare thing these days. Trust.'

'Agreed. Perhaps that's why we're having this meeting today.'

Christyakov took a sip of his coffee. 'Excellent. How might we build trust between our nations?'

'That's an excellent question. But I can think of a better one.'

'Which is?'

'How can we build trust between ourselves?'

'You mean, between you and I, personally?'

'Yes, of course. At the end of the day, politics is about people, not government. I need to be able to look a man or a woman in the eyes when I'm talking to them and know they're not shoveling horse hockey in my direction when they move their lips.'

Another smirking smile turned the Russian's mouth. 'You must be very frustrated, then, especially living in this city.'

'I like dealing with honest people. Makes life easier.'

'That is an admirable goal, Mr President. But I have found that most people are loyal only to themselves, and that honesty is a function of self-interest.'

'That seems rather cynical.'

'Honesty and cynicism are not incompatible.'

'But dishonesty and trust are.'

'I couldn't disagree more. I prefer the company of liars. A liar is a self-interested man, which means he is a rational man. He lies because he knows the *honest* truth bears a cost he's not willing to pay. But the honest man? He's the danger-ous one. He's the one who insists on telling the truth no matter the cost. Such a man is an irrational man that cannot be reasoned or bargained with. An honest man is either your best friend or your worst enemy. Usually your enemy. Most people can't handle the truth. If you tell them the real rea-sons why they're fat or poor or stupid or unsuccessful in life, generally they will hate you for it – and for the very reason it is the truth. If every congressman on Capitol Hill told the truth, the whole truth, for just one day, your empire would collapse in a heap of ashes.'

*The man likes to hear himself talk,* Ryan thought.

But he suddenly understood that Christyakov wasn't appointed just because of his family connections. He was a cold, cunning, ruthless son of a bitch. And someone to keep an eye on.

Christyakov saw Ryan's face darken.

'I see I have made you uncomfortable with my honesty. Does that mean you are more or less likely to trust me now?'

'I certainly have a clearer sense of who you are and how you think.'

'And is that more or less advantageous for me?'

'We'll have to wait and see.'

Ryan took a sip of coffee. 'I know you come out of the oil and gas business. How did you manage to do any deals with people you knew you couldn't trust?'

'Numbers don't lie. There is no ambiguity in a P&L statement. But of course, you come from the business world yourself. You built your first fortune on railroad stock speculation, I believe. And made millions more as a stock trader back in the day.'

'I got lucky every now and then. But even the stock trading business is about trust. We have a saying, "Figures don't lie, but liars figure." You need to be able to trust the guy on the other side of the trade for it to work.'

'Trust? Yes, of course. There must be trust for business to work, or politics for that matter.' The ambassador tented his fingers thoughtfully. 'But trust is different than honesty, and far easier to come by. A dishonest man will be completely trustworthy so long as he fears the consequences of betrayal.'

'I would rather deal with honest men than fearful ones, in business or in politics.'

The Russian's eyes widened. 'I'm surprised. I would have thought that your Mideast wars taught you otherwise. The mujahideen are honest about their faith and their hatred for you, and have killed thousands of your soldiers and citizens to prove that honesty. Better if they were more fearful than they were honest, don't you think?'

'I think we're talking apples and oranges here.'

Christyakov shrugged. 'People are the same everywhere, are they not? In my country, trust is rewarded, but lies are punished. The bigger the lie, the bigger the penalty. That doesn't make men honest, but it does protect the truth.'

Ryan well knew what that meant. Critics of President Yermilov had a nasty habit of suiciding themselves out of apartment windows or shooting themselves with bullets to the back of their own heads. *Truth is treason in the empire of lies,* Ryan reminded himself, citing his old friend Ron Paul.

The only 'truth' in Russia was that opposing Yermilov was a guaranteed death sentence.

*Time to change the subject.*

'Your uncle was quite successful in his oil and gas business.'

'He is very shrewd. His company employs quite a few Americans, actually.'

*Too many,* Ryan thought. The sons of two current congressmen and the daughter of an ex-senator sat on the boards of Christyakov corporations.

'He's a multibillionaire, I believe.'

'I thought success was a good thing, yes? Aren't we all good capitalists these days?'

'He's a friend of President Yermilov.'

'As are many people in Russia.'

*Including the top* vory *of the Russian mafia,* Ryan wanted to say. *And they're probably your friends, too.*

'Your uncle is an oligarch.'

The young Russian's mocking smile suddenly flashed daggers.

'An ugly word in some circles, and an unfortunate choice of one, if I may say so, Mr President. My uncle is a good man who raised me as his own son after the death of my father. Everything I have achieved I owe to him.'

*A career bought and paid for,* Ryan reminded himself. *Paved with stolen riches, on a path that someday might lead this man to the Kremlin itself.*

'I have a habit of speaking my mind and putting my cards on the table so that people know where I stand,' Ryan said.

'I was taught by my uncle that diplomacy is the art of leaving some things unsaid.'

It was Ryan's turn to shrug and smile. 'Whoever said I was a diplomat, Maksim?'

'Which is why I admire you all the more. So, please, what is the real purpose of our meeting today?'

'There are two things I'd like to discuss today.'

'Of course. How would you like to begin?'

Ryan needed to ease in, save the big ask for later.

'I'm concerned about Snow Dragon, the upcoming joint naval exercise you and China have scheduled in the Bering Sea next week.'

'Your country need not be concerned. We have no hostile intentions, and we are conducting all operations in our own national waters.'

'It's not my country I'm concerned about.'

Christyakov smiled. Smug and condescending. 'You must forgive me, but I'm rather new at all of this. I don't understand what you're saying.'

'You're too young to remember Zhenbao Island. Surely you've read about it?'

'An unfortunate skirmish that happened fifty years ago.'

'A skirmish launched by the Chinese against your country that nearly started World War Three. The Chinese have a long memory. You guys took Manchuria from them after the war. They wanted Manchuria back then and they want it back now. Hell, they want the entire Russian Far East, which is forty percent of your landmass occupied by only six million Russians. Russia will never be an equal partner with China; Russia will eventually become a colony of China. Your current relationship is a dangerous one, and just one spark can set off an explosion leading to all-out war.'

'Snow Dragon is merely a practical and natural evolution in our growing relationship. It will be the largest joint naval exercise our two countries have ever conducted. Three hundred thousand soldiers and sailors combined, including an amphibious landing of ten thousand Chinese Marines supported by Russian naval and air assets. But it will be no different than the many joint land-based exercises that have been conducted over the last few years – all very fraternal and cooperative.'

'Be that as it may, we'll be monitoring your exercises closely. Of course, the Chinese government will be collecting data on your military capabilities as well.'

'And we will collect data on them. As I understand it, that is how the game is played. "Trust, but verify" is what Ronald Reagan once said about the Soviet Union as I recall. Yes?'

'It's a very dangerous game you're playing with the Chinese.'

'Surely you realize that it has been your punitive sanctions against my government that have driven us into closer ties with Beijing, a decision that President Yermilov came to quite reluctantly.'

*Reluctantly? That sounds like an opening,* Ryan thought.

'Those sanctions came as a result of Russian incursions on Lithuanian and Ukrainian soil.'

'Russian forces were withdrawn, and no further incursions have resulted.'

*Yeah, after NATO forces kicked your asses.*

'Agreed. And it's a sign of progress in his relationship with the West that President Yermilov has limited his territorial ambitions. I hope that progress will continue.'

'I'm sure President Yermilov shares your hope of continued progress in our relationship. I will convey your message. What else concerns you today, Mr President?'

Ryan glanced over the Russian's shoulder at the portrait of George Washington over the fireplace mantel. *Why the hell didn't he have to smile?*

'Funny you should ask.'

'There have been rumors of pirates operating in international waters,' Ryan said. 'Have you heard of this?'

'Yes, of course,' Christyakov said. 'Off the coast of Africa, and in Asia, I believe.'

'I am referring to pirates operating in the South Pacific.'

'Interesting. This I have not heard.'

*Exactly what I would expect you to say if you were lying . . . or telling the truth,* Ryan thought.

'The Chinese have made great advances in their submarine technology, thanks to your country.'

'And others.'

'That's right. Some of it purchased, some of it reverse engineered. Some of it just flat-out stolen.'

'And so you suspect the Chinese are behind these piracy acts?'

'Unless you have a better idea.'

'I'm no military man.'

'But surely you are aware of your nation's submarine activity in the South Pacific?'

Christyakov was expressionless. 'Again, defense issues are not in my bailiwick. My background is in business, not naval affairs. I'm in Washington to improve business and political relationships with your country.'

'War is bad for both.'

The ambassador's blue eyes narrowed. 'What are you suggesting?'

'Wars sometimes happen by accident, unintentionally. Those are the worst kind and easily avoided, wouldn't you agree?'

'If they were easily avoided, why would such wars happen at all?'

'Well, here we are, back at the trust issue. If you bump into someone you like at a cocktail party, you laugh and say, "Excuse me." If you bump into your worst enemy, you might start throwing punches over it. Or worse.'

The younger, taller man sat back in his chair, crossing his legs. 'May I speak my mind, Mr President? Lay my cards on the table?'

'Please do.'

'My predecessor briefed me on you. He mentioned that you are a former Marine Corps officer, and that you are a single-minded American patriot, unafraid of violence at either the personal or national level.'

'I take all of that as a compliment.'

'He also said you were subtle as a snake, and just as dangerous, and that I should never do any business with you without a half-dozen senior FSB analysts on my elbow advising me on every word you speak.'

'Okay, now you're hurting my feelings.'

Christyakov laughed. 'Yes, and he said you were funny as hell, too. So let me cut to the chase. What is it that you want exactly, so that I can go back to my superiors and tell them, and then they can tell me what the hell it is I'm supposed to do about it?'

'Frankly, this meeting today was a chance for me to meet with you, to size you up. But the bottom line is this: I've dispatched the *Theodore Roosevelt* carrier strike group to the South Pacific. You said you're not a military man, so let me explain the significance of this. I'm sending some of my very best and most powerful weapons to the area, including two *Los Angeles*–class attack submarines. My intention is to find, capture, and, if necessary, kill the submarine or submarines that are behind the acts of piracy in the region. It would be better for all parties if the perpetrators withdrew before my strike group arrives.'

Christyakov frowned with confusion. 'And you're telling me this because you think my government is somehow involved?'

*If the kid is acting, he's doing a damned good job,* Ryan thought. *But he wouldn't be in the job if he wasn't a good actor, would he?*

Ryan stood, ending the meeting. So did Christyakov. 'I'm telling you this, Maksim, so you can pass along the information to your boss. Clarity is a virtue in diplomacy.'

Ryan extended his hand. The Russian took it.

'I will be sure to pass your information along, Mr President.' Christyakov's eyes locked with Ryan's. 'It was an unusual pleasure to meet you. You rose above my expectations, which were considerable, given your reputation.'

'I have a feeling we'll be seeing each other again soon, Mr Ambassador. I wish you much success in your new position.'

Ryan opened the visitor door and pointed the way out.

As Ryan took his seat, the door swung back open and Arnie came in.

'How'd it go?'

'Scott was right. We don't want to make the mistake of underestimating that guy, family ties or not.'

'He didn't cough anything up?'

'If I read him correctly, he's not aware of his government's involvement with the sinkings.'

'But they are involved, right?'

Ryan shrugged. 'That's still our presumption. I'm not willing to second-guess myself at this point. I gave Christyakov fair warning. If it's a Russian sub out there we're going to find it and, if necessary, sink it, unless they get the hell out before we show up. If we're lucky, they'll take the hint and vamoose.'

'And if they don't?'

'Then we might have a war on our hands.'

# 38

Lieutenant Bob 'Daisy' Callaway sat in the right-hand pilot's seat of the MH-60R (Romeo) Seahawk helicopter, the rotors on his bird slowly spinning up, preparing for takeoff. His helmet was festooned with daisy flower stickers, rainbows, and peace symbols, an inside joke among his air crew.

The first raindrops sparkled like rhinestones as they spattered on the windshield, illuminated by the overhead deck light. With his naked eyes, Callaway could barely see the blue-shirted chock and chain men kneeling down next to the LSE with his bird's gear in their hands. That was the first sign he was almost clear to take off.

The 'Grape' had just pulled the fuel hose, crouching low beneath the slowly turning blades, powered by two GE T700/CT7 turboshaft engines. They'd been ordered to find the *Glazov* ASAP. As per SOPs, the purple-shirted Grape had shown Callaway the fuel mixture she put in his tank – like he was ever going to object – and the red-shirted ordnance crew had pulled the safety pins from their load of four anti-ship AGM-114 Hellfires, and a Mark 54 air-launched, anti-submarine torpedo. It was designed to be a non-combat mission but the Navy liked to be prepared for all eventualities.

Especially the killing kind.

It was pitch black, and despite its bulk, the big *Ticonderoga*-class *Luzon* was yawing in a cool, stiff wind that whipped the water into a Pitch 3, Roll 3 situation. Manageable, but not ideal.

Callaway waited anxiously for the twenty-two-year-old LSE to clear him for launch before the weather got worse, and the night even darker. Night flying under the best of conditions – even with night vision – still induced maximum pucker factor for any pilot but especially a helo pilot. But that was the job he'd signed up for after graduating from Annapolis – Canoe U.

Tonight's mission was to find the sub and force it to the surface. Neither objective was easy.

Either could get you killed.

Callaway knew that finding an improved Kilo-class running on electric batteries while submerged was nearly impossible. Finding one ASAP was even more impossible, even with two Romeos on the hunt, the most advanced ASW helicopters in the air today.

The plan was to first drop their entire complement of AN/SSQ-101 ADAR passive sonobuoys in a wide grid pattern centered on the Russian sub tender *Penza*. Each device deployed a translucent, pentagon-shaped umbrella of hydrophones listening for known improved Kilo-class sound signatures.

With the help of the Romeo's onboard computer, Callaway's AWO would analyze the ambient sound forms to identify the *Glazov's* signature by comparing them to all known submarine signatures stored in the Navy's highly classified digital library.

Making the impossible even more difficult was the fact that Callaway's Romeo had been out of commission for several hours yesterday with a malfunctioning laser altimeter and the loss of hydraulic boost. That meant Callaway had to maintain seventy-five pounds of constant pressure on the left pedal just to keep it from yawing while also fighting the unboosted collective and cyclic inputs. Thanks to the constant training in 'loss of control' emergency scenarios, the sweat-drenched pilot and his crew made it back to the ship, but it was a close call. Thanks to the two dozen perennially shorthanded, sleep-deprived maintenance people, the machine got fixed.

It was nothing new for the maintenance crew. It was a 24/7/365 job to keep the helicopters aloft, and both seldom were, at least simultaneously. Keeping nearly twenty-four thousand pounds of machine and munitions in the sky without crashing was no easy feat while at sea. The salt air and water played hell with anything that could rust, clog, or corrode, and both were murder on the electronics gear, which was the primary weapon of the fabled helicopter.

Now it was up to Callaway and the other Seahawk to get to the search area and begin ASW operations, and to do it all at night. With the naked eye it was harder than hell flying just two hundred feet above the black water and beneath a black sky, with no horizon for reference. Unless you had the luxury of NVGs, night flying over the Pacific meant flying by instruments, and when the instruments failed, people died. Most of the folks back home, including Callaway's own parents, didn't realize how often those instruments failed, including night vision.

His wife did. Lieutenant Anne 'Snow White' Callaway flew the nearly identical MH-60S 'Knighthawk' airframe on vertical replenishment (VERTREP) and search-and-rescue (SAR) missions in the same carrier strike group. They were the first married couple ever assigned to their CSG. While fixed-wingers obsessed on call signs, most helicopter pilots eschewed them. It just wasn't their thing. But the CSG flight ops center had given the Callaways their call signs not only to be able to distinguish the two pilots with the same last name during flight operations, but also to let the two married partners know when the other one was flying.

*C'mon, for Pete's sake,* Callaway said to himself, keeping one eye on the signalman's red light wands and one on the pitching deck, which seemed to be pitching even harder now. His airborne tactical officer (ATO) and copilot was hyper-focused on the twin-engine readouts.

'Finally,' Callaway whispered in his comms as the enlisted landing signalman switched his red wands to green. The LSE extended his arms and lifted them up laterally, indicating to Callaway that he had permission to raise the Romeo into a hover position before taking off.

Callaway increased the throttle and raised the collective, holding his cyclic and pedals neutral to the stiff breeze buffeting the ship as he brought it into a hover. As the digital gauges swept and climbed across the glass cockpit, the ATO called out the numbers. 'Looking good,' he added hopefully, like a prayer, as he always did during liftoff. But his 'prayer' was routine, and pilots were devoted to their routines, especially ones that kept them from getting killed, even the superstitious ones.

The LSE then began twirling the green wands, granting permission for Callaway to begin his turn forty-five degrees right, and then power away. In reality, helicopter pilots ignored these instructions from the man on deck – his ass wasn't in the seat, and his feet weren't on the pedals. The transition from hover to forward flight was the most dangerous part of the flight. Helicopters needed forward momentum to actually fly, and physical forces trying to crash his aircraft played their hardest in the movement between the vertical and horizontal planes.

This transitional window was also the reason why the

ATO remained fixated on the readouts. The Seahawk was perfectly capable of flying on a single engine when it was traveling at speed and in a forward direction. But the Seahawk became a flying brick if one of the engines quit during the transition window. If Callaway couldn't get enough air speed when an engine quit, it meant crashing into the Pacific strapped to twelve tons of metal and munitions plunging toward the ocean floor.

'Gauges green, on the go,' Callaway said. He gently eased the cyclic forward and the collective farther upward as he hit the pedals to begin his turn out over the brooding waters of the rolling black Pacific.

Within moments, the helicopter rose to its cruising altitude, then turned full throttle, racing through the starless night just two hundred feet above the deck toward the target some two hundred and twenty miles distant.

One of the many features of the MH-60R Seahawk that made it such a formidable anti-ship and anti-submarine weapon was its Block III upgraded Light Airborne Multi-Purpose System (LAMPS). LAMPS was developed to extend the reach of surface vessels whose radar and sonar systems were limited by the physics of range and distance.

Putting Callaway's Seahawk two hundred miles in front of the *Luzon* allowed it to feed its data via LAMPS back to the ship in real time. This exponentially increased the *Luzon*'s ability to deal with surface and underwater threats beyond the horizon.

In effect, everything Lieutenant Callaway's Seahawk was seeing, optically or electronically, the CIC of the *Luzon* was also seeing.

It also meant that Admiral Talbot, several thousand miles away in Washington, D.C., was receiving the same real-time information. Because of the sensitive nature of the mission, President Ryan wanted his most experienced naval officer in charge of the operation. It was imperative that the *Glazov* be found and neutralized, but it was in no one's interest to start a shooting war with the Russians.

At least, not yet.

# 39

The heavy wipers slashed away the rain spattering the bridge windows but Captain Yevgraf still couldn't see a thing in the cloud-darkened night sky, including those damned American helicopters circling his ship high overhead – two MH-60R *Seahawks,* according to his electronic warfare officer.

Heavy cloud cover erased what little horizon he might have chased. A starless night lay like a blanket over the sea. Despite the heavy thrumming of his churning diesel motor belowdecks and the wind whistling in the rigging, Yevgraf couldn't help but feel if not hear the heavy beating of the Seahawk rotors booming above him.

He thought for sure they'd give up when the storm worsened. They'd dropped a dozen of their passive AN/SSQ-101 ADAR sonobuoys on their first run. His own sonar man had picked up the splashes of the three-foot-long, thirty-nine-pound devices. That meant the *Glazov* below heard the splashes, too – their sonar people were far superior to his own. And even a deaf sonarman would have heard the pinging of the Americans' active sonobuoys that followed.

*So what if the Americans had echo-located the sub?* Yevgraf chuckled. The *Glazov*'s captain was a cool customer – ice water for blood, and brass for balls. And smart. He just sat down there, waiting the Americans out. If he didn't move and didn't make a sound, the Americans would still have their doubts. And when the Seahawks finally left, he could surface and restock from *Penza*'s stores of food and fuel.

But rough seas delayed replenishment and the bastard choppers had returned.

The sound of the beating rotors was maddening. The grizzled Russian captain pulled the night-vision binoculars to his red-rimmed eyes. He scanned the sky again. Where the hell were they?

He couldn't see shit from inside the bridge. He barked at his XO. 'You have the conn.' He reminded the younger man to maintain course and speed, which was little more than holding their position against the tide. He didn't dare stray too far away from his comrade below with his batteries nearly expended.

Yevgraf pulled up the hood of his slicker and stepped out onto the starboard bridge wing some twenty-five meters above the water line. He cursed the roaring wind in his ears and the rain stinging his eyes. He felt more than saw a black shadow in an even blacker sky low in the distance.

He raised the binoculars to his eyes again – at exactly the wrong time.

Blinding light blasted his eyes.

The old Russian cursed violently, dropping his binoculars. He grabbed his aching eyes, praying the white-hot sunspot burning into his retinas would fade quickly. Rotor wash from the Seahawk hovering just six meters away from the bridge wing battered his body.

The blast from the Seahawk's thirty-million-candle-watt beam of short-arc xenon light was made worse because the dark had dilated Yevgraf's eyes, and the binocular lenses had magnified it.

Yevgraf's XO flung the bridge door open.

'Captain! The Americans are calling for you on the radio!'

Yevgraf's sight finally returned. He spun around and faced the fearsome helicopter, shielding his eyes from the blinding arc light. He could make out the shape of the four ship-killing Hellfires strapped beneath the port side stub wing pointed at his ship.

He flipped a bird at the helo and turned back inside the bridge.

Lieutenant Callaway fought the gusting winds with his controls to maintain his position parallel with the *Penza*'s bridge.

When the Russian captain flipped him off, Callaway and his copilot laughed.

'You see that, *Luzon*?' Callaway said in his comms. He knew the *Luzon*'s CIC was getting a live feed from his video camera, as well as the other Seahawk still circling overhead. The other bird had enough fuel for another fifteen minutes before needing to head back to the barn. His bird had forty. He hoped that was enough time.

'You think that old salt is pissed now? Just wait a minute,' *Luzon*'s radioman replied. 'But still, you better watch your six.'

'Roger that,' Callaway replied. The ATO killed the spot and they reengaged their night vision. Callaway saw three Russian two-man teams dashing out on deck, two armed with SA-25 'Willow' MANPADS, shoulder-fired anti-aircraft missiles, the other with an RPG. They each found covered firing points and raised their weapons skyward. The RPG team was focused on Callaway's bird. His ATO turned the spotlight on them and warned the other helo.

'You see those guys, Sara?' Callaway asked. With a short-handed air crew, AWO Sara Arendas was doing double duty tonight as both the bird's acoustic systems specialist and gunner, manning the pintle-mounted M60D 7.62 mm machine gun. She had a clear view of all three Russian teams through her NVGs.

'Got 'em, sir.'

Callaway heard Arendas racking the machine gun. 'Don't get an itchy finger just yet.'

'My finger's secured, sir. But say the word and I'll scratch those pukes right off the deck.'

If the Russians were that heavily armed, Callaway was glad he wasn't fast-roping SEALs or Marines onto the deck to seize the ship. Charging toward a rudder room below-decks with breacher charges and power saws was hard enough without getting shot at with automatic fire.

'Who the fuck is this?' Yevgraf demanded in thickly accented English.

'Lieutenant Commander Charles Ellis, U.S. Navy, commanding the USS *Luzon,* two hundred and twenty miles east-northeast of your position. Over.'

'And what do you want from me, Captain Ellis?'

'You are ordered to command the Russian Federation Navy submarine *Glazov* to surface immediately.'

'I have no idea what you're talking about, Commander,' Yevgraf shouted.

'Repeat, you are ordered to command the submarine *Glazov* to surface immediately.'

'You are mistaken, Commander. I am a civilian vessel. I am not —'

'Cut the shit, Ivan! You've got three choices in front of you. Two of them sinks your boat. One of them lets you sail back home in one piece.'

'This is an act of war. By what authority —'

'By the authority of the President of the United States.'

'I do not acknowledge your president's authority to attack my ship.'

'Acknowledged or not, it's going to happen. Ping *Glazov* to surface now or I will sink you. Then *Glazov* will have to surface and then I'll board him or sink him.'

'Even if I had the authority to comply –'

'Last chance, Captain. You have thirty seconds. I have sonobuoys in the water. I will know if you ping or not. Ping the *Glazov* up or watch your ship go down. Your choice. Over and out.'

Yevgraf swore violently as he slammed the radio mic back into its cradle. He shot a glance at his XO.

The executive officer knew that look all too well. Yevgraf wanted to fight. The old man had visions of dying gloriously for the Rodina.

The XO didn't.

'The *Luzon* will be here before the *Glazov* can be refueled and restocked, Captain. It'll have to surface no matter what. They kill us and the *Glazov* is stranded out here. *Glazov*'s only choice then will be to be boarded by the Americans or to scuttle.'

Yevgraf's eyes burned holes in the XO. He spat on the deck. *Coward!*

Nervous young crewmen froze at their stations. Everyone knew the old man was crazy.

The XO stood his ground. If he was going to die, he'd do it standing up to this broken-down old bastard. 'Our mission is to protect the *Glazov*.'

Yevgraf flashed a feral grin, then snatched up the intercom mic.

'Sonar room! This is Captain Yevgraf. Prepare to ping *Glazov*!'

# 40

The President held up the pitcher of water, offering to pour Arnie van Damm a glass.

Arnie sat on the couch, his face souring. 'Never touch the stuff.'

'Suit yourself.' Ryan filled a glass for himself and headed back over to the chair next to him.

'Admiral Talbot on line one for you, sir,' came over the intercom.

'Thank you, Betty,' President Ryan said. He stood and crossed over to his desk.

Arnie gestured as he rose from the couch that he'd leave but Ryan waved him back down. He punched the secure line and picked up.

'John, I hope this is good news.'

'The best possible news. We finally found the Ivan.'

Ryan grinned ear to ear. 'That's fantastic.' He threw a thumbs-up at Arnie.

'I won't bother you with the technical details,' Talbot said, 'but suffice it to say he's turned tail and run, and we're still on him. We'll track the *Glazov* all the way back to Vladivostok. If he tries to do anything stupid, we'll shove a couple of Mark 48s up his poop chute for the effort.'

'Make sure that everyone involved knows how much I

appreciate this and please congratulate them for me on a job well done.'

'I'll convey the message personally. Do I have permission to return the *Roosevelt* strike group to its original deployment?'

'As you see fit.'

'I'll contact Admiral Pike immediately.'

Ryan ended the call.

'That sounds like a win to me,' Arnie said. 'Score one for the Navy.'

'Yeah, feels pretty good, I have to admit,' Ryan said. 'It was a thousand-to-one shot.' His voice trailed off, his mind working a new problem.

'Jeez, don't break a leg jumping up and down for joy.'

Ryan glanced up. 'Say again? I wasn't listening.'

'You don't seem too happy.'

'I'm giddy as a schoolgirl.'

'Yeah, I can tell. What's the problem?'

'No problem. Not exactly.'

'Let me guess. You're worried that sub wasn't the pirate after all.'

'I've got no reason to think that.'

Arnie stood. 'Then it's time to celebrate. You probably just want more water,' he said, with a wink.

'Grab yourself a glass,' Ryan said, as he pulled open a desk drawer.

'Seriously, you're still worried?' Arnie said, crossing over to the service tray.

'We've tied a knot in the *Glazov*'s tail. We'll still have to deal with Yermilov on this but that's a problem for another day. For now, it's a win.'

Ryan uncorked the bottle of Jameson and poured a couple of fingers for each of them.

'As bad as this was, at least this thing was contained to the South Pacific. Imagine if it had gone global.'

'Amen to that.' Arnie lifted his glass. 'I propose a toast.'

Ryan lifted his.

'Arrr,' Arnie growled.

'Arrr.'

They drank.

It was a good day.

# 41

Aadhavan clutched the empty ice chest with one hand like his life depended upon it, because it did, and had, for the last two days. Its buoyancy sustained him as he drifted helplessly along with the current.

With the other hand he waved at the distant hull of a ship heading his way, or so his fevered mind had told him. Part of him hoped it wasn't true. If the ship was real and it passed him by, his soul would be poisoned by bitter disappointment on its journey into the next life.

The thirst tore at the inside of his throat like rats' claws beneath the unrelenting sun, even as the cool night breezes had chilled him to the bone despite the warmth of the water. At dawn, he had prayed to Lord Murugan to take him away from this living nightmare and give him the strength to simply let go and die. But he couldn't. He had two small children at home to feed and a wife with a crippled leg who couldn't work. He had to live, because they needed him. The sight of his children's small, hopeful faces made him want to weep with joy and grief all over again as he had for the last two days, but he had no tears left for them now. The water was all gone out of him.

And that was when his blurred eyes saw the smudge of oily diesel exhaust in the distance.

A ship. Surely it was real.

He tried to shout for help when he first saw it, but his voice was a ragged whisper, and all he could do was splash the water with one free hand and wave.

Thank the merciful gods he had persevered. Had not Murugan himself rewarded his faith by sending this ship to rescue him?

The blood on his scalp had finally dried, which meant he was no longer leaving a trail for the sharks to find him. But if he didn't get a drink of fresh water in the next twenty-four hours, he would die anyway and the big tiger sharks could have him.

He wondered if any of the killer fish had feasted on the friends he'd lost in the explosion. Probably not. The ship went up in a single, blinding blast that broke the vessel in half and sent them all to the bottom, where he would be now, too, if he hadn't been on the deck smoking a cigarette.

The explosion had tossed him over the railing headfirst, his scalp splitting open when it slammed into the rolled steel top rail before he hit the water. He swam furiously to escape the suck of the sinking boat that threatened to drag him down. But panic fueled his furious swimming and he escaped, barely.

He had swum back to the frothing swirl where the hull had slipped beneath the surface to search for survivors. There were none. But he found the watertight ice chest and clung to it for dear life as the current carried him away.

He realized he was hallucinating again. Was he even alive? Or in some perpetual watery hell for his sins?

He blinked his eyes, itching and dry despite the miles of ocean water surrounding him. He closed them for relief.

He was so tired. He felt his mind plunging toward a deep well of black, comforting sleep . . .

Aadhavan startled awake just as he heard a splash nearby.

Panicked, he turned toward the sound, ready to claw at the black eyes of the shark as it charged him. But he saw instead a young man, white like a fish, a smile on his face at the bow of a black rubber boat. Another man ran the outboard motor.

'Hey! You! Hold on!' the man in the bow shouted.

The sailor's eyes ached as he cried, or tried to, with relief. He couldn't believe his good fortune.

He had survived.

His wife and children would survive.

The sailor glanced up at his salvation. He shielded his eyes against the blinding morning sun. He could make out the shape of the great steel ship in the near distance. A fishing trawler. Men stood like shadows on the deck, leaning over the railing, staring in his direction.

The engine reversed hard and the rubber hull stopped on a dime near the sailor. The engine cut out.

The Tamil sailor reached up with one hand to grab the hull but there was no handhold. His fingers slipped away. He croaked in desperation as he released the ice chest and threw both hands toward the boat to save himself, but he was too weak.

*Splash!* The white man jumped in the water and grabbed the sailor from behind.

'Hold on there, fella! I got ya,' he said as he wrapped a nylon rope around the Tamil sailor's dark, emaciated torso.

The other man in the boat pulled the rope toward him, lifting the near drowning man above the surface.

'You speak English?' the man in the water asked.

'A . . . little,' the sailor whispered.

'Any of your friends out here with you?'

'None . . . sir.'

'You sure?'

Aadhavan nodded, his voice spent. His eyes pleaded, *Please haul me into the boat.*

'Okay, then. If you're sure,' the white man said, still supporting his torso in his strong arms. 'Time to take care of you.'

The sailor managed a weak smile, thinking of his children. 'Thank you . . . sir.'

His blinking eyes caught sight of the second man in the boat standing unsteadily by the motor, the sun behind his back. He lifted an anchor and tossed it over the side with a heavy splash. It sped toward the ocean floor.

Aadhavan was confused. The waters here were over four thousand meters deep. An anchor –

He felt the white man's grip release from around his chest just as the nylon rope jerked against his flesh.

Aadhavan's sickening cry was swallowed by the sea as his body was yanked beneath the surface.

The two men watched the last of the Tamil's air bubbles break the surface a minute later.

'Helluva thing,' the man in the water said, reaching up a hand. 'We need to call it in to *el jefe* and clear out of here.'

The man in the boat reached down and helped his shorter friend out of the water and into the Zodiac.

The taller one lifted a satellite phone to his ear as the short one cranked the big Suzuki engine. It was dirty work, but that was the job, the short one thought, the image of the Tamil's screaming face dragged down into the deep flashing in his mind. He shrugged it off. They'd be back on the trawler in fifteen minutes, and Cookie would have hot coffee and donuts waiting for them in the galley.

# October 28

# 42

*Washington, D.C.*
*The White House Residence*

He had given up much of his privacy when he took the oath of office, but President Ryan drew the line at his bed.

The idea of a stranger's hand shaking him awake as he lay next to Cathy in the middle of the night was abhorrent to him, a breach of matrimonial sanctity that he could hardly fathom. The few times it had happened it shocked him. He wasn't a young boot at Quantico anymore; he was a grown-ass man, and the commander in chief. Wasn't he entitled to this last, least bit of privacy?

Of course, he trusted the Secret Service detail with his life, and they had both the right and obligation to enter his bedroom and wake him under extreme circumstances. He'd defined 'extreme circumstances' to SAIC Gary Montgomery, the head of the PPD, to mean war, or extreme loss of life, or anything involving his wife and children. Other than that, the door stayed shut until business hours the next morning, starting at six a.m.

But Ryan wasn't so vain as to put his own personal comforts ahead of the national interest, and there were plenty of emergencies that needed to be addressed at the worst hours of the night. He gave Arnie van Damm and a few select others – his children, mostly – the right to call him on his private number anytime, day or night.

When his private cell phone rang with its distinctive Arnie van Damm ringtone at four a.m., Ryan's eyes bolted open.

'Arnie?'

'Don't shoot the messenger, boss.'

Jack rolled out of bed, careful not to pull the covers off his wife as he did so. He padded barefoot across the plush carpet and out of the bedroom, quietly closing the door behind him, and headed for the kitchen to make coffee.

'What's up?'

'You said to call you the minute we heard anything. I just got word from Admiral Talbot that there's been another sinking.'

'Where?'

'The Indian Ocean.'

Ryan shoveled scoops of Black Rifle Murdered Out extra-dark coffee into the paper filter.

'When?'

'Two days ago.'

'Why are we just hearing about this now?'

'Apparently it was out in the middle of nowhere, and the local port authority didn't bother notifying anybody that it didn't arrive until two hours ago.'

'Wasn't somebody monitoring the AIS signals when it disappeared?'

'Somebody was out on a smoke break when it happened or it could have been a software glitch. We don't know. Talbot's on the warpath and running this down.'

Ryan stuck the glass carafe under the running kitchen faucet.

'This isn't the way I wanted to start the day.'

'Not good news, I know. I thought you should hear it from me, and hear it right away.'

'You did the right thing.' Ryan sighed. He poured the pot

of water into the reservoir and hit the start button, willing the machine to begin wheezing out the first drops of liquid black gold.

'What do you want me to do, boss?'

'Call the group together. We've got a real problem on our hands now. Bad enough this thing was running loose in the South Pacific. Now it looks like we'll have to police the whole damn planet.'

# 43

*Barcelona, Spain*

Brossa pushed through the heavy door of the CNI office suites. She was greeted with a round of applause from Peña and the rest of the administrative staff.

'There she is. Our hero!' Peña said, still clapping.

Brossa blushed with embarrassment but shook hands with or hugged the staff that came over to congratulate her. The story had broken on the news the night before, with overhead helicopter images of Brossa and her digitally blurred head charging toward the farmhouse just before it exploded. But everybody in the CNI office knew it was her, and proudly shared in her achievement.

Drinks and pastries were set out for the celebration.

'Everybody, please, enjoy!' Peña said, pointing at the small buffet. He turned to Brossa. 'Something to eat or drink?'

'Just water, please.'

He handed her a bottled water and grabbed one for himself. He noticed the small bandage on her cheek. He frowned. 'You were wounded?'

'A scratch. It's nothing, really.'

'I spoke with Captain Asensio. It must have been terrible.'

'Can I have a word with you privately?' Brossa asked.

'*Por supuesto.* Let's go to my office.' He led the way.

Brossa endured more hugs and handshakes with a weary smile as she passed through the lobby. She was, indeed, grateful for their reception despite her bone-deep fatigue.

Peña motioned for Brossa to take a seat. He plopped down in the chair behind his desk.

'I wish you would have taken the day off, Laia. You must be exhausted from your ordeal. Besides, you're a hero. You deserve it.'

'I'm no hero, and there is still so much work to do.'

Peña chuckled. 'Which is why I knew you'd be in here today. Still, work fills the time allotted. Another day wouldn't matter, now that those *cabrónes* are dead, thank God. You must be very proud.'

'I'm glad that none of the Guardia Civil were killed. Those idiots in the farmhouse shouldn't have attacked us. I was surprised when they did.'

'Captain Asensio said that you were very brave. Of course, the news footage showed us that.'

'Asensio and his men led the charge. They were the brave ones. I just followed behind them.'

'Still, I think you can expect nothing less than a commendation for heroism. Perhaps even a promotion. I'm recommending both to Madrid later today.'

'That's very generous of you, but really, I was just doing my job.'

Peña pointed a fatherly finger at her. 'That's why I like you so much, Laia. So humble! But don't sell yourself short. A promotion means better pay, and a commendation for heroism moves you up the career ladder even faster.'

Brossa shrugged and smiled a little, uncertain as to what she should say. She took a sip of water.

Peña leaned forward on his desk, clasping his hands together. 'Asensio gave me a brief report about what happened. What's your take on it?'

'Things went very fast after we arrived on scene. For a moment, I thought everything would resolve itself peacefully.'

'Those animals didn't want peace. They wanted revolution.'

Brossa ignored his comment. 'They asked for a lawyer and promised to surrender peacefully if the warrant proved valid, which it was.'

'I assume the captain saw through their deception –'

'I'm not sure it was a deception.'

'You think they really would have surrendered peacefully?'

'We'll never know, will we?'

Peña waved a dismissive hand. 'Well, if that was the case, it falls on Asensio, doesn't it? He was the commander in charge. But any review board will defer to his combat experience, though I doubt there will be one. The case is closed now that the threat is removed, and justice is served. Madrid is happy. I am happy. You should be happy, too.'

'I am. But I can't help thinking that a lot of young Spaniards died yesterday.'

'Not Spaniards. Terrorist killers. They just happened to have been born in this country. Don't forget, they bombed a civilian target, and killed and wounded many civilians. And for what? Politics? It's beyond stupid. Seriously, Laia, I wouldn't lose a minute's sleep over them.'

'I suppose you're right. Still, it would have been better to arrest them and extract intel from them.'

'Yes, I agree. But you know how it is. We train. We take precautions. We make plans. We execute those plans. But in the end, you can't control outcomes, especially if the other party is intent on suicide. *Dios mío.*'

'It's so strange to me that they would rather commit suicide than fight their battles in court. They would have earned free publicity for their cause for months, maybe years, here, and all around the world.'

'If you want my opinion? They wanted to be martyrs. And

I think those bastards wanted you to charge in before they exploded that bomb to take the entire team out. That's why they threw the grenade. One of them must have panicked and triggered the bomb inside too early. You are all fortunate to be alive.' Peña quickly crossed himself in the Catholic manner, but sloppily.

'Yes, I know. Very lucky. I'm just frustrated that the case died with them. Hopefully we can pull more intelligence out when the rubble is cleared. I stayed until dark, but the stones and timbers were hard to move and there were no lights. And the blood . . .' Brossa's voice trailed off.

'I saw such things years ago when the *Vasco*' – Basque – 'were bombing the country. I know how you feel. It is quite distressing. You really should take some time off. Spend time with your father.'

'I'm fine. There are just some loose ends I still want to tie off. I think there's a possibility the Brigada Catalan was working with another group. We still haven't identified one man who was killed at L'avi' – she was referencing Runtso, only Jack still hadn't told her his name – 'and then there's this guy.'

Brossa reached into her purse and pulled out her phone. She opened up her message app and pulled up Jack's picture of the guy who broke into his place. The paper mask was on his face and the black Nike ball cap was on his head, but the hazel eyes really stood out. She handed her phone to Peña.

'Who's this?'

'No idea,' Brossa said. 'But he was near L'avi when the bomb went off. I have reason to believe he might be involved.'

'Reason? What reason?' Peña brought the phone closer to his face and expanded the picture.

'Maybe "reason" is too strong a word. More like a hunch.' Brossa shifted in her chair. 'I thought perhaps he was with

Brigada Catalan. But those eyes are hard to forget, and I have not seen them before. I've been back over the files of known Brigada members. He wasn't among them.'

'Yes, I see what you mean about the eyes. Perhaps our files are incomplete.'

'I was hoping you might recognize him.'

'I don't, but then again, my memory isn't what it used to be. But I agree with you, I don't recall this man in any of our Brigada files.' He studied the picture again. 'Where did you say you got this photo?'

'Jack Ryan sent it to me yesterday.'

'Ryan?' Peña rolled his eyes. 'I thought you told him to go home.'

'I did. He decided to stay a few more days.'

'I don't care what Madrid says. That American is a pain in the ass. The sooner he leaves, the better.'

'He's a nice man, even if he is a little pushy.'

'Where did he get the photo?'

'He didn't say. I was hoping this man with the hazel eyes was at the farmhouse and to interrogate him. But then the firefight happened. I tried going through the rubble to see if he was among them. But it wasn't possible, given the situation of the building and the condition of the bodies.'

'Do you have any reason why you think this man was in that building?'

'Ryan thinks he's the bomber.'

'Why?'

'I don't know. But it's a lead, and I'd like to find out, one way or another. If he was in the farmhouse, that means he was connected to Brigada, either directly or indirectly.'

Peña smiled with relief. 'That's an easy problem to solve. Once the remains are fully recovered and brought here, I'll tell the coroner to search for a pair of hazel eyes. Even if they are no longer attached to his skull, that will tell us something, right?'

'If his remains haven't been completely vaporized, we might be able to ID him, and perhaps link him to whatever organization he's with.'

'He might have been a loner.' He held up her phone. 'Will you forward me a copy of this photo?'

'Of course.'

She thought about Jack's insistence that Aleixandri wore a Bluetooth even though they never found it or her phone. She admitted to herself that it was odd not to find a phone on or near her because everybody under eighty had a cell phone these days.

It was also a strange coincidence that this hazel-eyed man wore a Bluetooth, as Jack reminded her in his text. If all of that was true, it seemed as if this mysterious man might have directed the L'avi attack, which meant he had some kind of authority or leadership. It seemed highly unlikely that Brigada would take direction from an outsider unaffiliated with any organization they could trust. And loners typically weren't leaders of organizations.

'I doubt he was acting on his own.'

'We'll have to wait and see what they find in the ruins.' Peña handed her phone back.

'But what if he was never in the ruins?' she said as she forwarded the Bykov photo to Peña's e-mail address.

'Suppose he wasn't. What would that tell you?'

'That our only other suspect is still on the loose, and if he is, I intend to catch him and find out exactly what this has all been about.'

'Or it could mean he had nothing to do with any of this.

He just happened to be in the area when the L'avi bomb went off, as were hundreds of other people.'

'It's impossible to know which, isn't it? So that's even more reason to find him.'

Peña laughed. 'Laia Brossa, you are relentless. It is your best quality. I trust you will remember your old friend Peña after you become the director of our illustrious organization?'

Brossa rubbed her head, trying to push away a headache. Peña frowned with concern. 'You're not well.'

'Just tired.'

'I wish you would go home and rest.'

She glanced at him, her eyes narrowed by the pain pounding inside of her skull. 'One last thing. This Sammler fellow. Is he still a dead end?'

'Completely. Whatever Ryan thought he heard was obviously wrong.'

She nodded. 'Perhaps you are right.'

'Of course I'm right. All that matters is that the people who killed Ryan's friend – and many other people, I will remind you – are all dead. Ryan wanted his justice, and now he has it. Next time you see him, tell him to go home.'

Brossa stood. 'I think I will take you up on your offer and take the rest of the day off. And please thank the office staff for the warm welcome.'

Peña rose from his chair. 'I will convey your thanks, and yes, please do take the rest of the day off. Tomorrow as well, if you need it. I'll handle all of the paperwork. And I promise you that if the coroner comes up with anything, I'll call you straightaway.'

She thanked him again. Peña escorted her to his office door, which he closed and locked after her.

He tracked her egress from the CNI suite to the street

260

below via the office security cameras. Once he was certain she was gone for good, he unlocked one of his desk drawers, removed a Faraday bag, and pulled out an encrypted satellite phone from it. A voice picked up on the other end.

Peña was to the point.

'We have a problem.'

# 44

*South China Sea*

Guzmán took another puff of his Marlboro, his pants gathered around his ankles. He was almost finished with his business in the cramped quarters of the captain's head, the only private shitter on the boat and, thankfully, his alone for the duration. He had needed the privacy. A dead galley refrigerator killed their beef stores two weeks ago. A steady diet of greasy fried fish and fish head soup since then had worked its toll on his gut.

The boat's actual captain had to do his duty with the others belowdecks.

*Rank hath its privileges,* he laughed to himself, taking his last drag. His encrypted satellite phone rang beyond the thin mahogany door.

Guzmán swore. That phone was only for emergencies. He needed to answer it. He quickly cleaned himself, yanked his filthy, fish-stained pants back on, and flushed the toilet, tossing the spent butt in after it. As it gurgled away into the black water tank in the hold of the ship – soon to be dumped into the ocean – he fought his way out of the confined space and into the wider but still cramped quarters, snatching up the ringing sat phone from the bed.

He saw that it was Peña. The Brigada killings had gone perfectly, according to Bykov. Why the call?

'*Digame.*'

'We have a problem.'

'Be more specific.'

'Brossa just left my office. She knows who Bykov is.'

'Impossible. How could she know?'

'She doesn't know his name, but she has a picture of him. She thinks he's connected to L'avi.'

'How would she know that?'

'That *hijo de puta* American has been sniffing around.'

'The one that Bykov was checking out? Ryan?'

Guzmán sighed through his broad nose, frustrated. It was too soon for DNA results, and the audio bugs had failed, thanks to Ryan's resourcefulness. What concerned him was that the big American went on the offensive and chased off Bykov, nearly capturing him. Whoever the hell this Ryan character was, he was dangerous.

'Brossa is relentless,' Peña said. 'She won't let go until she runs Bykov down.'

'Why are you telling me this? Take care of it.'

'Me? No, *jefe*. You don't pay me to kill people. You pay me for information. Let your man Bykov do the job. He's better equipped to handle it.'

'Fine. I'll instruct Bykov to take care of Brossa – and Jack Ryan. If Bykov calls you for assistance, I expect you to give it.'

'Of course. Any information I have, I'll pass along.'

'Excellent, Peña. Thank you for the call. Keep me posted.'

'Will do, *jefe*.'

Guzmán killed the call.

Peña was right. Bykov was singularly qualified to kill, unlike that buffoon Peña. Bykov was also loyal to the organization, his brothers-in-arms. Peña was the true mercenary, selling his services for cash. The Spaniard was both greedy and cowardly, and while greedy men aren't easily trusted, cowards were utterly untrustworthy, valuing their own skins above all other loyalties. Such men were treacherous in the extreme.

Guzmán picked up the satellite phone again and punched the speed-dial number for Bykov. Brossa and Ryan had to die.

So did Peña. Preferably in a manner worthy of his cowardice.

Bykov would enjoy that.

# 45

*Washington, D.C.*
*Situation Room, The White House*

President Ryan sat at the head of the long mahogany table again, surrounded by his same trusted advisers. Two days ago, they were dealing with an uncertain situation in the South Pacific. Today they were confronted by a full-blown global crisis. Their faces showed it. The same map of the oceans of the world was displayed on the big-screen monitor but now with an additional seventh green cargo ship with an *X* overlaid upon it. That seventh *X* sat in the middle of the Indian Ocean west of Australia.

Time to marshal the troops.

'Anybody here as pissed off as I am?' Ryan asked.

That elicited a few nervous chuckles.

'It was bad enough when we thought we were chasing a Russian diesel sub. We had as much chance of finding that as buying seven winning lottery tickets in a row – isn't that what you said, John?'

'Yes, sir. I did.'

'But we did it, didn't we?'

Heads nodded.

'And now, it looks like we're *really* screwed.' Ryan pointed at the wide-screen monitor. 'Whoever the hell was jerking our chain in the middle of the South Pacific has decided to expand his operations into the Indian Ocean. Any doubts they will spread out even farther if we don't stop them?'

Heads shook.

'I think this makes it even harder to find whoever's behind this.' Ryan's eyes scanned the room. 'But I don't give a damn about the odds, because I'm putting all my chips down on this table, on each of you, right now.' He stabbed the polished mahogany with his finger for emphasis. 'And I figure that puts the odds back in my favor.'

He leaned back in his chair, daring them to argue with him.

Arnie gave him a wink. *Good job, boss.*

'We're still tracking the *Glazov*, Admiral?' SecState said, breaking the silence.

'Yes, sir. Given the events in the IO, it's a safe bet he wasn't the culprit to begin with – but just in case, we're following him all the way back home.'

'Can we take the Russians off the board altogether?' the SecDef asked.

'Not if the Russians are using more than just one diesel-electric boat,' Talbot said. 'But given the fact the Russians called off the *Glazov*, I'd say they aren't our prime suspect at the moment.'

'How do we know that?' Arnie asked.

'We intercepted a Russian satellite comm to the boat. It wasn't secure.'

'Meaning they wanted us to know they'd called their dog off?' Arnie said.

'Exactly.'

'Should we dispatch a carrier group to the Indian Ocean? If nothing else, it sends a message,' SecDef said. 'Carrier strike group three is on station in the Arabian Sea. We could redirect.'

'Maybe that's the point of all of this. Keep us chasing our tails all over the planet,' Talbot said, 'and disrupt our current operations. I'd advise against it.'

'Agreed,' Ryan said. 'But where does that leave us?'

'Sunzabitches,' Arnie growled.

'Mary Pat, we ruled out the Chinese before. Any new information to change our minds on that?'

The DNI shook her head. 'No. None of our sources, inside or out, have found any mention at all of an operation like this.'

'Good. We've ruled out the NORKs, the Indians, and just about every other naval power with the capacity. Sounds to me like this isn't an officially sanctioned government operation.' Ryan rubbed his chin, thinking out loud. 'We already ruled out the possibility of a criminal syndicate or a terrorist organization. Do we need to revisit?'

'Would they have the ability to run submarine operations on a scale like this?' Adler asked.

'First thing they'd need is a submarine – more than one, as it turns out,' the SecDef said.

Talbot turned on a different video monitor and flipped through several screens until he pulled up what he was looking for – the Web page for Triton Submarines, a civilian manufacturer. They looked like round glass fishbowls on top of fat sleds. Some had exterior operating arms and claws.

'This is just one example from one company – Triton makes good rigs. They've got one that's rated to thirty-six thousand feet – it dives the Marianas Trench, the deepest place on the planet.'

'They look like spacecraft from a fifties sci-fi movie,' Arnie said. 'Not like weapons systems.'

'They're meant for exploration, maintenance – even eco-tourism. I'm not saying these subs are the prime culprits, only that there are significant civilian platforms that could accomplish the mission profile. But if you ask me, I'd say we're looking for a military sub design, not one of these.'

'Any possibility that a civilian could get ahold of a surplus military sub?' Arnie asked.

'For the right price, sure. Osama bin Laden was in the market for one before the FBI nixed the deal. The problem is, you need more than a boat. You need trained crews, supply vessels, maintenance facilities. It's not like driving a paddleboat at a city park.'

'The drug cartels have operated at least nine hundred narco-boats over the years. They're not subs, exactly, but they sit low enough in the water that they evade detection,' Foley said. 'Mainland Chinese car-smuggling gangs use something similar.'

'Those kinds of vessels don't have the range we've been talking about.'

Arnie laughed. 'Okay, I just have to admit it. I was messing around on the Internet last night thinking about this stuff and came across this crazy story about the Russian Navy using a beluga whale for underwater cameras or something.'

'We still have the U.S. Navy Marine Mammal Program. Hell, back in the day, we trained dolphins to do all kinds of combat operations,' Talbot said.

'What are we saying?' SecState Adler said. 'We're looking for a fish?'

'No, but, Arnie, I think you're onto something,' Ryan said.

'I am?'

'We're all loyal to our prejudices. We have the best technology in the world, but somehow, these assholes are beating us at every turn. Our prejudice is our high technology. What if these shitbirds are going low tech?'

'Low tech? How does low tech beat high tech?' Arnie asked.

'Ask the Afghanis how they beat the British and Soviet

empires, not to mention the fact we're going on nineteen years fighting them. It's called asymmetric warfare,' the Sec-Def said.

'Asymmetric is more about tactics and strategy,' Ryan said. 'I want to focus on tech for a moment.'

Ryan pointed at the admiral. 'John, how can a ship or submarine avoid radar and sonar?'

The CNO shrugged. 'Radar is easy to avoid. Get outside of its range or, easier still, go underwater. Radar waves don't propagate under the surface.'

'And sonar?'

'Sonar operates like radar but uses sound waves. Active sonar sends a signal out, hits a target, and the sound waves are reflected back to the source. Passive sonar simply listens for any sound waves generated by the target itself. You defeat active sonar by absorbing or deflecting the active ping, and you defeat passive sonar by remaining silent.'

'And how do you absorb or deflect sonar waves?'

'Diving deep never hurts, especially if the sonar source remains above the thermocline. But an easier way is what the Germans started doing in World War Two, which was using rubber coating on their sub hulls. We use more high-tech materials, but essentially, it's the same idea. Electric boats are quiet because of the electric engines but even nuke boats are getting damn quiet. Everything on a sub is designed for silence. Hell, submariners even wear rubber-soled shoes to keep from making noise when they walk. These boats are so quiet now that back in 2009 a British and a French boomer actually collided with each other even though they both had passive sonar up and running.'

'Anything else? I mean, low tech?' Ryan said.

'Low tech? How about no tech? The fact of the matter is, the bigger you are, the easier you are to find with either sonar or radar. It's a damn sight easier to see a basketball than a BB at two hundred yards. Smaller is always better.'

Ryan stood. 'So here's what I'm thinking. Something small. Something quiet – electric powered. Something that runs underwater to avoid radar. Something with sound-absorbing materials to avoid active sonar.'

'You're talking about a damned underwater drone,' Arnie said.

Ryan grinned. 'Not me, pal. That was you.'

'It was?'

'Yeah, you were thinking out of the box. You just didn't realize it.'

'But you said low tech. Drones aren't low tech.'

'Drones are *old* tech. Nikola Tesla had the first patent on one back in 1898 – a radio-controlled boat he called the "tele-automaton." Drones aren't new, they're just improved.'

'Come to think of it, the Germans had a remote-controlled explosive boat in World War One,' Talbot said.

'The damn Houthis have one now, running 'em in the Persian Gulf,' Burgess added. 'They take speedboats powered with Yamaha outboards and pack 'em with explosives.'

'Excuse me. Are we going back to the Poseidon idea?' Foley asked.

'No. I agree with John. They're too expensive and too untested for something on this scale,' Ryan said. 'And it's pretty clear to me now the Russian government isn't involved with this.'

'Drones can't be the answer,' the admiral said. 'Even the autonomous ones are short range – except for the new Orca XLUUV, which we're building now. Fuel cells give it a range of sixty-five hundred nautical miles. Nobody on the planet has that system now except for us.'

'I know. But I wasn't thinking long range.'

'Short range doesn't work.'

'Sure it does.' Ryan turned to Burgess. 'You remember the old Q-ships from World War One?'

'No, sir. I've got gray hair, but I'm not *that* old.'

A round of polite laughter rippled around the table.

Ryan grinned. 'Subs were the newest naval tech in World War One, and the Brits didn't have the ability to either find or sink them. So they started converting merchant vessels into sub hunters. They put up false superstructures to change their appearance, and hid deck guns behind the facades. U-boats would see them, think they were harmless merchantmen, and surface to take them out with their own deck guns, only to watch the facades drop and the Q-ship guns open up.'

Ryan stood and pointed at the bigger screen displaying the locations of the sunken vessels. 'John, can you pull up the map that displays all of the AIS ships currently at sea?'

'Sure.' He clicked a button on his laser pointer. Tens of thousands of arrowheads in a variety of colors swarmed across the sea lanes, mostly hugging coastlines, but many traversing the open waters.

Ryan nodded toward the screen. 'Our bad guys are out there in the middle of all of that, hunters hunting prey.'

'So you think Q-ships are behind this?' Arnie asked.

'Not Q-ships. Mother ships.'

'You mean, for the drones?'

'Yeah. And tell me this, where's the best place to hide anything?'

'In plain sight,' Foley said, thinking about the dead drops she used to use when she was a cowboy CIA operative in Moscow. She'd stuff coded messages inside of dead pigeons, dead rats, even dead cats. 'But disguised.'

'Exactly.'

'You think one or more of those ships on the board are a mother ship?' Arnie asked.

'Bingo. And if we can't find the drone – small, silent, invisible – we find the mother ship.'

'Do you think one mother ship can control drones in both the Pacific and Indian Oceans?' Foley asked Talbot.

'Not likely.'

Arnie pointed at the map again. 'Thirty thousand boats on the water right now. Could be any one of them. Container ship. Cargo ship. Tanker. Could be five, could be ten, could be a hundred of them.' He turned back to Ryan. 'You may have figured it out, but you haven't exactly solved the problem.'

'Like I said before, simple, not easy.'

He turned to the SecState and SecDef. 'This thing is too big for us to handle now. We need to start reaching out to people we can trust and get some help. You two get together with John and come up with a list of people who understand the gravity of the situation – and who know how to keep a lid on this thing. If we thought the markets might get rattled earlier, well, this will cause a firestorm.'

'Understood,' Burgess said. The others nodded in agreement.

He turned to Foley. 'Let's find someone over at DARPA. They're on the cutting edge of this stuff. Let's get some of their people noodling on this problem – but without blowing any whistles.'

'I know just the person to call.'

'Do it, please. And do we have any idea if Buck Logan has had any success with his efforts?'

'He's putting his security teams on his company-owned vessels, with automatic weapons and Stinger missiles,' Foley said.

'Do I want to know how you know this?'

'No, sir, you don't,' Foley said with a smile.

'Any other ideas?' Ryan asked the room.

Heads shook. 'Okay, then let's get after it.'

# 46

*Houston, Texas*

Buck Logan was a true paraplegic, having lost the use of his body from the L4-L5 lumbar region of his spine all the way down to the tips of his toes. His high-T libido still raged within his broken frame. He turned all of that frustrated sexual energy into building an empire, trading a lifelong commitment to one woman for an unbreakable bond with his destiny. He transformed his previous talent for feminine conquest into domination of his business competitors, doing to them in contract negotiations what he could no longer do to the buxom young cheerleaders he bedded as a youth.

While the lower half of his nerve-damaged body was unresponsive and weak, he religiously trained the upper half. He was in the middle of a German Volume Training exercise, doing ten sets of ten repetitions on a military press. His wheelchair was parked beneath a Smith machine with forty-five-pound iron plates on either side of the bar. Buck had the place to himself when he chose to work out there.

The door to the corporate gym pushed open. Phil Werley, his liaison to all things Fed, especially DNI Foley, came through the door.

Logan grunted out his last rep and rolled his wrists, slamming the hooks of the stop bars.

'Why the long face, Phil? Somebody cornhole your little sister?' Logan said, breathing heavily, speaking at Werley's reflection in the mirror.

'Just got word from a friend. Another boat's gone down. Not confirmed yet, but it seems to fit the profile of the other ones.'

Logan unlocked his chair, ducked his massive head beneath the weight bar, and spun around, his face reddened.

Whether it was reddened from the workout or the bad news, Werley wasn't sure.

'One of ours?'

'No, sir. Some Indian rust bucket. Went down west of Perth. The Aussies found the wreckage – or what was left of it. No survivors.'

'That's the IO, not the South Pacific. Guess these pukes are upping their game.'

'White House is pretty lathered up by it. They thought they had this thing nailed down when they cornered the Russian boat. Now they don't know who's behind it.'

'Goddamn it.' Logan swore long and low. 'So, I take it, still no witnesses, no radar tracks, no sonar hits, and no fucking clue at all who did this?'

Werley knew his boss wasn't actually asking him a question.

'They're putting their heads together in D.C. on all of this. My understanding is that they're working on a new plan and getting ready to roll it out.'

'What plan?'

'Moving air, sea, and space assets into place, where and when they can. It's high priority, but not at the expense of ongoing combat operations.'

'You mean Ryan's only putting his johnson halfway in.'

'It will take a few days. They're hoping for an electronic solution. There doesn't seem to be much chance of eyes-on at this point.'

'Ryan hasn't panicked? Called in the cavalry?'

'He's as worried as you are about roiling the markets. Until now, it's still just the Aussies, the Kiwis, and us who are tackling this thing, but now that it's moved to the Indian Ocean, all bets are off.'

'And our plans?'

'Rolling out as we discussed.'

'If the Russians aren't behind this, who is? Gimme your best guess.'

'My guess? The Chi-Comms. I think it's a test of one of their new weapons systems – and a test of our existing ones.'

'Not the Russians?' Logan asked.

Werley chuckled. 'Ivan? Are you kidding me? The Russian economy is smaller than Canada's – even smaller than Texas's. They don't want to pick a fight with us in the South Pacific, or the IO, for that matter. They're more worried about the PLA Navy than us.'

'If the Chinese are behind this, what will Ryan do about it?'

'Without proof? I wouldn't do a damn thing if I were him.'

'And when he gets his proof?'

Werley shook his head. 'I don't even want to think about it.' He snorted. 'Hope to God I'm wrong. I probably am. Even the Chinese can't be that crazy. I just can't figure out who else would have the capability of doing this – whatever the hell "this" is.'

Logan's eyes narrowed. 'Daddy always said, "Bad news comes in threes." Another shoe's gonna drop. I can feel it in my bones. It's just a matter of where, and when, and how bad.'

Logan dismissed Werley with a grunt as he turned back around to the Smith machine. He watched the door close behind Werley in the workout mirror as he wrapped his gorilla hands around the steel bar.

*The world can wait,* he thought. *The iron can't.*

He'd done his part.

# 47

## *Oak Ridge, Tennessee*

The drive over to the computer lab was another perk of the job. The green, pine-studded hills and crisp fall air of East Tennessee lifted her spirits this morning. Parsons's spirits had needed lifting, as she dreaded the so-called emergency meeting Rhodes had scheduled via text early yesterday.

Usually these emergency meetings were like nursing calls. Rhodes would hit the panic button and Nurse Parsons would run into his room fearing the worst only to discover that all he needed was his filthy bedpan emptied.

Rhodes was a trained physicist, for sure, and not without some talent in the lab. He was also a scratch golfer. The fact he had a Ph.D. in physics didn't mean he was good enough to drive the science at the lab any more than his par golf meant he could beat Tiger Woods at the Masters.

She pulled her pearl white Subaru Outback into the tree-lined parking lot. She found a space next to the sign announcing RESERVED FOR DIRECTOR RHODES, and his silver G-Class Mercedes wagon. She killed the engine, keeping her eyes on the Mercedes, a vehicle she'd like to own one day but never could on her government salary. Rhodes had been smart enough to segue into the private sector early. He made great money as a partner at a lobbying firm for a big defense contractor before transitioning back into the public sector.

Good for him.

The man might not have been a world-class scientist, but he was brilliant in his own way, discovering early in his career that he was a supremely gifted politician, both in the boardroom and on Capitol Hill. The DOE had decided they needed a man like him to run the program since it was a federally funded project. Quantum bits and entangled particles didn't fuel RAPTURE.

Money did.

That was okay by her.

Parsons smiled at the uniformed guard in the glass booth. He nodded back a little too eagerly, his wolfish eyes raking over her hard, lean body dressed in form-fitting slacks and a turtleneck sweater beneath a lambswool vest.

She passed by the sign in red letters, NO STICKER, NO PHONE, warning her that if her government-issued cell phone didn't have the required security sticker, it couldn't be taken into the area where she was heading.

No problem. Parsons was a stickler for the rules, particularly when it came to security.

Dr David Rhodes greeted Dr Kate Parsons at the door, holding a cup of black coffee out to her.

'I know it's early. I picked this up for you.'

'Thanks, David.'

'Please, have a seat.'

She sat in the buttery soft leather chair across from his desk as he took his seat. Her phone buzzed. 'Mind if I get this text?'

'Of course not.'

He watched her flip through her text one-handed, an unlacquered thumbnail scrolling through a block of words while sipping coffee with the other hand. She was a real worker.

Parsons was an attractive woman, for sure. Not cover-girl hot but striking nonetheless, he thought, with her short red hair and dark green eyes. Those were hard to miss. Parsons was the kind of woman that turned heads when she passed by. There was an energy about her, due in part to her incredible athleticism. He chided himself for paying a little too much attention to her shapely figure whenever she walked into a room, and especially when she walked out of it.

He was happily married, but he wasn't dead, was he?

But it was Parsons's incredible intellect that electrified a room. Beautiful women didn't intimidate him, but brilliant minds like hers did. He was no slouch in the education department – a Stanford Ph.D. meant something – but his brain didn't hold a candle to hers.

But it wasn't really her brains or her good looks that made him painfully self-conscious when he was around her.

It was guilt.

If IQ were the sole hiring criterion, Parsons would be running the RAPTURE project. But for all of her many and considerable assets, Kate was lacking in people skills. Sure, she was perfectly friendly, and an excellent communicator. She had done a great job leading the initial team and laying the foundation for a project that would likely change history, maybe more so than the Manhattan Project.

He always thought that it was fitting that RAPTURE was also being designed in Oak Ridge. Even the building they were sitting in was within shouting distance of the original graphite reactor. Ironic that the geniuses assembled to conquer nuclear power on the Oak Ridge campus so many decades ago didn't have a single computer to rely on, whereas RAPTURE was only and all about computational power.

Much like Parsons. She was nothing but computational power. Her eyes bore through you like a laser when she asked

279

you questions that you both knew you couldn't answer, and made you burn with shame. She was always the smartest person in the room. Everybody knew it and everybody hated her for it because she lacked the grace to hide the obvious.

Now that RAPTURE was a fully funded federal program, new skill sets were required. It meant lobbying on the Hill, shaking the right hands, and turning the impossibly complex into the understandable for Washington midwits.

For better or for worse, Rhodes was the face of RAPTURE now because he was the one testifying behind closed doors in subcommittee meetings. Of course, Parsons remained the genius behind the actual work. She really should be getting all the credit. But neither life nor government-funded science were fair. He didn't make the rules. He just played by them, and played by them very well.

He watched her close up her phone, grateful that she'd always been cool about the awkward situation they were in. He knew her second-class status had to be hard on her ego but she never showed it at work. She was a real pro and clearly dedicated to the greater cause of advancing human knowledge.

Thank God for that. Without Parsons, the project would die a long, malingering death.

Dr David Rhodes sat behind his polished mahogany desk in the wide corner office on the second floor, an expanse of pine trees and rolling hills framed in the giant picture window behind him. Photos of Rhodes posing with congressmen and senators whose names Parsons didn't know hung on the wall. There were also numerous awards and honorifics he'd earned over the years, mostly for philanthropic work. There was even a framed photo of Rhodes receiving an award from the hands of Neil deGrasse Tyson.

Rhodes's office was located just two miles away from the

Spallation Neutron Source facility where she had run into Tad/Ted two days before. A shiver ran down Parsons's spine, and other parts of her as well, after reading the text he'd just sent. The man showed promise.

She slipped the phone back into her purse.

'Sorry about that, David.'

'No worries.' He forced a smile. Something was obviously bothering him.

Rhodes was in good shape for his age, around sixty, she guessed, and good looking, in a game show host kind of way. He must have had something going on for sure, given the fact he'd been married for over thirty-eight years to his college sweetheart, a former beauty queen and mother to their six children.

Good for them.

'I appreciate you coming in a little early this morning,' Rhodes said. 'I'm afraid I have some bad news.'

She leaned forward. 'What?'

'I'm sorry to be the one to tell you this, but Dylan Runtso is dead.'

Her mouth narrowed. 'Oh.'

She sat back slowly, expressionless for a moment, eyes blinking as she processed the information. Finally, she said, 'That's terrible. How?'

'Four days ago, he was in a café in Barcelona when a bomb exploded. Maybe you heard about it on the news?'

She shook her head. 'I don't watch the news.'

'I know you two were close when he was here.'

'He was a brilliant guy.'

'Have you two stayed in touch?'

'No.'

'This must come as a real shock. If you need to take time off –'

'No. I'm fine. I mean, yeah. It is shocking. But we're already behind schedule.'

'Are you sure?'

'Of course I'm sure. The Russians and the Chinese aren't taking time off, are they?'

'No, I suppose not.'

Parsons knew what buttons to push. It was a three-way race to the finish line.

*God help us if we don't finish first,* Rhodes thought. RAPTURE was just weeks away from completion. The bad guys weren't far behind, according to his contacts on the Senate Intelligence Committee.

'I appreciate your commitment to the work, Kate. I really do.'

She stood, a small smile on her angular face. 'I'm a scientist, first and always. Personal feelings must come second. I'll work now and grieve later.'

Rhodes stood as well.

'If you'll excuse me, I need to get to the lab.' She started to turn.

'Oh, Kate. Just one other thing. Since you will be here today, I need to add something to your schedule.'

'Sure. Name it.'

'The FBI wants to speak with you.'

Her head cocked, like a bird spotting a worm. 'Me? Why?'

'About Runtso, of course. They have a few questions. But if that's a problem, I can wave them off.' He began reaching for his desk phone.

'No, not a problem at all. You know where I'll be. Send them along when they get here.'

Rhodes smiled sheepishly. 'They're already here.'

# 48

There was a knock on the open door.

'Dr Parsons?'

Kate Parsons stopped typing and glanced up from her computer.

'May I help you?' Parsons asked.

An East Asian woman and a Hispanic male stood in the open doorway, both in their mid to late thirties. Off-the-rack suits, store-brand leather shoes, cheap digital watches, Parsons noticed.

The Asian female held a synthetic leather folio in one hand and a leather billfold in the other, flashing her gold FBI badge and identity card with her name and badge number. The Hispanic agent did the same.

'I'm Agent Kang' – she pronounced it *Kong* – 'and this is Agent Silva. Is this a good time?'

Parsons forced a small smile as she stood, extending her hand.

'Sure. Why not?'

'Sorry to disturb you. Dr Rhodes told us to keep it short. We know how busy you are.' Kang pointed at the open chairs near her desk. 'Do you mind?'

'Please,' Parsons said. 'Something to drink? Water? Coffee?'

'We're fine, thanks,' the woman said.

Parsons sat back down behind her desk. 'Do you mind if I just finish up this e-mail?'

'No, not at all,' Kang said.

The two agents sat quietly, silently scanning the spartan office as Parsons finished up. No awards, no photos, no mementos, no diplomas. They exchanged a glance.

Parsons expected the visit. Rhodes had warned her they were coming. *Okay, not warned*, she reminded herself. They were just coming. A friendly visit to talk about Dylan. No doubt they were concerned about him. Nothing for her to worry about. She hadn't done anything wrong.

Technically.

They would ask her a few questions and leave. This wasn't her first rodeo with the Feds. She'd been interviewed by them before when she was getting her ANACI and SSBI security clearances, and many times since when they sought information about security clearance applications for other people in her department. She knew the drill. In fact, she probably could conduct this interview herself.

The questions were largely standardized. But there was one red flag to watch for.

When they asked specific and limited questions, it meant they were just tying off a few loose ends. No big deal.

But if they started asking broad and general questions, then they were hostile. Open-ended queries were just opportunities to say the wrong things, betray confidences, and confuse rehearsed stories. That meant they were fishing.

And you were the fish.

She finished the e-mail and hit the send button with a whoosh, then turned back toward her visitors.

'How may I help you?'

'Just a couple of questions,' Kang began. She opened her folio and clicked a pen.

'Of course. Anything.'

'I believe Dr Rhodes informed you of Dr Runtso's death.'

'Yes. He said it was a bomb. He thought it was a coincidence.'

'What do you think?'

*That was not a good question. Way too general,* Parsons thought.

'I have no idea.'

'Why do you think he was in Barcelona?'

'Again, no idea. I didn't even know he was in Spain.' Parsons's gaze turned aside, presumably to hide her grief. 'It's terrible. He was a brilliant guy. So young.'

'Yes, it's tragic. How long did you know Dr Runtso?'

*That's better,* Parsons thought. It was a very specific and quantitative question. An easy answer. She glanced up at the ceiling, calculating.

'I first met him when he interviewed for a position in my department twenty-eight months ago.'

Agent Silva fought back a smile. *What? Not twenty-seven and a half months?*

'And you hired him, why?' Kang asked.

Parsons couldn't decide if that was open-ended or not.

'He first came to my attention because of a paper he presented on quantum computing, his field of expertise. He also came highly recommended by a Princeton faculty member that I trust implicitly.'

Kang poised her pen over her pad. 'And that faculty member's name?'

'Dr Craig DeBell.'

Kang scratched the name down.

Parsons noticed that Silva never took his eyes off her, like he was conducting a visual lie detector test or something. She smiled at him. He didn't react.

'Why did Dr Runtso leave your employ?'

'He said at the time he had a better-paying opportunity in the private sector.'

'And what opportunity was that?'

Parsons felt the heat rise on her neck. There wasn't any doubt in her mind that Kang already knew the answer to the question.

'I believe he became a private consultant.'

'And who did he consult for?'

'I don't know. We didn't talk much after he left. I heard he was freelancing, but I have no idea who his clients were – obviously someone who valued his expertise. Something that took advantage of his top secret clearance, I'm willing to bet.'

'Any guesses as to whom he might have worked with? I mean, it's kinda weird a guy like that decides to live in Knoxville. I'd think he'd move to Silicon Valley, or even the Triangle.'

'Dylan loved Knoxville, especially the craft beer scene. With his skill set, he could travel anywhere to consult. I'm betting he did a lot of work from home.'

Kang nodded. 'Okay, that makes a lot of sense.' She made another note. 'When was the last time you saw him?'

Again, Parsons glanced at the ceiling, counting off the days. 'Six months ago, give or take a week. I bumped into him at a place in Knoxville. It was just a quick hello. He was with someone.'

'Who?'

'A woman. I don't know her.'

'What place was that?'

'Myrtle's Chicken and Beer. The one on Market Square. Best damn chicken and waffles around.'

'Oh, man. I love me some chicken and waffles,' Silva said.

*It speaks.* Parsons stifled a laugh.

'Can you remember the specific date?'

'Sorry, I wish I could.' Parsons smiled. 'Oh, wait. I get it.

You want the date so you can check security cameras and stuff. I saw that on TV once. Um, let me think. Yeah. I'm pretty sure it was a Sunday. That's about the only day we ever get off around here. Eleven-ish if I'm remembering correctly.'

'That's really helpful,' Kang said, noting it. 'And that was the last time you saw him?'

'He called me about two months ago. Wanted to go out for drinks and dinner, catch up. But I turned him down. I was just too busy at the time. But no, I didn't see him.'

'And you haven't spoken with him at all since?'

'No.'

'In the time you were still in contact with him, did you keep him apprised of the progress on the RAPTURE project?'

'No.'

'He was intimately involved with it for two years. I'd think he'd be interested.'

'Dylan would know better than to ask me something like that. He was no longer cleared for that kind of information and I take this work too seriously to risk either the project or my own security clearance. Besides, he walked away from RAPTURE. He lost his right to be curious about it.'

'Speaking of walking away, I'm just wondering, in the weeks or months before he left, did he exhibit any odd behavior?'

'You're in a building full of eccentric, high IQ people. You'll have to be more specific.'

'Oh, you know. Any kind of behavior that made you think something was bothering him.'

'Bothering?'

Kang shrugged. 'Was he acting guilty? Maybe becoming more distant or aloof?'

'Not that I recall.'

'Did he buy an expensive car? Maybe take a big vacation?'

'Vacation? Are you kidding? We're on a clock around here. Besides, they polygraph the shit out of us – counterintelligence and lifestyle. If he was engaged in any criminal behavior while at ORNL, it would have shown up, I'm sure.'

'So maybe he quit because of a growing sense of anger or frustration? The crappy hours, or lack of promotion?'

'No.'

'Did you see him coming to work late more and more often, or even missing days?'

'No, none of those things. He was a very diligent and con-scientious worker.'

'Was he on any kind of prescription meds?' She set her pen down. 'Maybe smoked a little weed to take the anxiety off?'

'Not that I was aware of. Dylan was into hot yoga, if that means anything.'

Kang scribbled a few more notes.

'How about his relationships? Did he get along well with the people he worked with?'

'Yes, absolutely. He had a tremendous sense of humor.'

Kang and Silva exchanged another glance.

Parsons's jaw clenched. She took a deep breath to calm herself.

'And I'm sure you've already been through his files at Human Resources.'

'We have, actually.' Kang smiled.

'Then you already know that Dylan and I were . . . friends.'

'Friends with benefits,' Silva said.

*It speaks again,* Parsons said to herself. She turned toward him. 'Fuck buddies, we used to call it in grad school. Nothing romantic. Strictly sexual. But nothing untoward. That's why we filed the mutual consent forms with HR. Dylan didn't think it was necessary but I did. It was important for me to do that because I was his supervisor.'

Silva offered a slight smile. 'That's very conscientious of you.'

Parsons wasn't sure if his grin was supportive or condescending. She had a hard time reading people sometimes. Well, most times.

'Look, we all work really long hours here. There isn't time for a social life, and we're told to avoid using apps like Tinder to meet people – that's where the bad guys hang out, right? Looking for lonely ORNL scientists to compromise?'

'That would be a really dumb idea for all kinds of reasons,' Kang said.

'Biology is primal. The drive to reproduce ourselves is coded in our DNA. We're all just paramecia, but with bigger brains and opposable thumbs to access Pornhub. Every now and then, we all have to burn off some energy. It's like a square dance. You pick your partner, you have some fun, get a little sweaty, then it's over and you get back to work. No harm, no foul.'

Kang nodded, and made more notes.

Parsons saw that neither Kang nor Silva wore wedding rings. 'Sort of like the way cops hook up, or so I've read,' Parsons added. It was a jab, for sure, but she really had read that.

'Yeah, I've read that, too,' Kang said without looking up. 'So, just to be clear, you haven't had any communication with Dr Runtso in any form in the last six months?'

*Oh, shit. Now they're trying to trip me up,* Parsons told herself. *Game on.*

'No, that's not accurate. What I said before was that I haven't *seen* him in the last six months. We spoke by phone two months ago when he asked me out.'

Parsons thought a moment. 'I can request the IT department to get you all of Dylan's e-mail and computer logs. The contents would be heavily redacted because you don't have the right security clearances but at least you'd be able to cross-reference the metadata against people, dates, or events you're concerned about. Would that be useful to you?'

Kang's eyes widened. 'That would be great. Thank you.'

'Saves you from having to get a warrant. Now, I don't mean to be rude, but I really do have a lot on my plate. Is there anything you need from me today?'

Kang and Silva stood. 'No, you've been more than co-operative.' She extended her hand. Parsons stood and shook it, and Silva's, too.

'If you don't mind my saying, you look tired,' Kang said.

'I'm working too many hours on a project that doesn't seem to want to end. But I don't care. I'm totally committed to completing it. I've given my life to it. I don't have any kids, and never will. It will be my legacy.'

'That's damned impressive,' Silva said.

Parsons smiled. 'I appreciate both of you as well, and thank you both for your service.'

Kang politely demurred. 'Thank you. It's our privilege to serve.' She turned to Silva. 'Don't you agree?'

'Oh, yeah. I love my job, and the chance to do the Lord's work.'

'That's awesome,' Parsons said, turning away.

'Oh, there is one more thing I forgot to ask,' Kang said.

Parsons forced a smile. 'Please.'

'You are willing to take a poly, right? About Dylan?'

'Of course. Anytime. I take them twice a year as it is. They don't bother me.'

Kang waved a hand. 'Yeah, you're right. Probably not necessary at all. I just wanted that in the record. You know how bosses can be, all up in your shit, micromanaging everything. If I don't dot my *i*'s and cross my *t*'s, I get written up.'

'Bosses. Tell me about it.'

'Okay, well, thanks again for your time.'

'Sure.'

Parsons sat down as Kang and Silva turned to leave.

'Oh, jeez. Where's my brain?' Kang said, turning back around. 'I forgot to tell you that someone broke into Dr Runtso's home and ransacked it.'

'What? That's crazy. You think it's related to his death?'

'Could have been a couple of tweakers stealing stuff. But my guess is that someone was trying to find whatever top-secret materials he might have had in his possession, or cover some tracks related to his death.'

Parsons's eyes widened. 'That's awful. Is my team in danger? Am I?'

'I'm sure there isn't anything for you or your team to worry about. But please do exercise extra precautions for the next few days until we can get to the bottom of all of this, okay?'

'That makes sense. Thanks for the heads-up.'

'And we've notified White Mountain Security here at ORNL and asked them to step up their game for a while, too. You know, just in case.'

'Thank you. I appreciate it.' Parsons's eyes turned to her keyboard.

Kang smiled. 'Okay, we're leaving now. For real.'

Parsons didn't hear her.

Her mind was somewhere else.

Kang climbed in behind the wheel of their high-mileage, government-issued Crown Vic, one of the last in the FBI's fleet. Silva rode shotgun.

'What do you make of Parsons?'

'Hard to read.' Silva chuckled. 'But judging by the number of mutual consent forms she's filed with HR over the last five years, I'd say she was one horny little professor.'

Kang turned the key. The eight cylinders coughed into life. She nudged the shifter into reverse and began pulling out. She started laughing so hard she had to hit the brake.

'What's so funny?' Silva asked.

'"Fuck buddies"? That's pretty lame. I was waiting for her to start quoting lines from *Friends*.'

'I took her for a cold piece of fish, but you can't always judge a book by its subtextual libido.'

Kang shifted into drive and hit the gas. 'Let's grab some breakfast. I'm starving.'

# 49

*Barcelona, Spain*

Brossa woke from a short nap and padded into her kitchen. Her father, Ernesto, handed her a cup of black coffee from the espresso machine. He wore a green woolen sweater and beige chinos, neatly pressed. Every hair on his handsome silver head was in place and his beard closely trimmed. That was a good sign.

'Thank you, Papa.'

'You're welcome.'

She took a sip. 'So good.'

'I pushed a button. You look terrible, by the way.'

She pushed her matted hair out of her eyes. 'A rough couple of days.'

'You never told me what happened on the raid.'

'It ended badly.'

'Violence always does.'

She kissed him on the cheek. She loved these rare moments of lucidity, when the father she grew up with appeared out of nowhere. Kind, literate, and thoughtful. He was a gentle soul. *No wonder my mama was crazy about him.*

He touched his face where she kissed him. 'What was that for?'

'Does there have to be a reason?'

*'Ex nihilo nihil fit'* – Nothing comes from nothing.

That was an even better sign. He'd only been speaking Català for the last seven months.

'Come sit with me on the patio while I drink my coffee and regale me with your Latin witticisms.'

The old man smiled, the crow's feet narrowing around his dancing eyes.

'Delighted.'

They sat on the patio overlooking the city. The sun glinted silver on the gray-blue Mediterranean.

Brossa laid back in her chaise lounge, her eyes closed, enjoying the warmth of a gentle sunshine.

Her father sat upright in a chair next to her, humming an old tune. She was still exhausted, but supremely happy. Perhaps he was turning a corner after all.

Peña was right, she decided. The Brigada case was closed. It was time to let go.

Her momentary bliss was shattered by the buzz of her silenced phone. Her eyes opened, painfully, as she reached for it.

'I hate those things,' her father said. 'Let me throw it away.'

'It's probably work.'

'I hate your work. I should throw that away, too.'

She smiled and shook her head. *Somebody has to pay the bills around here.* She could never say that to him, though. He was a proud man, and a good provider for his family while he could work.

'It will just be a moment.'

She saw the number. Part of her wanted to ignore the call. But part of her wanted to hear his voice. She didn't know why.

'*Hola,* Jack.'

'Hi. Sorry to bother you. I was hoping we could talk.'

'Sure. I have a few minutes.'

'I mean, I want to meet you somewhere.'

She glanced over at her father, who was staring at the distant sea, pretending not to listen. She lowered her voice.

'Why can't we speak on the phone?'

'I'm not sure it's safe.'

'Are you serious?'

'Yes. I checked at your office but they said you had left for the day.'

'I'm not feeling well.'

'I'm sorry. I wouldn't ask if it wasn't important.'

She sighed. She really wasn't feeling well, and she didn't want to leave her father. But Jack needed closure, too. It would be nice to be the one to deliver the good news in person.

'Okay, I'll text you an address and I'll see you there in thirty minutes.'

'Thanks.' He hung up.

'Who is Jack?' her father asked.

'An American.' She texted the address of a restaurant. 'I've been trying to help him.' She hit the send key.

'What is his full name?'

'Jack Ryan.'

'Ryan?' His eyes widened. 'You can't trust this man.'

Brossa frowned. 'Why not?'

Ernesto leaned over, wagging a finger.

'Because he is a spy!'

Brossa's heart sank. *So much for turning a corner.* She sat up.

'And why do you think he is a spy?'

'Because I worked with him when he was in Brussels, at NATO headquarters. I was a translator there with the Spanish Defense Ministry.'

She patted his spotted hand. 'I don't think Jack was old enough to work with you in Brussels. In fact, he wasn't even born yet.'

His face fell. 'You don't believe me?'

She stood, picking up her empty coffee cup. He rose on unsteady knees as well.

'Yes, of course I do. I believe you believe it. But perhaps it is just a coincidence of names.'

'Is he handsome?'

Brossa pursed her lips, thinking. She didn't want to feed his fantasy. But she could never lie to her father. 'Yes.'

'And is he young, about your age?'

'Yes.'

'And does he have blue eyes?'

How would he know that? Well, he couldn't. It was just another crazy coincidence. She hated to confirm that fact to him because it would feed his dementia, convincing him he didn't have it.

But a good daughter never lies to her father, does she?

'Yes, Jack does have blue eyes.'

'You see! It's him! *Un espía!*' His eyes beamed with pride.

She touched a hand to his bearded face. She smiled outwardly, but inwardly wept with pity. 'Thank you, Papa. That is good to know. I promise I will be very, very careful with this *espía.*'

'I have my pistol. I'll get it for you.' He turned toward the house but she stopped him with a gentle tug on his elbow.

'No need. He isn't dangerous. And besides, I carry my own, remember?'

'Of course I remember. I'm the one who taught you how to shoot when you were just a little girl.'

'And you taught me well. I won't be gone long. Perhaps an hour, no more than two. I will call the nurse.'

'Nonsense! I have my *fútbol.* Barça plays Granada today. I'll wait here by the television for you.'

She hugged him. He wrapped his long arms around her.

'I love you, Papa.'

'I love you, too. Stay safe.'

'I will. Always.'

# 50

Jack and Brossa sat at one of the window-side tables near the entrance to Els Quatre Gats – the Four Cats – in Barri Gòtic, waiting for the server to bring their coffees and *bombas*.

'Do you know the history of this place?' Brossa asked.

'Picasso displayed his first painting here at seventeen. The original owner discovered many other great artists. You could call it the birthplace of modernism.'

'I didn't know you were an art scholar.'

Jack shrugged. 'I read it on the menu.'

She glanced around at the stained-glass windows, brass fixtures, and period artwork.

'It can be touristy at times, but when it's quiet like this, I find it quite charming. Very fin de siècle. Something old and, yet, something new. It is very Catalonian.'

'Thanks for suggesting it. And thanks for coming down. How is your father?'

'He's home watching soccer. He's a hometown fan, of course. Thank you for asking.'

'You said you have good news for me?'

Brossa sat up, beaming. 'You saw the news yesterday about Brigada?'

'Yeah. All killed. Is it true?'

'Yes.'

'How can you be sure?'

'I was there.'

'You were the woman they showed charging that house before it blew?'

Brossa lowered her eyes, embarrassed by the attention. 'Yes, I suppose so. I didn't see the actual broadcast.'

Jack reached across the table and squeezed her hand. 'Are you okay?'

'Yes, of course. No big deal.'

'The newscast said they blew themselves up and tried to take you all with them.'

'That's exactly what happened. You should be happy.'

'Why?'

'Because those terrorists are all dead, and your friend has her justice.'

'Did you get my text? With the photo?'

'The man with the hazel eyes? Yes, of course.'

'Did you check the farmhouse? Was he there?'

'We couldn't get through the wreckage. It was too extensive. It's still being dealt with. The bodies are at the coroner's office at the Guardia Civil and being identified. That will take some time. A week, perhaps two. The remains were scattered by the blast. If he's there, I will let you know.'

'I appreciate that.'

Brossa frowned. 'I thought you'd be happy to know that the case is closed.'

'I am. I just hate loose ends. I'll be completely satisfied when the guy is found and identified.'

'Like I said, it will take some time.'

The server arrived with their coffees and *bombas*.

'*Gràcies,*' Jack said.

The college-age server smiled. She was cute and gave Jack another look as she walked away. Brossa saw this. Jack didn't.

'Well, your Català is getting better, I see.' She lifted her cup. 'To Renée. May she rest in peace now.'

'To Renée.'

They sipped in silence for a moment. Brossa cut her *bomba* with a fork.

'Do you know why they call this a *"bomba"*?'

'It means "bomb," doesn't it?' Jack really hadn't thought about it.

'Yes. It was invented because of the civil war. The round potato croquet is the bomb, and this little bit of garlic aioli cream on top is meant to be the fuse, and the hot red sauce is meant to be like an explosion in your mouth.'

Jack cut his with a fork as well. The tine crunched through the lightly fried potato, revealing the ground beef interior. He suddenly wasn't sure if he wanted to eat it. Yeah, it was a piece of culinary history, and delicious as hell. But Renée . . .

He set his fork down. 'What if he wasn't at the farmhouse?'

'Then I'll find him. I promise you that. You know I will.'

'I won't feel like the case is closed until we find him.'

Her voice lowered. 'Until *I* find him. You need to go home.'

'But –'

'Do you want to get me in trouble? I've already brought you too deep into this case, as a favor to you. Please don't put my job at risk. It means too much to me.'

'I'm not trying to put your job –'

Brossa's phone rang. 'It's my father. I need to take this.' She snatched it up.

'Of course.'

She spoke with him in a calming tone for a few minutes, but Jack could hear the rising anxiety in her father's voice over the phone's earpiece. Jack couldn't understand what they were saying, but he could read the emotions.

She rang off.

'Jack, I'm sorry, but I must go. My father is very upset and he –'

'You don't need to explain anything.'

'Thank you.' She reached for her purse.

'Forget it, it's on me.'

Jack pulled out his wallet as they stood and peeled off several bills, leaving enough for the food and an overly generous tip. Brossa started to leave. He stopped her.

'Let me walk you to your car and say a proper good-bye.'

She nodded. 'Of course. Forgive my poor manners. Thank you.'

'Let's go.'

They exited through the Gothic-styled archway and onto the narrow, paved walkway, heading east on Carrer de Montsió – hardly a street, save for the small delivery vans that navigated the pedestrian path.

It was crowded with people, including some tourists. But mostly locals, Jack saw, many of them with their independence flags draped over their shoulders like capes, as he'd seen before.

Another protest.

'We must hurry. My car is across Via Laietana.'

Jack knew the four-lane boulevard well. It was one of the main arteries in the old town. It had been the site of previous protests, judging by the melted street signs and burned trash cans that the city government hadn't yet replaced.

The pedestrian walkway changed its name to Portet where it widened into a two-lane thoroughfare, picking up more and more protesters as they went. A blue police van was parked at the end of it, fronting Laietana.

Jack and Brossa were carried by the flow of flag-draped bodies surging around the van and onto Laietana, which was now a river of humanity. The cars were completely stopped in all four lanes. Most drivers were smiling and pointing, and many honked their horns, all in support of the march.

Signs called for liberty, freedom of speech, and justice for the jailed politicians. Not many called for independence, Jack noticed. He supposed the independence flags with the white stars were loud enough.

'These things happen so quickly, like a flash mob,' Brossa said, smiling. 'I'm so proud of my people. Do you see? No violence! Only hope.'

'Which way?'

'Right, down to the traffic circle, left on Cambó.'

Jack took Brossa's hand as well as the lead, guiding them both through the swelling masses. People were laughing and shouting, and blowing whistles, too. Jack even heard a couple of trumpeting *vuvuzelas,* like at a soccer game.

Jack was half a head taller than most and broader shouldered but he still felt suffocated by the boisterous crowds and the people bumping into him as they squeezed past. It wasn't possible for Brossa to walk next to him. Bodies surged around them, propelling them forward, but trapping them as well. He felt her shifting back and forth at the end of his arm like she was a fish on the hook of his hand.

Jack kept his head on a swivel, glancing left and right as they marched, glad to be holding her fingers in his, knowing she was right behind him. He felt a sudden pang of sadness, knowing that in a few moments he'd put her in her car and likely never see her again. If he stayed around for a while, he knew they'd be good friends. Who knows, maybe even more.

And she was right. It was her case, and she'd be the one to finally close it once she found Crooked Nose, dead or alive. He only wished he could be there when she did.

What neither Jack nor Brossa realized was that the hazel-eyed man with the crooked nose – Bykov – was very much alive, and only a few feet behind them.

\*

'Jack –'

He barely heard Brossa's voice above the din, but it broke sharply, like a cry. A second later, her hand released, and Jack instinctively grasped it harder, only to feel the sudden weight of her body pulling him backward.

He turned around just as her body hit the pavement, her paralysed arms unable to cushion her fall as her head thudded like a melon against the sidewalk.

Bykov leaped over her body and lunged at Jack, thrusting a handheld jet injector like a rapier at Jack's bare throat.

Jack let go of Brossa's hand as he lunged backward, bumping hard into a shorter, broad-backed Spaniard, built like a stevedore, in a tank top and jeans.

The Spaniard shouted in protest and whipped around, knocking Jack aside just as Bykov thrust the poison-filled injector at Jack's face. The spring-fired device dumped a massive dose of nerve agent – Novichok – into the Spaniard's beefy arm. He yelped in painless shock and grabbed his wounded biceps as Jack hammer-fisted Bykov's extended arm, forcing him to drop the lethal cylinder onto the pavement.

All of this happened in the span of a couple of heartbeats. The Spaniard's last, it turned out, as the Novichok began its merciless work, killing his nervous system, destroying the connection between his brain and muscle tissues.

In eight more seconds, he'd be dead.

Bykov turned, and pushed his way back into the oncoming crowd, swimming upriver against the flow of bodies now surging around Brossa convulsing on the pavement. A young brunette knelt down next to her, feeling for a pulse.

Jack glanced back at the Spaniard, who was now crumpling to his knees, his watering eyes wide with terror, bowels and bladder loosed, his breathless mouth open in a silent shout, spilling with vomit.

Jack started to reach out for him, but his subconscious told him the Spaniard was beyond help.

He turned and chased after Bykov, pushing past the crowd gathering around Brossa's body twisted on the pavement, her now lifeless eyes open to the sky. Jack filed away his grief for later.

But not his rage.

Powerfully built, the young Russian operative dodged and stutter-stepped around the people he could, and bowled through the ones he couldn't, even tossing a few down behind him to slow Jack's pace.

Offended parties reacted to Bykov's rough treatment but not quickly enough to hurt him, let alone slow him down. In fact, it was Jack who suffered their wrath, as they seemingly blamed him for Bykov's behavior by reaching out with their hands to grab and slow *him* down. A few threw kicks and punches but the glancing blows didn't stop him.

Jack kept saying *lo siento!* – I'm sorry! – to people as he bulled his way behind Bykov, who somehow was threading the needle like a fullback on a broken tackle run, and pulling away fast.

Jack's only advantage was his height, and he was able to catch a glimpse of Bykov ducking off Laietana and onto an unmarked side street.

Jack powered through the surging protesters, ignoring the shouts of anger and fear behind him and the sound of a distant siren.

He finally made the turn into the narrow alleyway, but Bykov was gone.

Jack slid to a halt. *Shit! Where did he go?*

The stone-paved alley bent into a gentle curve, a narrow,

shadowed path between four- and five-story buildings, leading to a cross street two hundred feet ahead.

Jack charged forward, eyes scanning recessed doorways and alcoves, racing for the intersection.

A glint of steel swung out of the shadows. Jack turned, raising his forearm, blocking the downward strike of Bykov's arm.

But Bykov's momentum drove the two of them stumbling across the narrow alley into a niche crowded with garbage cans overflowing with the wet, fetid refuse of a Chinese restaurant.

The two of them crashed into the cans, bowling them over. Jack and Bykov fell between them, Bykov on top of Jack, his knees buried into Jack's thighs, pinning him to the filthy pavement.

Bykov raised his combat knife with one hand and grabbed Jack's shirt in the other as he plunged the serrated blade at Jack's heart.

But Jack snatched up one of the dented garbage can lids and raised it like a shield. The razor-sharp drop-point blade plunged into the aluminum lid up to the hilt, the knife's serrated edges catching in the metal.

Jack twisted the lid before Bykov could pull it out, wrenching Bykov's wrist with the torque and toppling him over in the same direction. Jack thrust his hips up and over, using the leverage to accelerate Bykov's fall, tossing him onto the greasy stones.

Both men sprang to their feet.

Both eyed the blade still stuck in the lid.

Jack lunged for it but wasn't fast enough to avoid the kick to his ribs from Bykov's boot, driving him backward into a wall.

Jack grabbed his ribcage as Bykov dove for the knife.

The Russian stomped a boot on the lid for leverage and ripped the blade out of the dented metal. He whipped around with the knife, going low and planting his rear foot to spring into a lunge at the big American.

As Bykov swept into his turn, Jack's fist plowed into his lower jaw, cracking his teeth.

The Russian dropped the knife, stunned. It clattered to the pavement. His face darkened with confusion and then disbelief as he grabbed his jaw with his hand.

He glanced up at Jack and flashed a smile at him through gritted teeth.

It was a smile Jack had seen before.

The big Dutchman, van Delden, had flashed the same *fuck-you* smile.

The hairs stood on the back of Jack's neck.

Bykov's eyes rolled into the back of his head as he tumbled to the ground, his strings cut.

Jack knelt down by the corpse, barely hearing the siren screaming into the alley.

# 51

*Knoxville, Tennessee*

Another late-night marathon in the lab. Nothing new.

Parsons seriously considered sleeping on the couch in her office for the next two days. Catnaps, anyway. There was a shower in the facility and even a decent selection of organics stocked in the kitchen pantry. Anything to save time, because time was the one thing she didn't have.

Phase One of TRIBULATION was scheduled to launch in less than thirty-six hours. The timeline was immutable.

So was she.

The project had come along nicely, but in this last final stretch she needed to have her own steady hand on the rudder. They were too close to the end for delegating responsibilities. It was *her* baby. She was the one who needed to climb into the stirrups and push for all she was worth, no matter the cost. That was a mother's duty, wasn't it?

Parsons checked her analog watch again – security protocols that she had implemented prohibited digital devices of any kind on this level. She sat in the conference room waiting for her Phase Two division heads to arrive for her first meeting of the evening.

The Ukrainian Matvienko headed up the Russian software interface, and his counterpart, the Taiwanese programmer Yu, ran the parallel Chinese effort. These were pioneering software geniuses on the cutting edge of a newly emergent branch of human knowledge.

They had made outstanding progress on Phase Two but there was still so much to do in so little time. She needed a progress report from them, and then later, the TRIBULA-TION systems engineers.

Failure was simply not an option.

She picked up her pen and began scribbling notes for the first meeting in her notebook but stopped, the thought of Dylan Runtso's body shredded like a plate of pulled pork flooding her mind. It was a sudden, violent death that ended the life of one of the most brilliant men she'd ever known, or fucked.

She smiled.

The greasy little bastard had it coming.

It was too bad. He would have shared in the glory to come, and the money, had he remained true to his loyalties, which at first had been her, and then later, TRIBULATION. Betraying one had betrayed both. That was something she couldn't abide. Dylan needed to be dealt with. She made a phone call. It wasn't emotional. It wasn't personal. It was only the simple computational instruction every programmer learned on day one; the most basic of all control flow statements: *if, then.*

This was the most rational and primary means by which the decision to execute a code could be made.

Code, or people.

It was simple, pure, binary.

*If* a certain condition was true (guilt), *then* the prescribed course of action was taken. *If* a certain condition were not true (innocence), *then* the prescribed course of action was not taken.

Dylan actually executed himself. He chose his condition when he betrayed TRIBULATION – or attempted to – and thus his execution was inevitable.

Cause and effect. Linear and inexorable.

But Parsons knew quantum mechanics stood outside of linearity because it was non-localized in either time or space. Israeli scientists had proven that in 2013 when they swapped an entangled pair of temporally separated photons – one future, one past – and detected the polarization of the future photon before the past one was even created.

Effect, then cause.

Dylan had executed himself the day he decided to betray her.

She rubbed her eyes and stretched to push away the failed musings of her amateur philosophizing. It had been a long damn day and the FBI grilling hadn't improved her mood. She knew she'd passed their oral examination with a decent grade.

The only thing that disturbed her was the idea that Dylan's death had been made known so quickly. His true identity was as invisible as a quark to almost everyone on the planet, thanks to the DOE's identity-scrubbing program. How he'd been identified so quickly in Spain was troublesome, but not worth her attention at the moment. Security wasn't her department. She'd left that to others. Perhaps that was another reason she felt no guilt over Dylan's death. There was no blood on her hands, was there?

She saw Matvienko and Yu in deep discussion, heading her way. Her mind snapped into focus. She opened her laptop and pulled up the project management flow chart she'd been using for nearly two years. It looked like an underground metro map in the world's largest city, with huge decision nodes like metro stops sprawling across a succession of digital pages. Each decision node was connected by intricate track lines of responsibilities, timelines, and sub-decision points. More than ninety-eight percent of the chart had been executed and displayed in red. But it was these last few precious stops that led toward the final destination they needed to check off tonight. Judging by the smiles on both men's faces as they stepped into the conference room, those last decision nodes were about to turn red.

*Hallelujah,* as her mother used to say.

There was, however, one pubic hair in the organic hummus. Her stomach suddenly sank as if she were falling off a rooftop.

Could these two men be trusted?

Could anyone on this project be trusted?

Dylan Runtso's betrayal had nearly killed everything she'd worked her whole life to achieve. TRIBULATION would change the world forever. Dylan's treason was a stunningly selfish act, a betrayal of science itself. She'd thought he was as committed to the project's success as she was if only because he was as committed to the science as she had always been. Perhaps that was the reason why his betrayal was the 'black swan' event she hadn't predicted or prepared for.

What had suddenly frightened her was the obvious and secondary question. Didn't swans usually travel in flocks?

# 52

## South China Sea

The Vietnam People's Navy patrol boat cut two of its three diesel engines a hundred meters out, and reduced the third to slow ahead as the skilled helmsman maneuvered it toward the *Don Pedro*, Guzmán's fishing trawler.

Guzmán was surprised it had taken this long to be pulled over and inspected by one of the national services. He'd passed through the waters of four countries in the last two weeks, mostly to take on supplies, gather intelligence, and reinforce the 'legend' that his purse seiner ship was, indeed, a working fishing vessel. It was. At least, in part.

The *Don Pedro*'s actual captain was a stoic, barrel-chested sailor named Järphammar with twenty years' service in Baltic waters as an officer in the Swedish Royal Navy. Järphammar showed little concern when he was first hailed by the Vietnamese vessel, speaking in English to them through teeth clenched around his perpetually lit meerschaum pipe.

After requesting and confirming the *Don Pedro*'s identity from its AIS signal, the Vietnamese captain, Lieutenant Commander Phan, ordered the trawler to stop engines and prepare to be boarded for inspection.

Järphammar complied, readily.

The Vietnamese patrol boat was a familiar Russian design that the sturdy Swede had encountered before during his time of military service. Technically, it was half a meter shorter than the *Don Pedro*, but more than made up for its lack of stature with, among other armaments, a forward-mounted AK-630, a six-barreled 30mm rotary cannon similar to an American M61 Vulcan. Expending upward of five thousand rounds per minute, the AK-630 could shred the *Don Pedro*'s thin steel plating in a matter of seconds. Compliance was both logical and inevitable.

'We look forward to your visit, Commander,' Järphammar replied.

*We do, indeed.*


The *Don Pedro* was fishing in international waters currently undisputed between China and Phan's own country, but close to it.

*Too close,* the Vietnamese captain thought.

The Chinese had been aggressively and illegally overfishing traditional Vietnamese waters for the last five years. Worse, the Chinese Maritime Militia (CMM) had become an active and effective arm of the PLA Navy. Drawing on China's huge private fishing fleet, the PLAN had recruited nearly *two hundred thousand* civilian fishing vessels. PLAN variously supplied them with advanced electronic equipment, weapons, and training to carry out asymmetrical naval warfare duties. These fishermen-soldiers not only illegally fished Vietnamese waters, but harassed other nations' fishing and naval vessels. They also hauled ammunition, weapons, and personnel to various PLAN outposts. And they supported the development of the 'artificial islands' now permanent and prevalent throughout the South China Sea.

The Vietnamese People's Navy, like every other regional navy, had become alarmed by the CMM's activities. It was originally feared that the *Don Pedro* was one of these vessels in disguise. Phan was ordered to check it out.

From his bridge, Phan scanned the deck of the *Don Pedro*

with his binoculars as his patrol boat approached. The blue-and-white civilian vessel appeared to be a working boat, with cranes and masts to support deepwater commercial fishing. The men on deck were either working or cleaning equipment. They all appeared to be men of fighting age and, it seemed, in good shape, which most deepwater sailors had to be. It was strenuous and dangerous work.

None of them appeared to be Chinese. An interesting mix of Europeans, Hispanics, and, he presumed, a few Africans.

'Oh,' Phan said aloud as his binoculars swept over the front deck. He nudged the naval infantry sergeant standing next to him and handed him the binoculars.

'Extreme danger, Sergeant. Better warn your men.'

The dour infantryman put the glasses to his eyes and scanned the deck, then broke out into a grin.

Three young women lay sunbathing on chaise lounges in string bikinis, leaving little to the imagination.

*Perhaps this boarding won't be so bad after all,* Phan thought, taking back the glasses for a second long look at the young women.

Fifteen minutes later, lines had been secured and the two boats were lashed together, separated only by the *Don Pedro*'s heavy bumpers that squeaked with friction as the two ships bobbed in the gently rolling sea.

Lieutenant Commander Phan jumped the short distance between the vessels. He was followed by the sergeant and three more armed naval infantrymen with AK-74 rifles strapped to their chests. Phan and his men were greeted on deck by Captain Järphammar, who led Phan and his four men to the *Don Pedro*'s spacious bridge, equipped with the latest navigational equipment.

Järphammar introduced Guzmán as the ship's owner. Guzmán offered up a friendly smile, an unopened bottle of Jack Daniel's Black Label, and glasses.

Phan's flint-faced demeanor softened slightly at the sight of the Jack Daniel's. 'No, we can't while on duty, but thank you.'

'I understand,' Guzmán said, cracking open the bottle.

At that moment, two of the statuesque young women Phan had seen sunbathing earlier, one blonde, the other brunette, appeared in the cabin doorway carrying a huge ice chest between them. They were now both dressed in clean coveralls and introduced as the *Don Pedro*'s cooks. Both were taller than the Vietnamese men standing on the bridge.

They set the ice chest down on the deck and the blonde opened the lid. Thick slabs of pink tuna steaks and bottles of chilled Filipino Red Horse beer sat on top of the crushed ice.

'Japanese sushi chefs say that the southern bluefin is the best tuna for sashimi,' Guzmán said. 'I prefer mine grilled with butter and pepper over a pit barbecue.'

'What is this?' Phan asked. It was enough food and drink for each member of his crew.

'The benefit of being a fishing boat is that we catch a lot of fish. Please accept this small token of our appreciation for keeping the oceans safe and allowing us to do our jobs and feed our families.'

The commander's eyes fell on the tuna steaks. His mouth watered. 'That is very generous of you. But I must inspect your ship.'

'We insist on it,' Järphammar said. 'We need your documentation to prove that we are operating legally in these waters, unlike the goddamned *Chinese.*'

Phan's jaw clenched when he heard 'Chinese,' the name of his nation's ancient mortal enemies with whom they'd been warring for a thousand years. His father had fought against the Americans in what the Vietnamese called the American War. But even his badly wounded father saw the Chinese as far worse enemies of his people than the American invaders, despite the millions of Vietnamese who had perished in that war.

Phan nodded his appreciation. 'Then I thank you for your generous gift.' He turned to his sergeant. 'Have your men carry this back to the ship.'

'Excuse me, sir,' the blonde said in accented English, shutting and securing the lid. 'But we have a very special way we'd like to prepare the tuna if you will allow us to do so.' The two strong young women picked up the chest with ease. No need for smaller men to do it.

Phan exchanged a conspiratorial glance with his sergeant.

'We look forward to it,' Phan said. 'I'll inform our galley that you are on the way.' He turned back to his sergeant. 'You and two of your men will begin the inspection, the other will escort these ladies to our galley.'

The sergeant smiled, turned, and barked his orders.

The youngest Marine led the way off the bridge with a smile as the two tall women bearing gifts followed behind him toward the stairs. The sergeant and the two other enlisted Marines exited the bridge as well to begin their inspection.

Phan turned to Järphammar. 'Your papers, sir?'

Järphammar heard the Marines' boots clanging on the steel steps as he pulled a thick leather folio from a nearby desk and handed it to him.

Guzmán brought over a glass of smoky bourbon to Phan, then handed one to Järphammar.

The Vietnamese officer glanced up, annoyed.

'Since we're alone now.' Guzmán winked. He lifted his glass in a toast. 'To the sea, and all that she gives.'

'Oh, what the hell.' Phan smiled. 'To the sea!' He threw back his shot. It burned in the best kind of way, warming him all the way down his throat.

'Another?' Guzmán asked, holding up the bottle.

'No, thank you. That is quite enough.'

'A cigar?' Guzmán held out a thick Cuban Cohiba.

Phan wavered, then gave in. 'Perhaps for later.' He accepted the cigar and pocketed it.

Guzmán reached under Järphammar's desk and pulled out an unopened box of Cubans and handed it to the commander. 'For you and your men, of course. Perhaps after dinner.'

Phan took the box and tucked it under one camouflaged arm. 'The men will enjoy this.' He turned serious, suddenly remembering his duty. 'Now, shall we proceed to our inspection?'

Järphammar nodded. 'Follow me.'

Järphammar led Phan and Guzmán down the stairs toward the main deck, following the path the Vietnamese Marines took.

Guzmán saw that the Marines were sniffing around bins and holding tanks, pulling up tarps, checking equipment lockers. Nothing too aggressive, but thorough. His men were disciplined enough to cooperate enthusiastically, even joking with the soldiers as they worked.

Järphammar pointed out the features of his vessel to Phan, his voice booming with pride. He described its speed and endurance characteristics, the amount of fresh fish cargo it could hold in ice thanks to its onboard $CO_2$ refrigeration system, and a host of other nautical features Guzmán couldn't care less about.

Neither Phan nor his men paid attention to the women

following the young Marine as they crossed over to the Vietnamese ship and headed into the bowels of the patrol vessel with their ice chest.

'Shall we head belowdecks so that you can inspect our equipment?' Captain Järphammar asked.

Phan waved the sergeant and his two Marines over to join him, then turned back to the beefy Swede. 'Lead the way, Captain.'

Järphammar headed down the steel stairs first, followed by the three enlisted men, then Phan, and finally Guzmán. The smell of diesel and hydraulic fluid wafted up the staircase as they descended.

Järphammar stopped on the first level and pointed down the hallway. 'Crew's quarters.'

'How many?'

'Eighteen souls, all good seafaring men – and *women,* as you saw.' Järphammar laughed and winked, and gently punched the much smaller Vietnamese.

Phan nodded, nearly blushing.

Järphammar pointed to the descending staircase. 'This way, gentlemen.'

Phan led the way, followed by his men. Guzmán and Järphammar were the last down. The Vietnamese commander heard and smelled the workings of some kind of machine shop, which struck him as somewhat odd. When he reached the lowest deck, he stopped, taken aback by what he saw. His men stood to one side. Järphammar and Guzmán stood close behind them.

More fighting-age men and a few women in great physical shape, including the third sunbather he'd seen earlier, were at their respective stations. Some were soldering motherboards, others constructing electronic equipment with fine tools. Still others sat at various computer screens monitoring AIS ship traffic, radar tracks of ships and aircraft, weather patterns, and other data. It looked like a combat information center. In the middle of the room was a twenty-foot-long steel table, and lying upon it was something out of a science fiction movie.

'What is this —'

Phan's last words were choked off by the razor-sharp wire garrote that sliced through his windpipe.

Before the other three surprised Marines could react, Järphammar's knife stabbed with lightning speed, like a needle on the end of a runaway sewing machine. All four men fell into a bloody heap on the rusted steel deck.

The men and women working on the floor hardly looked up.

Guzmán watched Järphammar wipe the blood off his Fairbairn-Sykes fighting knife, a double-edge stiletto designed for surprise attacks, first made famous by the British commandos in World War II.

Guzmán nodded with an approving smile. 'You are fast with that blade, *amigo.*'

'You should see what my wife can do with it.' The big Swede laughed, referring to the brunette 'cook' who was now on the other boat.

And definitely not cooking.

The tall blonde peeked around the corner of the door into the patrol boat's bridge and called out, 'Hello?'

The XO stood by the helmsman, trying to reach his commander on the radio. When he heard her voice, he turned around, frowning.

The blonde flashed a big toothy smile and came out fully from behind the wall holding out a bottle of chilled beer with her right hand, her left hand held casually behind her back.

'Commander Phan wanted you to have this.' She tossed the bottle at the Vietnamese officer. He instinctively reached out and caught it.

The bottle exploded in his hands as the frangible nine-millimeter round plowed through it and into his gut. The lead bullet dragged microscopic shards of glass along with it as it shredded his bowels. Two more shots barked out of the blonde's cold, wet pistol as he fell backward.

At the same time, thirty .45-caliber hollow-point slugs tore around the confined space, ripping into the unprotected flesh of the helmsman and three other crewmen, their eyes wide with shock.

The bridge quickly filled with bitter blue gun smoke, the ice-chilled grip of the Heckler & Koch UMP machine pistol clutched in the brunette's hands. She stood just behind the blonde, a wisp of smoke still curling from the crown of her SIG 365XL pistol.

The blonde's ears rang from the deafening noise. She touched her own cheek with the barrel of her SIG, telling the brunette, 'You've got a little blood . . .'

The brunette reached up and wiped off the arterial spray that had splattered on her face after knifing the young Marine escort and the killing spree belowdecks that followed.

'Call it in,' she said to the blonde. The *Don Pedro*'s assault team had boarded the Vietnamese vessel after the first shots rang out in the galley. The assaulters killed the rest of the crew as the women worked their way toward the bridge.

The blonde radioed over to Guzmán on her comms. She shouted loudly, nearly deaf from the ringing still in her ears. 'We're clear. Send the sappers.'

One of the *Don Pedro*'s assaulters scrambled up behind the

brunette, breathing hard, his carbine in hand, his face anxious.

'What's the problem?' the brunette asked.

'Your man Sablek. He's gone.'

Later that night, Guzmán leaned over the rail on the stern of the ship, smoking one of the fat Cohibas, the copper blades of his boat's single propeller frothing the dark water behind them like a ribbon of light.

Järphammar stood next to him with his pipe, nursing a beer, commiserating.

'These things happen in war, my friend. He was a good soldier and died doing his duty. That's an epitaph I'll take any day.' The Swede took another puff on his pipe.

The thin moonlight exaggerated the deep puncture scars in Guzmán's round face, making them look like shadowed craters on a brown, fleshy moon.

'Sablek was just a kid. And we're not at war.'

'He was a 2nd REP para with the Legion' – the French Foreign Legion – 'and tough as nails. He knew what he was getting into when he joined with them. And he knew what he was getting into when he joined with us.'

'He was only twenty-six.' Guzmán took a long pull on his cigar and exhaled. The blue smoke wafted away into the dark behind them. 'That's too young to die for money.'

'He didn't die for money. You know that. He died for us, as we would have died for him.' Järphammar took another swig. 'We were his family. That means something, doesn't it?'

'Not to his widow.' Guzmán examined the stub of his cigar, turned up his nose at it, and tossed it overboard. 'I will see to it she gets a double share for his trouble.'

'That's good of you, *patrón*.'

'A family takes care of its own.'

Järphammar worried for his boss. He'd seen these dark moods before in his years as his number three in the Sammler organization. He knew not to try and talk him out of his despair.

'Still no word from Bykov?' Guzmán asked.

'No, sir.'

Guzmán was now certain that Ryan was connected to van Delden's death. Bykov had been sent to kill the big American for that but he hadn't reported back in. This was worrisome as well.

Guzmán took the loss of one of his people like it was the loss of one of his own children, of which he had none. But van Delden's death hit him hardest. The big Dutchman had been Guzmán's first European recruit and a close friend.

'Did Harte make the AIS swaps?' Guzmán asked for the second time in the last ten minutes.

The Swede didn't know if his boss was being extra cautious or if he was just distracted by his grief. It wasn't like him to repeat himself.

'As you ordered. He swapped ours out and put it on the Vietnamese boat and killed their VDR before we scuttled it. The world will think the *Don Pedro* sank with all hands lost somewhere in the South China Sea.'

'And our new AIS is online and broadcasting?'

'You are now the proud owner of the *Lupita,* under a Panamanian flag.'

'And what did you do with the Vietnamese AIS?'

'Harte decided to put a battery on it and launch it on a weather balloon. At last report, it was traveling due east at fifteen knots.'

'A weather balloon? Won't that be a problem?'

'AIS doesn't measure altitude. It's strictly GPS. Longitude and latitude only.'

He clapped Guzmán on the arm as his broad face broke into a wide smile. 'But it would be funny if the Vietnamese thought their patrol boat was sailing along at seven thousand feet.' The Swedish captain swore that a small grin was tugging at Guzmán's troubled face but in the dark it was hard to know for sure.

'I'm heading for my bunk. Notify me when we reach the next waypoint.'

'Aye, aye, sir.'

Järphammar watched Guzmán climb the ladder toward the bridge and his private stateroom. The Swede polished off the last of his beer, then tossed the empty into the churning wake behind him, knowing it would sink eventually somewhere out in the dark.

# October 29

# 53

*Barcelona, Spain*

Jack's ankles were cuffed and shackled to the steel chair bolted to the floor. His hands were cuffed and shackled to an iron bracket in the middle of the steel table, its top scratched with graffiti. He wondered if the jailhouse artists got their justice, whatever that was.

His wrists hurt where they cuffed him, a little too tight – on purpose, no doubt. Jack had taken a swing at the first cop who approached him in the alley with a drawn gun, not realizing it was a cop. Thank God he only put the man on his ass instead of on an autopsy table. The other cops that swarmed him didn't seem quite as grateful. They rang Jack's bell pretty good, putting him on the ground and cuffing him, even after Jack had surrendered and apologized for hitting the other cop.

Jack's ribs still hurt, too, where Crooked Nose had kicked him. The image of that *fuck-you* smile looped in Jack's brain like a bad movie trailer. He'd punched him hard, but not hard enough to kill him. Why the smile?

But the other image that wouldn't leave his mind's eye was Brossa, dead on the pavement, her lifeless eyes wide to the steel gray sky. She deserved better. So did her father, wherever he was.

It had all happened so fast. He'd replayed the scene in his mind a thousand times. What could he have done differently? He should have let her lead the way. He should have been more aggressively searching for Crooked Nose, after the fight he'd had with him in his parked car. But he never suspected the man would try to kill him and Brossa. Jack assumed he was just a surveillance guy. Had he wanted to kill Jack earlier, he could have done it easily instead of planting the bugs he never got to use.

Brossa's death dragged his soul down even deeper as Liliana's horrific death clawed at his heart. He'd failed her, too.

A hard Spanish face appeared in the steel door's small, wire-reinforced window. The dark eyes scanned the room, then fell on Jack, holding on him for a while. Maybe the cop wanted to come in there and tune him up while no one else was around.

If he did, there wasn't a damn thing Jack could do about it.

Keys jangled in the lock and the door swung open.

Dellinger spoke in Spanish to the guard, who shrugged and shut the door behind the CIA man, then locked it. Dellinger approached the table where Jack was shackled but remained standing.

'Jack, how you doing, son?'

Jack raised his shackled wrists a few inches, as far as they could go. 'Good thing I don't have to pee.'

'Well, if you do, don't ask me to hold it for you.'

'Not part of your cultural affairs responsibilities, I take it.'

'No. But getting you out of here is.'

'That's why I called you instead of a lawyer. Speaking of which, didn't you bring one?'

'You don't need a lawyer. I've made all the arrangements. A Guardia Civil escort is going to drive you and me straight to the airport and put your ass on a plane to fly you home to Dulles. You can pay for your own damn Uber back to wherever you want to go after that.'

'I'm not going anywhere until this case gets fully and finally resolved.'

'I guess you're not hearing me. This isn't optional. There are three dead people lying in your wake today, two Spaniards, including one of their federal officers. They intend to hold you for questioning as a person of interest – and here's the fun part – they're going to hold you without bail for as long as they need until they wring everything out of you.'

'I didn't do anything wrong. I didn't kill the Spaniards. That other guy did.'

'Which is what you say. Right now, there are witnesses that think you were responsible, since you were the one standing closest to both victims.'

'That's ridiculous.'

'That's the nature of eyewitness testimony. Just about the most unreliable kind of testimony there is. But it's out there, and the Spanish authorities have a legal obligation to take it under advisement.'

'And the third guy? The one with the crooked nose?'

Dellinger leaned on the table like a bad cop. 'The one that could have proven you innocent if you hadn't killed him?'

'Yeah.' Jack smiled. 'That one.'

'As far as I know, smartass, the Spaniards are still trying to identify him. So far they've come up with at least seven aliases and four nationalities for this joker. The last alias he used was Bykov. And do you know what the real head-scratcher is?'

'I have a feeling I can't stop you from telling me.'

'Turns out, you killed a dead man.'

'Run that by me again?'

'Bykov was reported dead three years ago. Interpol ran his photo. They think he was ex-Russian military and ex-Wagner, but they can't be sure. Do you know what Wagner is?'

'Russian mercenaries.'

'You know a lot about the world for a finance guy.'

'I know how to read a newspaper. I also know that most cultural attachés don't carry.' Jack nodded at the shoulder holster underneath Dellinger's sport coat.

Dellinger frowned, frustrated he'd been that careless. He straightened up.

'You must throw one helluva punch, kid, to kill a man with one shot to the mouth.'

'Lucky, I guess. Well, not for him.'

'Or you. Look, the bottom line is that the Spaniards are very curious and very unhappy with the situation, and the only fall guy they can find within arm's reach is you.'

'I'm not guilty of anything. I'm not worried about what their investigation might turn up.'

'I knew you weren't listening to me. I believe you when you say you had nothing to do with the death of the two Spaniards, and that the death of this Bykov character was accidental because you were just trying to defend yourself. Okay? I'm on your side here. Do you believe me or not?'

Jack nodded reluctantly. 'Yeah. I guess so.'

'Good, because I am. So, please, pay attention.' Dellinger pulled on his own ear. 'And *listen* to me. You might not be worried about *what* the Spaniards might turn up on you. But you need to be very worried about *how long* it will take them to find you innocent. It could be months. It could be years. And if they decide to link you up with the L'avi bombing, that makes you a terror suspect, and then all kinds of new rules and procedures come into play.'

'If the Spaniards think I'm the prime suspect, why are they willing to cut me loose?'

'Because, like the rest of us, they've discovered you're a real pain in the ass.'

Jack fought back a laugh. That's a title he'd take any day. He'd been a pain in the ass to tangos and shitbirds for years, and he was damn proud of it.

'Ass pain notwithstanding, you need to be a little more clear.'

'Somehow this boss of yours, Gerry Hendley, has gotten involved in this, and apparently has a lot of pull with the State Department. You are just about to cause a minor international crisis between our governments, which means a crisis within NATO, and that's something nobody wants.'

'Sounds like I have leverage.' Jack wasn't referring to his dad. He would never use his relationship with POTUS for personal advantage, even if that meant getting out of this jail.

Dellinger pointed at Jack's handcuffs. 'Yeah? You got so much leverage, try standing up right now.'

'Then how come you can get me out of here?'

'Because our two respective governments have worked out a deal. But there's a time stamp on it. If you agree to leave with me right now and let me take you straight to the airport and you return immediately to the States, the Spaniards are willing to accept your version of events. But if I walk out of here today without you, you're on your own, back alley garbage stink and all.'

Jack sat back as best he could. He blew out a long sigh, thinking. 'I just need to know what really happened to Renée Moore.'

'You and I both know what really happened to her. She was killed in an explosion from a bomb detonated by a member of Brigada Catalan.'

'But this Bykov guy. He's connected to it, too. And if he's ex-Wagner –'

'Bykov's dead. You killed him, remember? Case closed.'

'But he was tied to Brigada –'

'Brigada's all dead. Believe me, I know that because I was there when it happened. Case *closed.*'

'But –'

'Case *fucking* closed. Don't you get it?'

'Yeah, I get it. I know it's closed. Laia said the same thing. But there was another American at L'avi who was killed. A guy named Runtso. Dr Dylan Runtso.'

Dellinger's face flinched. 'How do you know about him?'

'He bumped into me as he was coming into the place and I was going out. He said, "Sorry, man" as we passed.'

Dellinger's eyes narrowed. 'Don't you worry about Runtso. And by the way, there were a lot of other people killed and wounded that night, not just two Americans.'

'Yeah, I know. I was there, remember?'

'One more thing you haven't considered. There's another corpse that's attached to your name, at least by extension.'

'Who?'

'Do you know who Gaspar Peña is?'

'Never heard of him.'

'He was with the CNI. Brossa's boss. They found him a few hours ago, extra crispy. He was handcuffed to the steering wheel of his burned-out Audi R8 Decennium, which is one helluva car and about as shitty a way to die as I can think of.'

'You know I have nothing to do with that.'

'I know it. You know it. And wherever the hell Peña is, he knows it, too. But how long will it take the Spanish authorities to figure it out as well?'

Jack shrugged, Dellinger's logic falling on him like a heavy woolen blanket.

'So, what's it gonna be, Jack? Sit on your ass in a Spanish gray-bar hotel for the next six months and get your gringo ass molly-whopped by local talent until they finally cut you loose? Or do you want to walk out of here a relatively free man and get back to your life in the good ol' US of A?'

Jack folded his hands together, rattling the chains, thinking. He knew the moment he left Spain, the case really was closed. But he couldn't shake the feeling that there were still a few loose threads that he needed to tug on to get closure.

But Dellinger was right. All the cards were stacked against him. The best possible outcome was that he'd waste the next several weeks, if not months, in jail, unable to do any kind of investigative work anyway. The worst case was too terrible to consider – somehow convicted of one or more killings, even if only by association or intent. False convictions weren't exactly a myth, even in Western democracies.

Worse, several weeks in jail – innocent or guilty – meant he'd be off the shelf as far as The Campus was concerned. And for what? The case really was closed. Renée's killers were dead. So were Brossa's. And knowing his father, there wasn't any chance he wouldn't get involved at some point to get his oldest son out of the hoosegow, especially if he was innocent. If POTUS got involved, that surely meant his identity as the son of SWORDSMAN would be revealed. That would definitely kill his future as an undercover operative with The Campus.

'Okay, you win. Let's get the hell out of Dodge.'

Dellinger grinned. 'Smart boy.'

He pounded on the steel door with the palm of his hand, telling the guard to let them out.

In a few hours, Jack would be somewhere over the Atlantic, far from Spain, a free man.

# 54

True to his word, Dellinger got Jack out of jail almost as fast as he could walk him through the front doors and into the fresh air and sunshine.

An unmarked Guardia Civil Nissan SUV stood at the curb with the rear door opened. The international business intern Jack had spooked earlier stood by it holding Jack's leather satchel stuffed with his clothes and his laptop bag.

'Who told you you could break into my place?' Jack said, still reeking and disheveled like a man who'd just broken out of a dumpster.

The college-age kid blanched at Jack's tone and pointed at Dellinger. 'He sent me.'

'We didn't have time to waste,' Dellinger said, motioning for Jack to get in the car as the Guardia Civil plainclothes detective climbed into the driver's seat.

'How'd you know I'd take your offer?'

'Because I figured you weren't stupid. Get in. We're late for your flight.'

Jack snagged his satchel and laptop from the intern and fell into the backseat next to Dellinger. They slammed the doors behind them as the Nissan rocketed toward the airport.

Dellinger and the Guardia Civil detective-driver both escorted Jack into the giant glass and steel Barcelona–El Prat airport southwest of the city. Thanks to his Spanish escort, Jack and Dellinger were both passed through to the front of the long check-in and security lines. Their movements were tracked by the angry, jealous eyes of the passengers lined up like cattle in pens waiting for slaughter.

Jack was then led to his departure gate and ushered to the gate agent's desk. The agent was forced to reopen the jetway when the detective flashed his badge, though it was against company policy to do so.

Dellinger offered Jack a firm hand that was as much a warning as a pleasantry along with 'Good luck, son,' before Jack disappeared into the jetway.

The Spanish detective escorted Jack to his seat, turning curious heads as they strode through the wide first-class aisles and back to the narrow ones in coach. Jack stuffed his carry-on into the crowded overhead and shoved his laptop under the seat in front of him. He then fell into his chair and buckled in. The detective flashed Jack one last angry glance before he turned around and marched back off the plane.

The middle-aged flight attendant for Jack's section was a real pro. She hid her concern over Jack, unlike the passengers near him who squirmed uncomfortably in their narrow seats, trying desperately not to look at – or smell – the large, bearded man suddenly thrust into their presence by a police escort.

Jack perused the drink card, searching for something hard.

It was going to be a long damn flight.

After three glasses of Jameson Irish whiskey, Jack was finally numb to his frustration and grief.

He felt like shit that Brossa had died but at least he'd killed the asswipe that did it. How he killed the man with a single punch to the face still confused him. According to Dellinger, the Spaniards would get around to an autopsy in the next few weeks, and he promised to let Jack know what the results were as if that was some sort of consolation over Bykov's death. It wasn't.

Jack didn't need any.

Now winging his way back home, Jack was leaving both physically and emotionally drained. Renée was dead and nothing would change that but at least the people who claimed responsibility for her death were all dead, along with the man Jack believed to be the real bomber, even if he wasn't with Brigada Catalan.

He hated to admit it but the case really was closed. It felt like a betrayal of Renée and especially Brossa but he had done everything he could in the short time he had. His heavy eyelids began to flutter. He reclined his seat as far as it would go and gave in to the sleep that had eluded him for the last twenty-four hours.

Maybe it was the booze or something else that fueled his dream but Jack found himself back inside L'avi. This time the crowded restaurant was full of street protesters jammed in so close that Jack could hardly breathe. He fought his way toward the exit, desperate to escape the suffocating mass of flesh. Just as he reached the cool, fresh air pouring in at the doorway, he bumped into a long-haired Runtso, only this time, it was Jack who said, 'Sorry, man,' instead of the shorter, hapless man. Runtso said nothing but only stared for a long moment at Jack with eyes full of unspeakable sadness, then finally he turned away, trudging in slow motion – not into a crowded restaurant, but instead into a shrieking wall of fire, his body vaporizing in flames so hot that it made Jack's skin tingle.

# 55

## Knoxville, Tennessee

Parsons was beside herself. She rubbed her bare arms, her skin literally tingling with anticipation.

In eleven hours and forty-eight minutes, she would make history.

She couldn't stop smiling. She felt like the yearning, libidinous gymnast she'd once been, waiting by her locker for the high school quarterback to whisk her away in his cherry red Camaro.

She blushed at the memory. *That was a hell of a good day, too.*

The last staff meeting had just concluded. All of the department heads showed up, eager and grinning – always a good sign. Every department reported in as ready. Each division head guaranteed that every hardware and software system had been stress tested and double-checked, and that all personnel were ready and in place. Everything had gone according to plan. Everything was on schedule.

To hell with RAPTURE.

TRIBULATION was about to change the world.

*'And to hell with you, Dr David Rhodes, you worthless, backslapping, glad-handing, thieving prick,'* Parsons said in a quiet whisper.

Rhodes took RAPTURE from her. He had talent enough for that. His soft, manicured hands were strong enough to stab her in the back and twist the knife. He'd stolen all the credit for her work, her genius. He'd stolen her baby.

Sure, it was just another case of politics and patriarchy biting her in the ass again. But it was his name that would have gone down in the history books. *Would have.* She laughed to herself.

But nobody remembers second place. That's just first place for losers.

RAPTURE wouldn't be first.

TRIBULATION would have that honor.

*She* would have that honor.

And Rhodes would be standing around with his tiny dick in his even tinier fingers wondering how she had stolen it from him.

Parsons crossed over to the Viking refrigerator in the break room and pulled out a cold Fiji water, savoring her moment to come.

Rhodes would look like the biggest idiot in the world. The ultimate dupe. The completely clueless chucklehead that let a woman kick him in his diminutive nutsack.

She cracked open the bottle and took a long pull of cold, clear water.

And to think she'd nearly walked away from it all.

'You'll never make a good decision while you're angry,' her Sunday school teacher mother had always said.

For once, the old bag had been right.

Parsons was practically out the door – already circulating her incredible CV – when the call came that changed her life.

She could hardly believe it. At first, she thought it was a test. Maybe even a trap laid out by the Feds.

It wasn't.

It took some time for him to prove himself and to earn

her trust. But he did. He proved that he had the funding. He showed her that he was risking as much as she was, if not more. He certainly had the motivation. And he had a plan.

A hell of a plan.

But most important of all, he *believed* in her. He told her how significant she was, and he wasn't just blowing blue smoke up her skirt. He'd followed her research and knew about RAPTURE, and all about Rhodes and how he had played the Jacob to her Esau and stolen her birthright. How he'd known about all of it she could never figure out. But that just spoke to her about the power of his reach and his incredible resources.

Her patron clearly understood her contributions to the work. He was no scientist but possessed an impressive command of the subject for a civilian. He told her how her name would rank in the pantheon of all great scientists – not just women scientists, but all scientists. He appealed to her vanity, no doubt, and she was vain. Except it wasn't vanity because what she believed about herself was absolutely true.

And it was. She was a genius.

So she finally agreed to the plan. He would build an alternate facility, not too close to Oak Ridge, but not so far away that she couldn't be there on a regular basis to oversee the work. He would provide a list of vetted scientists, programmers, and engineers but she would have the authority to hire and fire them. He would provide all of the security, and all of the materials, and all of the resources needed. All she ever needed to do was send him her list of needs, human or material, and he would provide it.

Her contributions were materially minimal but the most significant. She would continue to plow ahead at Oak Ridge and push the RAPTURE project forward, extracting every ounce of information and insight from it that she could and then bringing it over to the TRIBULATION program. Of course, there were certain expectations he put upon her. But they were reasonable, given the outcome.

First, he told her, TRIBULATION must be completed and ready to deploy on a certain date and time. No exceptions. He named both.

'Do you agree?'

'Of course.'

'And you believe it's absolutely possible?'

'I do.'

'Are you willing to bet your life on it?'

'I am.'

'Then you just did.'

The threat was neither unexpected nor particularly frightening. It also showed that he was serious, which she admired. Parsons was certain she'd meet the deadline, as certain as she was the sun would rise in the morning, or that energy could be neither created nor destroyed.

She expected to get paid something at some point but was surprised that thirty million had already been deposited into an encrypted account for her. This was immediately available for transfer to another account of her own choosing, and in any denomination or medium of currency she preferred.

If for whatever reason *he* decided to cancel the project, she would keep the money without condition.

It was also expected that she would say nothing about TRIBULATION to anyone outside of the lab where it was being built. After TRIBULATION was launched, she still couldn't reveal her involvement for exactly three hundred and sixty-five days.

'Why?'

'For your protection, and mine. Time to allow us to find places to hide in the world where we can never be found.'

She didn't question it further. A year wasn't much of a delay in relation to the fame that would accrue to her forever afterward. Her brilliance would be her defense if she decided to come back into the world. And if she decided to remain in hiding? Well, she wasn't looking for celebrity anyway. Only the universal acknowledgment that she had won, and TRIB-ULATION would prove that.

A final expectation was that she would carefully and surreptitiously sabotage progress on the government's RAP-TURE project. The reason was obvious. The only possible threat TRIBULATION faced would be the launch of RAPTURE, the only other true, universal quantum machine on the planet.

But what utterly delighted her was the fact that Rhodes's reputation would be ruined.

TRIBULATION would change the world because nearly every form of modern military and civilian operations, intelligence gathering, information processing, and communications all relied heavily, if not exclusively, on digital data.

All of that data was the lifeblood of global human activity and, increasingly, of individual human activity, no matter how pedestrian or mundane. Whether it was Alexa on your kitchen table, the phone in your pocket, or the hearing aid in your ear, computers were proliferating at an alarming rate – tens of billions of ordinary items were coming online; the so-called Internet of Things.

For all of the convenience, efficiency, productivity, and promise that the digital age was providing, the great sword of Damocles hanging over everyone's head was the insecurity of all of that data. Data was the gold stored in every device.

Relentless thieves, including governments, criminal syndicates, and individual hackers, hungered to steal that gold.

Early on, cyberthieves succeeded. New defenses were raised. Cybersecurity was born.

By the early part of the twenty-first century, an extremely secure form of cybersecurity had been achieved through sophisticated encryption algorithms. These algorithms were analogous to a passcode, like a three-digit number for a lock on a gym locker. A simple three-digit locker passcode only has one thousand possible combinations.

But a 128-bit AES cipher passcode would require a conventional computer capable of a 'brute force' attack of one trillion 'combinations' per second for nearly eleven quintillion years (eighteen zeros) to break through.

The hackers lost the 'brute force' arms race because it was far easier to create more complicated software algorithms than it was to produce computer hardware fast enough to beat them.

Thus, cybersecurity made the world safe for commerce and governments.

Until TRIBULATION.

TRIBULATION would soon be what RAPTURE could have been if the thieving politicians had left Parsons alone to finish the work she had started.

But they didn't, so she created TRIBULATION, the world's first true, universal 128-qubit quantum computer.

Google's 72-qubit quantum machine Bristlecone recently solved one particular mathematical calculation in less than four minutes. The fastest conventional supercomputer would have required at least ten thousand years to solve the same problem. Impressive by any measure. Google claimed quantum supremacy.

Google was wrong.

TRIBULATION was far superior to the Google machine by orders of magnitude. And it wasn't only about the quantity of qubits.

Generally speaking, there were two types of quantum computers: annealing and universal. D-Wave deployed a 2,000-qubit annealing machine but despite the larger number of qubits, its architecture limited its range of operations.

But universal quantum machines like Bristlecone and TRIBULATION were virtually unlimited in their applications. What made 128-qubit TRIBULATION exponentially more powerful than 72-qubit Bristlecone was that each of TRIBULATION's 128 qubits was also quantumly 'entangled.' This yielded more than 340 undecillion ($2^{128}$) combinations of output states – a number so large it was nearly incomprehensible to the human mind. And TRIBULATION, unlike Bristlecone and other competitors, operated flawlessly, with a zero error rate.

The significance of quantum computing was poorly understood outside of scientific circles. Sci-fi movie fans, doomsday preppers, and self-described 'futurists' insisted that artificial intelligence (AI) was the greatest threat to humanity.

They were wrong, too.

In just over eleven hours and forty-three minutes, TRIBULATION's quantum computer 'key' could unlock any encrypted door on the planet.

Nothing – absolutely nothing – that was digitized and stored accessibly would be secure once TRIBULATION came online.

Parsons shut her laptop and headed for the computer room located in the most secure building, which was also the cleanest and coldest.

To function properly, TRIBULATION depended upon the controlled spin of superpositioned quantum particles, i.e., qubits.

To maintain that controlled spin without interruption or interference, the machine required millikelvin temperatures to operate – temperatures approaching absolute zero, the point at which nearly all molecular activity ceases. If TRIBULATION was a juggler spinning plates – qubits – on the ends of her fingers, she couldn't have a monkey – unwanted molecular movement, i.e., heat – jump on her arms and start grabbing her hands because she would lose control of the spinning plates and they would crash.

Of the many breakthroughs Parsons's teams had accomplished, stable, near-zero operations had been one of the most important.

Parsons wanted to take another look at her machine. She could peer at TRIBULATION's magnificent architecture through a pane of tempered glass. She knew she would feel the love and longing of a mother gazing at her newborn daughter lying in an incubator, unable to touch her. But it was worth it.

Parsons knew that in all likelihood, it would be the last time she'd see her creation, at least for a good, long while. No matter. When the time was right, she'd be back to take full credit for whatever TRIBULATION had wrought upon the earth, for good or for ill.

# 56

*Washington, D.C.*
*Dulles International Airport*

The Lufthansa/United Airlines Airbus A321 touched down three minutes ahead of schedule, the wheels hardly kissing the tarmac.

Jack's mouth was full of cotton and spiders, or so it seemed to his aching skull and bleary eyes. He counted three little Jameson bottles stuffed in the seat pocket in front of him but he couldn't remember how many of the free Heinekens he'd downed before, during, and after the teriyaki chicken dinner now souring in his gut. At least the booze had knocked him out. He slept like a log . . . but he felt like he'd been sleeping under one. One that had fallen on him from a great height.

He could smell his own stink. He hadn't showered in over thirty-two hours, including a twelve-hour stint in a Spanish jail, not exactly a French perfumery. He wanted to get out of his dirty clothes, take a long, hot shower and wash away the last few days before hitting the sack for about a week. He wasn't scheduled to report for duty with The Campus for another few days.

As the plane taxied toward its jet bridge, the flight attendant announced that it was okay to turn on electronics. Jack powered up his phone and saw that Gavin had texted.

**TEXT ME WHEN YOU LAND. I'LL PICK YOU UP.**

Jack groaned. The last thing he wanted to do was deal with the lumpy IT executive. A sweet guy, sure, and a nice enough offer, but Jack didn't need a buddy right now. Just an Uber. Or a Lyft.

Jack texted back.

THANKS BUT I'LL JUST GRAB AN UBER. TALK TOMORROW.

The plane stood still on the tarmac waiting for the jet bridge to clear. His phone dinged. Gavin again.

I'M ALREADY HERE.
COULDN'T WAIT TO SEE YOU. SO MUCH TO TELL YOU.

Jack shook his head.

TELL ME NOW.

Gavin replied.

IT'S TOO GOOD NOT TO TELL YOU IN PERSON. ALSO, SECURITY.

Jack rubbed his throbbing skull. After all that Gavin had done for him, this wasn't much of an ask.

AWESOME. CAN'T WAIT.

Jack checked for other messages but nothing important had come over the transom. His stomach rumbled. He hoped he wasn't going to blow his cookies before he got off the plane.

Jack climbed into Gavin's blood-red Chevy Silverado crew cab idling at the curb and tossed his laptop and carry-on into the back. The truck was so new it still had temporary paper plates. The cab was full of that new-car smell, too.

Also, the smell of french fries.

Jack noticed several wadded-up fast-food bags tossed in the backseat. He suddenly didn't feel so badly about smelling like a garbage truck.

'Didn't take you for a truck guy, Gav.'

Gavin fired up the beefy 3.0L turbo-diesel engine. 'Used to own a Dodge panel van tricked out like I had back in high school. But the last girl I tried to pick up for a date saw me pull up to the curb and wouldn't come out of her house. I figured she thought it was a little too serial-killery.' He paused, adding, 'The girl before that one, too. So I decided it was time to change my ride.'

'Makes sense.'

'So I upscaled to this cowboy Cadillac.'

'It's a beautiful rig.'

'Comes in real handy at the Renaissance fairs, too, let me tell ya.'

Jack pulled out his wallet to pay for the parking as they rumbled up to the booth.

Gavin pushed his wallet away. 'Friends don't let friends pay for airport parking.'

Ten minutes later, they were rolling along in silence on the wide, four-lane VA-267 back toward Jack's apartment in Alexandria. Gavin was practically bouncing in his seat, bursting with excitement. But he was too polite to interrupt Jack's brooding thoughts.

Jack's mood was as sour as his gut but he finally relented.

'So, what is it that you wanted to tell me?'

'Gosh, I dunno where to start. There's so much to talk about.'

'Try the beginning.'

'Okay. I'll start with Sammler.'

Jack sat up. 'You found him?'

'No. You did. That guy you killed? Bykov?'

'Wait. How did you know that I killed him?'

'Dellinger uploaded a report on you. He was nice enough to include the Bykov autopsy photo, which is how I ran down his ID. My face re-creating program wasn't cutting it.'

'You hacked into the CIA mainframe?'

'Had to. I'm on overwatch, keeping an eye out for my buddy in the field.'

'Well, thanks for that. So why do you think Bykov is Sammler?'

'I don't. Sammler isn't a person, it's an organization. I mean, it's all rumors and hearsay. But if half of what's out there is true, these guys are way beyond the pale. They break a lot of things and hurt a lot of people for anybody for the right price. Or used to.'

'What do you mean?'

'They dropped off the radar a few years back. Rumor was they disbanded. But these people are evil. Like, Evil Empire storm trooper evil. The kind of evil that doesn't just quit. Think of Wagner, only worse.'

'Dellinger told me just this morning that Bykov was ex-Wagner, ex-Russian military, and reported dead long before I killed him.'

'You killed a dead guy? That's gotta be some kind of record.'

'I'm starting to see why you think Bykov was Sammler. He was ex-military. Most contracting outfits recruit those kinds of guys and Sammler is a contractor.'

Gavin's eyes widened. 'Oh, man, these Sammler guys aren't like any other contractors you ever heard of. They're real old school. They're all about the money, for sure, but not just the money. They've got some kind of a loyalty cult. Sort of a cross between the samurai Bushido code and *Legio Patria Nostra*.'

'"The Legion is our homeland," the motto of the French Foreign Legion.'

'Yeah. And toss in a little Mafia *omertà* on top and a dose of *Fight Club* and all of a sudden you have a band of super secret, super loyal, psycho-killer blood brothers who never talk about themselves or what they do.'

'That explains why it was so hard to find van Delden before. Maybe he was with Sammler, too.'

'Get this. They're so serious about their honor and loyalty that they do that Cold War thing where they put a cyanide capsule under a false tooth in order to take themselves out rather than get captured.'

Jack suddenly saw the puzzle pieces falling into place. 'After I punched Bykov in the mouth, he rubbed his chin and gave me this weird little smile before he dropped dead.'

'I'm waiting for the Spanish coroner to file his complete autopsy report, but I'll bet you a bag of Popeyes fried chicken sandwiches that it'll show cyanide or some other poison.'

Jack's mind flashed back to the steel mill. 'Now that I think about it, van Delden slammed his fist into his jaw a couple of times just before he jumped over the railing. I couldn't figure out why. I guess when his capsule didn't work, he knew the only way he wasn't going to get captured was to kill himself the hard way. I'll be damned.'

'And if Bykov really was with Sammler, you know what that means.'

'It means Sammler is responsible for Renée's murder. And Laia's. And Peña's. What the hell are these guys up to?'

'And maybe Runtso's murder, too. Unless Runtso was only collateral damage.'

'Speaking of Runtso, any progress on the RAPTURE project?'

'Oh! Yeah. That's the second thing I wanted to tell you about.'

'Go for it.'

'Well, I'm still not exactly sure *what* RAPTURE is but I know *where* it is – Oak Ridge, Tennessee. It's connected to the Oak Ridge National Laboratory.'

'Oak Ridge, as in, the Manhattan Project?'

'Yup. More brainiacs per square mile than, well, I dunno where. Nuclear weapons research. Fusion research. Quantum mechanics. Materials science. Aerospace engineering. Precision manufacturing. You name it, they do it all, and they do it for the DoD, DoE, NASA, and even the private sector.'

'Maybe I should head down to Oak Ridge.'

'Only if you want to get arrested and renditioned out to a Romanian secret prison. There's no way anyone not in that program can know about that program. You will be presumed guilty of espionage until you can prove your innocence, which is kinda hard to do when you're shackled to a basement wall with a car battery jumper-cabled to your McNuggets.'

Jack's head still throbbed but a shot of adrenaline suddenly cleared his mind.

'You said before that Runtso was some kind of consultant? What company was he consulting for?'

'He was his own boss. His work address is in Knoxville, Tennessee.'

'That's not too far from ORNL,' Jack said. 'Or the University of Tennessee.'

'Go Vols!' Gavin said, pumping one fist.

'You are full of surprises tonight. I had no idea you were a football guy.'

'I'm not. Women's basketball is where it's at. Pat Summitt

was one of the greatest NCAA coaches of all time. My mother used to play there. Mom and I never miss a game.'

They rolled along for a few minutes, Jack's mind turning back to Runtso.

What was a nuclear physicist doing in Spain? Why sneak into Barcelona?

Was it a coincidence that a CIA operative working for a technology front was in the same restaurant as he was?

Or was he intentionally coming there to meet her?

Or was he there to meet Aleixandri?

Was Runtso delivering some kind of a warning about RAPTURE to Renée or selling secrets to Brigada Catalan?

Did Sammler intend to kill Runtso or was he collateral damage?

And maybe the most important question of all:

Was Sammler somehow connected to RAPTURE?

'Questions are more powerful than answers,' his dad always used to say. Right now, he'd settle for answers. Questions like these only made his head hurt more than it already did, especially when the answers were so far out of reach.

Jack knew that the key to answering those questions was to figure out whether Runtso was a patriot or a traitor. And the answer to that question wasn't going to be found in the cab of a Chevy Silverado.

'I've got to go to Knoxville and chase down this lead on Runtso.'

'I'm going with you.'

'I don't think so, Gav. You never know what kind of trouble might be waiting down there.'

'The team's not back yet. You're the only operator in the area. And you know the rules. You never go in alone.'

'Gav —'

'Look, RAPTURE is technical, whatever it is, and you're,

349

well, physical. I'm the technical guy. So you go do the physical stuff, I'll take care of the rest.'

'I want to head out first thing tomorrow morning.'

'Let's get you back to your place and you can take care of your business, and maybe even take a shower. I'll make all of the arrangements and text you with the flight schedule as soon as I have it. Deal?'

Jack's head hurt too much to argue.

'Deal.'

# 57

*Labrador Sea*
*345 miles due south of the Greenland coast*

The tip of the shark's dorsal fin slipped beneath the surface of the frigid water.

Had anyone seen it, they might have thought it odd. The location was approximately nine hundred miles north of where RMS *Titanic* struck an iceberg and sank in April 1912.

No icebergs were floating around in the area this time of year. Most of the glacial calving on the coast of Greenland happened in the warmer temperatures of late spring and early summer.

Favoring warmer waters where food sources thrived, tiger sharks were frequently found in tropical and subtropical areas like the Caribbean or the Gulf of Mexico. But they were commonly seen in the Pacific waters near Australia, New Zealand, and the islands of the South Pacific. They have also been spotted in the colder waters of the northern Pacific and the Atlantic. Known to live as long as fifty years, these great fish are capable of circumnavigating the globe in the course of their lifespans.

The tiger shark is one of the largest predatory shark species on the planet, just slightly smaller than the more famous great white. They are nomadic animals who mostly follow the warm water currents. Their insatiable hunt for food includes all manner of fish and also giant sea turtles, dolphins, octopi, manta rays, sea birds, sea lions, and even other sharks. Fishermen have split open the stomachs of these ravenous beasts and discovered in whole or in part rats, cats, horses, monkeys, cushions, coats, car tires, and even explosives.

A pelagic species, tiger sharks usually inhabit the deep waters beyond the continental shelf, sometimes over four hundred feet below the surface. Sometimes they venture closer to the coast. They are perfectly designed for long journeys in deep water, and capable of short bursts of speed on the attack.

The largest tiger shark ever caught was just under twenty-four feet in length and weighed nearly seven thousand pounds. Typically, they are half that length and a third that weight.

In overall shape, length, and weight, the average tiger shark is quite similar to the human-designed Mark 48 torpedo.

The Canadian-owned freighter *Emerald Glory* was a Liberian-flagged vessel. The term of art was 'flag of convenience,' which was quite apt. Registering a vessel under the Liberian flag was a legal and convenient way for the owners to avoid the burdensome costs of additional taxes, environmental regulations, union wages, and maintenance requirements that a Canadian flag would have necessitated. This saved the owners over three million dollars per year.

The *Emerald Glory* had been loaded in the port of Montreal with a variety of cargoes, most of it in containers, but not all. Shipments of forklifts, excavators, gas turbines, plywood, fiberboard, and fuel wood were all bound for Aberdeen, Scotland, and Grimsby-Immingham, on the east coast of England, the busiest port in the UK.

The *Emerald Glory* was making just over eleven knots on a northerly route in the frigid waters of the Labrador Sea, a decent speed for her aging and fuel-inefficient engines. Her current location, speed, direction, and ports of destination were all broadcast on her AIS and available on a variety of commercial websites.

There were a number of people who monitored her live AIS broadcast, including those who intended to destroy her.

The tiger shark swam at a very low rate of speed, just above that of the eastbound current that carried the *Emerald Glory* along. The shark was, in fact, exactly in line with the ship as it approached from some two thousand yards away.

This particular shark was more than eighteen feet in length and weighed nearly four thousand pounds, neither of which was particularly unusual for the species.

Had the fish been hauled aboard one of the many fishing trawlers that harvested the fruit of the North Atlantic waters, they would have discovered several differences between this tiger shark and those typical to the species.

The single biggest difference was simply this:

The tiger now diving below the surface of the frigid waters of the Labrador Sea was an autonomous drone.

God – or nature's god, evolution, depending upon one's metaphysical orientation – was the world's greatest designer, and few designs exceeded the hydrodynamic efficiency of the tiger shark.

Biomimicry was widely adopted in many forms of drone technology. Rather than try and reinvent the wheel, the designers of the tiger shark drone let nature be their guide. Whereas actual tiger sharks were designed to hunt for food and reproduce, the tiger shark drone was designed to destroy commercial shipping vessels. This necessitated a few changes in God's design, not that it needed any improvements in form, only in function.

That function was not unlike the American-designed and -manufactured Mark 48 torpedo, one of the world's great undersea weapons. A lone sonar-guided, high-speed Mark 'fish' was capable of single-handedly destroying a surface or submerged warship.

The latest Mark 48 models weighed about thirty-five hundred pounds including a six-hundred-and-fifty-pound payload of high explosives. Much of the torpedo's remaining weight was due to the onboard liquid fuel propellant that drove the heavy swash-plate cam engine. The Mark 48's high-speed, pump-jet propulsion produced speeds exceeding sixty miles per hour underwater. The internal components and high-speed performance necessitated a metal skin and rigid architecture to maintain the torpedo's structural integrity from launch to impact.

The other requirement for the Mark 48 torpedo system was a delivery platform, which included every submarine class in the U.S. inventory. Delivery platforms like submarines and surface vessels were extraordinarily expensive, complex, large, and heavily crewed.

In short, the brilliant engineers at the U.S. Naval Surface Warfare Center designed the Mark 48 to attain high speeds, dive to great depths, and overcome defensive countermeasures in order to seek and destroy fast-moving, deep-diving enemy subs, their primary targets.

The challenge for the designers of the tiger shark drone was to combine the hydrodynamic efficiencies of the shark with the destructive potential of a torpedo.

While these two design characteristics were seemingly at

odds – God versus the Naval Surface Warfare Center – in fact, the solution was relatively straightforward.

The tiger shark drone design variations from the Mark 48 torpedo all stemmed from the variation in targets.

The Mark 48 weapons system was designed for combat against fast, stealthy, deep-diving submarines capable of high-speed defensive maneuvers. This required fast, deep-diving torpedoes with advanced target acquisition capabilities.

But the tiger shark drone targets were slow-moving, non-diving commercial cargo vessels that deployed neither stealth nor any other defensive countermeasures.

That made commercial cargo vessels extremely vulnerable to slow-moving weapon systems like the drone shark.

With that kind of target, the tiger shark drone design solutions immediately suggested themselves.

First and foremost, a slow-moving drone could carry a larger payload – twenty-six hundred pounds of high explosive, four times greater than what the Mark 48 deployed.

Slow-moving targets allowed a slow-moving weapon. This meant the drone required lower energy output and energy use. The battery-powered, electric-motored tiger drone had plenty of both in reserve.

When first described to Sammler, the chief design engineer compared the four-thousand-pound, sixteen-foot tiger drone to a submersible 2020 Tesla Roadster – but with fins instead of tires. The all-electric Tesla Roadster was capable of achieving zero to sixty miles per hour in 1.9 seconds, and could travel over six hundred miles at highway speeds on a single charge of its 200 kWh lithium-ion battery.

But the tiger shark drone wasn't turning four tires at maximum speed on high-friction asphalt in order to chase down a fast-moving target. In fact, the drone didn't have to move at all. It could simply drift for hours, if not days, without expending any energy whatsoever as it waited for its target to arrive at the drone shark's location. Even if it ran continuously at its average speed of thirteen knots per hour, it would still have a range of over twenty-four hundred miles on a single charge. Thanks to its eight-hundred-volt architecture stolen from the Porsche design bureau, it could recharge eighty percent of its capacity in just fifteen minutes.

A particular genius of the tiger shark drone system was its targeting program. In fact, the drone relied on the commercial vessel to target *itself* – via its own AIS transmissions. Once the target was selected, the tiger drone positioned itself somewhere along the vessel's path via the drone's onboard AI program or by remote human operation.

Whereas a conventional submarine and torpedo system had to find and chase an enemy vessel, a deployed tiger drone passively awaited the arrival of its target.

There were many other advantages to the tiger drone design, including its stealth capabilities. Noise, heat, size, wave propagation, and magnetic anomalies were the primary means of detecting submersible and surface vessels. The tiger drone avoided or mitigated all of these.

First, its primary means of propulsion – a swishing tail – produced one-tenth the acoustical noise of a conventional propeller, though the shark had one of these for emergency use or for microbursts of speed.

Second, the tiger drone's outer hide was comprised of just four millimeters of bubble-infused ('bubble wrap') latex skin. This dampened sonar signals by as much as ninety-nine percent, and reduced radar wave detection by a factor of ten thousand. A secondary layer of rubber added extra stability and helped shield the few metallic internal components, including its two small and nearly silent electric motors weighing just seventy pounds each.

Third, the skeleton of the fish was comprised of non-metallic polycarbonate 'bones' and the propeller shaft and propeller were constructed from German-designed carbon fiber reinforced plastics (CFRP).

Finally, the dorsal fin of the drone served as its antenna, able to send and receive encrypted comms and location signals. It was also able to independently receive and track the AIS signals of any commercial vessel worldwide. And, of course, high-def digital cameras were located behind the clear lenses of the drone's eyes.

Taken altogether, the tiger drone was practically invisible to sonar, radar, heat, or magnet anomaly detection. But in the extremely unlikely event one of them popped up on screen or scope, the size and shape of the signature would indicate exactly what it appeared to be: a lone shark in the water, not a fast-moving, metal-skinned submarine or torpedo.

Biomimicry at its best.


The research lab that designed the tiger shark drone knew that another significant technical problem still faced them: the delivery platform.

Because of their limited range, Mark 48 torpedoes were delivered to combat areas by submarines and launched from tubes within the vessel.

While the tiger shark had far wider range than a torpedo, it wasn't capable of completely independent movement. Eventually, its battery would be exhausted, or mechanical issues might arise. And given its slow speed, it would take many days if not weeks to arrive in its zone of operation if launched from its point of origin.

The delivery system option was even more obvious to the

designers than the biomimicry 'fish' solution for the weapons platform itself.

What better delivery system for a drone fish than a fish trawler?

These 'trawler' mother ships were, in fact, converted deepwater fishing vessels, with all of the appropriate gear to pass any unlikely inspection. Modern fishing vessels deployed sonar, radar, navigation, and comms that did double duty as drone support equipment.

In addition, these disguised mother ships possessed both battery recharging platforms for the sharks and drone repair facilities. In the event of an emergency, the sharks could be 'caught' by the mother ships, and either towed or brought on board and redeployed elsewhere.

In the unlikely event one of the tiger shark drones was captured by an enemy vessel, the onboard munitions would self-destruct when the machine was lifted vertically unless the gyroscope motion detector was deactivated by its mother ship commander.

There were five mother ship vessels deployed around the world, and each deployed six shark drones. Once deployed in the water, the sharks were given an AIS signal to track. The drone's onboard computer automatically attacked the vessel in question. The shark drone dove under the hull and exploded, breaking the spine of the ship and destroying its structural integrity with a single but massive charge equivalent to four Mark 48 torpedoes.

Without question, the tiger drone weapon system would have been of limited value in direct confrontation in a wartime scenario with a major seafaring power. But that wasn't its purpose.

The tiger drone program was a new kind of piracy, operated by a new kind of pirate. Lucrative, yes, but temporarily so. It was a means to an end. Its primary purpose was to distract the United States from an even more dangerous and terrifying operation that had only begun to unfold.

The *Emerald Glory* broke apart instantly, its two halves sinking in less than seven minutes. Miraculously, three crew members survived the blast. Without lifeboat or vests, they treaded the bone-chilling waters for less than twenty minutes. Each died in turn as their numbing muscles failed. Helpless to avoid slipping beneath the surface, they perished swallowing the sea in whimpering gasps, their corpses blueing in the water as they waited for a rescue that never came.

# October 30

# 58

## *Alexandria, Virginia*

Jack stood ready at the curb in front of his house checking his watch, shaved, showered, and rested. He was waiting for Gavin, who finally pulled up in his Silverado an hour before sunrise.

Jack tossed his buffalo leather carry-on in the cab and followed in after it.

'You're late.'

'Can't be late if we're the only passengers,' Gavin said with a smile as he sped off for the airport. 'And I wanted to get you a coffee.' Gavin pointed at the large black Dunkin' Donuts coffee in Jack's cupholder. Jack saw the flakes of croissant on Gavin's shirt and assumed another crumpled bag now lay in the back.

'Appreciate it.'

'Next stop, Knoxville.'


Jack and Gavin boarded the Cirrus G2 Vision Jet parked at Signature, the Dulles FBO. The nice thing about flying private, particularly on a Hendley plane, was that Jack could carry his weapon, a single stack slimline Glock 43 nine-millimeter. He carried it in a BlackDog IWB deep concealment holster beneath his sport coat, along with a spare six-round mag.

The new Cirrus G2 was a powerful but diminutive 'personal' one-pilot jet with seating arranged for just two passengers that morning. Hendley Associates purchased the G2 as an alternative to its giant fuel-guzzling Gulfstream G550 used for international flights.

The V-tailed, single-engine G2 was fast, powerful, and economical. It had a glass flight deck and side sticks that looked like something from a *Star Trek* episode with automated flight controls to match. Jack was impressed with its luxury comfort and visibility in the small cabin. His flight-phobic dad would have loved the safety features. These included an emergency one-button Safe Return autoland and the one-lever parachute system that landed the aircraft in an upright position.

Captain Helen Reid, the senior pilot for Hendley Associates, was at the controls. She'd already been scheduled for a trip to Knoxville later in the week for the G2's annual maintenance at the Cirrus facility at McGhee Tyson Airport in Alcoa. She was happy to switch her schedule on short notice for Gavin and Jack.

They reached their cruising altitude of thirty-one thousand feet in short order.

'I wanted to bounce an idea off you,' Gavin said.

'Shoot.'

'I couldn't get to sleep last night, so I did some messing around on one of my tech blogs, catching up on the latest goings-on. Have you ever heard of Chris and Cari Fast?'

'No, can't say that I have.'

'They were two of the most important researchers at Google's AI quantum labs in Mountain View. They were found murdered just four days ago. Some kind of crazy satanic ritual.'

'That's sick.'

'Yeah, it is. And apparently they left their entire thirty-million-dollar estate to a no-kill animal shelter in San

Francisco. That's what the board was buzzing about, bitching that it should've gone to the homeless instead.

'But their murders got me to thinking so I started nosing around, and then I found an NSA internal memo on the suicide of Dr Stanley Hopkins. That really bummed me out. I actually met him once at a London conference a few years ago. He was lecturing on the challenges of cryptography in a post-quantum world. Dude was spooky smart, emphasis on spooky.'

'Meaning?'

'Meaning he was a spook. Or at least, working at GCHQ.'

'Keep going.'

'Yeah. Two points make a line. So I followed the line. And you know what else I found? There are five other world-class researchers all connected in one way or another to quantum cybersecurity that have died in the last year.'

'And no one else has made that connection?'

Gavin shrugged. 'They all happened in different countries, and all the deaths were completely different. Ritualistic murder, suicide, motorcycle accident, drowning, accidental overdose, an armed robbery gone bad, and carbon monoxide poisoning. Even if you were looking for a connection, you wouldn't have necessarily found it. But then again, genius is seeing the obvious.'

'Well then, friend genius, who's the obvious culprit behind these killings?'

'Still working on that one.'

They rode along for a moment. Jack said, 'Do you think Runtso could be another link in that chain of killings?'

'Depends on whatever it was he was doing at ORNL with the RAPTURE project.'

'Given his background, do you think he could have been working in cybersecurity?'

'I don't see why not. He could have been working on the hardware side of things, since he was a physicist.'

'And if Sammler is behind Runtso's death, then maybe they might be responsible for these other deaths, too.'

'I can see that.'

'But Sammler is just a crew of hired guns. We definitely need to find them, but we really need to find who hired them.'

Jack sighed, frustrated. It was déjà vu all over again. He was right back where he started with van Delden, his first dead end, then Bykov. Also a dead end.

'We don't have any more links in the Sammler chain,' Gavin said. 'It's like we're free-climbing the face of El Capitan. No way to get to the top.'

'No, but we've got Runtso. If we can figure out exactly why he was killed, that might be a handhold we can work with.'

'And if Runtso is just another dead end?'

'Then I start pulling out pitons and driving them into somebody's skull.'

# 59

After they landed and Captain Reid secured the G2 at the Cirrus maintenance hangar, Jack and Gavin grabbed the rental waiting for them outside the Cirrus offices. It was a four-door silver Jeep Wrangler soft-top with a high-end Warn Zeon winch fixed to the front bumper.

'I picked the Wrangler in case we want to explore the Smoky Mountains while we're here,' Gavin offered. 'And I thought we'd look cool in it.'

Jack climbed in behind the wheel and Gavin punched the business address he'd found from Runtso's tax records into the Garmin GPS navigator. The Garmin sent them north on the 129 Alcoa Highway toward Knoxville. Runtso's office was just fifteen miles distant. But the roads were red-lined all the way up because they were hitting morning rush hour traffic, miles of construction slowdowns, and navigating at least one wreck on the highway. Add to that the stop-and-go traffic on Kingston Pike, and what should have taken twenty-four minutes was now costing them more than an hour.

Jack checked his frustration. It wasn't as if they were in a rush. There wasn't a ticking clock pointed like a gun at their heads. They were just chasing the one lead they had, not even exactly sure of what they were looking for, let alone what they might find when they got there.

\*

What they found when they finally arrived was entirely underwhelming.

The address led them directly to a UPS Store. As expected, when they went inside, Jack and Gavin found that the suite number of Runtso's business address was just the number on a mailbox, one of dozens. There was no window on the mailbox and therefore no way to tell if it was full, empty, or even in use.

'Now what?' Gavin said.

'Follow my lead,' Jack said, ginning up his seductive powers. He approached the middle-aged, heavyset woman behind the counter. She wore black stretch pants, a blue oxford work shirt, and bright green eye shadow.

'May I help you?' she asked behind a pair of thick glasses.

Jack smiled broadly, locking eyes with her. 'A friend of mine has a business address that's located here, in one of your mailboxes. His name is Dr Dylan Runtso. He owns a consulting firm.'

'Synergy Solutions,' Gavin said, standing just behind Jack.

'This Runtso fella must have a lot of friends.'

'Oh? Why do you say that?' Jack asked.

' 'Cuz you're not the first ones to stop by and ask about him. What is it that you want exactly?'

'He's out of town and he's asked me to come down and fetch his mail out of his box.'

The woman's eyes narrowed. 'I'll tell you what I told the others. Unless you're on his paperwork as an authorized user, I can't let you do that.'

'What if I told you he gave me permission?'

'Do you have anything in writing?'

'He called me. Just a few minutes ago.'

'Then how about you call him right back and I'll talk to him?'

'I wish I could. He just went into an important meeting and can't be reached.'

The woman parked her big fists on her even bigger hips. 'Honey, do I look like I just fell off the turnip truck?'

Gavin barked a laugh, like a circus seal. The woman glanced over Jack's shoulder and gave Gavin the stink eye. He withered and turned aside.

'No, ma'am, you don't,' Jack said. 'But this is really important.'

'I'm sure it is.'

Jack pulled out a billfold and flashed a fake ID, along with a fake badge. He held it up to her face and she grabbed it with both of her red-nailed hands and read it while he was still holding it.

'U.S. Department of Homeland Investigations.' She let go of Jack's billfold. 'Another Fed.'

*Another?*

'Can we see the contents of that mailbox?'

'I'll tell you what I told those FBI people. Unless you have a warrant signed by a judge, I can't let you in there.'

Jack pocketed his phony credentials. 'Then I guess I'll have to go and get one.'

'No use, hon.'

'Why not?'

'Don't you Feds talk to each other? The FBI already came back with one and emptied out that box two days ago. Wasn't much in it, near as I can tell. Not that I read my customers' mail, mind you.'

Jack shook his head, feigning disgust. 'You know how it is back in D.C. It's just one giant goat rodeo.'

'Ain't it the truth,' she said, nodding in agreement. 'Wait a minute.' The woman searched beneath her counter, then came up with a business card and handed it to Jack. 'That was the FBI lady in charge. She and another fella came in here.'

The woman touched her red index nail to the name. 'She spells it *K-a-n-g* but she pronounces it "Kong." Give her a call. She was nice enough.'

The bell on the glass door tinkled as another customer came in.

'Thanks. That's really helpful.' Jack pocketed the card. 'Sorry to bother you.'

'No bother at all, hon. Good luck. And thank you both for your service.'

*Ouch.*

# 60

## Washington, D.C.
## Situation Room, The White House

For this emergency meeting, the long mahogany table was crowded with more principals. The chairs along the walls were occupied by department and agency staffers, mostly military.

Each principal had given a brief summary of their findings and concerns. The latter was a considerable list. It all amounted to a seemingly insoluble challenge.

Ryan called this latest meeting as soon as he got word about the Labrador Sea sinking from Admiral Talbot before his day had even begun.

They all had been lulled into a false sense of victory after the *Glazov* was forced to the surface and perp-walked back to Russia three days ago. But the sinking of yet another ship in the Indian Ocean had shattered that illusion.

Now the news of this additional sinking in the Labrador Sea proved the crisis was spinning out of control. Nobody knew who was behind the attacks, how they were conducted, or where the next ones would take place.

'It's like we're boxing with blindfolds and earplugs,' was the way Arnie put it. 'And the ring just keeps getting bigger and bigger.'

These escalating attacks by an unknown hostile deploying an assumed but as yet unidentified weapons system threatened to destabilize the global economy. This was the worst crisis Ryan's administration had ever faced.

And he took full responsibility for it.

Ryan needed more hands on deck if he hoped to get ahead of this thing.

DARPA sent over a department head and two leading researchers working on extra-large unmanned undersea vehicles (XLUUVs), and Admiral Talbot flew two officers in from the Naval Undersea Warfare Center in Keyport, Washington: the commander of Submarine Development Squadron (DEVRON) 5, and the commander of the newly formed Unmanned Undersea Vehicles Squadron (UUVRON) 1.

Ryan scanned the room. All eyes were on him. These were earnest, serious people looking for guidance and, more important, confidence. They were scared. So was he. Ryan knew they weren't looking for answers because there weren't any. They wanted leadership.

Ryan stood.

'We're standing right in front of a brick wall, no two ways about it,' Ryan began. 'A wall so tall and wide we can't comprehend it. Randy Pausch was right about brick walls. They're there to show us how badly we want something. And they only stop the people who don't want it badly enough.

'I know most of you in this room, and more important, you know me. You know how badly I want to find and stop whoever is behind these attacks. I don't know how we're going to do it. I don't know how long it's going to take.

'What I do know is that the Labrador incident is the first lucky break we've had because it's the first sinking we've been able to detect in real time, thanks to SBIRS picking up the thermal flare.

'The second lucky break is that it appears to be a simple, conventional chemical explosion, and definitely not nuclear, according to MASINT.

'The third thing we know is that no known hostile

combat aircraft were in the area, and no cruise, ballistic, or hypersonic missiles were detected before, during, or after the attack.

'Which I believe is connected to the fourth thing in our favor. DNI Foley has assured us that there has been no Chinese or Russian chatter about these events, and SecState Adler has not received any back-channel communications from either principals or opposition from within their respective governments. We still don't know who is behind all of this but we are now reasonably confident it isn't the Russians or the Chinese, which takes a World War Three scenario off the table.

'Now it's time to roll up our sleeves, and find a way to get our tails over, under, around, or through this goddamn brick wall. Who's coming with me?'

Ryan sensed rather than heard a collective sigh of relief around the table. Nodding heads and smiles told him he won the room over.

'We're with you, Mr President. All the way,' Foley said.

More nodding heads. Even a few laughs.

*Not a bad little pep talk,* Ryan thought. *If only I believed it myself.*

The room's secure door opened, and Ruby Knox, the temporary lead agent of the Presidential Protective Division, approached him.

That wasn't good.

The PPD knew exactly how important this meeting was. Nothing short of an even greater national emergency should be interrupting it.

'Excuse me,' Ryan said to the table as he stepped closer to Knox and out of earshot from the others in the room.

'What is it?' Ryan asked in a low voice.

'The Treasury secretary is in the Oval, along with the chairman of the Federal Reserve. They've requested a meeting with you ASAP.'

Ryan frowned, genuinely confused.

'I've got more important things on my plate right now than worrying about the ECB dropping interest rates a quarter point next week.'

Knox nodded. 'I explained that to them, sir. But they're quite insistent.'

'Did they tell you what it's all about?'

'I'm just the hired help, sir.'

'What do you think?'

'I think SecTreas Hodge is going to stroke out if you don't get up there pronto, and if I'm not mistaken, Chairman Moorcroft has already pooped his pantaloons. Sir.'

# 61

*The White House*

Agent Knox opened the northeast door leading from the President's secretary's office into the Oval. SecTreas Stephen Hodges and Chairman Wesley Moorcroft were sitting together on one of the long couches.

Both men bolted to their feet when the door opened and President Ryan and Arnie van Damm marched in. Knox closed the door behind them for privacy – and security. The two financial executives each wore expensive, tailored gray suits. Hodges wore a silk rep Harvard tie and held a leather folio in a white-knuckled grip. Moorcroft wore a bright yellow bow tie and glasses.

Ryan beelined to the two men and waved them back to their seats on the couch. Both executives were in their mid-sixties and in good health, and known for their steady nerves and keen minds navigating the turbulent world of global and domestic finance.

It scared the hell out of Ryan that both men were visibly shaken.

'Gentlemen, please. Let's forget the formalities. What's going on? You two look like you've seen a ghost.'

Ryan took one of the chairs and Arnie grabbed the couch opposite the two financial wizards.

Hodges opened his folio, pulled a letter from it, and handed it to Ryan. He also gave Arnie a copy.

'Mr President,' Hodges began, 'our offices simultaneously

received this letter approximately one hour ago. You can read the details in full later. But the letter claims – and unfortunately, my office has verified that claim – that five *trillion* dollars has been stolen from the accounts of the world's one hundred largest banking institutions.'

No one moved. No one breathed. They couldn't.

'Now wait one goddamned New York minute,' Arnie said. He leaned forward, his face a welter of confusion. 'Did you really just say five *trillion*? With a *t*?'

'I'm afraid so,' Hodges said.

'And it's already stolen? Gone? Just disappeared?'

'Yes.'

Arnie threw his hands in the air. 'That's utter bullshit.'

'Unfortunately, it's not,' Moorcroft said. 'It's absolutely accurate. We've verified with over forty-two banks so far, and others are reaching out to my office even as we speak.'

'I've already been contacted by the presidents of Bank of America and JPMorgan Chase,' Hodges said. 'Eighteen of the world's largest banks are Chinese, including the top four. The U.S. has twelve of the largest banks; Japan eight; France, South Korea, and the UK each have six; Canada, Germany, and Spain five.'

'My counterparts at the European Central Bank and Bank of Japan reached out to me within minutes of the letter,' the Federal Reserve chairman said. 'England, Canada, Australia, and New Zealand as well. These are all sober and imperturbable men and women, and I'm telling you, they are scared witless.'

'What about the Chinese?' Ryan asked.

'When I didn't hear from them, I took it upon myself to reach out to the governor of the People's Bank of China. I hope I didn't overstep my authority, but time is not our friend.'

'You did exactly the right thing,' Ryan said.

'Thank you, sir.'

'What did the Chinese say?'

'The governor hasn't responded to my repeated calls. They're clearly stonewalling. Not surprising, really, given the way they work. The PBOC is an organ of the Chinese Communist Party, like almost everything else over there. In a crisis like this, the governor isn't going to communicate with any outsiders without official instructions from the higher-ups.'

'Unless they're the ones behind all of this,' Arnie offered.

Ryan thought of that, too. 'And what about the Russians?'

'They only have one bank in the top hundred, Sberbank,' Hodges said. 'We have, shall we say, third-party access to their organization. Apparently, they have *not* been hit.'

*Interesting,* Ryan thought. *Fits perfectly with the improved Kilo-class scenario.*

He couldn't share that with the finance men, though he would need to read Hodges in to that crisis soon, before word got out about it and *that* crisis started a global economic panic.

'Five trillion?' Arnie asked again. 'It's mind-boggling. How is that even possible?'

'Digitally, of course,' Hodges said.

'Only eight percent of global money is actual physical currency these days,' Ryan said. 'The other ninety-two percent is just ones and zeros on a hard drive somewhere.'

Hodges pointed at the piece of paper in Arnie's hand. 'Read the letter, Mr van Damm. It appears the thieves have acquired the technical means to break into each of these banks and rob the till, so to speak. Whoever it is used a computer they call TRIBULATION.'

Ryan pulled on his reading glasses and scanned the letter. His eyes fell upon one particular passage. His blood ran cold.

*. . . Your best interest is to make arrangements to cover my theft. Do not pursue me or I will RETALIATE. You are dealing with the person who created the first true quantum computer. Everything is open to me: all of your secret files, all of your official lies, all of your weapons systems and energy grids . . . every savings account, every retirement account, every investment account. Corporations and governments are equally exposed. Everything is open to me.*

*But I'm not greedy. Five trillion dollars is enough for what I have planned. Within the next several months, I'm confident that the world will have developed quantum cyberdefenses against me so my window of opportunity will close – which is your only hope.*

*And now, gentlemen, please convey this special message to President Ryan: Do not pursue me. You will fail.*

*If you attempt to pursue me, I will burn your world to the ground, starting with a press release detailing my theft. My silence is your only protection.*

*As proof of your commitment not to pursue me, you will personally instruct Chairman Moorcroft to deposit one hundred billion dollars into the account described below by nine a.m. EST. We both know the chairman has the power to do that. After all, didn't he print sixteen trillion dollars out of thin air to bail out your 'too big to fail' bankster buddies?*

*If you fail to make the deposit by nine a.m. EST, I will unleash unimaginable chaos.*

'I don't understand,' Arnie said. 'Is he saying that if we pay the one hundred billion he'll return the five trillion?'

Ryan shook his head. 'No. He – or she – is keeping the five trillion. That's an all-out assault on the world. But the additional one hundred billion dollars is directed at me, jerking my chain. Somehow this is personal.'

Hodges said, 'If he really has constructed the world's first true quantum computer, he's perfectly capable of overwhelming the encryption security protecting the world's largest financial institutions, just as he claims.'

'What does the theft of five trillion dollars do to these banks? To the global monetary supply?' Ryan asked. The questions were rhetorical. His background in Wall Street investing gave him a firm grasp of markets and money.

'For the banks, it's absolutely devastating,' Hodges said. 'Their primary function is lending money. Without money, their function ceases. If families and businesses can't borrow money to buy homes or make products, the global economy collapses.

'The only good news I've heard from the banks so far is that they have each been left with enough operating capital to last them the rest of the week,' Hodges said.

Moorcroft added, 'For the global money supply, it's a somewhat different story. Global money supply is approximately ninety trillion dollars. The choice of the five-trillion-dollar figure is an interesting one. The theft has removed only about five and a half percent of that total.'

'You make it sound like it's no big deal,' Arnie said. 'A nickel out of a dollar.'

'Oh, no, Mr van Damm. It's a really big deal. Maybe the biggest of all time. If people discover their life savings and college funds and checking accounts have all been emptied out, they'll lose complete confidence in the monetary system as we know it. It will be the end of capitalism.'

Hodges leaned forward for emphasis. 'We're not talking about a temporary banking or stock market or real estate crisis like we've experienced over the last few decades. Those were bad, sure, but they were part of the business cycle, and we bounced back from all of those. But this? There won't be any bouncing back. If there's a global economic collapse, and trust in the currency is destroyed, capitalism will be irretrievably discredited. And I think we all know what comes next.'

'Lenin, Hitler, Stalin, Tojo, Mussolini. They were all products of economic collapse,' Ryan said. 'And the result was war: civil, regional, global.'

'We're talking an economic apocalypse,' Moorcroft said. '*And* a political one.'

# 62

Sectreas Hodges and Chairman Moorcroft stared ashen-faced at the President. Ryan shared their concern. But now was not the time to quail.

Ryan tried to hide his rage along with his growing sense of panic. Every major government in the world was chasing quantum computing. A quantum computing arms race was raging across the globe.

He had convinced Congress to take the threat seriously and help speed along the research rather than simply wait for the private sector to figure it out. The stakes were too high to let a bad actor acquire quantum computing first – as today was proving out. Quantum computing would be the technological equivalent of nuclear weapons for the twenty-first century, and suddenly, the United States was completely disarmed.

'He's put a countdown clock on us, Mr President. Two, actually. First, as you've just read, he demands we deposit a sum of one hundred billion dollars into an account he's specified within the next' – Hodges checked his Patek Philippe Geneve watch – 'forty-seven minutes as proof you'll not pursue him.'

'He's badly mistaken if he thinks I won't hound his ass to the gates of hell and back. But to buy time, I'm authorizing you to make the deposit.'

'Very good, Mr President. I assumed you'd agree to his condition, and I've prearranged everything. One call and the transaction will be completed.'

'And the second ticking clock you were talking about?' Arnie asked.

'The banks I've spoken with are fully aware of the scale and scope of this crisis. I've received personal assurances from each of them that they won't act unilaterally but they will only give us until end of business today to work out some kind of a solution.'

'And I've reached out to my counterparts at the ECB and the BOJ,' Moorcroft said. 'They also agree to abstain from any unilateral action until we can coordinate our response. The question remains, what is it we want to do?'

'How long do we have to fix this thing?'

'The sooner the better.'

'Obviously. But what's the absolute outer limit of time we have to come up with something?'

'It's Wednesday,' Hodges said. 'If we could come up with some plausible reason for an extended global bank and market holiday through the weekend, we'd be pushing it. I'd say before markets open Monday morning would be the absolute outer limit. And that's assuming we can get the Russians and Chinese on board.'

Ryan checked his watch. 'Just under one hundred and nineteen hours to save the world? No wonder you guys were sweating buckets when we came in.' Ryan rubbed his chin, thinking. 'Can your technical people come up with some kind of story about a computer virus that's playing havoc in the international banking community?'

'That kind of news could cause a panic all on its own,' Hodges warned.

'Not if we say it's contained, that all records are digitized and in order, and that no one has lost any money. We'll tell them that in order to purge the system we need to shut it all down. Something along those lines. I'm not a computer guy.

It just has to be believable to the average joe to avoid a mass run on the banks and a general panic.'

'We can get the big banks and Wall Street behind this,' Arnie said. 'They can make announcements in support of all of this, and they'll do it because it's their bacon in the frying pan.'

'Assuming we can convince the whole world to stop banking until next Monday, then what?' Hodges asked. 'How do we restore the five-trillion-dollar losses to the banks?'

Ryan smiled.

'That's the easy part.'

'Easy?' Arnie asked. 'How?'

'We create our own five-trillion-dollar string of ones and zeros,' Ryan said.

'What? Just create five trillion dollars' — Arnie snapped his fingers — 'like that? How is that even possible?'

'Modern money is a kind of fiction. It's a story we tell ourselves to keep away the scary monsters of our uncertainties,' Ryan said. 'Digital money — those ones and zeros on a hard drive — has value because people *believe* it has value.'

'You're waxing a little too poetic, boss. Simplify it for a knuckle dragger like me.'

'Currencies like the U.S. dollar used to be based on something tangible, like gold. From 1834 until FDR outlawed the private ownership of gold in April 1933, you could trade in $20.69 American for one ounce of gold, and vice versa. That way you knew that your paper dollars were always worth something of real value.

'Not anymore. It's all fiat currency. The only thing sustaining the U.S. dollar is the "full faith and credit" of the U.S. government. In other words, psychology.

'Same with every other government using fiat currency,

which is all of them. If you trust the government to protect your money, you trust your money. If the government says that digital dollars are safe, then they're safe.'

Arnie nodded, suddenly seeing the bigger picture. 'And if someone steals all the money, it means your government can't keep the money safe, which means people think that money has lost all of its value, and all economic activity grinds to a halt.'

'It also means we've lost the "full faith and credit" of the American people,' Moorcroft added. 'And if they lose confidence in our ability to protect them on this most fundamental level – the means to feed and clothe and house their families – then I shudder to think what the political aftermath of that might be.'

'We can avoid all of this if we can prove that those digital dollars really *are* safe,' Ryan said. 'All we have to do is create five trillion new dollars and replace the stolen ones with it.'

Moorcroft frowned. 'What about inflation? Interest rates? What about –'

Ryan held up his hand, cutting the chairman off. 'I would only do this as a stopgap until we can recover the stolen five trillion. When we get it back, we'll toss it in the desktop trash can, so to speak, and balance the books.'

'But no government has ever done anything like this before. I'm afraid you'll open up a Pandora's box with this precedent,' Arnie said.

'I think you're forgetting about quantitative easing,' Moorcroft said. 'And the other tools in the Federal Reserve's toolbox. Just as the letter said, we created sixteen trillion dollars "out of thin air" during the banking crisis.'

'But that's different,' Arnie said. 'That was done to stimulate the economy. If Congress thinks they can just start printing "free" money for votes, then all bets are off.'

'They already do. It's called twenty-three trillion dollars of national debt,' Hodges said. 'But at least that took them over two hundred years to figure out.'

Ryan shook his head. 'I can't worry about what politicians might do in the future, Stephen. All I know is that this move will buy us time and may prevent the collapse we're all afraid of. I think it's worth the gamble, unless one of you has a better solution.'

Hodges nodded, reluctantly accepting the logic. 'Perhaps you're right, Mr President. But if word of this gets out to the general public, it will still cause a panic, and a crisis in confidence in global currencies, and still lead to the collapse we're trying to avoid, even if we promise to restore the five trillion in losses.'

'Agreed.' Ryan turned to the chairman. 'Wes?'

The chairman shrugged. 'This is a dangerous course of action that poses considerable risks over the long run. But I'm at a loss to offer a superior solution to the immediate crisis. I think it's the way to proceed.'

'Arnie?'

'Sounds crazy enough to work, boss. But only if you can get everyone involved on the same page by Monday. Frankly, I don't think that's going to happen. You'd have a better chance of herding a hundred frightened cats all into the same litter box to take a shit together. And it doesn't solve your bigger problem.'

'I know. We've got to find the bastard who did this or it could happen all over again tomorrow.'

# 63

*Knoxville, Tennessee*

Jack knew it was a felony to impersonate a federal agent, even if it was a fake agency like the Department of Homeland Investigations. But he was desperate and it was the only move he could come up with back at the UPS Store. He also felt guilty about lying to the nice UPS lady, especially after she thanked him for his service. But deception was as important a weapon in his business as the Glock 43 in his holster. Thankfully she bought the ruse, otherwise she might have felt compelled to call this Agent Kang and put her on his tail.

Since the FBI had been to Runtso's 'office,' Jack assumed they'd already paid a visit to his home. They'd probably cleared out anything useful. But maybe they missed something that could tell him about Runtso's work or any connection he might have to Sammler or even Bykov. Something that tied him to Renée would be great, too. Any intel he could find on RAPTURE would be a home run. It was a real long shot but worth the try.

Jack followed the Jeep's GPS back east on Kingston Pike to Neyland Drive. He followed the winding curve of the Tennessee River along the back side of the University of Tennessee campus, checking his mirrors for unwanted friends.

Gavin nearly jumped out of his seat as they passed Thompson-Boling Arena, where the national champion Lady Vols basketball team played. Gavin had only ever seen the inside of it on a television screen. He made Jack promise they'd come back later and tour the arena, then grab pulled pork sandwiches at Calhoun's on the River nearby.

From Neyland they made their way up to the Henley Street Bridge and headed south on Chapman Highway. They made the turn onto Druid Drive past Berry Funeral Home, a stately, mountain stone building and into a historic, tree-lined neighborhood.

Following the narrow two-lane roads, Jack and Gavin navigated past dozens of cozy, well-kept homes. It was a workday morning and there were few signs of life save for a half-dozen parked cars in driveways or on the street. Jack assumed those belonged to stay-at-home moms, working self-employed and remotes.

'There it is,' Gavin said, pointing at one of the few river rock houses on the street. Jack gently lowered his arm. 'No pointing, Gav. It's rude. It's also a big red flag.'

'Oh, gee. That was stupid. Sorry.'

Jack could see the yellow NO ENTRANCE sign taped to the red front door in his peripheral vision as they passed by. No doubt put there by the FBI.

He took one more trip around the neighborhood just to make sure there wasn't a government car parked somewhere or anyone watching from a living room window. Reasonably sure they weren't being watched, Jack pulled into Runtso's leafy driveway and around toward the back of the house, where a one-door garage stood, out of sight of the street.

'Keep your eyes open, Gav. And let's not give the neighbors any reason to call the cops.'

'You got it,' Gavin whispered, slinging his messenger bag over one of his narrow shoulders.

Jack glanced around one more time for prying eyes but didn't see any. He and Gavin snapped on pairs of latex gloves before Jack pulled out his lockpick set and easily opened the back door. They stepped inside the small kitchen.

Not good.

The kitchen was trashed. Drawers had been pulled out and crashed on the floor, along with silverware, pots, pans, and lids. Cabinets were opened, as were the pantry, the doors beneath the sink, and the utility closet. Everything in them had also been thrown to the floor. Someone had gone through this room like a hurricane. Judging by the effort, Jack assumed they had done the same to the rest of the house.

He was right. They went room to room in the old house, including two small bathrooms, a formal dining room — with a pool table — and two bedrooms. Each had been thoroughly tossed. Furniture cushions, pillows, and mattresses had been cut open. Drawers, cabinets, and closets were also torn apart.

The only good news in all of this mess was that the whole house wouldn't have been torn apart if whatever they were looking for had been found easily, if at all.

Jack also knew it wasn't the FBI's style to tear a place apart like that. If they had, they would have attempted to bring it back to some kind of order. That told him someone else had been here besides the Feds.

*Probably Sammler.*

The largest bedroom was the last they checked and it had been converted into a game room and office. A file cabinet stood in one corner, its drawers opened and files tossed on the floor, along with a smashed router and a broken laser printer. A green leather couch was shoved against the far wall, its cushions cut open. A busted shadow box lay on one of the ripped cushions.

'Jeepers! Look at that!' Gavin dashed over to the couch

and picked it up. The two-foot-wide, one-foot-tall, six-inch-deep display case was glassed-in but the glass was cracked. Inside of the case was an object that looked to Jack like an old computer keyboard. It was thick and beige with brown keys.

Jack didn't get it. *Why is Gavin so fired up?*

'What's the big deal?'

'Are you kidding? That's an old Commodore 64! I had one of those when I was a kid. How freaking awesome is that?'

Jack shrugged. 'Couldn't say.' He pointed at a cut-up padded chair, tossed on its side. 'What's that?'

Gavin looked at Jack like he was the village idiot. 'That's a reclining racing simulator cockpit driving seat with a gearshift, steering wheel, and pedal mounts. Dude must have been a serious racer.'

'As in computer games?'

Gavin's eyes said, *Duh,* even if his mouth didn't.

Gavin set the broken display case back down on the couch gently, as if it were a rare Egyptian artifact, then pointed at the eighty-five-inch LG TV on the wall.

'Runtso sure had an awesome setup.' Gavin walked over to the shelving beneath the TV. He pointed at the rectangular dust outline on the top shelf. 'They took his game machine.' Gavin bent close to the dust outline. 'Judging by the size of the imprint, I'd say this was an Xbox One X.' He glanced around the room and pointed to a broken controller lying in the corner. 'Yup. Definitely a One X.'

'Why?'

'Game consoles are serious machines, especially this one. It has a one-terabyte hard drive, twelve gigabytes of RAM, and a whopping six-teraflop GPU. If I was hiding files, that's where I'd put them.'

Jack kicked aside one of the dozens of emptied game

poly-boxes. Most of the titles were racing games, especially cars. 'Took the DVDs, too.'

'Yeah, an even better place to stash stuff.'

Jack swore. Whatever Runtso might have stored anywhere in the house had probably been found and taken away, either by the FBI or, more likely, Sammler.

'HEY!'

Gavin's high-pitched shriek spun Jack around on his heels. He reached beneath his sport coat. By the time he faced Gavin, the Glock 43 was in both of Jack's steady hands at low ready.

Gavin's eyes went wide as dinner plates. 'Wow! That was a Wyatt Earp fast draw if I ever saw one.'

'A scream will do that.' Jack holstered his weapon, half angry, but mostly relieved. 'What'd you see?'

Gavin bent over and picked up a cracked photo frame and handed it to Jack. It was a photo of Elon Musk with his signature, addressed to Runtso.

'How cool is that?'

Jack frowned, unimpressed.

Until he had a thought. He glanced around the room again and handed Gavin the photo frame back. 'What do you make of that?'

'He must have met Elon. That would be awesome.'

Jack shook his head. 'Look around you. What do you see?'

Gavin did as he was told. His face lit up with a smile. He held up the photo. 'You're right, Jack. Runtso was into cars. I bet he even owns a Tesla.'

'Let's go.'

Jack led the way back out through the kitchen, stopping briefly at the door to make sure no one was watching them. Then he and Gavin dashed over to the garage and pulled open the door.

No car.

The garage was completely empty. Just a couple of rakes and a shovel hanging on nails on the walls. Gavin tugged at the messenger bag that kept slipping off his shoulder.

Jack pointed at the floor. 'Looks like there were storage boxes in here. A lot of them.'

'Whoever took them thought there was something in them.'

'Something that had to be gone through with a fine tooth comb. My guess is tax records, business records, that sort of thing. They took them because otherwise they'd be standing in here for hours going through them.'

'Makes sense, Jack. But where's his car?'

'The only thing I can think of is at the airport, where he left it before his trip to Spain.'

'No, I mean, if he's a car guy and he has a garage but he uses it for file storage, where does he keep his car?'

'That's a great question.'

'I have an idea.'


'We're looking for a key fob,' Gavin said, stepping over pots and pans on the kitchen floor, his head on a swivel. 'Tesla has a phone app that will open your car and start it at a distance, but they also make fobs. Find the fob, we find the car.'

'How do we find the car with the fob?'

'You find the fob. I'll find the car.'

Gavin went over to a key rack screwed into the wall. A couple of lock keys were on it, and probably a spare house key.

'I didn't see a fob when we went through before,' Jack said.

'Me neither. But I think I can find it.'

Gavin reached into his messenger bag and pulled out a handheld electronic device.

'Fobs put out a constant RF signal that communicates with its paired vehicle. In North America, that signal broadcasts at 315 megahertz, plus or minus two-and-a-half megahertz, depending on the make and model.' He held up the device. 'And this, my friend, is an RF signal detector, tuned to the same wavelength range.'

'Seriously? You just happen to carry one of those around?'

Gavin patted his messenger bag. 'I have all kinds of goodies in here. Like I told you before, you're the physical, I'm the technical. Just cross your fingers that Runtso wasn't paranoid and parked his fob in a Faraday bag.'

Gavin switched on his device. 'If Runtso was just a little paranoid, he'd know not to keep it near a door, where thieves can stand outside and capture the signal, amplify it, and send it to another thief standing by the car with a transmitter imitating his fob.'

'Yeah. Everybody knows that.'

'Yeah. Everybody in this house not named Jack. C'mon.'

Gavin found the fob signal and within five minutes found the fob, tucked inside a toilet paper roll lying on the bathroom floor. 'Okay, so he was a little paranoid. But there ya go.' Gavin pulled it out and handed it to Jack.

'What good is this if we don't know where the car is? Don't you have to be like three feet away for this to work?' Jack hit the button. Nothing.

'You need to be three feet away. I don't.'

Gavin walked over to a street-facing window and pulled back the curtain. He then pulled out another device and held it up. 'Note, one aforementioned amplifier.' He turned it on. 'Hit the button again.'

Jack did. They both saw it. A pair of headlights flashed dimly beneath a plain car cover just two hundred feet up the street.

'You didn't hear the engine start because it's electric,' Gavin said in a professorial tone.

'Thanks, Elon. I might have worked that one out for myself. We need to check out the car. It might have just the clue we've been looking for.'

Still confident they weren't being watched by killer mercenaries, FBI agents, or even curious neighbors, Jack and Gavin lifted the car cover, folded it up, and tossed it into the back seat of the sporty Tesla Midnight Silver Model S.

Jack handed Gavin the keys to the Jeep. 'Meet me at the funeral home we passed earlier. We can't leave it here.'

'Gotcha.'

Jack climbed into the Tesla and drove the short distance back to the Berry Funeral Home parking lot. He pulled the Model S into a spot toward the back where they could work undisturbed and camouflaged by other parked cars. Gavin parked next to him and climbed into the passenger seat next to Jack with his messenger bag in tow.

It only took them a few minutes to pull up the Tesla's onboard map. From there, Gavin hacked into the car's hard drive and downloaded all of its GPS records onto his tablet. The GPS data only went back eight months, which was when Runtso had apparently purchased the vehicle.

With the Tesla data on his tablet, Gavin pulled up a map of the area and downloaded the GPS coordinates onto it, generating thousands of blue lines traversing roads all over Knoxville and the areas surrounding it. Two giant nodes stood out far and above all of the others. Runtso's home, and one other location.

'What's this place?' Jack asked.

Gavin pulled it up on Google Maps. 'No name. Looks like some kind of an industrial park or a distribution facility.'

Gavin dropped the little yellow street-level man on the location. The pictures that came up were blurred.

'Wow. Didn't expect that,' Gavin said. 'That's either a top-secret government facility or somebody paid big bucks to do that.'

'I think it's time we paid a visit to Runtso's real office.'

# 64

Jack and Gavin took the Wrangler for the sixteen-minute trek toward the travel node they identified as Runtso's primary workplace. They left Runtso's Tesla parked at the funeral home but took the fob with them in case somebody else finally figured out what Gavin had already put together.

Jack reminded Gavin to play it cool on the drive-by. No finger pointing or phone cameras or even long stares at the place were allowed. He didn't want to draw any attention from their security people as the two of them made their surveillance run.

They drove past the main gate. The property was protected by a fifteen-foot-high chain-link fence topped with razor wire. Tall lampposts were planted like trees everywhere and lights were fixed to the warehouse walls. The place lit up like a Christmas tree at night, Jack assumed. Security cameras were everywhere.

A simple white sign facing the road displayed three letters: *WML,* along with the street address. A uniformed guard stepped out of his booth and approached an eighteen-wheeler that had just pulled up. It wasn't hard to see the pistol on the guard's hip, even from the road. Several other freight trucks were backed into loading bays. Civilian workers loaded and unloaded the trailers with forklifts and dollies. Jack spotted at least one security man on the loading dock as well, wearing civilian clothes. But his short-cropped hair, physical build, and determined gait gave him away.

It looked like the main offices for the facility were located at this first building. White decal letters with the same *WML* were stuck on the glass doors leading inside.

Jack drove on farther down the road past a second gate and more security guards. Freshly painted military combat and support vehicles were parked in rows in the expansive yard. A freight train rumbled slowly past behind the property inside the fence. From where he sat on the road, it seemed to Jack that the railroad track was elevated, along with the rest of the property, above the wide and greenish river. Power lines paralleled the train track as well.

Jack kept driving, following Gavin's tracking program. It beeped when they passed a third gate, indicating that this was the place where Runtso had driven to so many times in his Tesla.

A tanker truck hauling liquid nitrogen was parked just outside the closed gate. The driver was showing ID to an armed uniformed guard while another security man in civilian clothes climbed up into the cab. A second uniformed guard examined the undercarriage of the truck with an inspection mirror.

A dozen refrigerated trucks were unloading. Several were branded with familiar food company names. Jack saw forklifts driven by men wearing insulated coveralls inside the open rolling doors. The same freight train rolling past the other building was now approaching this one, its brakes and steel wheels screeching to a coupler-clanging stop.

Jack kept driving. He knew that security cameras pointed at the road captured every vehicle entering and exiting the gate of this more secure facility. And almost certainly every vehicle driving on the frontage road. He put another mile between him and the distribution facility before pulling into a vacant lot on the side of the road.

'What'd you see, Gav?'

'Pretty big place. Three entrances. Armed guards, which I guess isn't that big of a deal for a place storing lots of stuff.'

'Did you notice the undercover guards? Not your typical rent-a-cops.'

'Not really. My peripheral vision kinda sucks.'

'Some of those guys were strapped. Real operator types.'

'That second facility had military vehicles parked there,' Gavin said. 'Maybe that's why.'

'What about the refrigerated facility? Why do you need armed guards there? And they seemed to be the most paranoid.'

'They must be guarding something *really* valuable. I'm guessing it's not the trailers full of Stouffer's Meat Lovers Lasagna – my personal favorite, by the way.'

'So tell me about Runtso. Why would a brainiac like him work in a frozen food warehouse? The transition from ORNL to here doesn't make a whole lot of sense to me.'

'Unless they're working on a top-secret frozen pizza recipe inside of that place, I don't think they'd need the kinds of clearances he had.'

'And he wouldn't need a physics degree to work in there. So what would he have been doing at ORNL?'

'It was redacted from the records. But he was working on a project even your dad would have a hard time accessing. It had to be something on the bleeding edge of national defense. Next-gen nukes? Directed-energy weapons? Electromagnetic railgun? Something like that.'

'At ORNL, sure. But at a frozen food warehouse?'

Gavin scratched his flaky scalp. 'I know. It doesn't make sense. We need to get in there but the security was too tight back there to try and fake our way in. And there's only two of us, so it's not like we're going to fight our way in.'

*Fight* our *way in?* Jack fought back a smile. 'Good call.'

'I think we should call the FBI or DoD and have this place checked out.'

'And what would we tell them? There's a warehouse full of Swanson TV dinners that pose a threat to national security you need to investigate?'

'Yeah. I guess it does sound kind of stupid.' Gavin's stomach gurgled like a jar of fermenting kimchi. 'I'm getting kinda hungry. How about we go hit up Calhoun's? I think it's only like fifteen minutes from here.'

'Sure. Why not? Give us a chance to regroup and plan our next move.'

Jack put the Jeep in gear and checked for traffic in his rearview mirror.

A big refrigerated truck rumbled past, throwing brightly colored leaves, heading back toward Knoxville. As soon as it cleared, Jack pulled back onto the two-lane and followed him, his mind working on the problem at hand while Gavin scrolled through Calhoun's online menu.

They rolled along at the posted thirty-mile-an-hour speed limit for a few miles. Suddenly, Gavin shouted.

'I'm such an idiot! How can I have been so stupid?' He thumped his forehead with the palm of his hand.

'Whoa, Gav. Take it easy. It's just lunch.'

'We need to get back to Runtso's.'

'Why?'

'Now, Jack. We need to get back now!'

# 65

Jack pulled into the back of Runtso's house again, keeping the Wrangler out of sight from the street.

Jack and Gavin each pulled another pair of gloves on, then made their way back into the house and into the gaming room. Gavin led the way.

'Jeez, Gav. What's got your tail knotted up?'

Gavin ran over to the broken shadow box with the Commodore 64 and picked it up. He stared longingly at it through the cracked glass, like he was reuniting with a lost love.

'Do you have a knife, Jack?'

Jack pulled out his EDC blade, the same Kershaw Blur he'd plunged into van Delden's thigh back at the steel mill. He snicked the razor-sharp steel open and handed the knife to Gavin, handle first.

Gavin turned the shadow box over and set it facedown on the carpet. He took the knife and carefully cut away the backing, revealing the power plug and connecting cords and cables. There was another, thicker backing that supported the computer on the other side. There were also three small packages wrapped in plain brown paper.

'Oh, baby.' Gavin opened the first wrapped package carefully, as if he were handling an original version of the Constitution.

Gavin sighed with deep satisfaction, even reverence. 'And it has the cartridges, too.'

'And that's a good thing?'

Gavin then wedged the tip of the blade beneath the thin,

twisted wire ties that held the computer in place against the thick backing.

'Is this really the time to play a game of Pong?' Jack asked, watching Gavin proceed with surgical precision.

'Runtso's a genius. I know, because I'm one, too,' Gavin said. 'And every young genius that could get his or her hands on one of these babies did so, or drove their parents crazy trying.'

A minute later, Gavin had the Commodore 64 removed. He picked it up along with its accessory parts and the cartridges and carried it over to the big-screen TV that was attached to a wall mount. He set the sacred objects down like a priest placing a sacrifice on the altar. He pulled the TV away and exposed its back and connecting ports.

'Runtso thought of everything,' Gavin whispered. He turned to Jack. 'He was one of the good guys. I just know it.'

'Because he played old video games?'

'Just watch.' Gavin hooked up the Commodore 64 and powered it up. 'Come to Papa,' Gavin whispered as the machine's start-up screen displayed on the TV.

**\*\*\*\* COMMODORE BASIC V2 \*\*\*\***
**64K RAM SYSTEM 38911 BASIC BYTES FREE**
**READY.**

'Now watch this.' Gavin inserted one of the gaming cartridges into the slot on the side of the unit. The TV display pulled up another screen:

**PASSWORD?**

'Aha! I knew it!'
'What?'

'You don't password games, Jack. Not back then. He's hiding something.'

'Can you hack this thing?'

'*Pffft.* I'm hurt, Jack. I really am. Runtso's a gamer, just like me, and a gamer's gotta game. So I know how this dude thinks.' Gavin's chubby fingers began dancing on the keyboard.

'You keep on that. I'm heading back to Runtso's job site. Call me if you find anything.'

'Will do.' Gavin glanced up at Jack, worried. 'Careful, okay?'

'You keep your ears open, too. No telling who might be coming back.' Jack pulled his Glock and held it out, butt first. 'You might need this.'

Gavin glanced at the pistol and shook his head. 'I think you might need it more.'

After studying the map, Jack made a turn onto a side road five minutes away from the distribution center, a plan forming in his mind. His phone rang. It was Gavin.

'How'd it go?'

'I got in.'

'Fantastic! You really are a gen –'

'It's far worse than we thought, Jack. Dear God.' Gavin's voice cracked with emotion.

'Worse? What? How?'

'Runtso was working on a project called TRIBULA-TION.'

'TRIBULATION? We're looking for RAPTURE.'

'TRIBULATION *is* RAPTURE, but not exactly. They're both quantum computer projects. Universal QPUs, entangled particles, the whole nine yards. Only, RAPTURE is the ORNL project and TRIBULATION is a parallel project – stolen, basically, by Runtso and a lady named Parsons.'

'Is a true quantum computer even possible?'

'It must be, since they did it.'

'That's not good. A quantum computer that powerful changes everything.'

Jack knew something about them from his time in Singapore when he busted a Chinese attempt to steal quantum software technology. But the stuff they were doing back then was nowhere near this powerful.

'Yeah. It does change everything,' Gavin said. 'And in the wrong hands, it changes everything for the worse. There isn't a computer in the world today that can withstand a quantum brute force attack.'

'What else?'

'It gets worse.' Gavin filled in the details.

Gavin was right.

It was far worse than they could ever have imagined.

# 66

President Ryan was sitting at the Resolute desk when his private cell phone rang. The people who had access to that number were a privileged few, including his wife and kids. They knew to only use it for an extreme emergency because they knew he'd answer it, no matter what, even if the world was on fire.

It was Jack Junior.

'Son, what's wrong?' He could barely hear Jack for the interference.

'I don't have time to explain but Gavin and I just found out that there's going to be a five-*trillion*-dollar robbery any time now. It's an operation using a quantum computer called TRIBULATION. And there's more –'

Ryan was stunned. *How did Jack find this out?*

'You're too late. It's already happened.'

'What?'

'Son, I'm putting you on speakerphone. I'm here with Secretary of the Treasury Stephen Hodges and the chairman of the Federal Reserve Board, Wesley Moorcroft. Tell them what else you know about TRIBULATION. We still need more information about which banks were hit.'

'The banks? Forget the banks. Gavin can fill you in on that later. Right now we've got a real DEFCON situation about to hit us.'

'What do you mean?'

'TRIBULATION's next target is a joint Chinese-Russian military exercise in the Bering Sea called Snow Dragon. They're going to use TRIBULATION to hack their systems. These assholes want to start World War Three.'

'When?'

'Now!'

The color drained from Ryan's face.

'So we're too late?'

'Not necessarily. The intel said the launch date was today. I'm assuming it's happening now. Or maybe we still have a little time. All I know is that we've got to shut it down now no matter what.'

'How?'

'TRIBULATION is in Knoxville. That's where I am, too.'

'There's an FBI SWAT team in Knoxville,' Ryan said. 'What's the address for this TRIBULATION thing?'

He grabbed a pad and pen from his desk and wrote the address down as Jack recited it. He ripped the paper from the pad and shoved it into Arnie's hands. 'Call Director Medina. Tell her to get her SWAT team to this address ASAP. Fill her in on what you've heard and have her call me for anything else she needs – and get Scott, Bob, and Mary Pat up here pronto.'

'On it, boss.' Arnie bolted into action.

'One more thing, Pop,' Jack said over the speakerphone. 'Get an FBI team down to Houston.'

Ryan shouted at Arnie, halfway out the door. 'Arnie, hold up.' He turned back to the phone. 'Why Houston?'

'Because Buck Logan is the asshole behind all of this.'

'Logan?'

'Gavin can fill you in. But you better grab Logan before he hears about Knoxville.'

'You catch that?' Ryan asked van Damm.

'I'll put the call in to Medina right now.'

'Son, any chance you can get over to that address, be our eyes on the ground? It'll be at least thirty minutes before the FBI can saddle up.'

'Get there? I'm already here.'

'Sit tight, then. I'll get back to you when I know more. You did good, son. Son?'

Jack's line was dead.

# 67

*Sulu Sea*
*Off the coast of Mindanao, the Philippines*

Guzmán leaned on the starboard rail of the *Lupita* admiring the luminous full moon shimmering in the boundless dark of the infinite sea.

He smoked his cigar, contemplating his next move. TRIBULATION had launched according to the encoded text from *el jefe,* though the meaning and purpose of it had never been fully explained to him. The same text also confirmed that another payment had been deposited into the Sammler account. Sablek's widow would get her husband's share, and his as well. Money meant nothing to Guzmán.

Loyalty was everything.

His people would end this mission with enough cash to walk away if they wanted to. Many of them would.

He could not.

He'd thought long and hard about van Delden's death as well as Sablek's and Bykov's, now confirmed. Death was not such a bad thing, he'd decided. It was the negation of suffering, and the end of fear.

Unless, of course, there was a hell. Then suffering and fear would only be the beginning. But he'd given up on the concept of such things long ago. This life was hell enough.

He felt strangely content. The mission he'd been hired to do had been accomplished. The next two weeks were secondary. He'd complete those as well.

And then the next job.

He blew a cloud of smoke into the cool night air and tossed the butt into the water near the hull.

It bounced against the oily gray hide of a tiger shark . . .

Halfway across the world, a digital monitor displayed four red icons in oceans around the globe. They represented four Sammler mother ships. A fifth, located in the Sulu Sea, the *Lupita*, was still yellow.

It turned red in that instant.

The technician smiled. She had remotely activated the automatic return homing devices in the tiger shark drones. She had also deactivated the mother ships' drone-tracking devices and ignored requests for technical assistance.

The nearest drone sharks returned undetected to their respective mother ships and, on command, detonated as instructed. Guzmán's was the last. The remaining sharks also self-detonated, destroying all evidence of their existence.

Everything had gone exactly according to plan. All of the loose ends were tied off.

She sent an encrypted text to her employer.

### GUZMÁN DEAD – PROJECT TERMINATED

She shut down her computer, smirking with satisfaction at a job well done. She would receive one heck of a bonus for this.

She stretched and yawned but the sound of automatic gunfire outside shut her pretty little mouth.

She leaped to her feet and grabbed her backpack with her wallet, passport, car keys, and a Ruger .327 LCR. There was a hidden emergency exit in the back of her office that led to the underground garage.

As she turned to run, her office door blasted open, nearly tearing the hinges off.

An FBI agent in tactical gear and bump helmet stood in the doorway, flecks of blood on his face.

She dropped her backpack.

The SWAT leader pointed his M4 carbine at her chest.

'Where the hell is Logan?'

# 68

*Knoxville, Tennessee*

After studying the map earlier, Jack located a service road with an underpass beneath the elevated embankment that took him near the river. As soon as he exited the underpass, he turned off the service road and onto the narrow dirt track that ran between the river and the embankment. The big knobby tires on the Wrangler splashed dark mud and bright leaves as it raced toward the distribution center. He was hidden from view the entire way, including when he passed the razor wire demarcating the massive WML distribution complex.

He slammed his brakes and skidded to a halt. He was opposite the engine of the train he'd heard pulling to a stop at the frozen food warehouse earlier when he and Gavin did their drive-by. The Wrangler was still below the elevated railroad embankment and hidden from sight on the other side.

Jack jumped out and disengaged the release lever on the winch and unspooled the high-capacity rope. He pulled on the steel winch hook and coiled the rope around his shoulder as he went. After he unspooled the entire eighty-foot length, he freed the other end attached to the winch drum by cutting the small-diameter Dyneema loop spliced to the end of the rope with his knife.

With eighty feet of twelve-thousand-pound capacity rope secured across his chest like a bandolier, he scrambled up the embankment. He dropped to his stomach near the fence, peering beneath the train's big steel wheels, checking for guards or workers who might be in the area. The last several cars of the long train were being unloaded with forklifts and work gangs, too far away to be of any concern — at least for now.

So far, so good.

Now for the fun part.

Razor wire.

Jack pulled off the rope coil and set it on the ground, took off his sport coat, and picked up the rope coil again. Slipping his index finger through the hanging loop in the back of his coat, he grabbed the fence and started his climb. The big diesel train engine shielded him from any eyes that might be watching for him on the other side.

When he reached the razor wire on top, he threw his sport coat over it and climbed over, then worked his way down the other side, dropping to the ground for the last few feet.

He dropped to his stomach again and did another scan. Everybody seemed to be going about their business around the yard. Nobody was in close proximity to Jack. If something as catastrophic as TRIBULATION was going on inside the frozen warehouse, these people outside were obviously unaware of it.

Jack scuttled toward the front of the engine, opposite of his target, the building just on the other side of the train that stood next to the warehouse itself.

The HVAC building.

Jack put together a stupidly simple plan. *Emphasis on stupid*, he whispered to himself, kneeling down by one of the train's big steel wheels.

He didn't have any other options. Shutting TRIBULATION down immediately was the objective, and he knew the FBI was still twenty minutes out. He couldn't risk waiting for them. Hell might be breaking loose even now.

Without the other Campus gunfighters to assist, without blueprints and schematics of the facility, and outnumbered by at least ten armed security men, all operators by the look of them, he could only come up with one wild-ass, long-shot, Hail Mary solution.

Gavin's brief to him on the phone about TRIBULA-TION included one interesting fact. The computer they built relied on super-low temperatures. 'Almost absolute zero,' Gavin had said.

The only thing Jack could think of was the HVAC unit he'd spotted from his drive-by. He thought about taking out the power lines that ran along the track, but a computer with that kind of sensitivity would have some kind of power backup like a generator. There was no way to kill the power to any of the facility for any length of time.

That left one option.

Jack crawled beneath the engine in the space between the giant diesel tanks, the rope still looped around his shoulder. Luckily, the rail car immediately behind the engine had already been freighted. All of the loading activity was still taking place far in the back, far away from him. Everyone associated with the train was focused there. It was go time.

Now or never.

Jack scanned the area one last time, then dashed out from beneath the train and sped over to the cinder-block HVAC building. He dropped down low behind it, once again finding cover from eyes and cameras that might be searching the area.

Or so he hoped.

He turned the corner and tried the steel doorknob into the building. That would be the easy way in.

But it was locked. He swore and returned to the back wall again. He then slipped a quick peek at the wall opposite the door.

Bingo.

A service ladder was bolted on the outside of the building, leading to the roof.

Jack dashed over to it and scrambled up like a monkey on crack. He reached the top and dropped to his belly again. The big refrigeration unit's massive compressor roared inside its aluminum housing. Hot exhaust blew through the long metal louvers.

And the electric motor that ran the whole thing hummed furiously next to Jack.

*Thank you, baby Jesus.*

Jack pulled the rope off his shoulder and unwound it enough to be able to grab the steel winch hook. He secured it through the massive eyebolt welded to the top of the motor casing used to pick up the heavy device for installation and removal.

Jack scanned the yard again. He was still undetected. He pulled the remainder of coiled rope back over his shoulder and let it out as he climbed down the ladder, retracing his steps to the train. He quickly knotted the other end around a steel I-beam of the engine's undercarriage and then stopped himself.

The rope was rated for twelve thousand pounds of weight. The electric HVAC motor weighed a thousand pounds at most.

But the motor was bolted to the rooftop of the building. Was the rope strong enough to bust those bolts?

Maybe not.

*Shit!*

He made a quick calculation.

It should work.

Jack untied the rope and instead of securing it, looped the end of it around the same undercarriage steel I-beam, then pulled the end of the rope and brought the rest of the rope through it. He double-checked to make sure he was clear, then dashed back up the ladder.

He ran the end of the rope through the eyebolt a second time.

He scrambled back down the ladder to tie the end off again beneath the engine.

And slammed into a security guard.

The guard's hand flew to his sidearm as he shouted, 'What the fu —'

But Jack was faster, and a throat punch cut the man off mid-sentence.

Gasping for air and grabbing his broken larynx, the man crumpled to his knees. Jack smashed his own big knee into the man's lower jaw, flopping him back into the dirt, knocked out cold.

Jack snatched the man's pistol out of its Kydex holster and shoved it into his own waistband, then scurried back under the train and finished tying off the rope. It might have been a really dumb idea but at least now he had twenty-four thousand pounds of pull to work with instead of just twelve.

Jack scrambled back to the fallen guard. He grabbed the stocky man by the shoulders and dragged him back underneath the train, then pushed him down the embankment. Jack couldn't tell if he was still breathing. Any other day he might have stopped to try and help him but right now one man's life wasn't worth the millions at risk. Especially a Sammler puke.

*If that's what he was.*

Only one thing left to do.

The train engineer slept like a log in his seat, his watch alarm not due to go off for another twenty minutes. But the shock of cold steel pressing into his ear woke him early.

He turned in his seat. His groggy eyes widened at the sight of Jack's Glock pointed at his gray-bearded face.

'What's this?'

Jack pointed around the engineer's side of the cabin. 'This is a train. And you're an engineer. Let's get this thing moving.'

The man sat up. 'Moving? Where? I can't –'

Jack pressed the pistol against his forehead.

'Now. Move this rig.'

'Where?'

'About a hundred feet should do it.'

'Look, mister –'

Jack pointed at the control panel with his pistol. 'That's the brake release, that's the throttle, and that's the dead man's handle. Either you can run this thing or I can blow your brains out and run it for you. Decide which it's going to be before I finish squeezing this trigger.'

'Okay! Okay!'

The four-thousand-horsepower General Electric EMD 710 series V-16 diesel motor roared into life as the throttle engaged to the first position.

Couplers banged as the wheels began moving. Loaders way back down the line started cursing and shouting, wondering what the hell was going on.

The train inched forward, pulling forty-five cars and flatbeds along with it, creating chaos with the guys still inside or on the forklifts.

The double-tied rope that Jack had fixed to the undercarriage strained as the train lurched ahead. Ten feet later the rope was taut as a violin string. The train kept moving.

The big eyebolt on top of the electric motor began to bend, threatening to shear off as the motor mount bolts held fast to the concrete platform.

But the cheap Chinese iron bolts that held the motor to the platform gave way first, snapping like twigs.

The electric motor tipped over. The drive belt running from the motor to the HVAC unit inside slipped off its drive wheel. The train rolled on.

Thirty seconds later, the big electric motor crashed to the dirt, dragging down its thick power line along with the transformer it was connected to.

Jack had killed the HVAC compressor.

No more deep freeze.


Klaxons blared. Jack had definitely kicked the hornet's nest with this one.

He turned around just as a pair of heavy boots clanged onto the steel deck of the cabin behind him. The uniformed guard was breathing heavily from his sprint to catch the slow-moving train, and the scramble up its eight-foot ladder to engineering. He saw Jack's pistol in his hand and reached for his own.

A 147-grain nine-millimeter bullet from Jack's Glock 43 plowed into the man's forehead. Brain tissue and bone fragments splattered the fire extinguisher on the wall behind him. The guard dropped to the floor.

Bullets suddenly spanged inside the train cab, fired from outside through the window facing the warehouse. A few bullets ricocheted inside.

Like hornets.

The engineer screamed and grabbed his wounded arm.

'Let's get out of here,' Jack said, grabbing the man by the shoulder. 'We're done here.'

Jack dragged the engineer out of his seat. When the engineer's hand left the 'dead man's handle,' the train's brakes engaged. Steel wheels screeched. Jack and the engineer stumbled as Jack hauled him by the shoulders toward the door.

Another guard was climbing up the ladder. Jack kicked him just beneath his nose with the toe of his boot. Even through the heavy leather, Jack could feel the crunch of snapping bone and cartilage. The man flew backward, hitting the ground like a rag doll, his unconscious mind unable to brace his body for the fall.

Jack dragged the engineer forward but the older man jerked away, still clutching his wounded arm. 'Shoot me here or leave me alone.'

'I can help you.'

'Go to hell. You've helped enough. I can take care of myself.'

'Suit yourself. Thanks for the ride, old-timer.'

'Shove it, asshole.'

Jack slid down the ladder, stopping himself at the last rung, then jumped off. He lost his balance and fell to the ground.

Bullets kicked up the dirt near his face.

He was a dead man.


Jack rolled hard away and down the embankment, bullets marking the spot he just vacated.

He reached the bottom and rose to his knees, pointing his pistol up where he knew his attackers would appear.

A quick glance showed him the Wrangler was a good three hundred feet away. If only he could get to it.

The first guard appeared at the top of the embankment, an MP5 in his hands. He raised it to fire –

His head exploded.

An FBI sniper had found his mark.

# 69

*Croatia*

Parsons's new identity, complete with her new Montenegrin passport and biometric data to match, had gotten her all the way to Dubrovnik, where she boarded a private helicopter.

She'd been a nervous wreck until she'd cleared Italian airspace and crossed the Adriatic. She monitored the news but nothing was mentioned about TRIBULATION. Neither a global financial crash nor a shooting war had occurred nor seemed imminent.

No matter. That was all Logan's affair. She had achieved her dream. Everything else was in the past.

She'd covered her tracks and made her arrangements. Her spirits rose with the Eurocopter as it lifted into the sweet golden light of a glorious sunset. In less than half an hour, she'd arrive at her final destination, a small town of twenty thousand on the crystal blue Adriatic coast, surrounded by Venetian walls and filled with Mediterranean charm. Peace, quiet, beauty, and no extradition treaty were just a few of the benefits she intended to enjoy in her early retirement.

The only luggage she brought with her was a small, inexpensive carry-on with just enough personal items and protein bars to make the twenty-four-hour trek. She left her electronics and her worries behind.

The handsome, blue-eyed pilot had greeted her in the small but efficient office of the FBO where he operated. She was warmed in all the right places by his charming smile and runner's physique, but she knew this wasn't the time to break character. She did, however, accept his offer of a gin and tonic before boarding. Her favorite.

Now some five hundred feet above the white-capped water, she felt utterly safe. The adrenaline surge of the last twenty-four hours finally caught up with her. She felt herself suddenly tired sitting in her seat, the rhythmic pulse of the beating rotors lulling her to sleep. It had been a long journey, but now she was free. She blinked heavily. The blue-eyed pilot was in the left seat navigating. He turned around and smiled at her again.

'Tired?' he asked.

'Terribly.'

'Just close your eyes. I'll wake you when we arrive.'

But she was already asleep.

The blue-eyed pilot whispered a command into his headset to the other pilot, a woman. She nosed the EC145 into a gentle dive, dropping altitude to just fifty feet off the deck. She stopped in midair, hovering.

The blue-eyed pilot unbuckled himself and climbed back to the passenger compartment. He felt for a pulse. She was still alive, her breathing long and deep. She wouldn't wake for hours.

In fact, she wouldn't wake at all.

He reached behind her seat and pulled out a heavy duffel. He secured a thirty-kilo dumbbell to her right wrist with a pair of handcuffs, unbuckled her seatbelt, opened the sliding door, and shoved her out.

The dumbbell hit first, dragging Parsons by the right arm into the bright blue water, her body following like an arrow shot into the sea.

He closed the door, climbed back into his seat, and buckled in for the short flight back home.

# Days Later

# 70

## *Camp David, Maryland*

Jack Junior and his dad stood at the number one position on the skeet range, just beneath the high house.

The range officer, Mike Cravy – a three-time NSSA national champion shooter – pointed at both men. 'Ready?'

Jack and his dad both nodded back. 'Ready.'

'You won the toss,' Ryan said.

Jack took his stance and raised his shotgun, a Benelli SuperSport Performance Shop semiauto. He smashed the oversized red release button and the bolt slammed home with a satisfying *thunk*.

'Pull!'

The first bird flew out of the high house behind him. Jack fired, smashing the bird, just as the second bird darted from the low house. He shattered that one, too.

'Nice job, son.'

'The first station's easy.'

'No, I mean everything else.' He looked his son in the eyes. 'Thanks to what you and Gavin did, we avoided a global economic apocalypse, recovered the five trillion, and stopped a potential holocaust.'

Jack shrugged. 'That was more Gavin than me. You're up.'

Ryan took his position, a case-hardened Caesar Guerini Summit Limited over and under in his hands. A real beauty, a recent anniversary gift from his wife. Another classic beauty.

The President laughed. 'That train thing you did was pretty slick.'

Jack grinned. 'I always said it's better to be lucky than good.'

'I think it was a little of both.'

Jack's decision to take out the warehouse refrigeration unit was based on Gavin's intel that the computer could only operate at millikelvin temperatures.

What Gavin *didn't* tell him was that those near-absolute-zero temperatures were achieved through a process known as 'laser cooling,' not freon and a compressor like an old Maytag making ice cubes.

Destroying the warehouse HVAC unit had no effect whatsoever on the quantum computer's subatomic cooling. But tearing out that motor, the transformer, and the electrical lines along with it temporarily disrupted the power supply to the building. That disruption lasted less than two seconds before the emergency backup generator kicked on. That was just enough time to disrupt the laser cooling mechanism. Once disrupted, the TRIBULATION system completely shut down and had to be rebooted.

Jack's attack also distracted the warehouse security team long enough to give the FBI SWAT a window to insert and seize everything before TRIBULATION could resume operation. They grabbed the scientists, programmers, and hardware before the five trillion could be disbursed and before the attack on Snow Dragon, scheduled for launch just seven minutes after the moment Jack disrupted the power.

Ryan raised the shotgun to his eye, lining up the Bradley white front bead on top of the silver mid bead like a little snowman. 'Pull!'

Cravy hit his remote and the orange clay disk shot out of the high house. The twelve-gauge jerked on Ryan's shoulder.

The bird exploded in a cloud of orange dust just as the low house bird launched out of its thrower. Ryan fired.

Missed.

The clay crashed harmlessly into the grass behind them.

'Maybe it's time for shuffleboard, old-timer.' Jack smiled.

Ryan looked at Cravy. 'I'll take my extra here.'

'Yes, sir.'

Ryan loaded a single shell into the top chamber and stepped up to the square.

'Pull!'

The low house bird sped into the sky. Ryan crushed it. He turned back to his son. 'Back to even, *boyo*,' he said with a wink.

Cravy grinned. He liked working with the Ryans. Good guys. Not like some of the congressional pricks the President sometimes brought out here.

Jack and his dad marched over to the second station.

Jack reloaded two more shells and stepped into the square. He punched the release button, racking his first round, then raised his Benelli to his eye. He put the front red optic and brass mid beads together into their figure eight.

'Pull!'

The high house bird darted across the sky. Jack led it and pulled the trigger, busting the clay. The second bird flew past in the opposite direction. Jack nailed that one, too.

'You missed your calling,' Ryan said. 'You should go pro with that thing.'

'Two stations does not a champion make,' Jack said. He turned to Cravy. 'Right, Mike?'

Cravy grinned. 'Well, two in a row's a good start. You just gotta work your way up from there.'

'How far up?' Jack asked.

'Oh, I dunno.' Cravy scratched his chin thoughtfully. 'A couple ten thousand more oughta do it, for starters.'

'I'll be lucky to hit the next one,' Junior said, stepping out of the square, changing positions with his dad.

The President barked, 'Pull!'

Killed two clays.

'Oh, so I guess now we're getting serious,' Jack said.

'I'm always serious. I thought you knew that.'

Jack laughed. 'That move of Logan's, putting the near-kelvin-zero operation inside of a frozen food warehouse? Makes me think he must have watched a lot of *Breaking Bad*.'

He led the way to the third station. His dad followed.

'It was a damned smart play. The whole operation was. Logan knew to begin his drone attacks in the area where SBIRS had been knocked out. DoD's still looking into it but they think his people might have been the ones to disable it.'

Ryan sighed, frustrated.

'The bastard really bamboozled us. Hell, who am I kidding? He got the better of me is what it boils down to. White Mountain Logistics and Security was the perfect cover for his plan. He was in deep with the federal government, and his operations were global. He could move any kind of material to any location of his choosing without raising any suspicions because he was a trusted and security-cleared defense contractor. And I bought into it, hook, line, and sinker.'

'Can't blame yourself for that one, Pop. What he planned was so freaking crazy, no one could have predicted it.'

Jack stepped into the square at the third station. He saw the set of his dad's jaw. He was taking this all really hard. Time to change the subject.

'I never did hear the rest of the story on Runtso. Gavin thought he was one of the good guys.'

'Those birds aren't gonna shoot themselves.'

'Fine.' Jack stepped up and loaded two more shells into his shotgun.

'Pull!'

*Bang, bang.* Two dead clays.

Jack shrugged. 'So, what about Runtso?'

'The FBI went over those cartridges Gavin found with a fine-tooth comb. It led them to some other files stashed in other interesting places. The bottom line is that Runtso totally bought into what he called the "Heist of the Universe." It was a real ego trip for him. But when he found out about Logan's war plan, he got cold feet.'

'So, not exactly a good guy.'

'Not exactly. He helped let the horse out of the barn and tried to chase it down after the fact. If he hadn't shown up in Barcelona to meet with your friend Renée while you were there, Logan's plan might have actually worked.'

The President stepped into the square, yelled, 'Pull!' Killed two clays.

'Next station, gentlemen,' Cravy said, pointing at number four. They headed over.

'Whatever happened to the Parsons woman?' Jack asked.

'Interpol found a corpse that might be her washed up on shore in Montenegro. It's hard to tell from the level of decomp, so they're running DNA tests.'

'That's too bad. A real waste of genius.'

'Genius doesn't matter as much as character,' Ryan said. 'Heraclitus said that character is destiny. But I think it's loyalty that's destiny. Logan loved himself more than his country and was willing to destroy it. Parsons loved her own ambition more than her science, and it got her killed. I'll take an honest man or woman over a smart one any day.'

Jack took his position, loaded his weapon. 'Pull!'

Cravy let fly. Two puffs of red dust hung in the air.

Jack changed positions with his dad.

The Caesar Guerini barked twice. Two birds shattered.

427

The Ryans followed Cravy over to the fifth station. They didn't speak. Jack's mind was clearly somewhere else.

'What's bugging you, son?'

'Logan. Where the hell did he go?'

Ryan darkened. 'We may never find the bastard.'

'I can't let it go until we do.'

'Well, don't let it ruin your game today, *old man*. You're up.'

Jack stepped into the box. He pulled two more shells out of his pouch and loaded them.

The President laid a hand on his son's broad shoulder.

'I also wanted you to know that Renée Moore is getting her star at Langley. She died in service to her country, trying to bring Runtso in. There's a ceremony next week, if you'd like to attend.'

'Yeah, I would.'

Ryan smiled and squeezed his neck. 'I'll join you, if you don't mind. I read her service jacket. She was a real patriot, one of our best and brightest.' He looked at his son. 'You two went to school together, didn't you?'

Jack looked at his dad and nodded slightly, unable to speak. He took a deep breath and gathered himself up. Ryan stepped back.

Jack brought the gun to his eye.

'Pull!'

Two clays flew.

Jack missed both.

# 71

## Gulf of Mexico

The *Dulces Sueños* cruised due north some eleven miles north-northeast of Cancún at minimum speed to conserve fuel. It was scheduled to round the tip of the Yucatán Peninsula before sunrise.

Despite its security contingent of cartel *sicarios* on board, the resin-infused carbon fiber vessel remained a very soft target. Logan knew that speed made a soft target hard – or at least, harder to hit. He was as restless as the tide these days, trapped on board his Mexican-flagged luxury yacht. He was unable to risk going ashore even under the cartel's protection. America's eyes were everywhere. He still needed to hide. A luxury yacht near the Mayan coast was just another platinum needle in a haystack of platinum needles.

Despite the late hour, he couldn't sleep. The rumble of the boat's big diesel engines calmed his nerves a little. The two-hundred-and-eighty-foot four-deck cobalt blue vessel remained far enough from shore to avoid any landward threats, and just inside the outer bounds of Mexico's territorial waters to remain under her jurisdiction. The *Uxmal,* a lightly armed twin-diesel Mexican Navy *Tenochtitlan*-class vessel, half the size of his own, patrolled these waters on a disciplined schedule like a vigilant sheepdog.

Logan knew that Ryan wouldn't risk a shooting war with Mexico over something as trivial as his arrest, especially since the TRIBULATION project had been completely defeated. The President was many things but he wouldn't risk America's national interest to satisfy his personal need for vengeance.

With Sammler destroyed, Logan turned to his most important criminal ally, the infamous Gulf Cartel, under whose protection he now lived as he plotted a return to the stage. He'd stashed away enough money, resources, and weapons to secure his future, despite the fact Ryan's government was seizing White Mountain assets and shutting it down.

The only thing that kept him from losing his mind was imagining the look on Ryan's face when he realized Buck Logan had played them all and nearly ran the table, all on Ryan's watch.

The HALO jump was timed to the patrol route of the *Uxmal*, now at its maximum distance from Logan's vessel. Speed and silence were key to the operation. So was the covering darkness of the moonless night.

Adara was the first to splash into the dark water two miles due north of *Dulces Sueños,* a fifty-five-pound float bag leading her way. Once in the water, she shed her chute, pulled on her fins, opened the bag, and began assembling the vehicle inside.

Thirty seconds later, the rest of The Campus team dropped into the Gulf, less than a quarter mile from Logan's luxury vessel. Three landed due east, the other two due west of the big boat. Like Adara, they were kitted out in neoprene scuba suits.

But strapped to each of their chests in specialized harnesses was a 77-pound Rotinor DiveJet RD2, along with suppressed H&K MP7A1 automatic PDWs, firing 4.6x30mm armor-piercing rounds. They also carried full underwater diving and boarding gear – along with a few other surprises.

Once in the water and clear of their chutes, Clark, Ding,

Dom, Midas, and Jack unharnessed their DiveJets, pulled on the rest of their dive gear, and checked their comms – waterproof Sonitus tactical mics attached like a retainer to their upper back molars, utilizing bone conduction through the jaw for both transmitting and receiving radio signals. The Campus started using them after seeing them deployed by a Marine FAST platoon in Indonesia.

'Alpha ready?' Clark asked.

'Alpha ready,' Adara replied.

'Bravo and Charlie are ready. See you in twenty.'

Clark gave the signal. Each of the men in Bravo and Charlie grabbed the control grips of the four-foot-long, lithium-ion dive sleds and slipped beneath the waves, tracking on a swift and silent intercept course for their target.

The Bravo and Charlie divers stopped on their first timed mark and stripped away their tanks, then rose just enough to breach the surface. At one hundred yards they were still far enough away that searching eyes would struggle to see the black forms in the black water. Each man swapped his scuba mask for NVGs and pulled his suppressed HK.

'Bravo and Charlie are in position,' Clark said. 'Alpha, you are good to go.'

'Launching now.'

Clark acknowledged. The clock was ticking.

It wouldn't be long now.

In less time than it took for Clark and the others to get into position, Adara had removed, unfolded, and assembled the waterproof UAV and its controller from the float bag. She pulled on her own pair of waterproof NVGs and shoved the rolled-up bag between her thighs to add to her buoyancy.

Time to rock and roll.

Weighing just fifty-five pounds, the Songar UAV lifted swiftly into the air. The drone's night-vision sensors, camera, and laser range finder fed its data in first-person shooter imagery into the gaming-styled, handheld controller. The drone was hovering in position one hundred feet above the water when Clark reported that both teams had reached their waypoints.

Lying directly in the path of the oncoming vessel, Adara needn't fly the Songar any farther. The sound of the UAV's whirring blades was masked by the gentle rolling Gulf waters and the rumbling diesel engines coming toward her.

She zoomed in on the brightly lit forward bridge on the third deck of the magnificent super yacht, bought and paid for with dirty narco-money and crewed by narco-killers. She felt no guilt when she set the reticle on the man standing at the helm and pressed the trigger.

The helmsman never heard the shot or the sound of the breaking glass as the 5.56 NATO round tore into his abdomen. He fell to the floor with a scream, grabbing at his burning guts.

The captain dashed out from behind a door just as more bullets – fired in three-shot bursts – shattered more of the bridge-wide glass. Two of the rounds struck him in the chest. A third ripped out his throat, splattering blood against the polished mahogany bulkhead as he dropped to the deck.

The first shots startled the starboard guard out of his waking slumber on the second deck. He was no coward. The other *sicarios* were shouting behind and below him as more shots rang out from the distance.

He unslung his AK-47 *cuerno de chivo* – goat horn – and charged forward toward the sound of the gunfire coming from high and ahead of the boat. He raced at a dead run toward the bow and raised his rifle at the sparks flashing like angry fireflies in the night sky. But the sparks changed position, pointing at him.

Bullets clawed his chest open.

The brave *sicario* died before he could even scream.

Clark waited for the sound of AK-47 fire – the weapon of choice of assholes everywhere – before giving the 'go' signal.

All five men simultaneously revved their silent DiveJet engines and sped toward the yacht. Their eyes were locked on the *sicarios* charging forward on all three decks, firing their weapons at the Songar drone dancing in all directions off the bow and sniping at them from out of the dark.

Thirty seconds later, all five Campus operators had reached the port and starboard sides of the slow-moving vessel, avoiding the spinning props at the stern. They slapped boarding hooks onto the rails, the first man up clearing the way for the others to follow. They scrambled aboard completely undetected by the distracted gunmen, leaving their DiveJets behind.

They'd already studied the yacht's schematics. Clark and the others knew where they had to go, and what they had to do.

Jack most of all.

As Clark and Bravo team cut down the *sicarios* Adara hadn't already killed on the outer decks, Charlie team – Dom and Jack – began clearing the interiors, Jack in the lead.

One fat, hairy gunman, naked save for his bikini underwear, leaped out of his stateroom with a gold-plated Desert Eagle, aiming it at Jack's face as he bolted past the door. A bullet from Dom's HK tore off the man's jaw before he could fire his pistol. He fell to the floor, mewling in agonizing pain.

Dom did him a favor and put a second one in his skull.

Jack raced up the three flights of interior stairs, reaching the fourth deck, where Logan's private quarters were located.

Logan reached for a mag to slam home into his daddy's ivory-handled .45 Colt just as Jack turned the corner into the door, his PDW held high ready.

Jack charged forward and knocked the pistol out of Logan's meaty hand with the butt of his HK. The Colt crashed to the floor with the *thunk* of heavy metal. Jack pulled his weapon back to his eye.

Jack heard the calm, professional chatter of his team echoing in his skull, and the sharp retorts of the last 4.6x30mm rounds dispatching the remaining *sicarios*.

Logan looked at Jack like a wounded child, slapped around by an angry parent.

'I wasn't gonna use that on you, boy.' He glanced at the pistol on the floor. 'It was for me.'

'No shit.'

Jack's finger slipped onto the HK's two-and-a-half-pound trigger. It would take more energy to scratch his nose than to kill this son of a bitch where he sat.

But his dad's orders were clear.

Alive, not dead.

'No easy way out for you, Logan. Instead, you're going to spend the next forty years of your miserable life in a cement hole somewhere, tied into your chair and crapping in a baggie in the dark.'

Logan squared up in his chair, puffing out his chest, defiance burning in his eyes.

'I don't care what you do to me. It won't change the fact I kicked the President's ass. My name will still go down in history.'

'As an asterisk, at best.'

'I did what was right.'

'Are you kidding? How does setting the world on fire constitute "right" in any sane universe?'

Logan sat up straighter. 'Sane? Sane? Two hundred and forty-four trillion dollars of global debt is sane? The whole financial system needs one giant flush. A Year of Jubilee for the whole world, to start everything all over again. That's what I was gonna do.'

'And the five trillion you stole was just a finder's fee, right?'

'A man's gotta get paid, doesn't he?'

'Forget your Freakonomics. A world war isn't a fresh start for anybody.'

Logan leaned forward, his face reddening.

'I make no apologies for trying to defend my country. Extreme threat demands extreme action. I'm a loyal American patriot. It was my duty to try and destroy America's enemies before they destroyed us. In less than a decade, the Chinese and the Russians will have the means to wipe us out. They already have the will to do it.'

'You just forgot one thing. The Chinese and Russians might have blown themselves to bits in the Bering Sea, but they would've figured out pretty damn quick that someone else was behind it – and they would've blamed us.'

'That's why I did it! I put the ball in the red zone. First and goal. All Ryan had to do was punch it into the end zone and win the game once and for all. I knew he didn't have the balls for a first strike. So I was gonna do it for him because I sure as hell do.'

'The only problem, Logan, is that you aren't the President and never will be.'

Logan chuckled with disgust. 'Don't I know it.' He sat back. 'It was my destiny to be President. I was born and bred for it.'

Logan's big hands rubbed the armrests of his hated wheel-chair. 'But the hell of it is, sometimes fate makes the wrong man king.'

Clark gave the order to stack the dead bodies into the yacht's first-floor deck compartment away from prying eyes until they got deeper out into the Gulf, where they'd toss them overboard, chum for the hungry sharks patrolling the deeper waters.

Clark, a former chief boatswain's mate, knew how to han-dle a boat, even one as big as the *Dulces Sueños*. He maneuvered it closer to Adara, still in the water, the Songar already packed for the trip home. Dom helped her on board as Ding made the call to the CV-22B Osprey, a SOCOM tilt-rotor bird winging its way toward them from its base at MacDill AFB, Florida. The others pulled the DiveJets from the water and secured them, then prepped the yacht for the journey across the Gulf to Houston.

Jack arrived on the aft deck with a handcuffed Logan slumped in his chair just as the tilt-rotor Osprey arrived overhead. Its twin turbo-shaft Rolls-Royce engines rotated to ninety degrees to vertical, converting the airplane into a helicopter in just twelve seconds.

The pilot's voice echoed clearly in Jack's skull. The Soni-tus mics eliminated the ambient noise of the roaring turbines and beating rotor blades.

Jack confirmed. The clock was ticking the moment the Osprey entered Mexican airspace, something a hostile Mexi-can government wouldn't look kindly upon. Interceptors would be launched within minutes if the Osprey didn't clear back out pronto.

Clark reported the yacht's onboard radar showed the *Uxmal* making a turn, and heading back their way at flank speed.

'We need to get this tub moving, fast!'

A rope was lowered from the hellhole in the belly of the Osprey. A dual Y strap was attached to the rope with carabiners on each arm of the Y.

Jack snapped the carabiners to the D-rings on the shoulder straps of Logan's STABO extraction harness.

'He's on the string,' Jack said.

'Roger that,' the pilot said.

A winch inside the Osprey turned. Logan lifted out of his chair helplessly, his dead legs dangling, his cuffed hands immobilized. He cleared the deck five feet, then ten. The big, crippled body began slowly spinning in the prop wash.

'If you like fishing with live bait, he's all yours,' Jack said. The pilot had been briefed on his cargo's criminal actions.

'Too bad I forgot to bring my fishing license.' The pilot laughed as he signed off.

The Osprey's big engines roared again as it leaped into the sky, Logan still dangling from the rope. No time to wait and pull him into the Osprey. The accelerated speed and rotor wash spun him like a top as he rocketed into the moonless air. The pilot swung away at a steep angle, pointing his machine toward home.

Jack's eyes tracked Logan into the dark that finally swallowed him up.

Logan was still alive. Mission accomplished.

A wide grin creased Jack's face.

He could still hear Logan's screams.

# Epilogue

*Washington, D.C.*
*The White House Residence*

Jack came in the private entrance, his face shielded by an umbrella and the two PPD agents that accompanied him. There wasn't any press standing around in the rain, and if there had been, the PPD would have shooed them away.

To maintain his cover, Jack never appeared in current family photos or at public events with his parents. But he loved hanging out with his folks. It was too much trouble for them to come to his place, so he came to them whenever he could. Especially when his mother offered to make her famous Burgundy beef stew and apple pie for dinner, his favorites. His three siblings were all out of town. He wished they could be there, too.

Jack came into the kitchen and hugged his mom, holding her for a little longer than usual.

'Are you feeling all right, son?' She touched his bearded face with her palm. The gesture was equal parts motherly and medical. 'I hope you're not coming down with anything.'

'Nah, I'm fine. Just tired. Smells good in here. Let's eat.'

Jack helped his mom set the table and serve the food. Senior said grace. The three of them dug in.

Cathy worried about her son. Renée Moore's star ceremony had been that morning. Her husband told her earlier that Jack took it harder than he expected.

'They must have been closer than I thought,' Ryan said.

Cathy wanted to take her son's mind off the memorial.

'So, I never did hear about your trip to Spain,' she said. 'Tell me about it.'

Jack perked up a little bit. 'Amazing country. Wonderful history. Fabulous food. I can't wait to go back. Maybe someday we can all go there together as a family. I mean, later, of course.'

'Sounds like a plan,' Ryan said. 'I always wanted to see a bullfight.'

'You meet anybody interesting?' Cathy asked.

Jack's faint smile vanished. He took a long, slow breath, thinking of Brossa.

'Yeah. I did.'

'Anyone you'd like us to meet?' she asked hopefully. She was antsy for grandkids.

'Honey . . .' Ryan said, frowning.

'Probably won't happen.' Jack's voice fell away. He set his spoon down, lost in thought. It had been a rough day.

'I'm sorry, Jack. I shouldn't have asked.'

Jack shrugged. 'No, it's fine.'

He took a sip of water, then sat up straighter, gathering himself. The shadow on his face passed away.

'So good,' he said with a smile to his mother as he picked up his spoon.

He shoveled a heaping bite into his mouth and chewed a chunk of succulent beef with gusto.

Cathy studied Jack's face. Senior hadn't told her what her son had been up to recently, only that he was one helluva kid. But the pride in her husband's cracking voice when he said it spoke volumes. Jack must have risked everything to accomplish something that really mattered. Just like her husband had so many times in the past.

She'd seen the expression on Jack's face before. It was the same one her husband wore after he'd come home from long

439

trips he couldn't talk about with her. She knew in her heart that behind the hard, confident mask they both wore in public lay an inexpressible grief for things and people lost.

She ached for her son's sorrow.

But her heart skipped a beat as she glanced first at her husband and then her boy. Pride washed over her. The two of them were so alike.

Jack was truly his father's son.